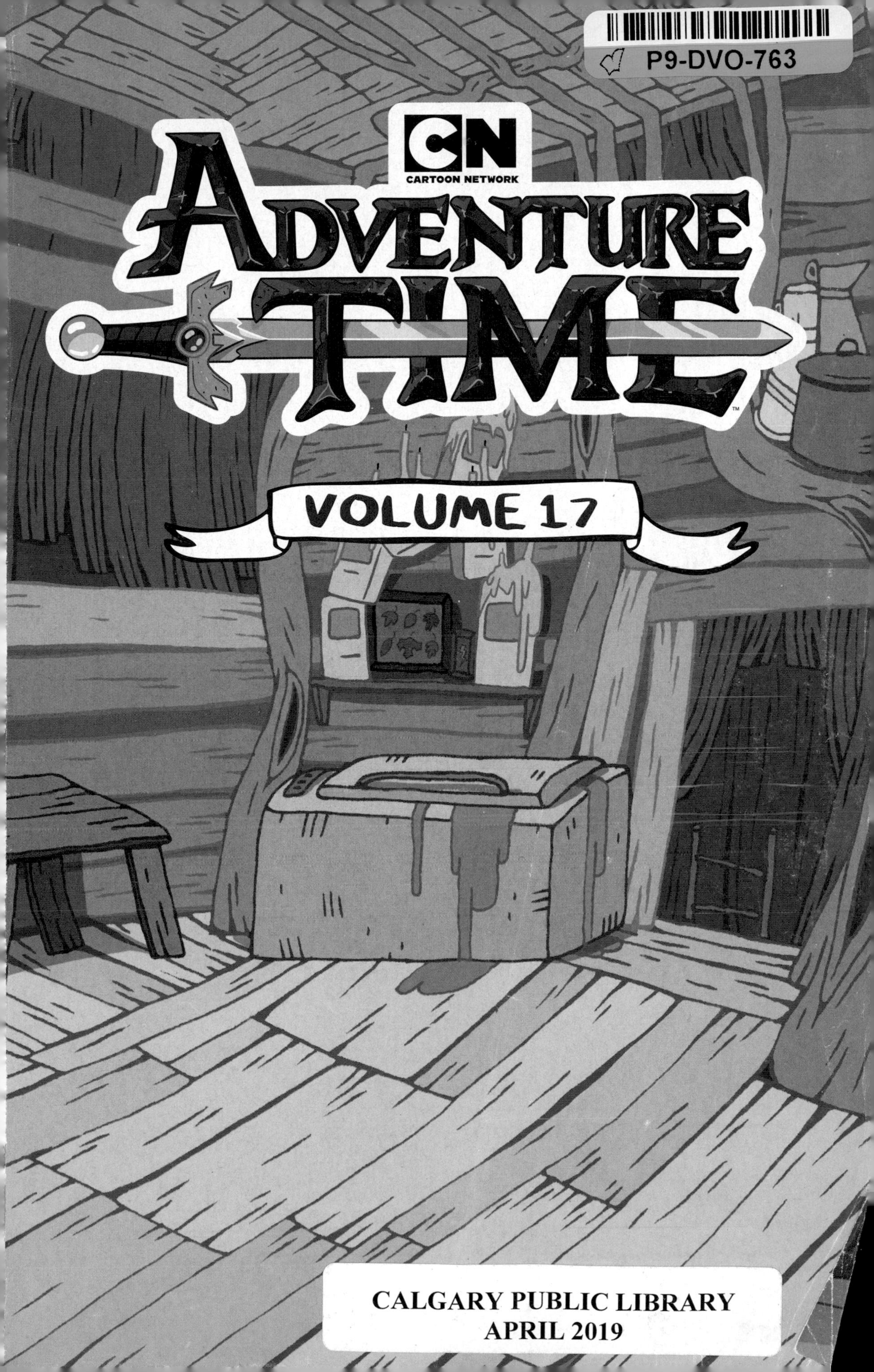
CN
CARTOON NETWORK
ADVENTURE TIME™
VOLUME 17

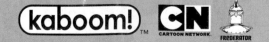

ADVENTURE TIME Volume Seventeen, April 2019. Published by KaBOOM!, a division of Boom Entertainment, Inc. ADVENTURE TIME, CARTOON NETWORK, the logos, and all related characters and elements are trademarks of and © Cartoon Network. A WarnerMedia Company. All rights reserved. (S19) Originally published in single magazine form as ADVENTURE TIME No. 74-75, ADVENTURE TIME WITH FIONNA AND CAKE 2018 FREE COMIC BOOK DAY SPECIAL. © Cartoon Network. A WarnerMedia Company. All rights reserved. (S18) KaBOOM!™ and the KaBOOM! logo are trademarks of Boom Entertainment, Inc., registered in various countries and categories. All characters, events, and institutions depicted herein are fictional. Any similarity between any of the names, characters, persons, events, and/or institutions in this publication to actual names, characters, and persons, whether living or dead, events, and/or institutions is unintended and purely coincidental. KaBOOM! does not read or accept unsolicited submissions of ideas, stories, or artwork.

For information regarding the CPSIA on this printed material, call (203) 595-3636 and provide reference #RICH - 830538.

BOOM! Studios, 5670 Wilshire Boulevard, Suite 400, Los Angeles, CA 90036-5679. Printed in USA. First Printing.

ISBN: 978-1-68415-331-2, eISBN: 978-1-64144-184-1

CREATED BY
Pendleton Ward

Issue #74

WRITTEN BY
Conor McCreery

ILLUSTRATED BY
Jorge Monlongo

Issue #75

WRITTEN BY
**Christopher Hastings,
Mariko Tamaki, & Ryan North**

ILLUSTRATED BY
**Zachary Sterling, Ian McGinty,
& Shelly Paroline & Braden Lamb**

COLORS BY
Maarta Laiho

LETTERS BY
Mike Fiorentino

"WHAT'S THE PUNCH-LINE?"

WRITTEN BY
Kiernan Sjursen-Lien

ILLUSTRATED AND LETTERED BY
Christine Larsen

COVER BY
Shelli Paroline & Braden Lamb

SERIES DESIGNER
Grace Park

COLLECTION DESIGNER
Chelsea Roberts

ASSISTANT EDITOR
Michael Moccio

EDITOR
Matthew Levine

With Special Thanks to Marisa Marionakis, Janet No, Becky M. Yang,
Conrad Montgomery, Kelly Crews, Scott Malchus, Adam Muto and the
wonderful folks at Cartoon Network.

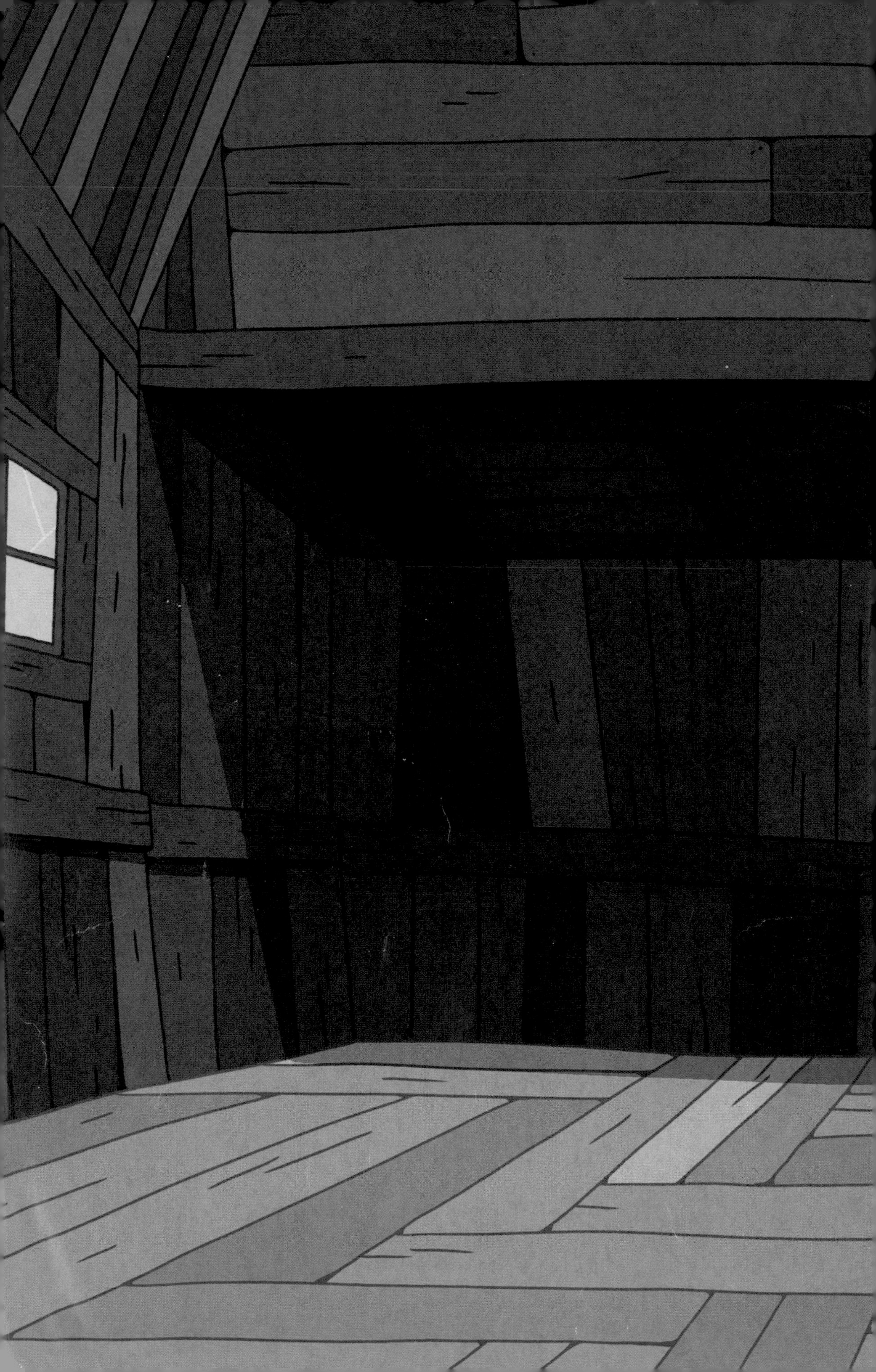

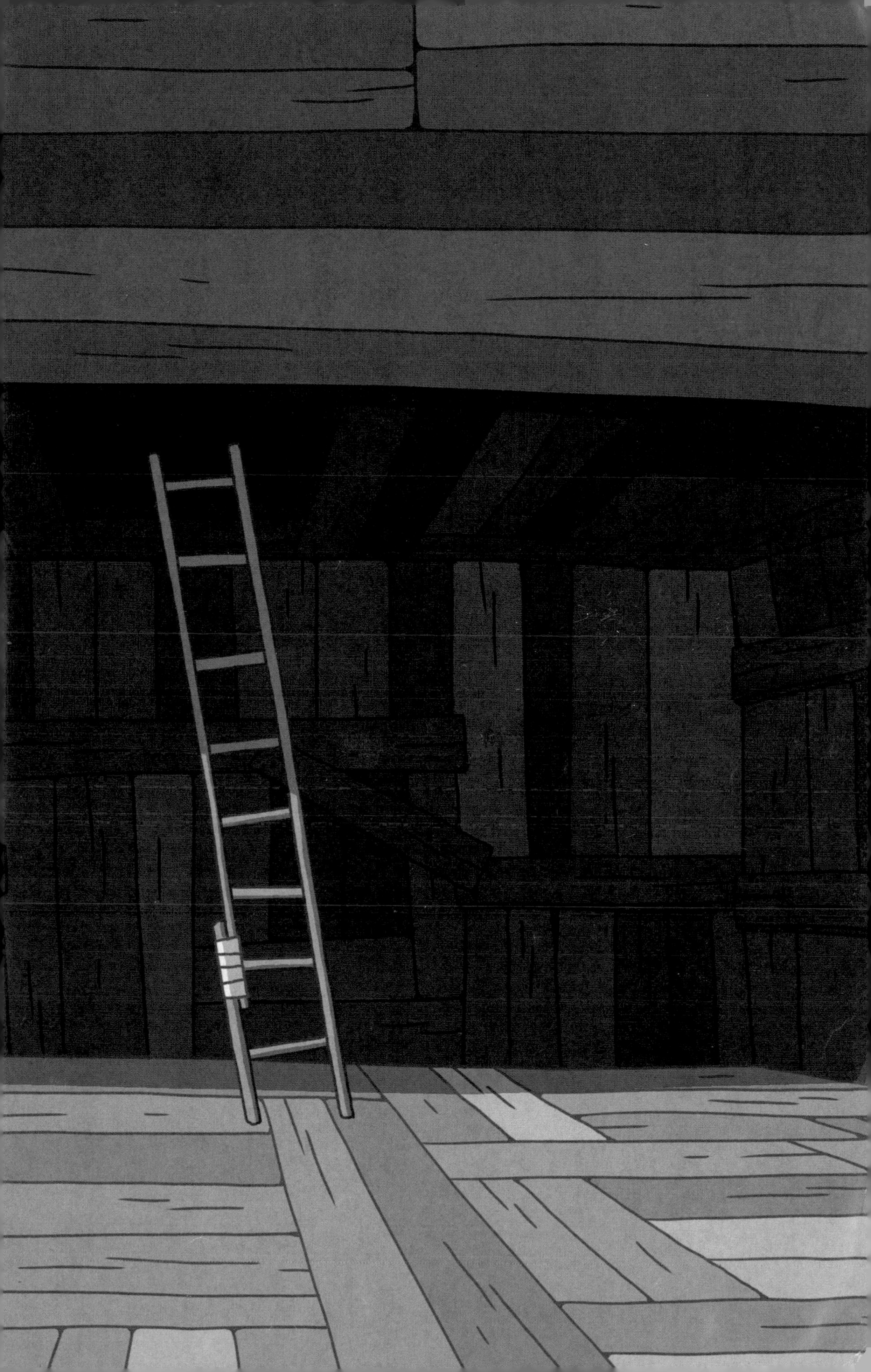

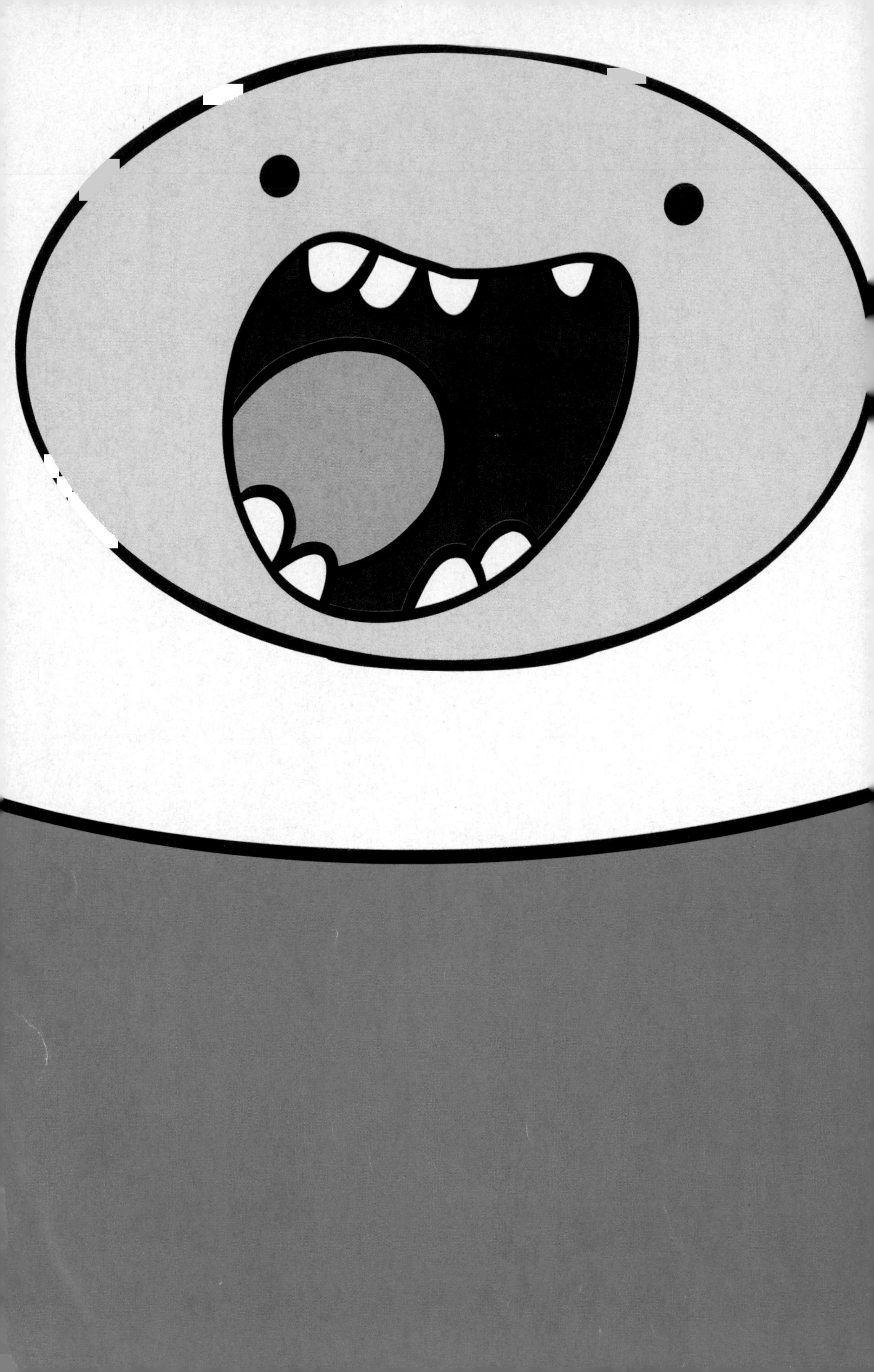

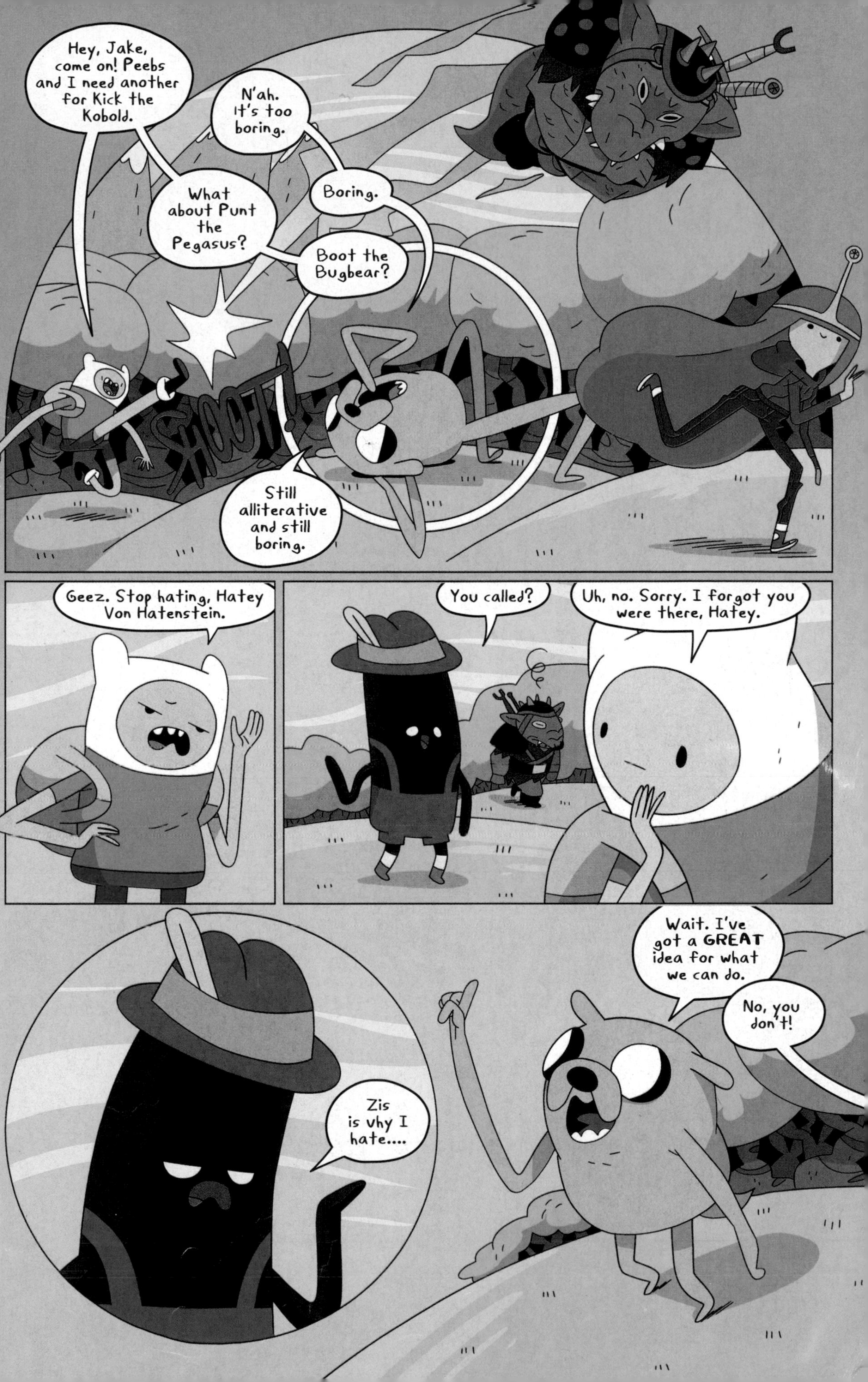
Hey, Jake, come on! Peebs and I need another for Kick the Kobold.
N'ah. It's too boring.
What about Punt the Pegasus?
Boring.
Boot the Bugbear?
SHOOT!
Still alliterative and still boring.
Geez. Stop hating, Hatey Von Hatenstein.
You called?
Uh, no. Sorry. I forgot you were there, Hatey.
Zis is vhy I hate....
Wait. I've got a GREAT idea for what we can do.
No, you don't!

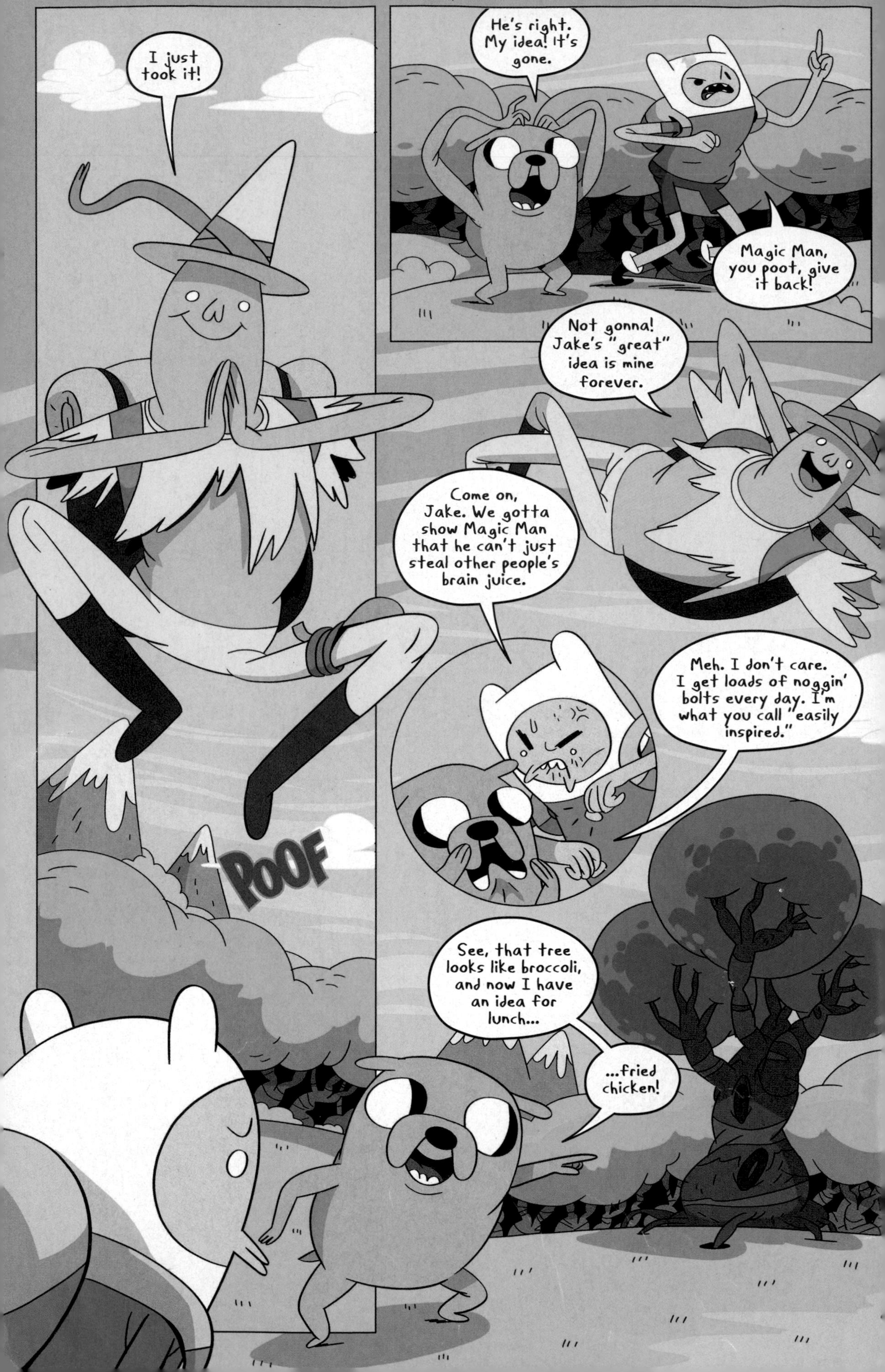
I just took it!
He's right. My idea! It's gone.
Magic Man, you poot, give it back!
Not gonna! Jake's "great" idea is mine forever.
POOF
Come on, Jake. We gotta show Magic Man that he can't just steal other people's brain juice.
Meh. I don't care. I get loads of noggin' bolts every day. I'm what you call "easily inspired."
See, that tree looks like broccoli, and now I have an idea for lunch...
...fried chicken!

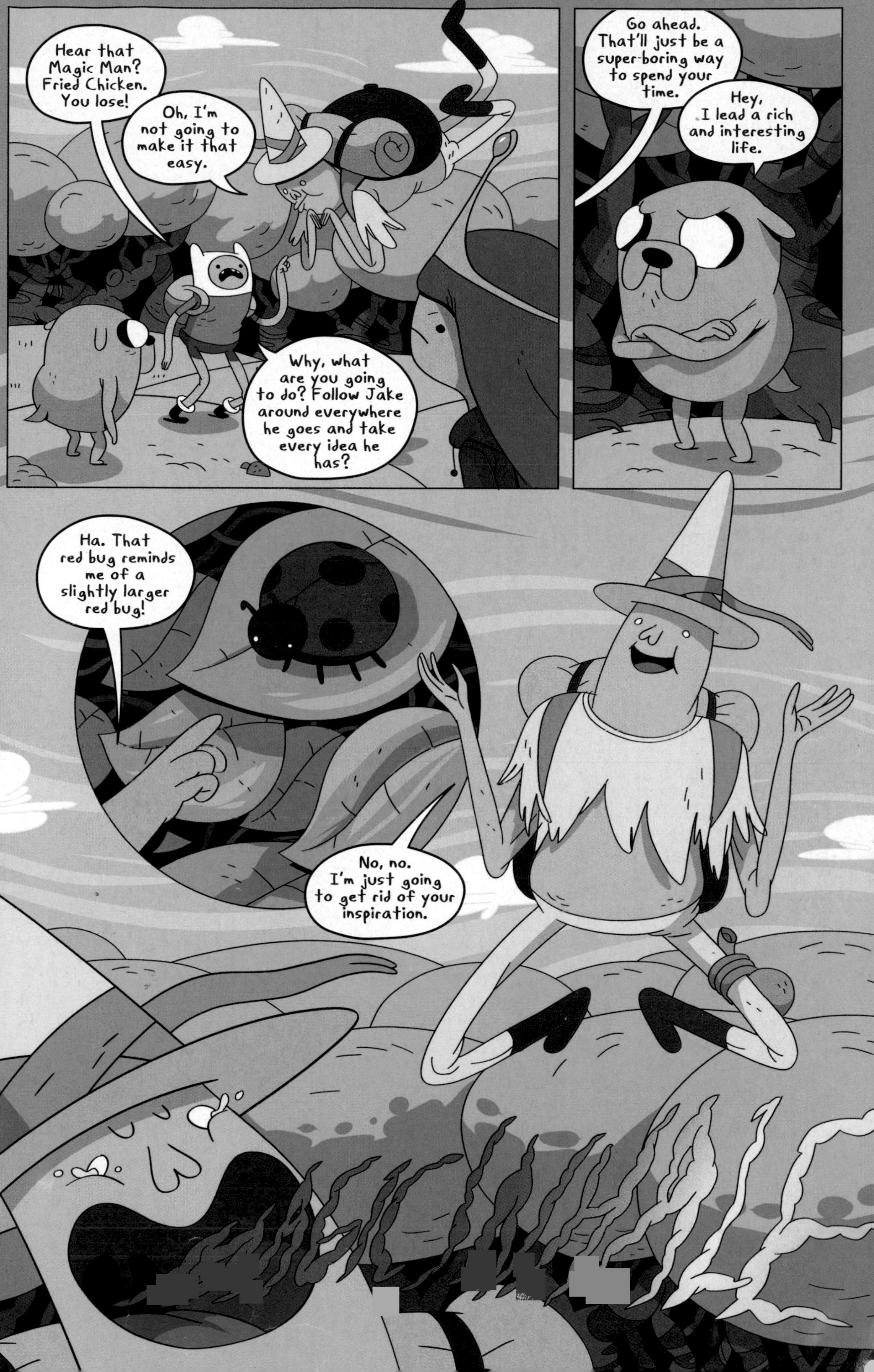
Hear that Magic Man? Fried Chicken. You lose!
Oh, I'm not going to make it that easy.
Why, what are you going to do? Follow Jake around everywhere he goes and take every idea he has?
Go ahead. That'll just be a super-boring way to spend your time.
Hey, I lead a rich and interesting life.
Ha. That red bug reminds me of a slightly larger red bug!
No, no. I'm just going to get rid of your inspiration.

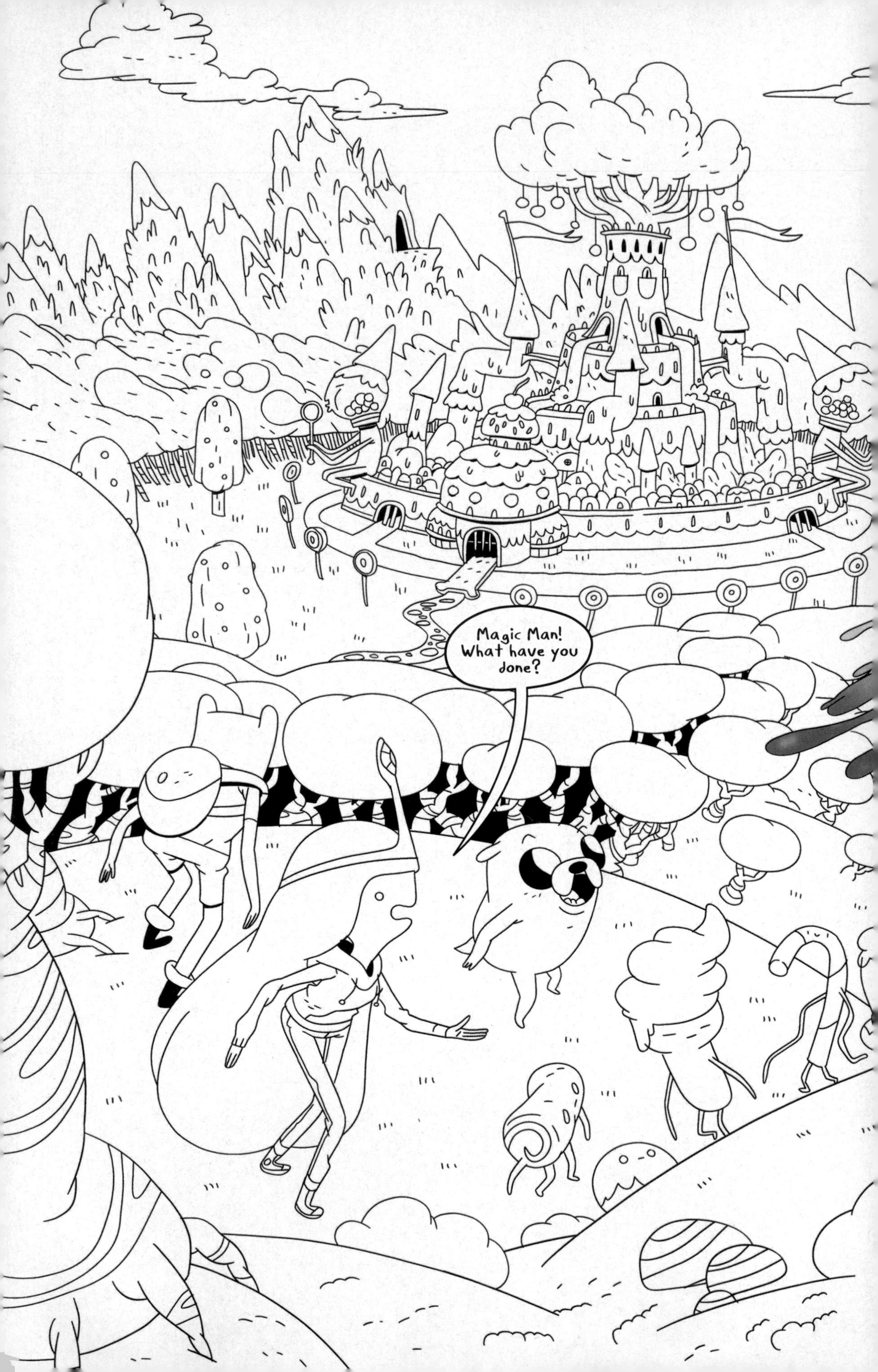
Magic Man! What have you done?

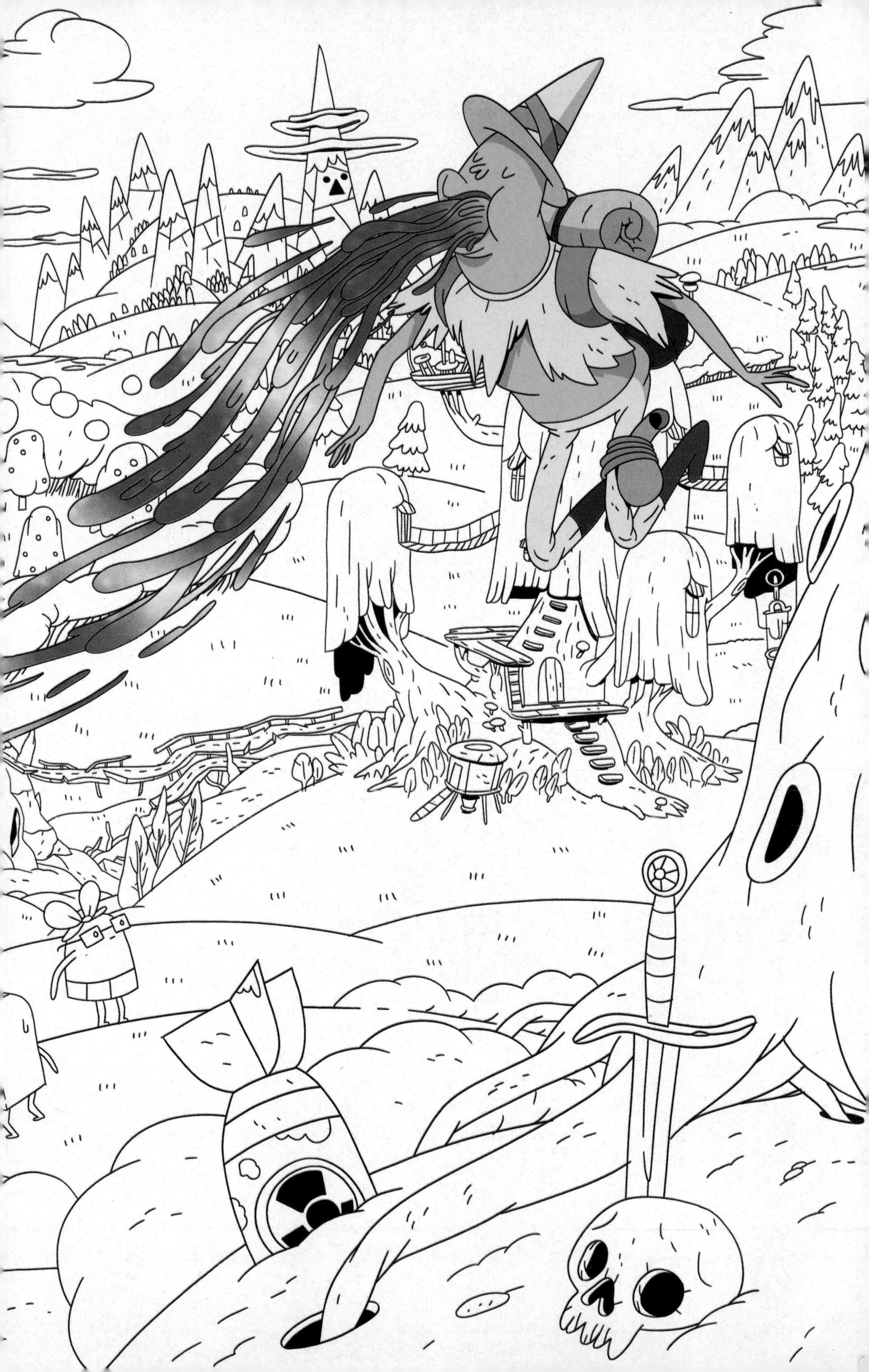

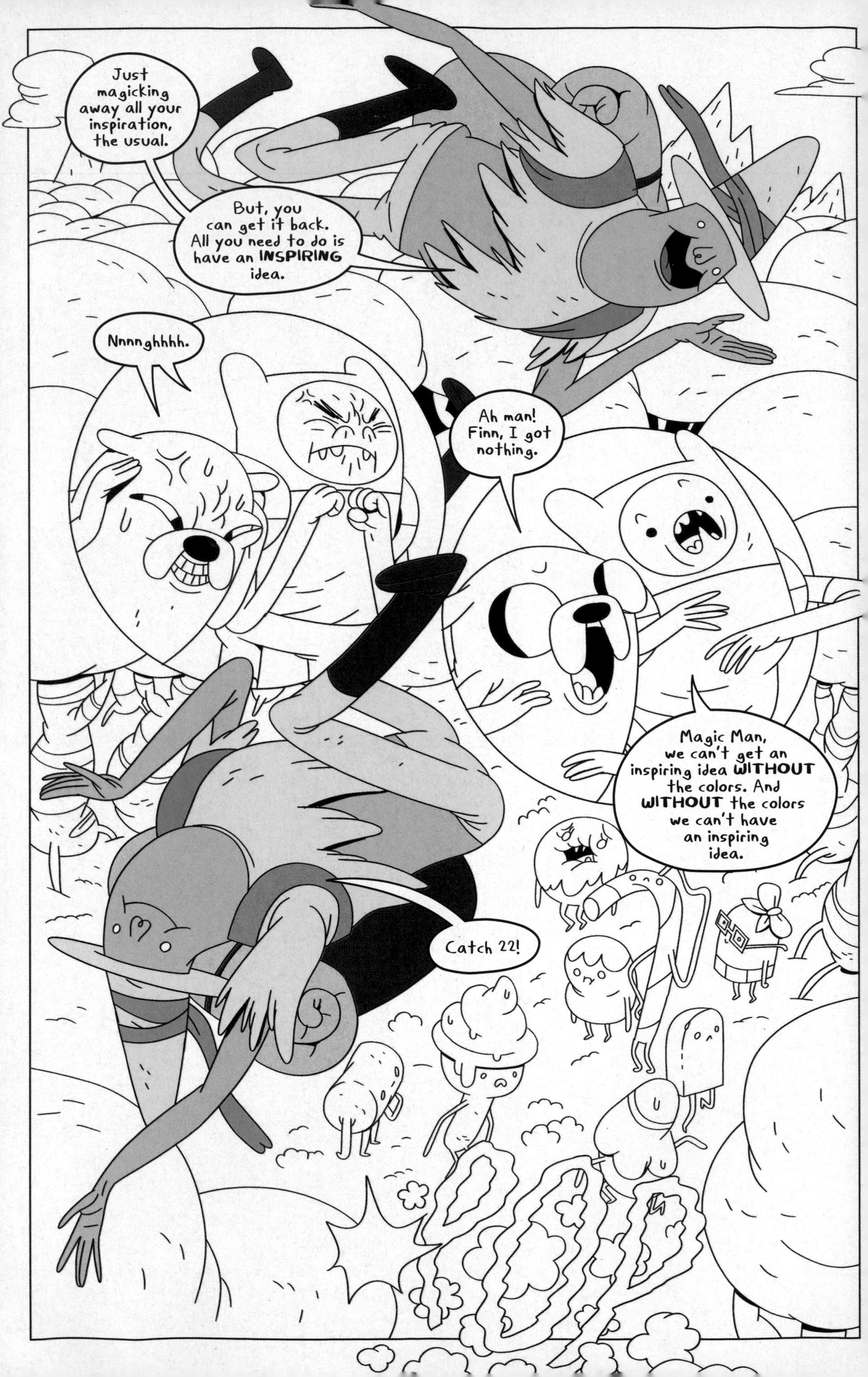

Just magicking away all your inspiration, the usual.
But, you can get it back. All you need to do is have an INSPIRING idea.
Nnnnghhhh.
Ah man! Finn, I got nothing.
Magic Man, we can't get an inspiring idea WITHOUT the colors. And WITHOUT the colors we can't have an inspiring idea.
Catch 22!

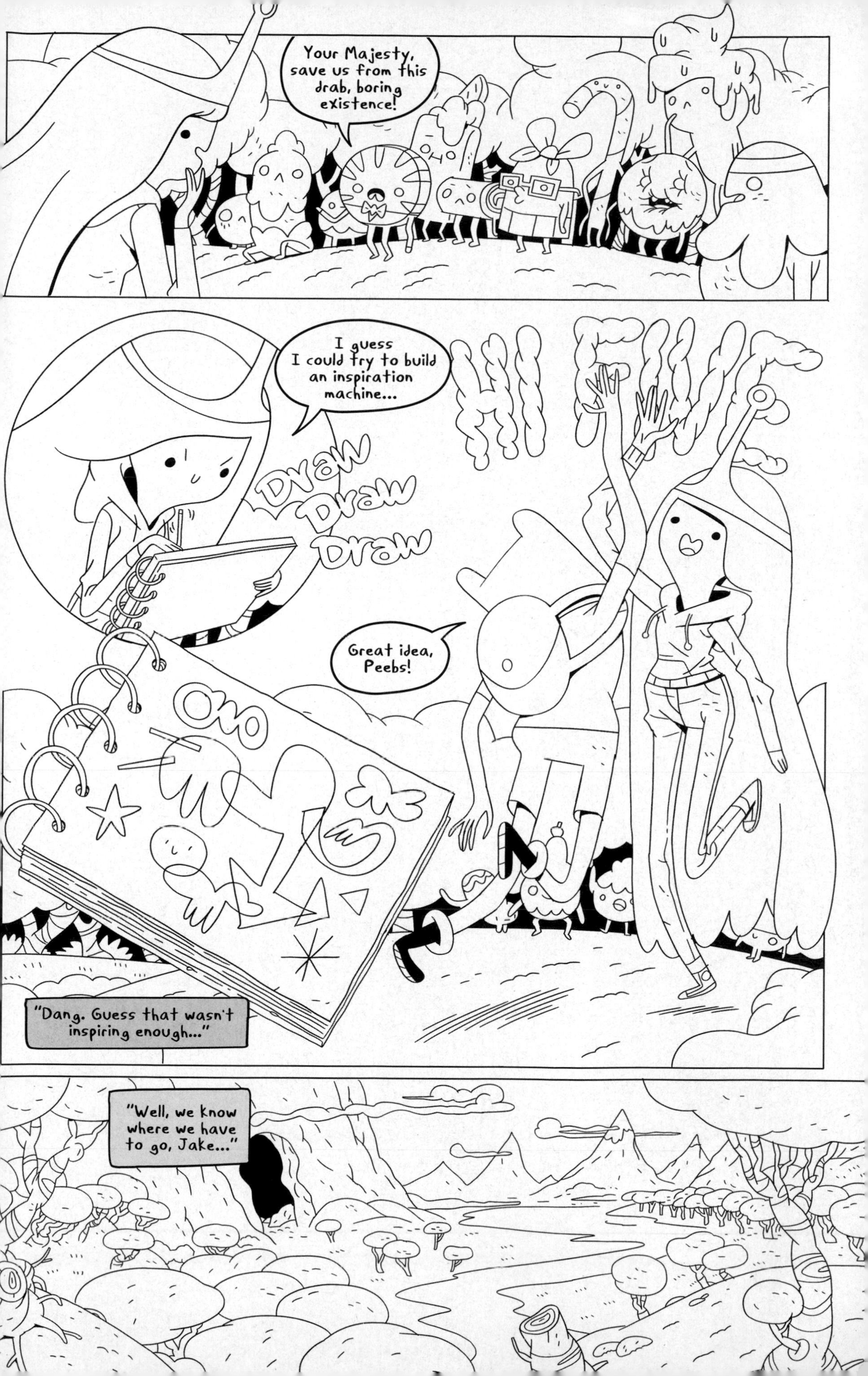
Your Majesty, save us from this drab, boring existence!
I guess I could try to build an inspiration machine...
Draw Draw Draw
Great idea, Peebs!
"Dang. Guess that wasn't inspiring enough..."
"Well, we know where we have to go, Jake..."

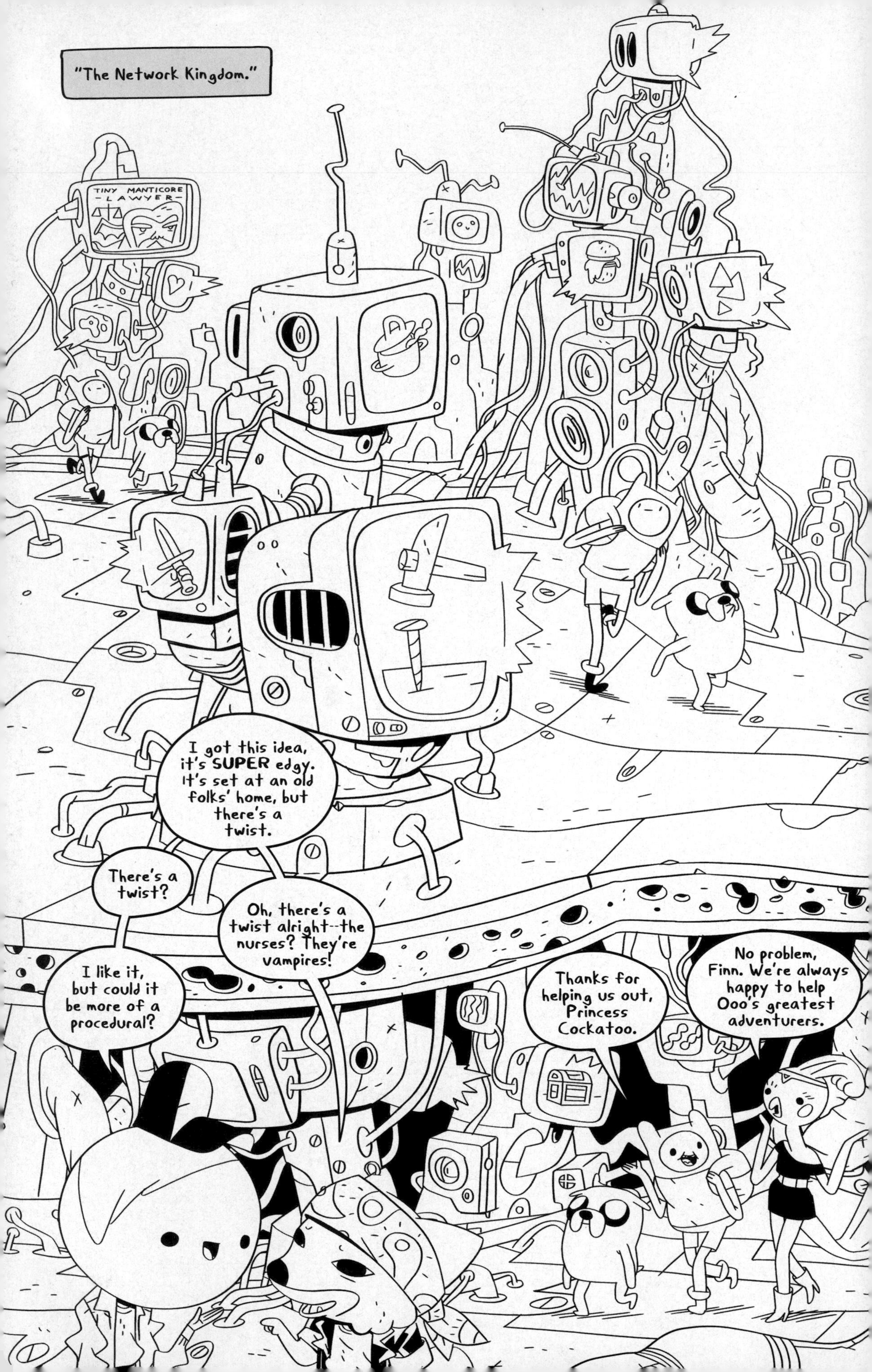
"The Network Kingdom."
TINY MANTICORE -LAWYER-
I got this idea, it's SUPER edgy. It's set at an old folks' home, but there's a twist.
There's a twist?
Oh, there's a twist alright--the nurses? They're vampires!
I like it, but could it be more of a procedural?
Thanks for helping us out, Princess Cockatoo.
No problem, Finn. We're always happy to help Ooo's greatest adventurers.

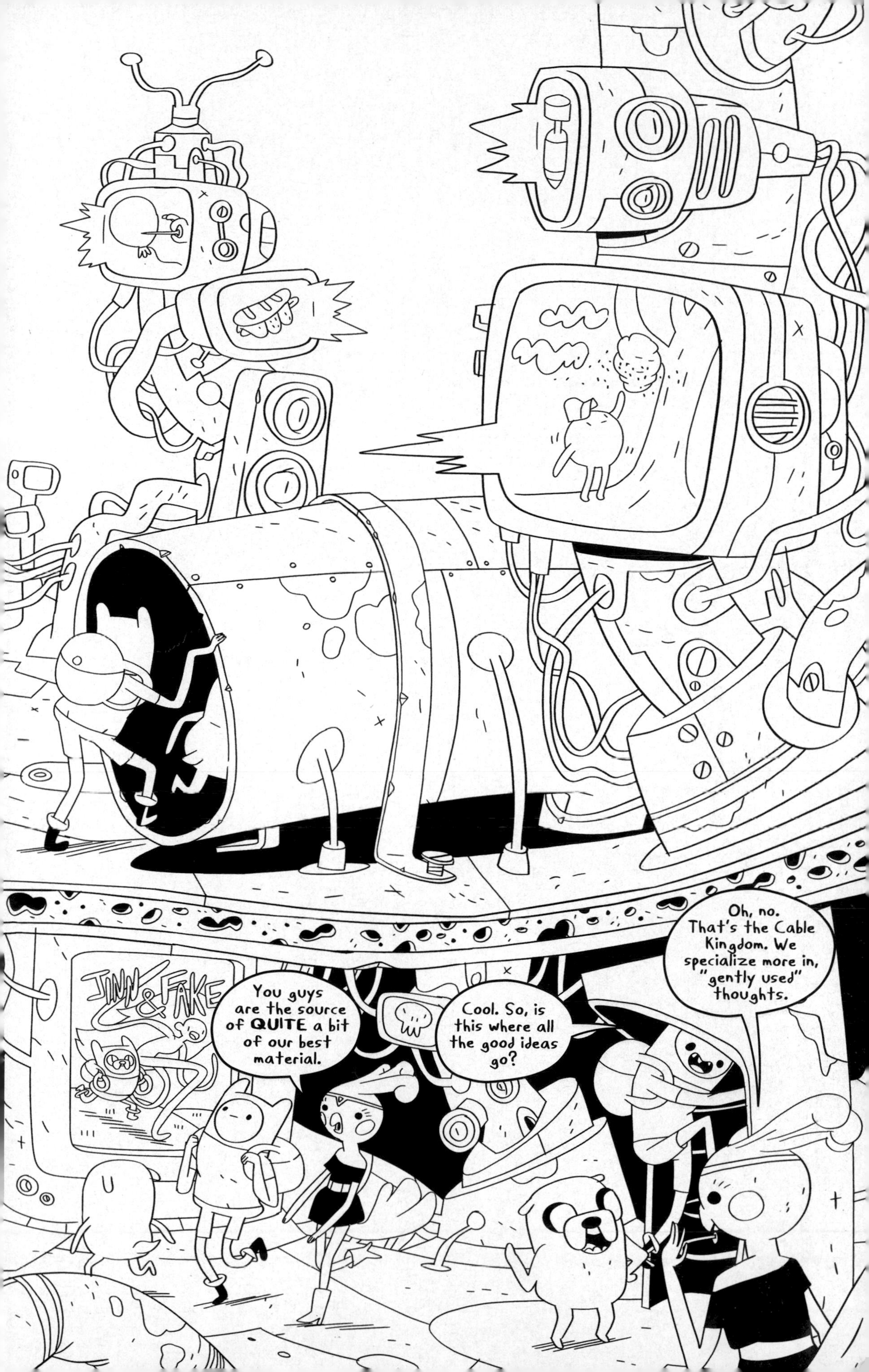
JINN & FAKE
You guys are the source of **QUITE** a bit of our best material.
Cool. So, is this where all the good ideas go?
Oh, no. That's the Cable Kingdom. We specialize more in, "gently used" thoughts.

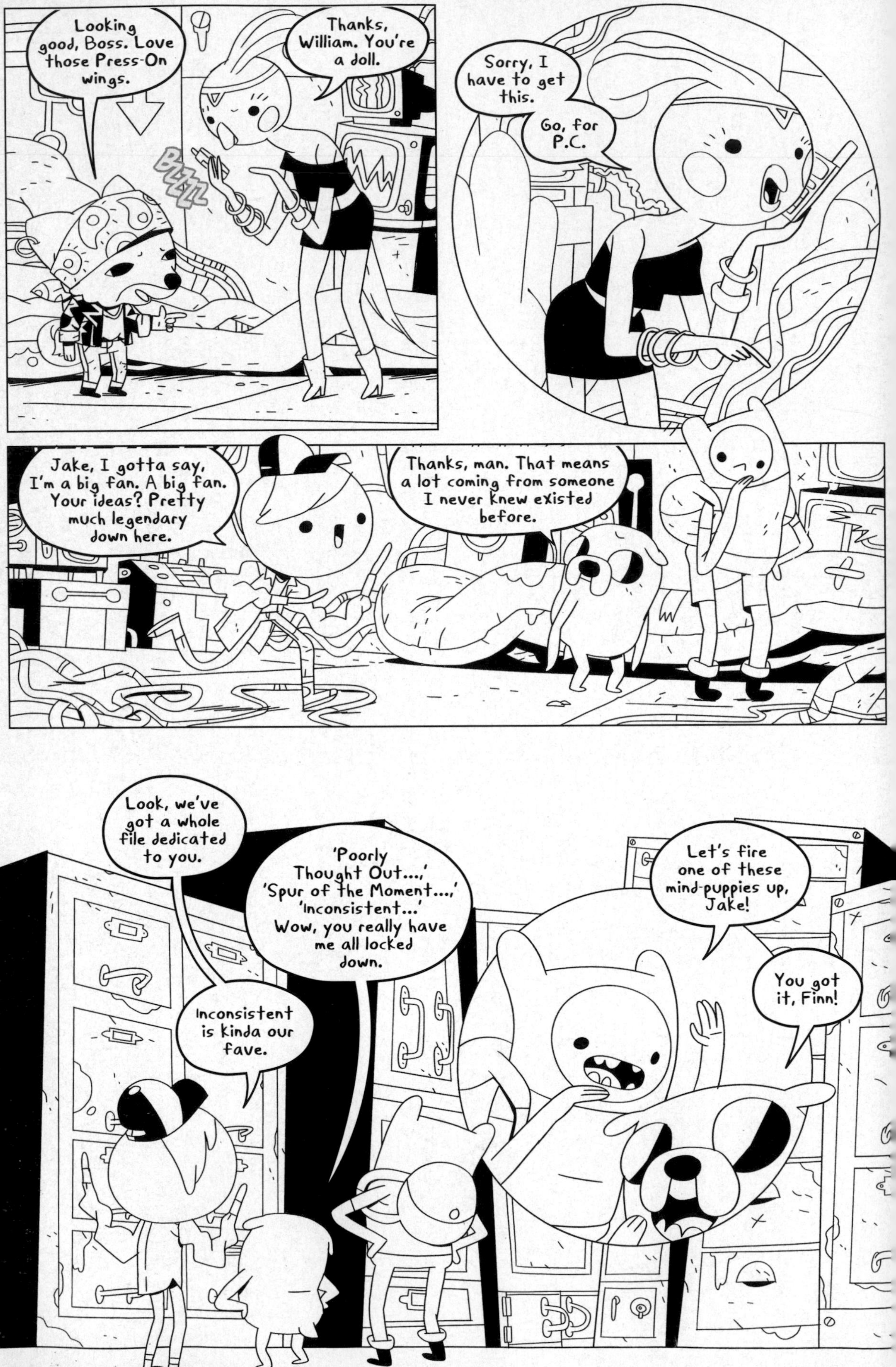

Looking good, Boss. Love those Press-On wings.
Thanks, William. You're a doll.
BZZZ
Sorry, I have to get this.
Go, for P.C.
Jake, I gotta say, I'm a big fan. A big fan. Your ideas? Pretty much legendary down here.
Thanks, man. That means a lot coming from someone I never knew existed before.
Look, we've got a whole file dedicated to you.
Inconsistent is kinda our fave.
'Poorly Thought Out...,' 'Spur of the Moment...,' 'Inconsistent...' Wow, you really have me all locked down.
Let's fire one of these mind-puppies up, Jake!
You got it, Finn!

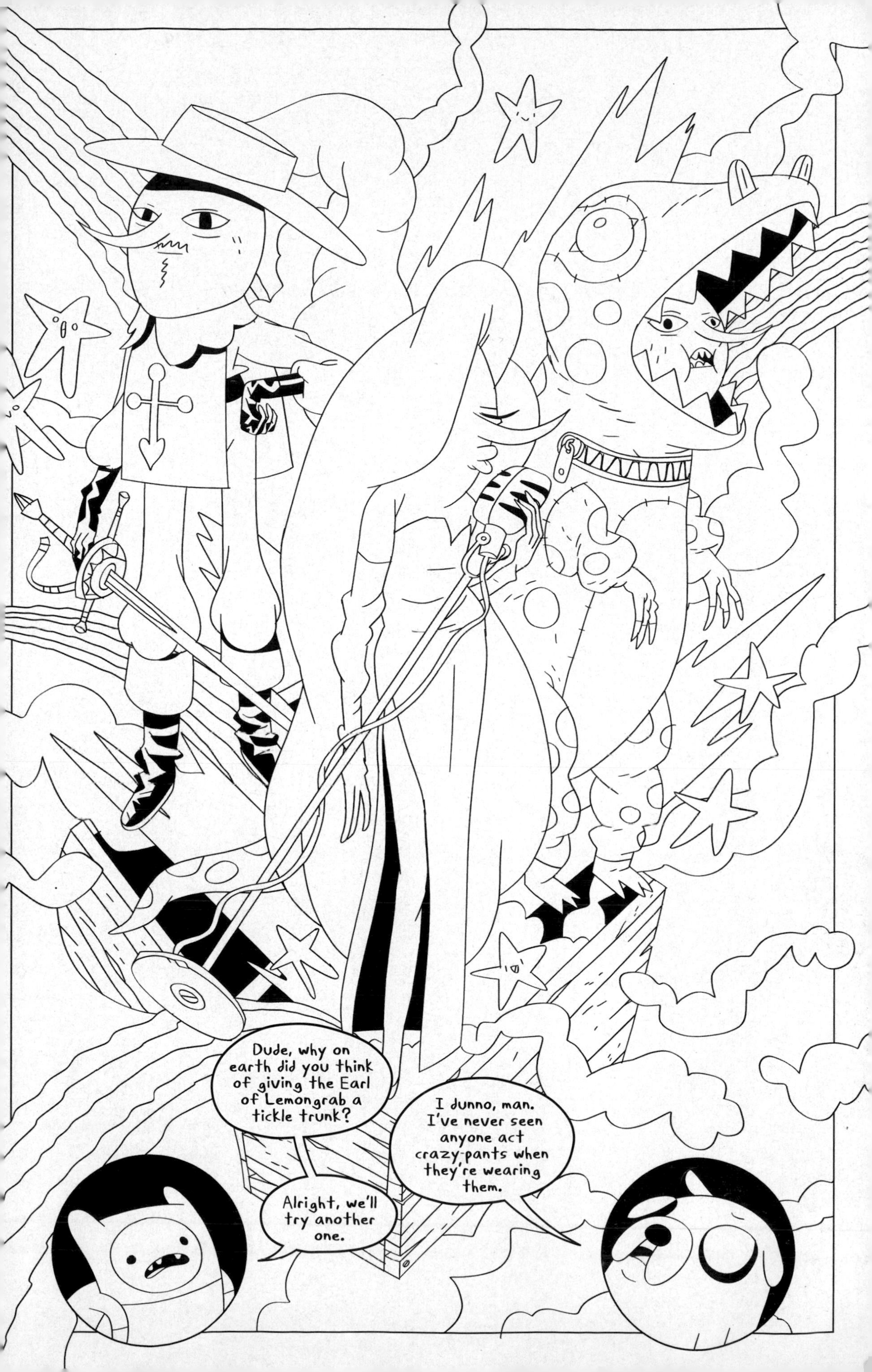
Dude, why on earth did you think of giving the Earl of Lemongrab a tickle trunk?
I dunno, man. I've never seen anyone act crazy-pants when they're wearing them.
Alright, we'll try another one.

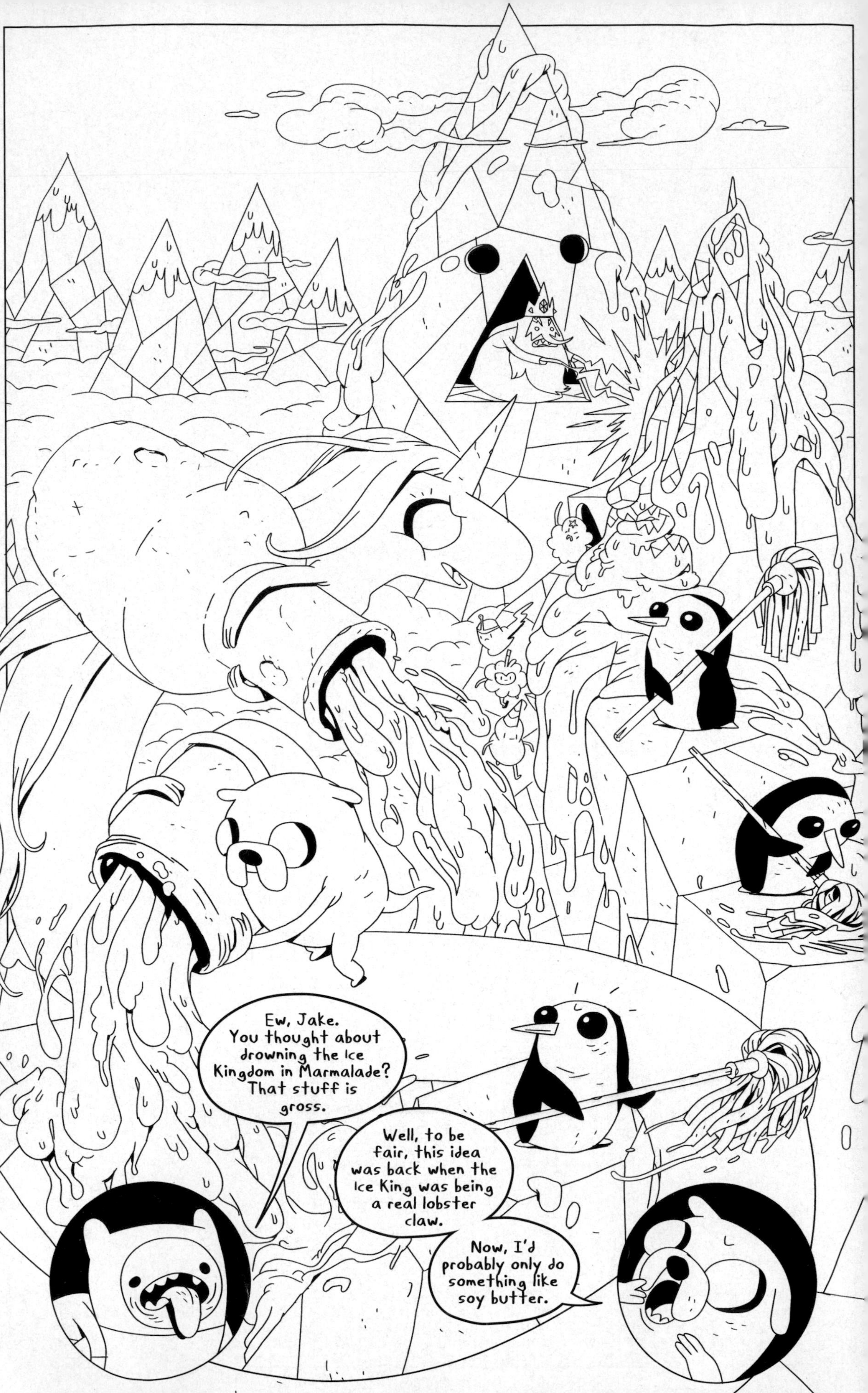

Ew, Jake. You thought about drowning the Ice Kingdom in Marmalade? That stuff is gross.
Well, to be fair, this idea was back when the Ice King was being a real lobster claw.
Now, I'd probably only do something like soy butter.

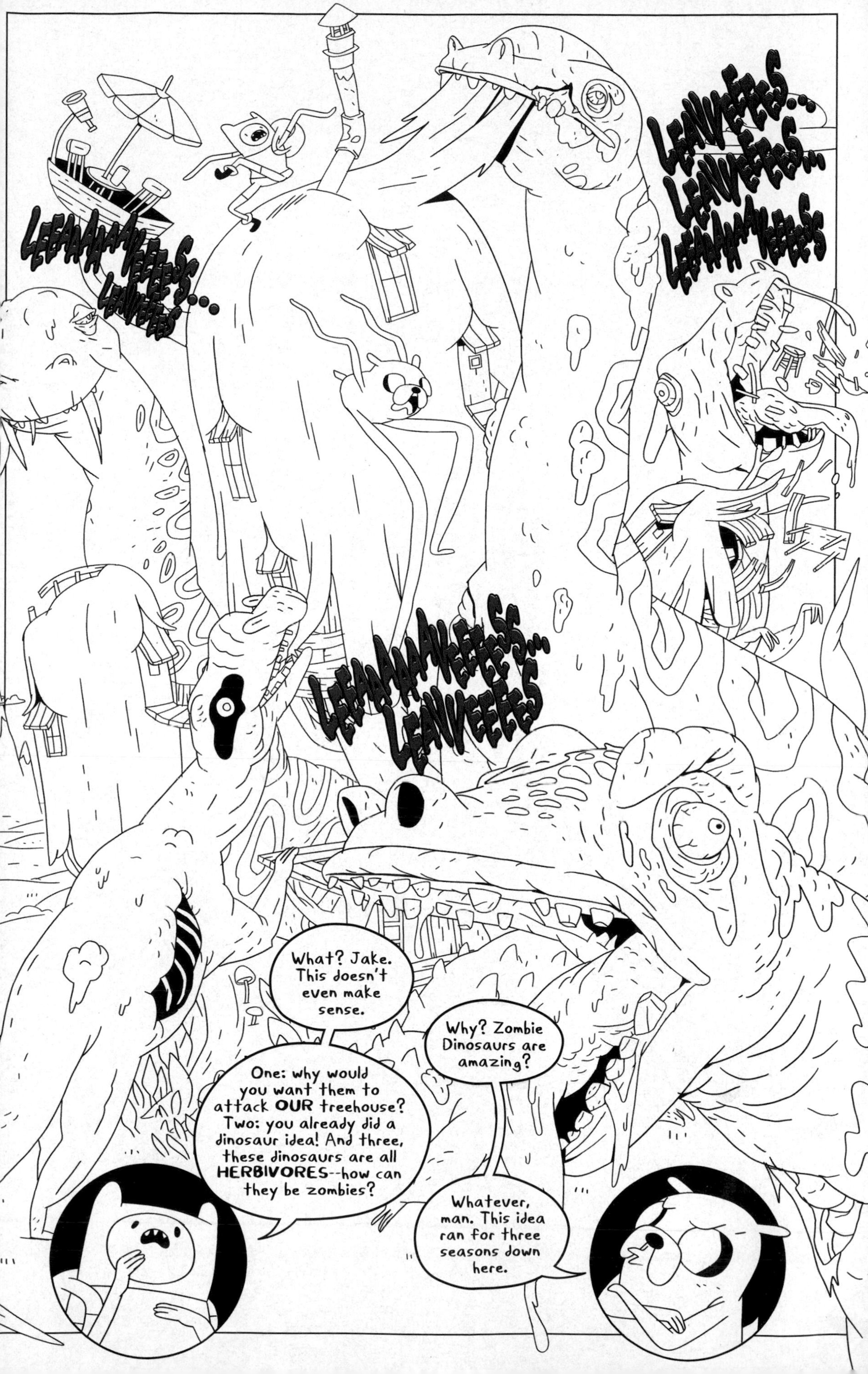

LEEAAAAAVEEEES...
LEAVEEES
LEAVEEES...
LEAVEEES...
LEEAAAAAVEEEES
LEEAAAAAVEEEES...
LEAVEEEES
What? Jake. This doesn't even make sense.
One: why would you want them to attack OUR treehouse? Two: you already did a dinosaur idea! And three, these dinosaurs are all HERBIVORES--how can they be zombies?
Why? Zombie Dinosaurs are amazing?
Whatever, man. This idea ran for three seasons down here.

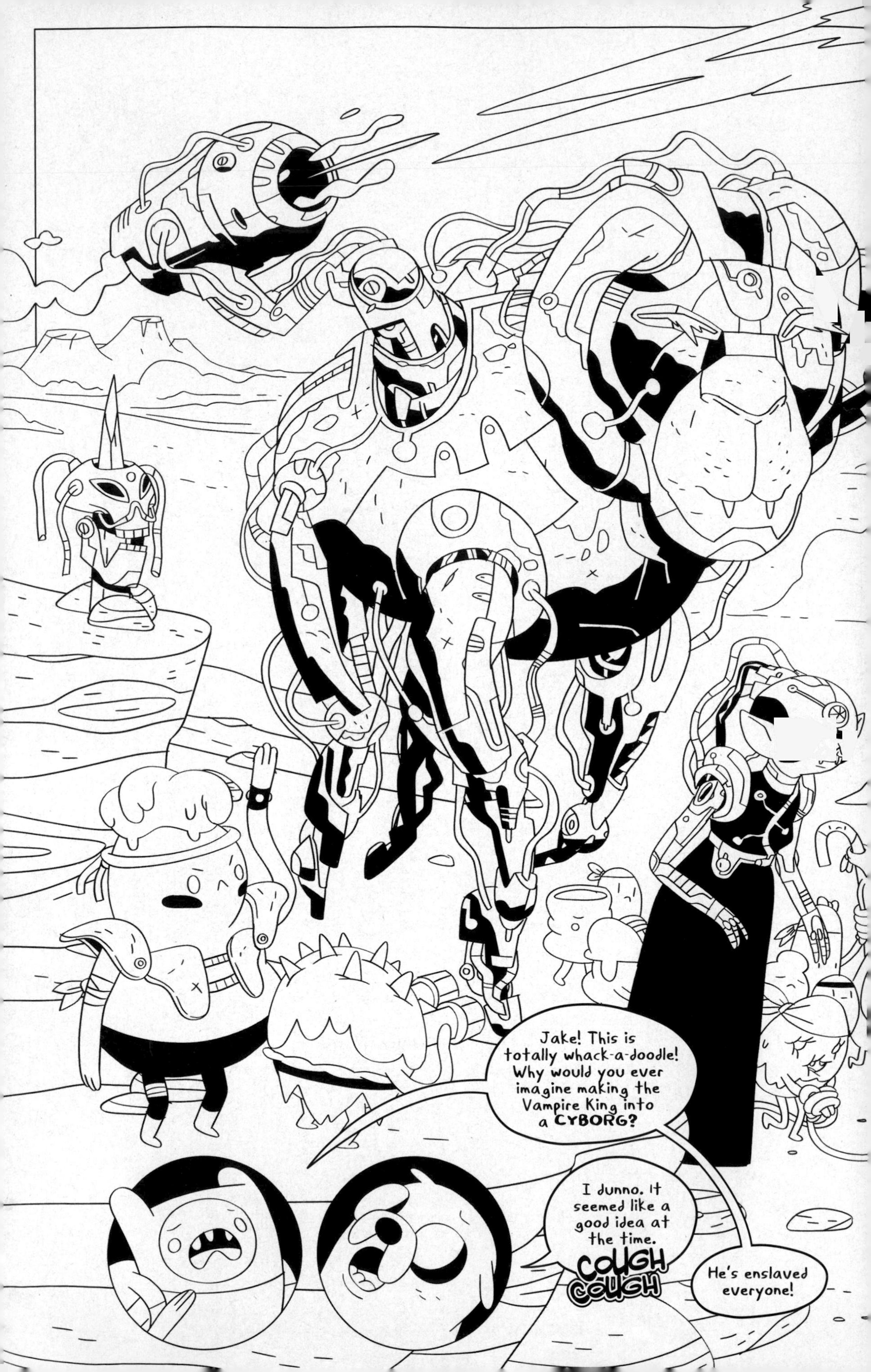
Jake! This is totally whack-a-doodle! Why would you ever imagine making the Vampire King into a CYBORG?
I dunno. It seemed like a good idea at the time.
COUGH COUGH
He's enslaved everyone!

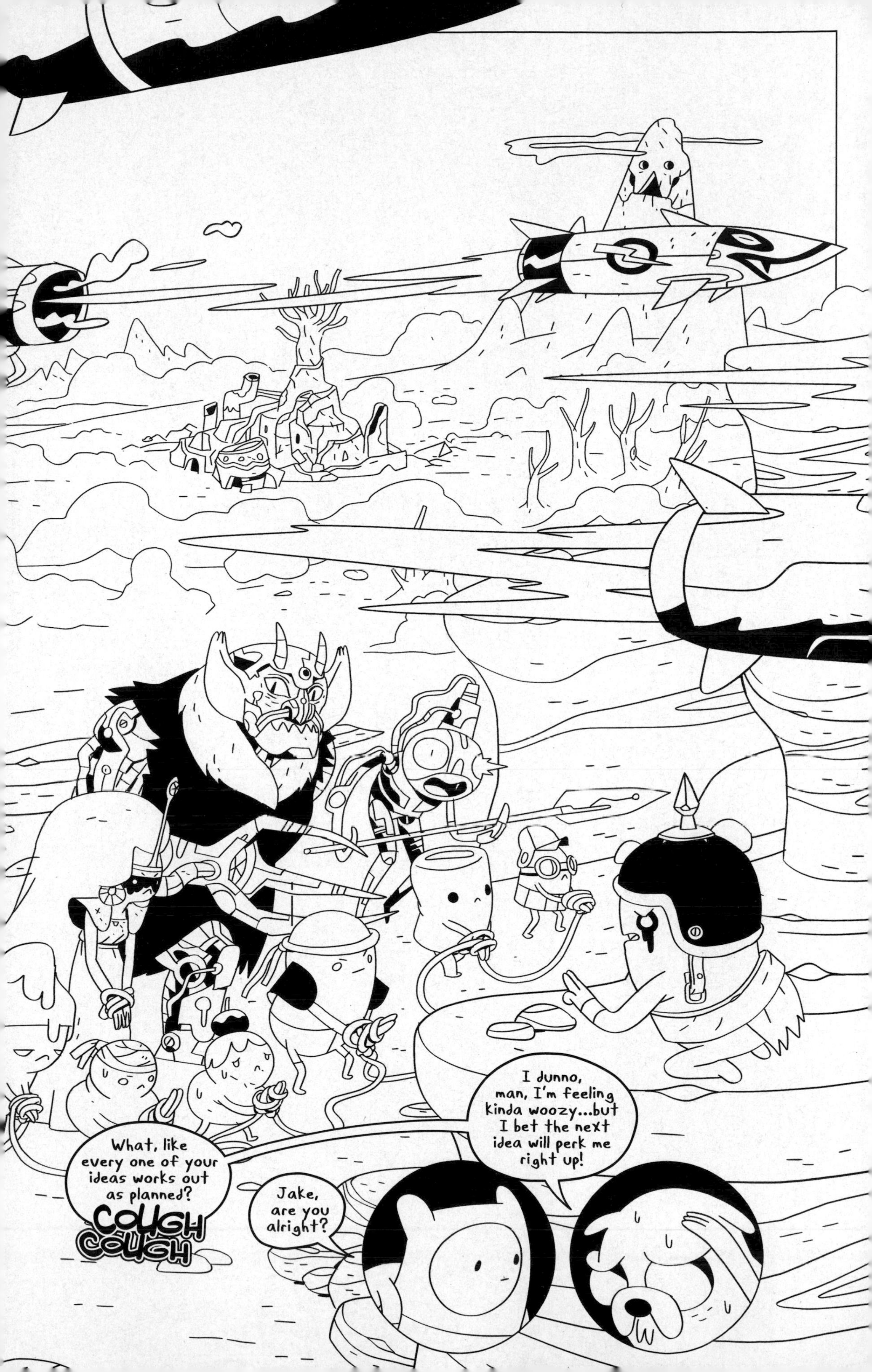

What, like every one of your ideas works out as planned?
COUGH COUGH
Jake, are you alright?
I dunno, man, I'm feeling kinda woozy...but I bet the next idea will perk me right up!

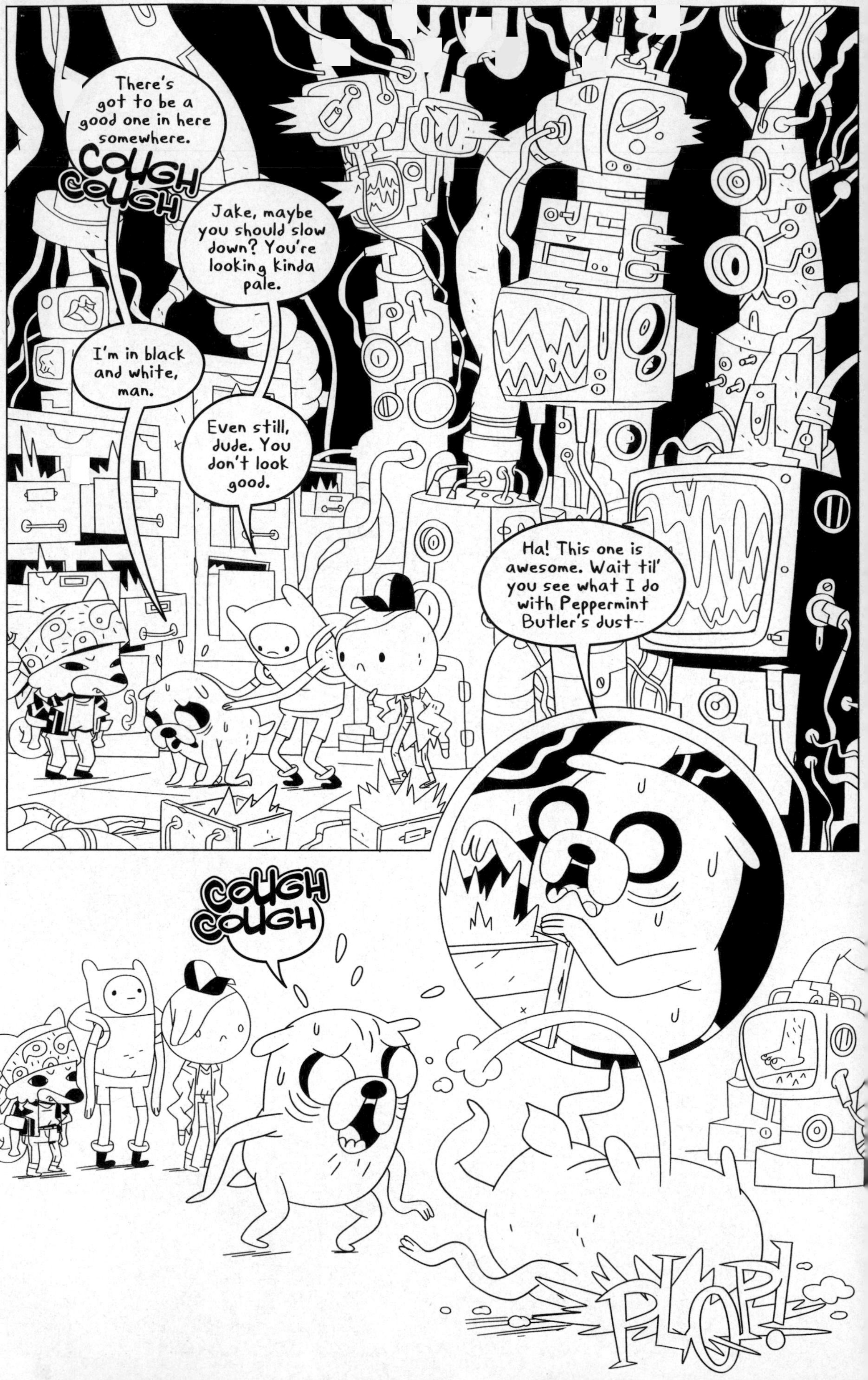
There's got to be a good one in here somewhere.
COUGH COUGH
Jake, maybe you should slow down? You're looking kinda pale.
I'm in black and white, man.
Even still, dude. You don't look good.
Ha! This one is awesome. Wait til' you see what I do with Peppermint Butler's dust--
COUGH COUGH
PLOP!

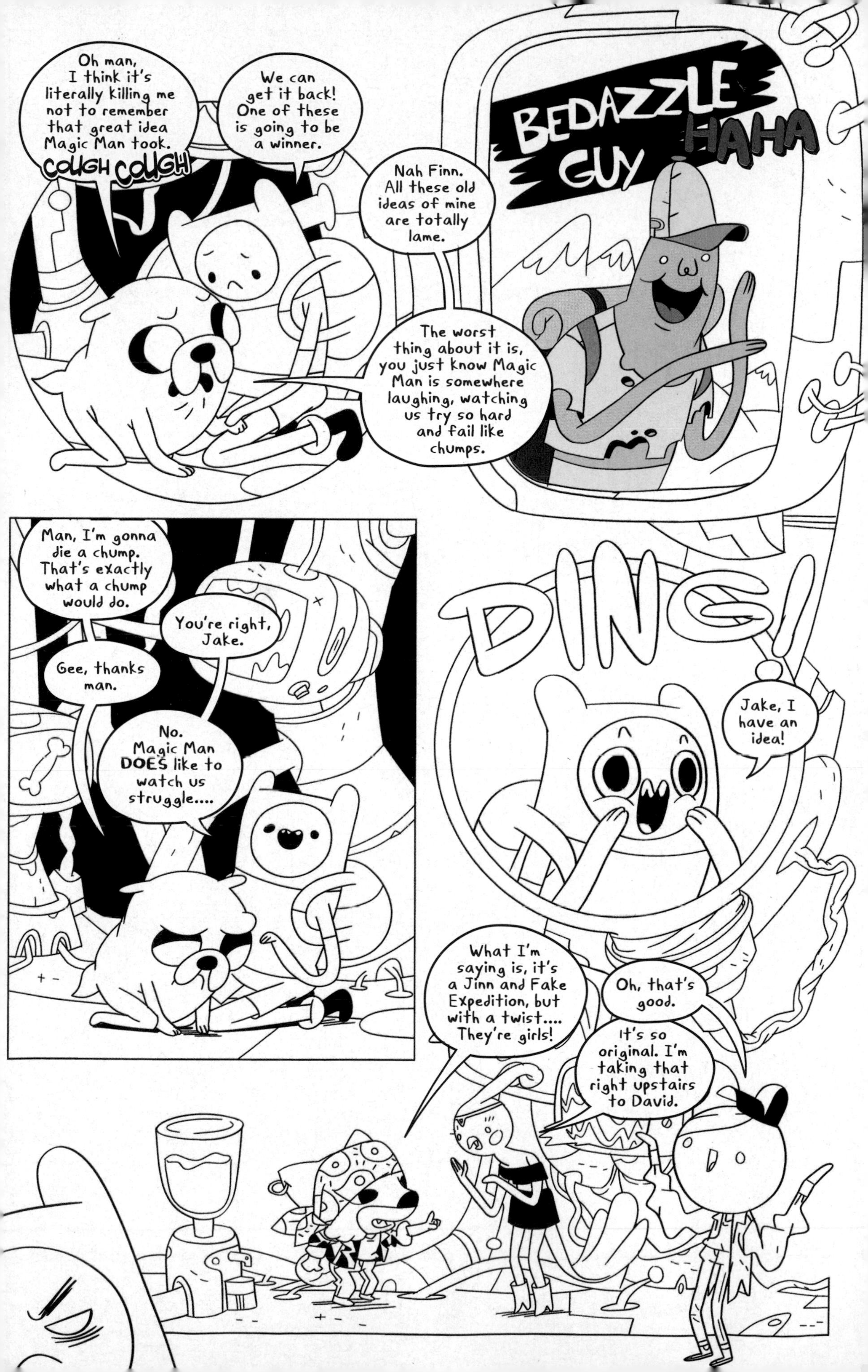
Oh man, I think it's literally killing me not to remember that great idea Magic Man took.
COUGH COUGH
We can get it back! One of these is going to be a winner.
Nah Finn. All these old ideas of mine are totally lame.
The worst thing about it is, you just know Magic Man is somewhere laughing, watching us try so hard and fail like chumps.
BEDAZZLE GUY
HAHA
Man, I'm gonna die a chump. That's exactly what a chump would do.
You're right, Jake.
Gee, thanks man.
No. Magic Man DOES like to watch us struggle....
DING!
Jake, I have an idea!
What I'm saying is, it's a Jinn and Fake Expedition, but with a twist.... They're girls!
Oh, that's good.
It's so original. I'm taking that right upstairs to David.

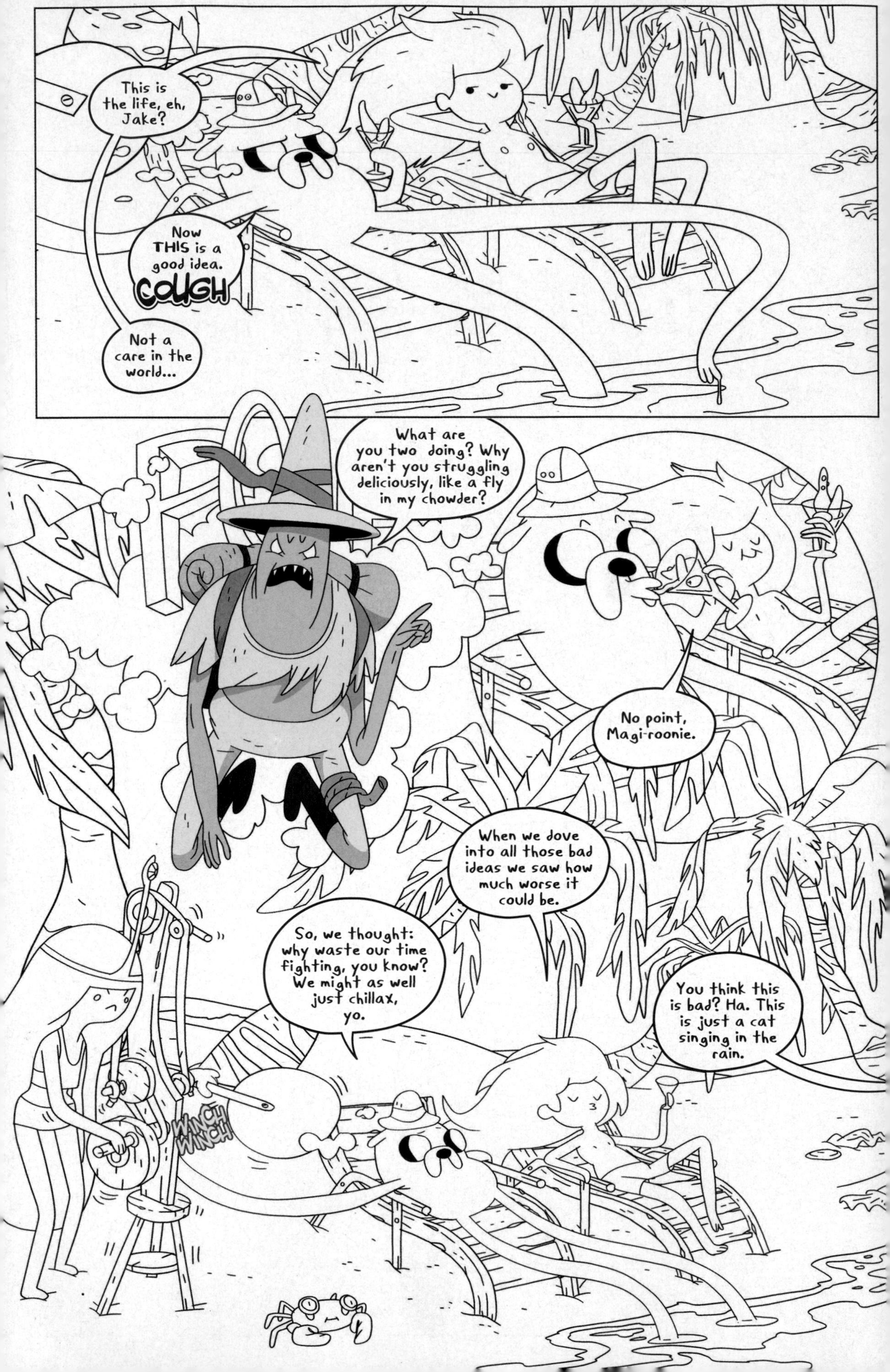
This is the life, eh, Jake?
Now THIS is a good idea.
COUGH
Not a care in the world...
What are you two doing? Why aren't you struggling deliciously, like a fly in my chowder?
No point, Magi-roonie.
When we dove into all those bad ideas we saw how much worse it could be.
So, we thought: why waste our time fighting, you know? We might as well just chillax, yo.
You think this is bad? Ha. This is just a cat singing in the rain.
WINCH WINCH

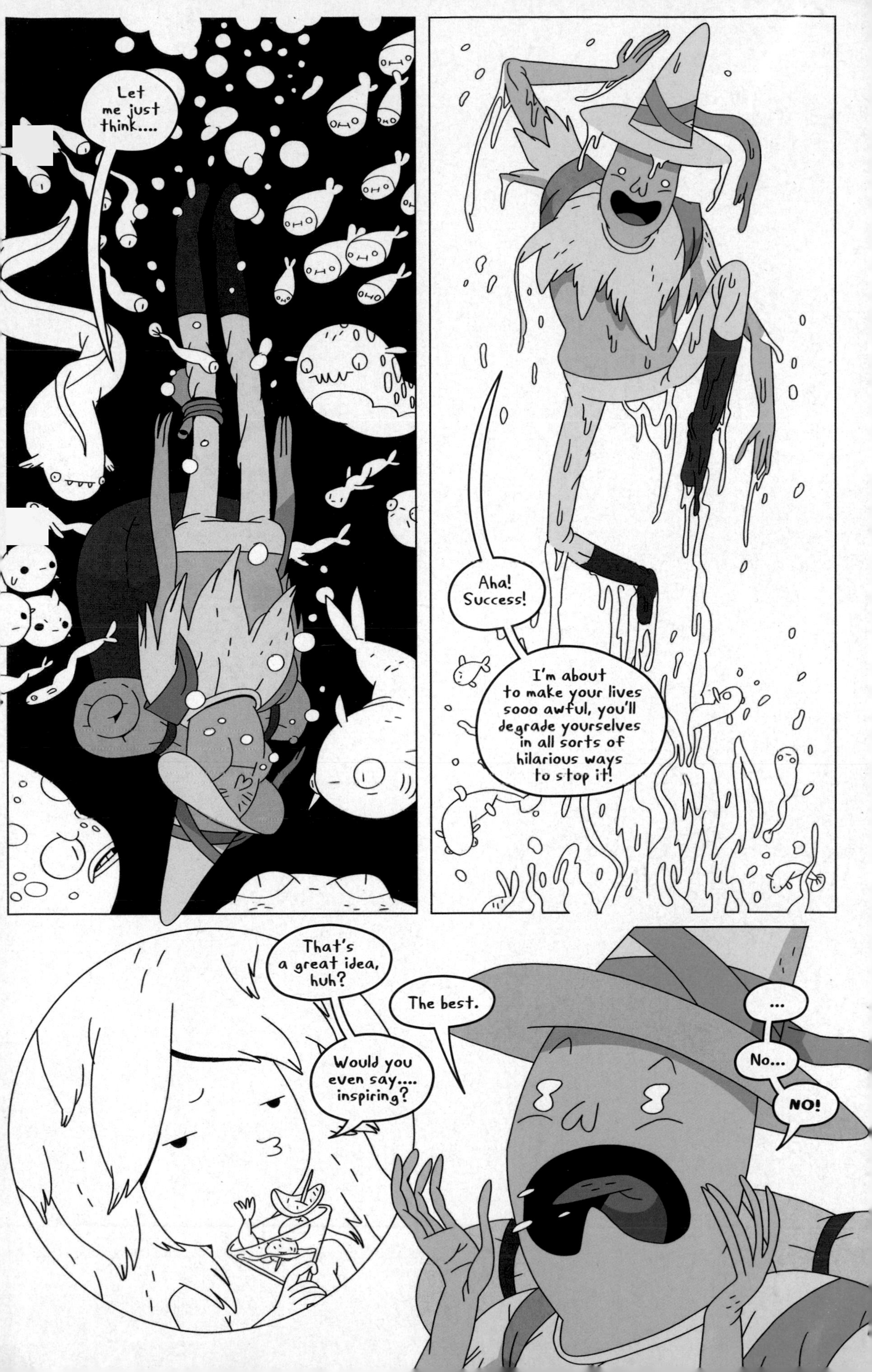

Let me just think....
Aha! Success!
I'm about to make your lives sooo awful, you'll degrade yourselves in all sorts of hilarious ways to stop it!
That's a great idea, huh?
Would you even say.... inspiring?
The best.
...
No...
NO!

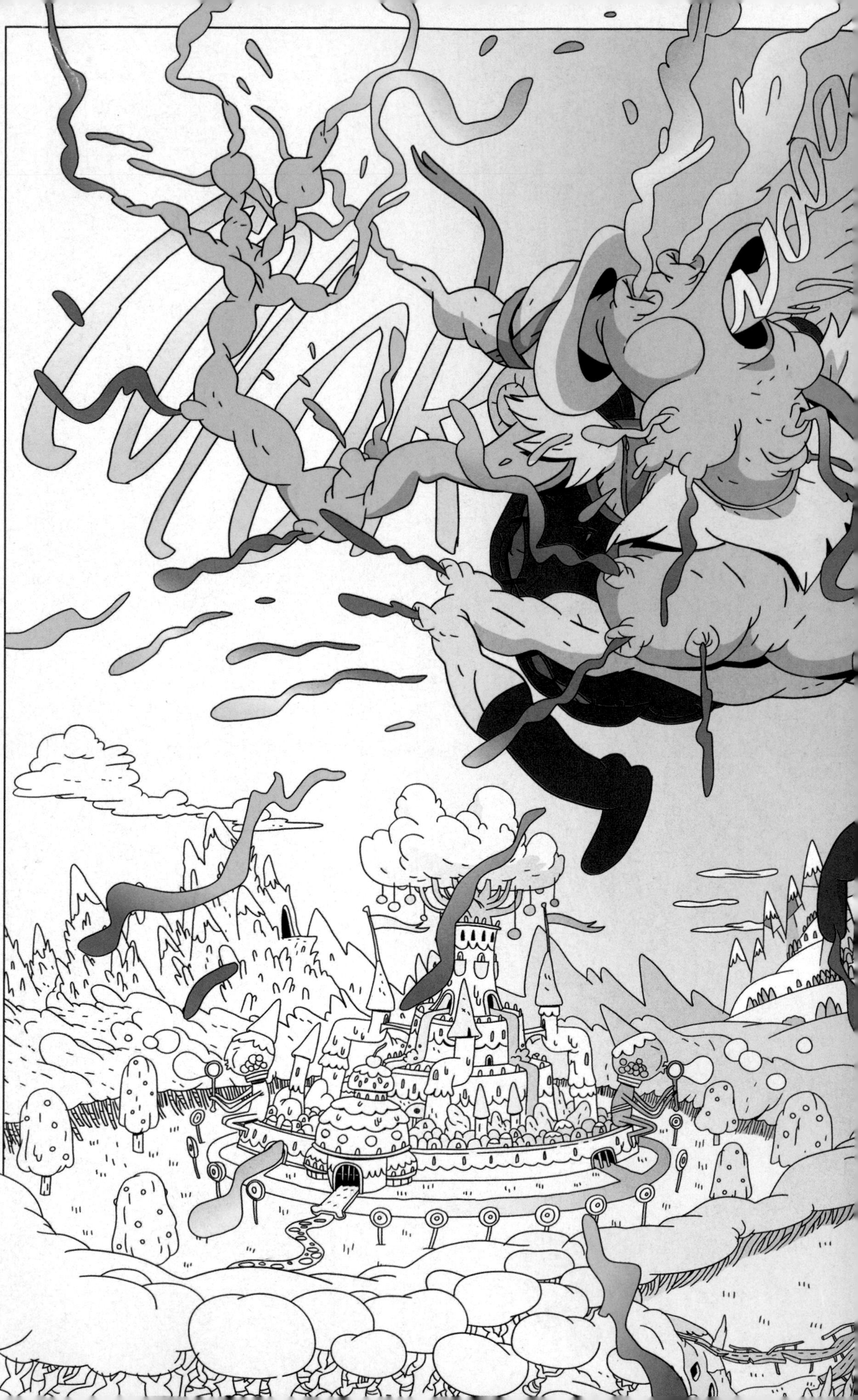
NOOOO

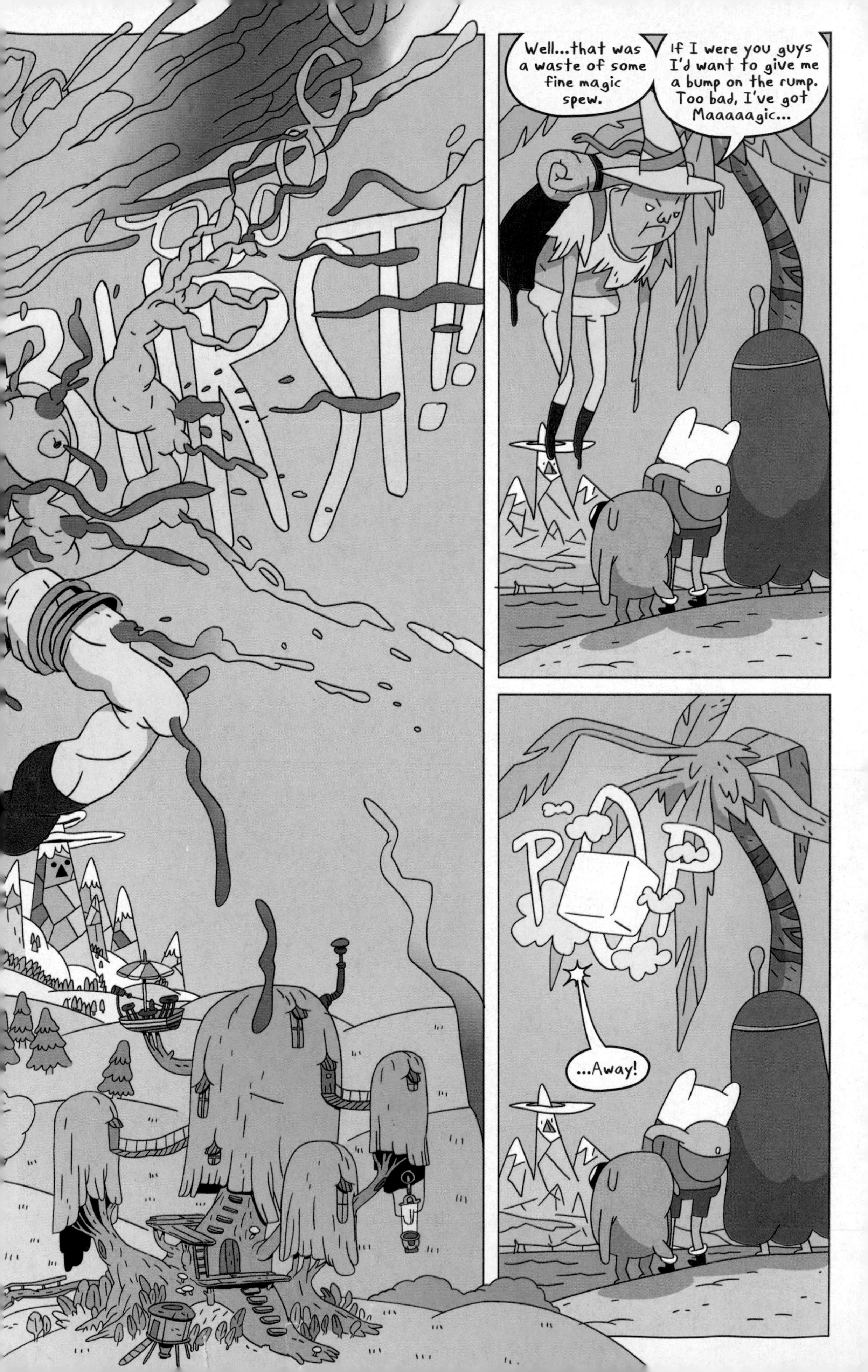
Well...that was a waste of some fine magic spew.
If I were you guys I'd want to give me a bump on the rump. Too bad, I've got Maaaaagic...
POP
...Away!

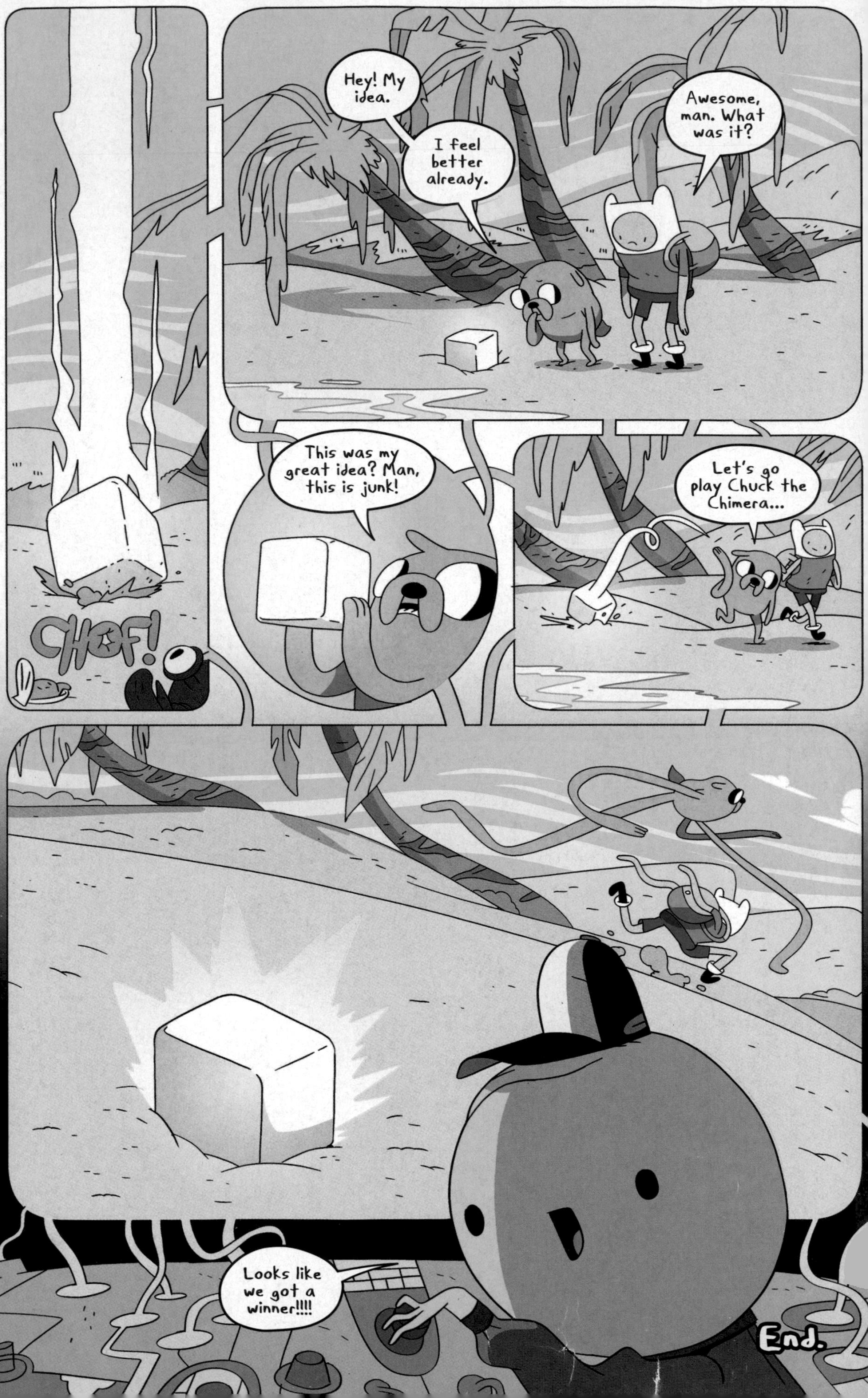

Hey! My idea.
I feel better already.
Awesome, man. What was it?
CHOF!
This was my great idea? Man, this is junk!
Let's go play Chuck the Chimera...
Looks like we got a winner!!!!
End.

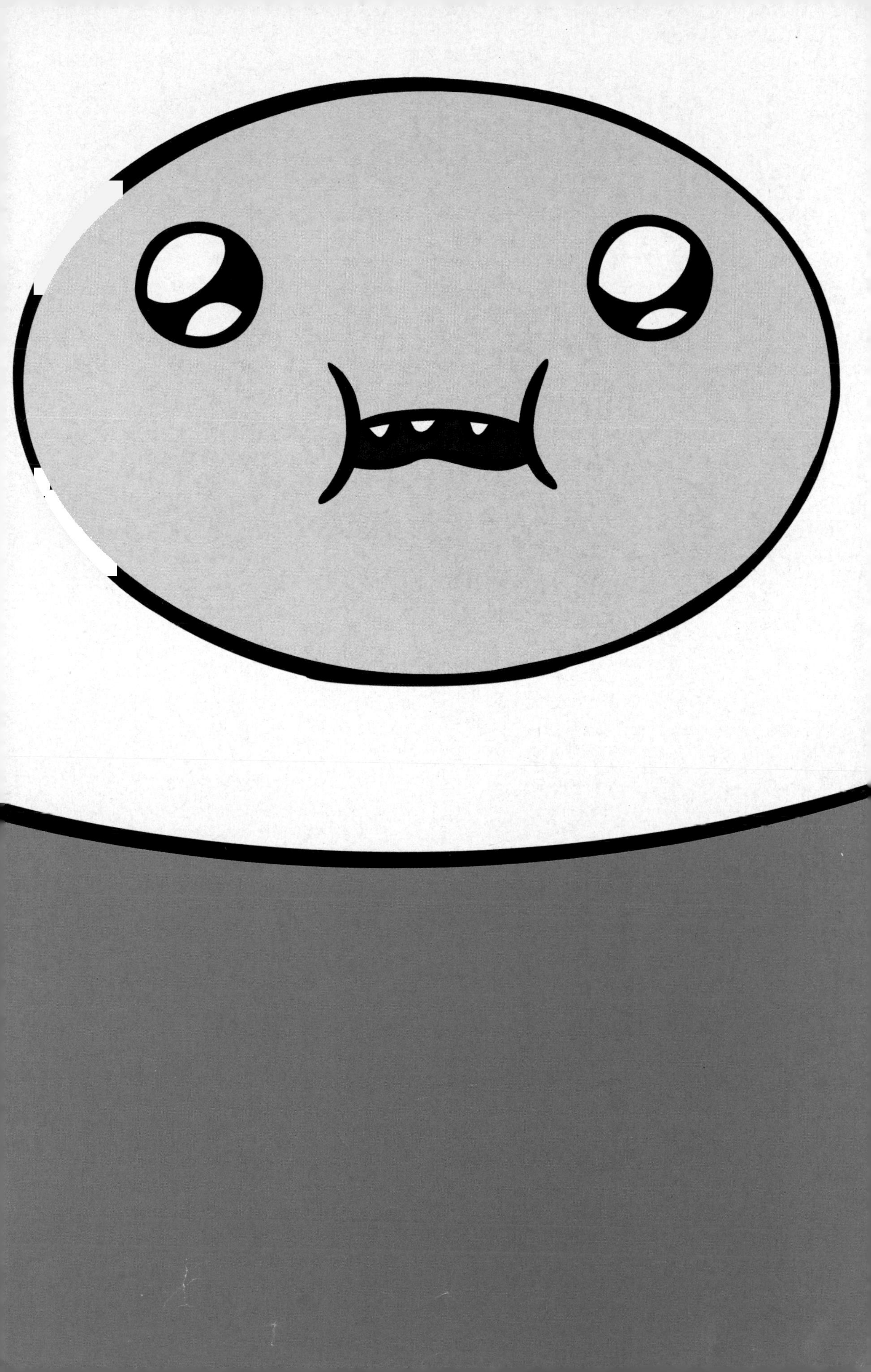

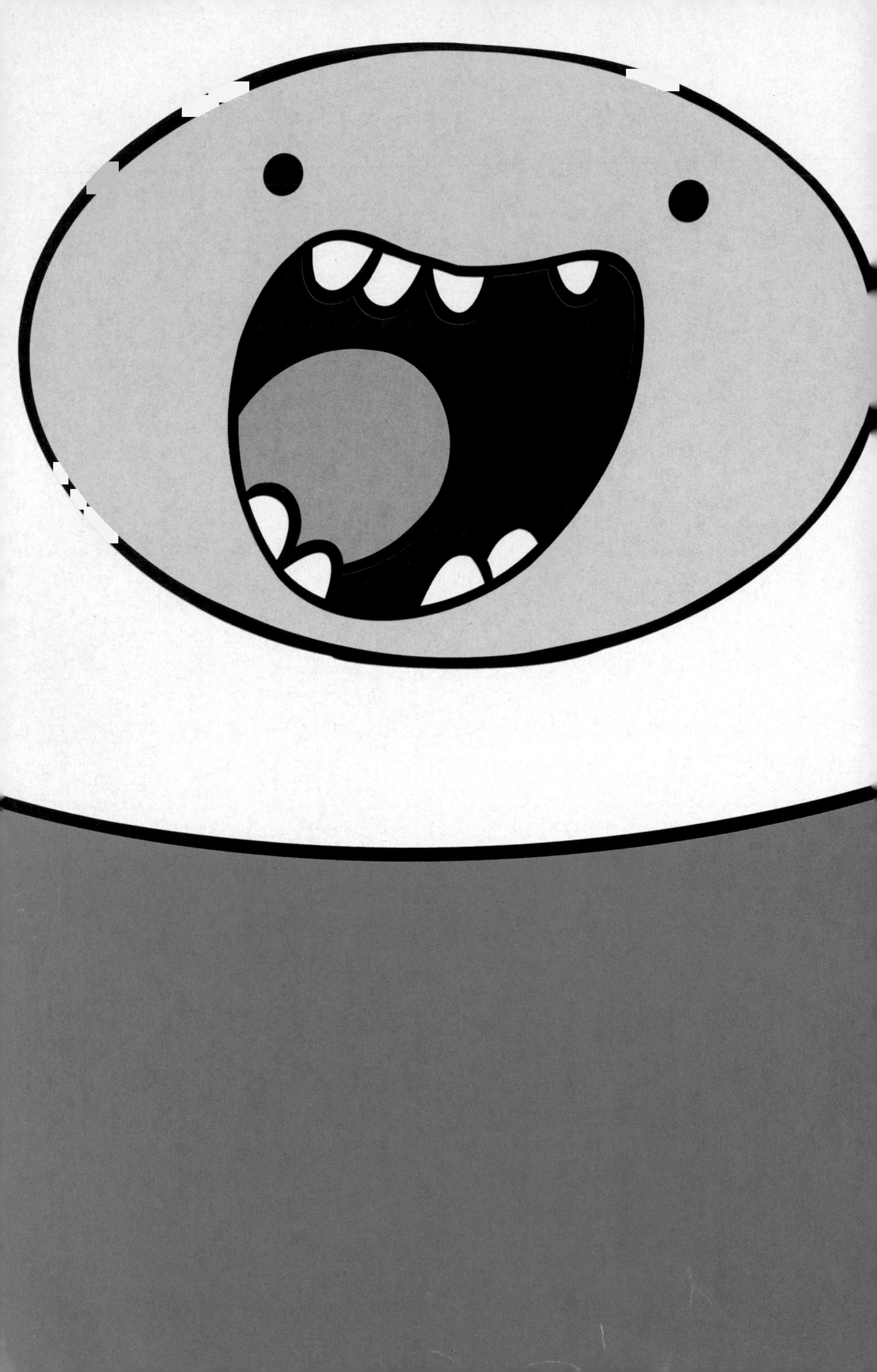

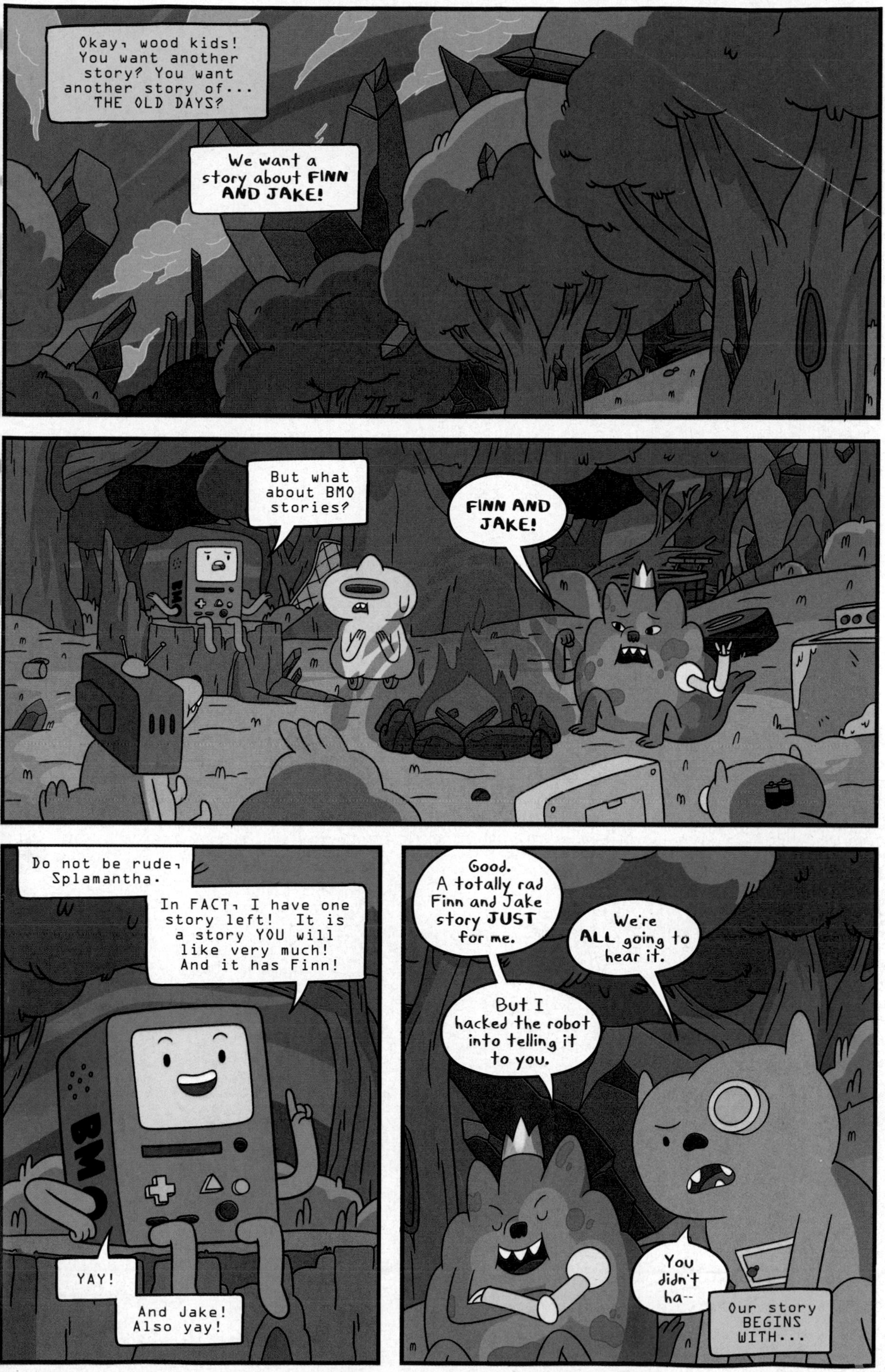
Okay, wood kids! You want another story? You want another story of... THE OLD DAYS?
We want a story about FINN AND JAKE!
But what about BMO stories?
FINN AND JAKE!
Do not be rude, Splamantha.
In FACT, I have one story left! It is a story YOU will like very much! And it has Finn!
YAY!
And Jake! Also yay!
Good. A totally rad Finn and Jake story JUST for me.
We're ALL going to hear it.
But I hacked the robot into telling it to you.
You didn't ha--
Our story BEGINS WITH...

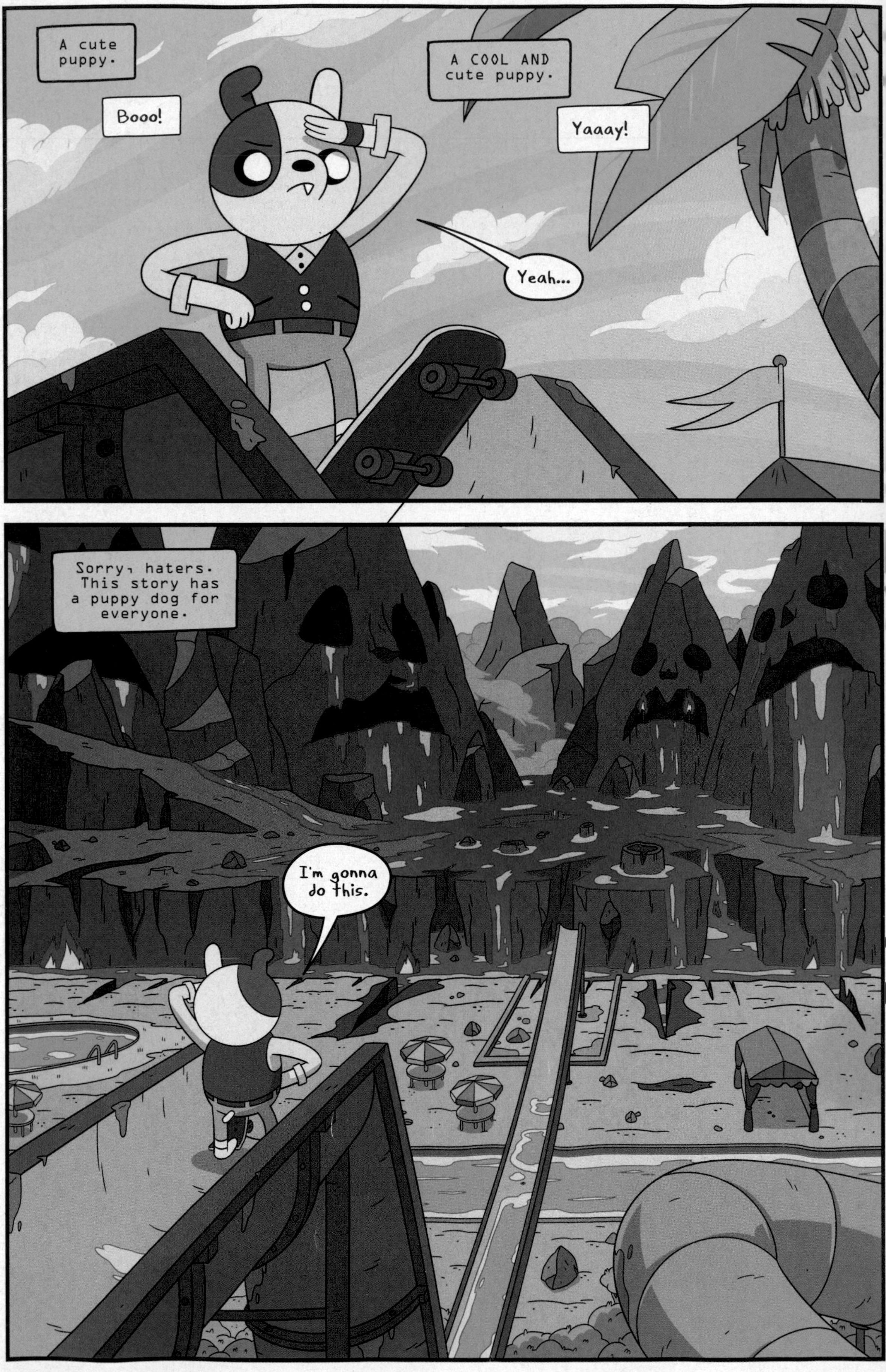

A cute puppy.
Booo!
A COOL AND cute puppy.
Yaaay!
Yeah...
Sorry, haters. This story has a puppy dog for everyone.
I'm gonna do this.

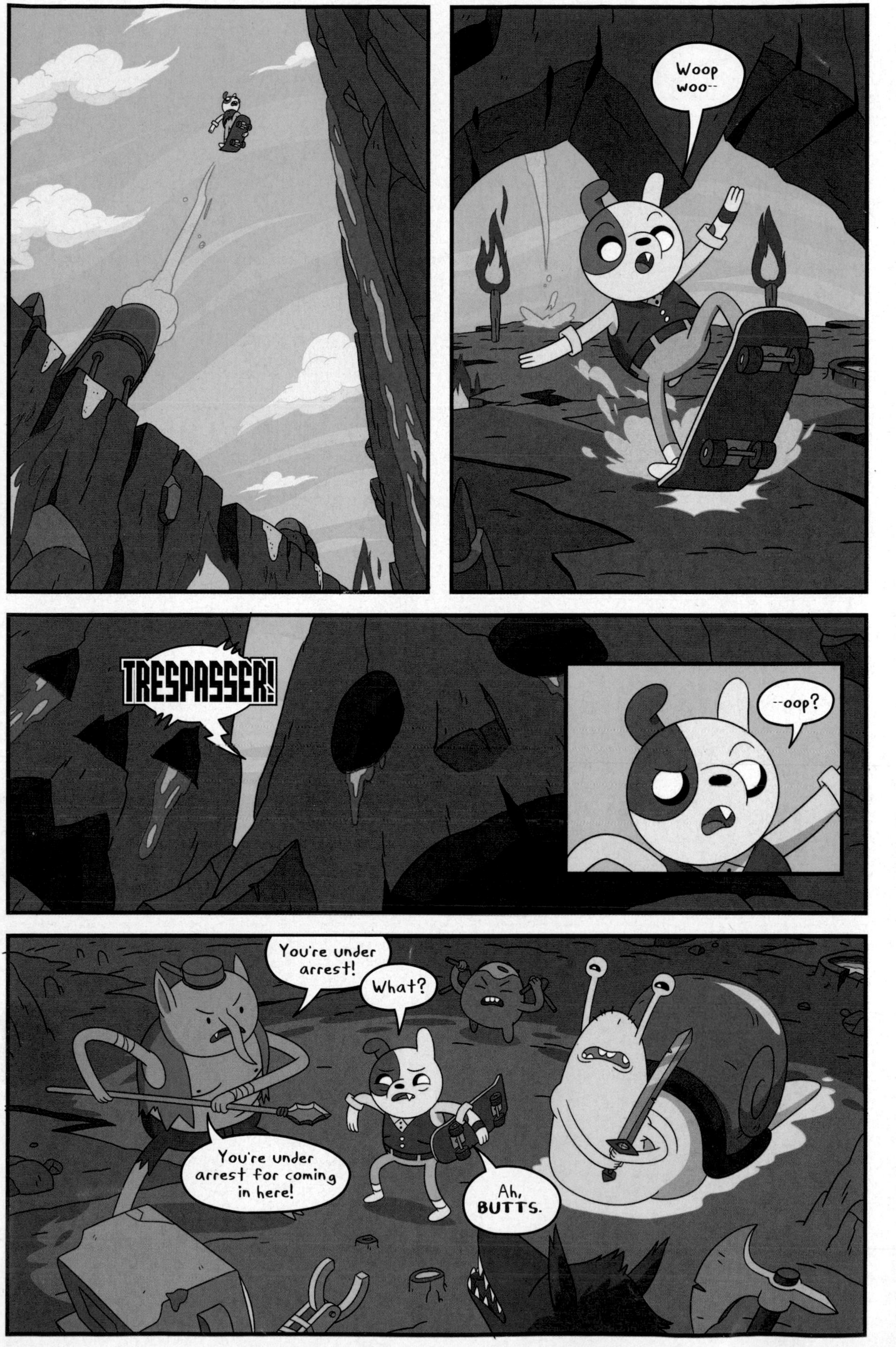
Woop woo--
TRESPASSER!
--oop?
You're under arrest!
What?
You're under arrest for coming in here!
Ah, BUTTS.

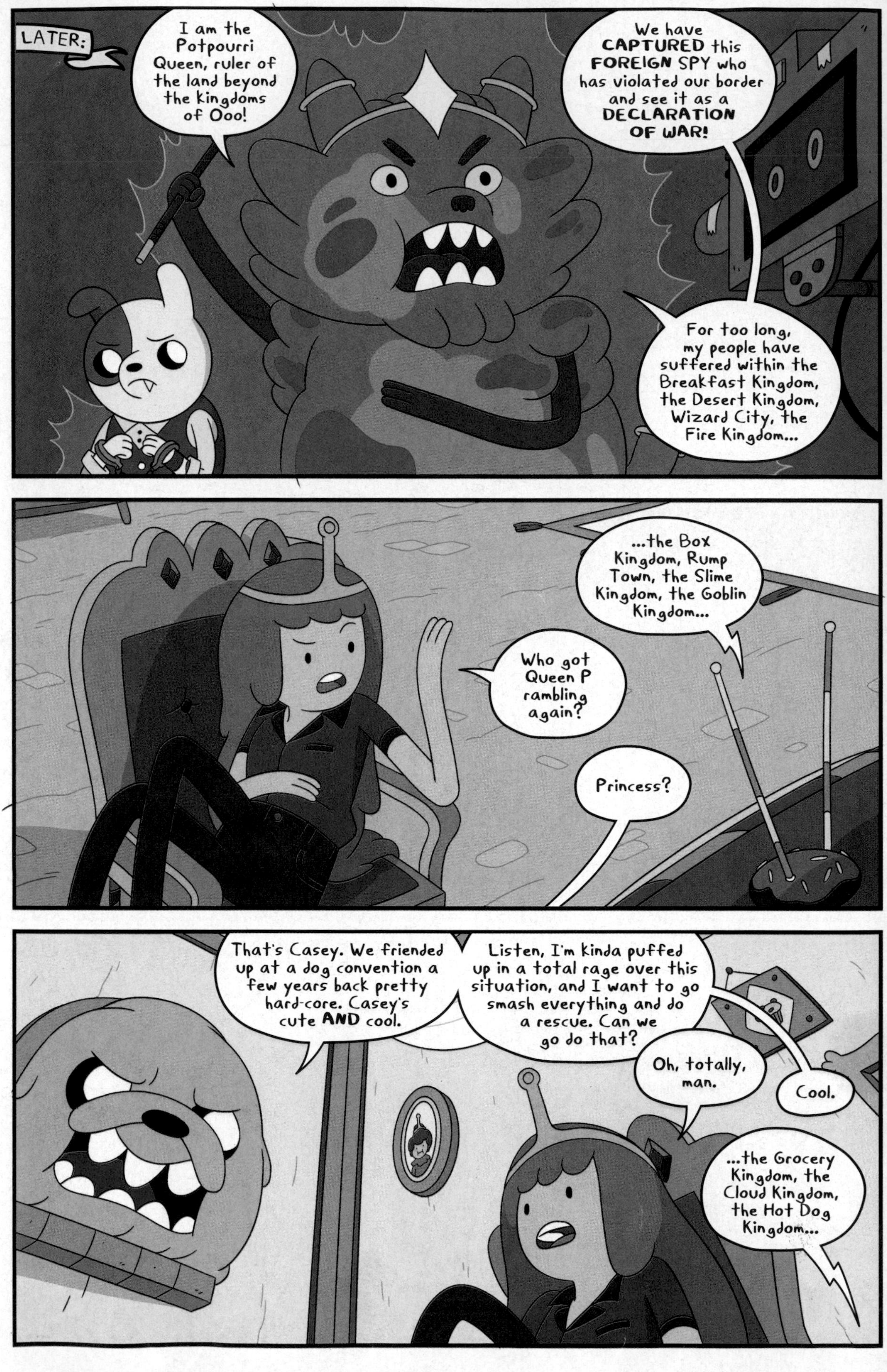

LATER:
I am the Potpourri Queen, ruler of the land beyond the kingdoms of Ooo!
We have CAPTURED this FOREIGN SPY who has violated our border and see it as a DECLARATION OF WAR!
For too long, my people have suffered within the Breakfast Kingdom, the Desert Kingdom, Wizard City, the Fire Kingdom...
...the Box Kingdom, Rump Town, the Slime Kingdom, the Goblin Kingdom...
Who got Queen P rambling again?
Princess?
That's Casey. We friended up at a dog convention a few years back pretty hard-core. Casey's cute AND cool.
Listen, I'm kinda puffed up in a total rage over this situation, and I want to go smash everything and do a rescue. Can we go do that?
Oh, totally, man.
Cool.
...the Grocery Kingdom, the Cloud Kingdom, the Hot Dog Kingdom...

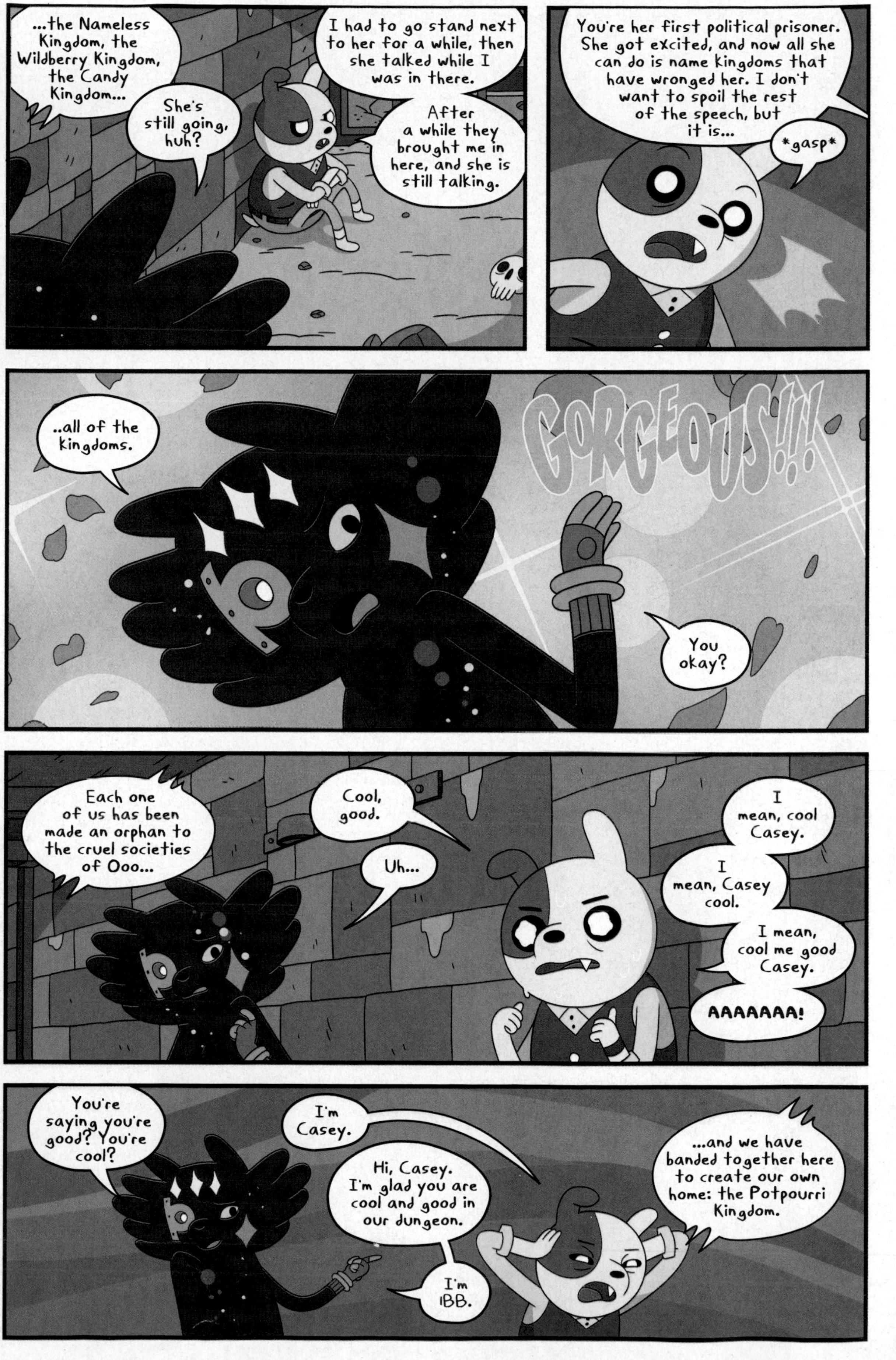
...the Nameless Kingdom, the Wildberry Kingdom, the Candy Kingdom...
She's still going, huh?
I had to go stand next to her for a while, then she talked while I was in there.
After a while they brought me in here, and she is still talking.
You're her first political prisoner. She got excited, and now all she can do is name kingdoms that have wronged her. I don't want to spoil the rest of the speech, but it is...
gasp
..all of the kingdoms.
GORGEOUS!!!
You okay?
Each one of us has been made an orphan to the cruel societies of Ooo...
Cool, good.
Uh...
I mean, cool Casey.
I mean, Casey cool.
I mean, cool me good Casey.
AAAAAAA!
You're saying you're good? You're cool?
I'm Casey.
Hi, Casey. I'm glad you are cool and good in our dungeon.
I'm IBB.
...and we have banded together here to create our own home: the Potpourri Kingdom.

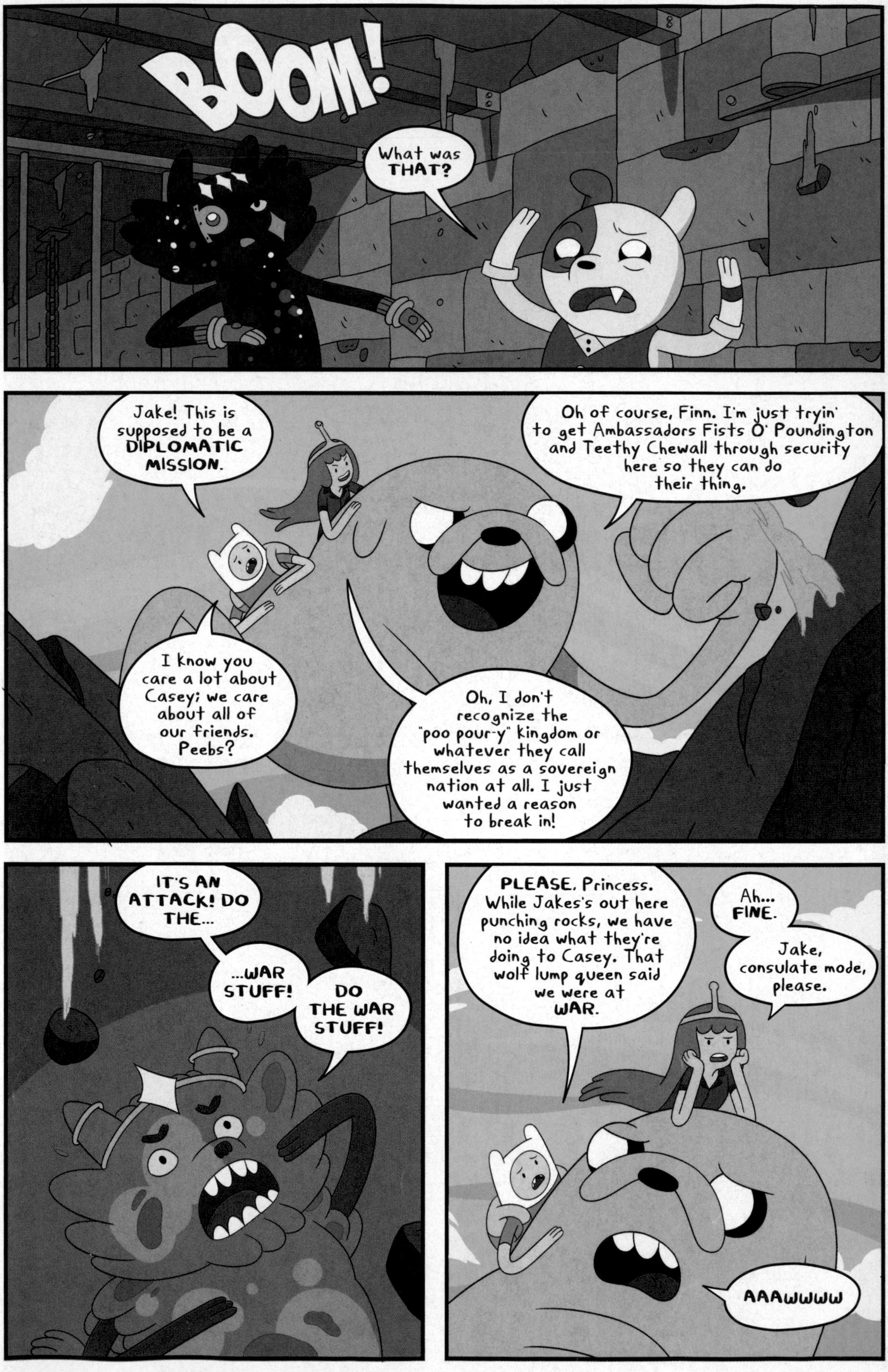
BOOM!
What was THAT?
Jake! This is supposed to be a DIPLOMATIC MISSION.
Oh of course, Finn. I'm just tryin' to get Ambassadors Fists O' Poundington and Teethy Chewall through security here so they can do their thing.
I know you care a lot about Casey; we care about all of our friends. Peebs?
Oh, I don't recognize the "poo pour-y" kingdom or whatever they call themselves as a sovereign nation at all. I just wanted a reason to break in!
IT'S AN ATTACK! DO THE...
...WAR STUFF!
DO THE WAR STUFF!
PLEASE, Princess. While Jakes's out here punching rocks, we have no idea what they're doing to Casey. That wolf lump queen said we were at WAR.
Ah... FINE.
Jake, consulate mode, please.
AAAWWWW

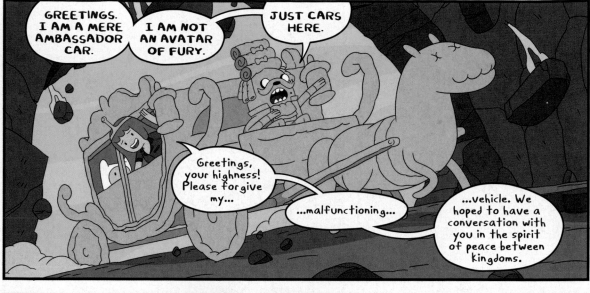

GREETINGS. I AM A MERE AMBASSADOR CAR.

I AM NOT AN AVATAR OF FURY.

JUST CARS HERE.

Greetings, your highness! Please forgive my...

...malfunctioning...

...vehicle. We hoped to have a conversation with you in the spirit of peace between kingdoms.

You just SMASHED APART THE WALLS TO MY HOUSE!

Again, this vehicle is WHACK. Sorry.

It's my brother! He's a dog. And also an alien.

MEANWHILE:

...and over the years, all sorts of people who weren't crazy about their homelands wandered about, got together, and eventually ended up here.

It's kind of funny that left to your own devices you still end up making a kingdom with a princess and everything, just like everyone else.

HEY.

She is a QUEEN.

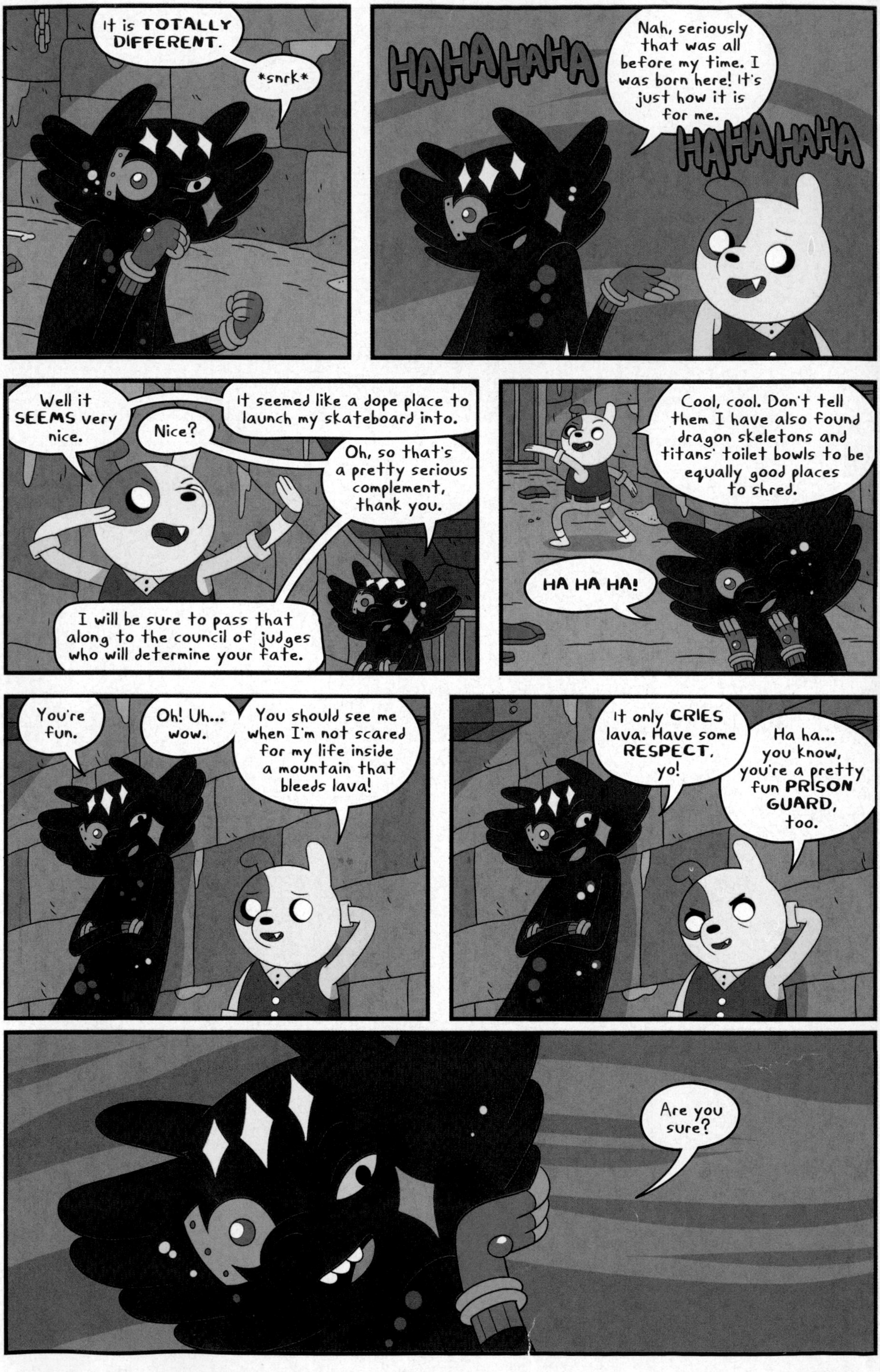
It is TOTALLY DIFFERENT.
snrk
HAHAHAHA
Nah, seriously that was all before my time. I was born here! It's just how it is for me.
HAHAHAHA
Well it SEEMS very nice.
It seemed like a dope place to launch my skateboard into.
Nice?
Oh, so that's a pretty serious complement, thank you.
I will be sure to pass that along to the council of judges who will determine your fate.
Cool, cool. Don't tell them I have also found dragon skeletons and titans' toilet bowls to be equally good places to shred.
HA HA HA!
You're fun.
Oh! Uh... wow.
You should see me when I'm not scared for my life inside a mountain that bleeds lava!
It only CRIES lava. Have some RESPECT, yo!
Ha ha... you know, you're a pretty fun PRISON GUARD, too.
Are you sure?

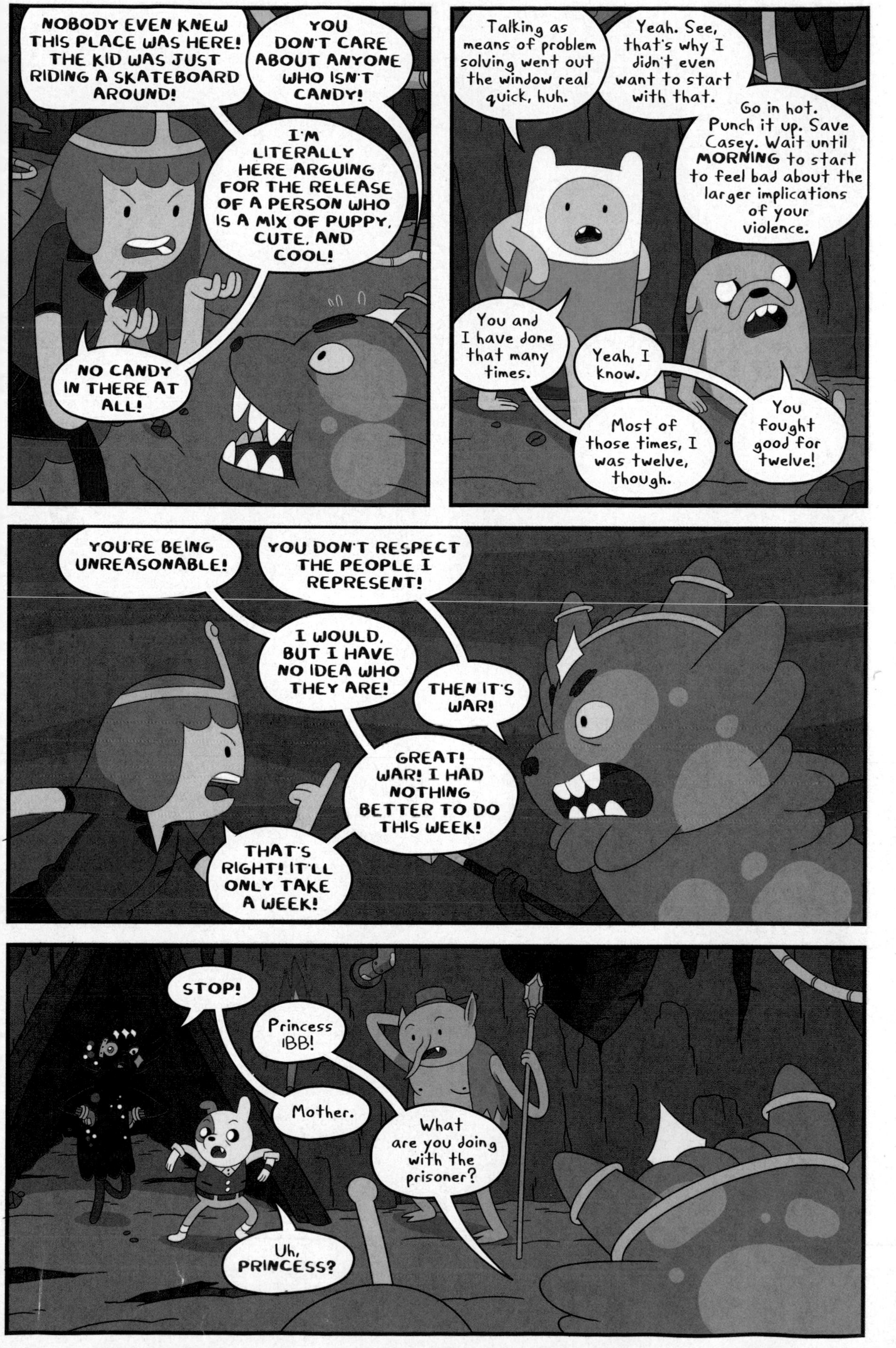
NOBODY EVEN KNEW THIS PLACE WAS HERE! THE KID WAS JUST RIDING A SKATEBOARD AROUND!
YOU DON'T CARE ABOUT ANYONE WHO ISN'T CANDY!
I'M LITERALLY HERE ARGUING FOR THE RELEASE OF A PERSON WHO IS A MIX OF PUPPY, CUTE, AND COOL!
NO CANDY IN THERE AT ALL!
Talking as means of problem solving went out the window real quick, huh.
Yeah. See, that's why I didn't even want to start with that.
Go in hot. Punch it up. Save Casey. Wait until MORNING to start to feel bad about the larger implications of your violence.
You and I have done that many times.
Yeah, I know.
Most of those times, I was twelve, though.
You fought good for twelve!
YOU'RE BEING UNREASONABLE!
YOU DON'T RESPECT THE PEOPLE I REPRESENT!
I WOULD, BUT I HAVE NO IDEA WHO THEY ARE!
THEN IT'S WAR!
GREAT! WAR! I HAD NOTHING BETTER TO DO THIS WEEK!
THAT'S RIGHT! IT'LL ONLY TAKE A WEEK!
STOP!
Princess IBB!
Mother.
What are you doing with the prisoner?
Uh, PRINCESS?

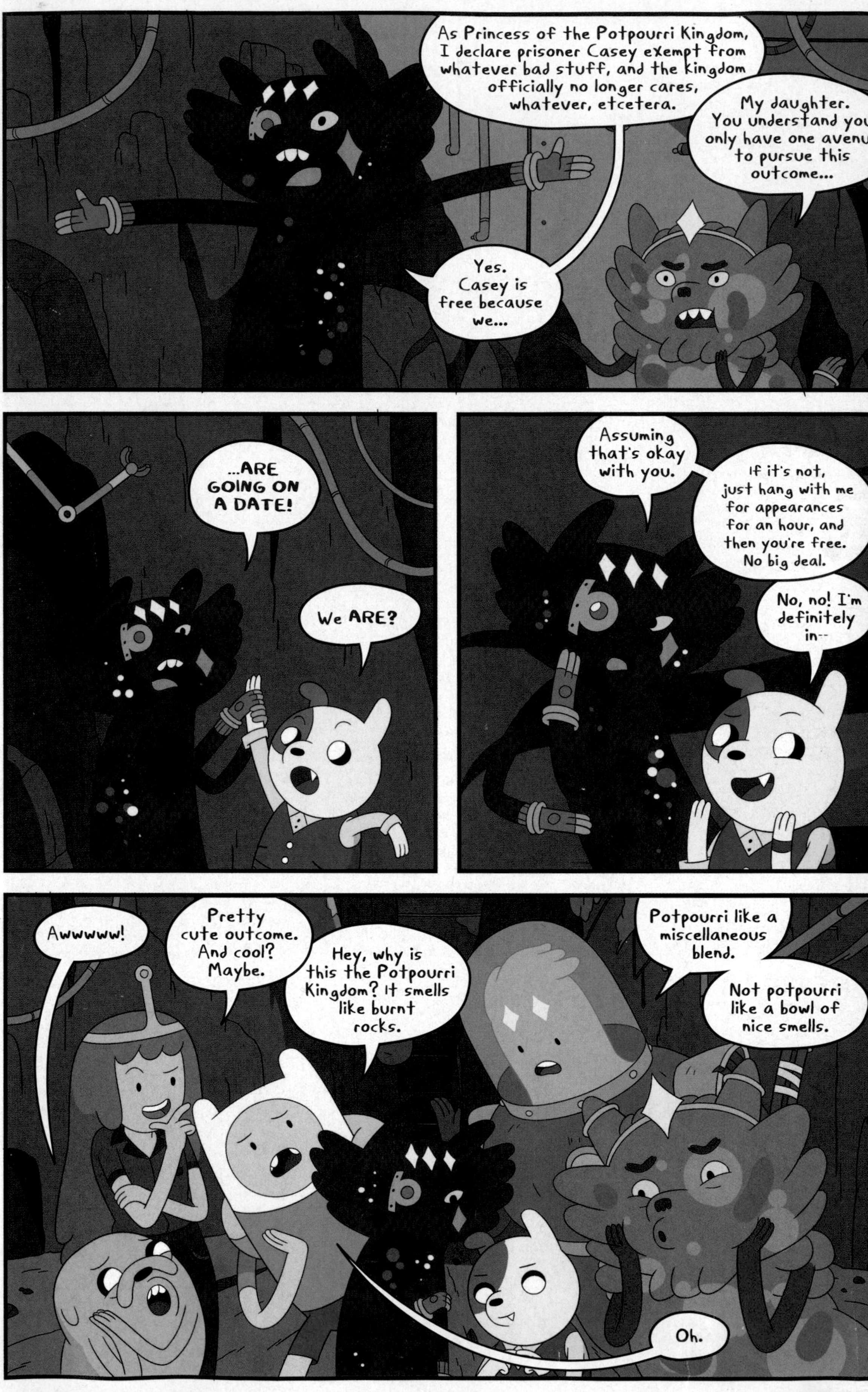

As Princess of the Potpourri Kingdom, I declare prisoner Casey exempt from whatever bad stuff, and the kingdom officially no longer cares, whatever, etcetera.
My daughter. You understand you only have one avenue to pursue this outcome...
Yes. Casey is free because we...
...ARE GOING ON A DATE!
We ARE?
Assuming that's okay with you.
If it's not, just hang with me for appearances for an hour, and then you're free. No big deal.
No, no! I'm definitely in--
Awwwww!
Pretty cute outcome. And cool? Maybe.
Hey, why is this the Potpourri Kingdom? It smells like burnt rocks.
Potpourri like a miscellaneous blend.
Not potpourri like a bowl of nice smells.
Oh.

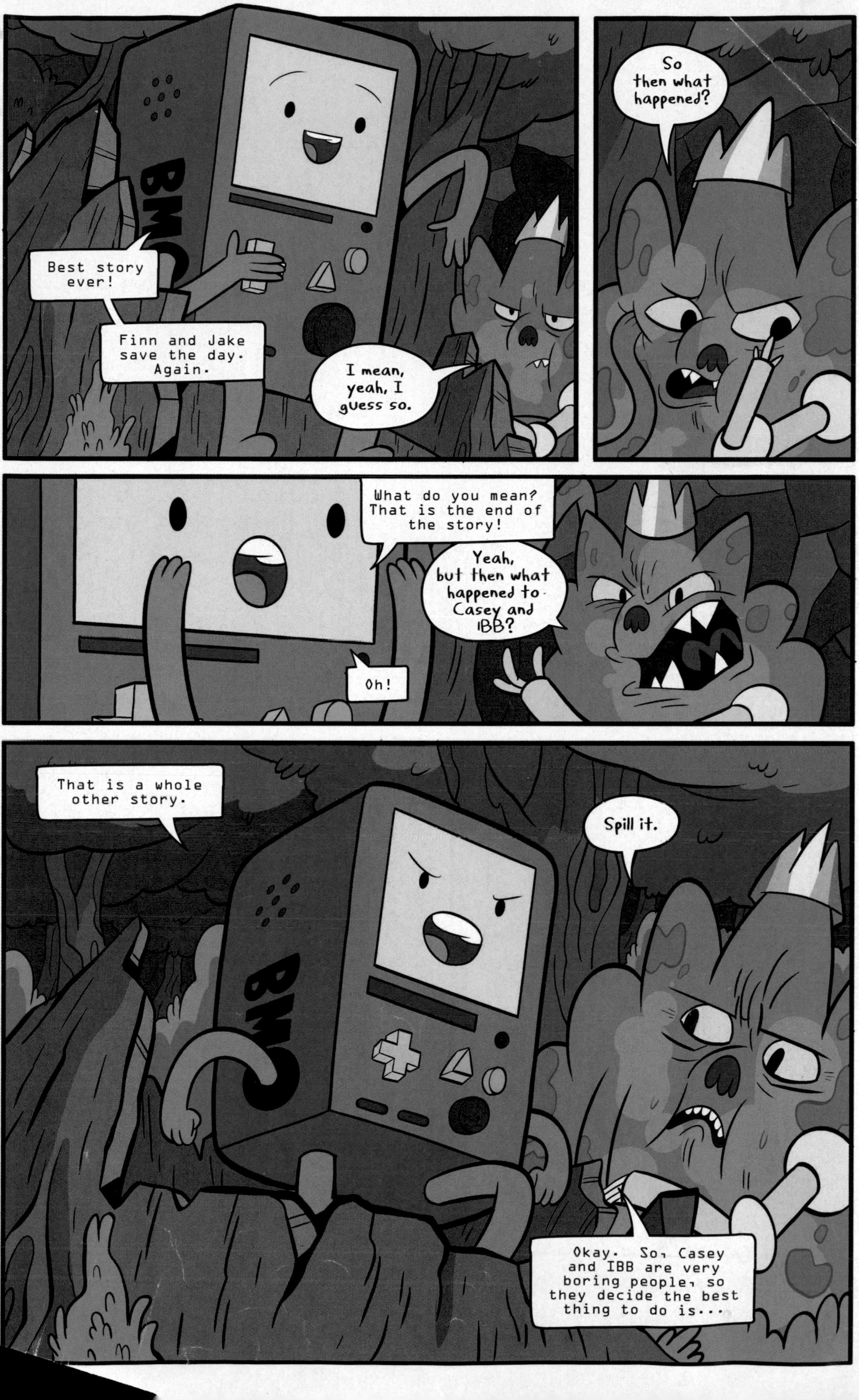
Best story ever!
Finn and Jake save the day. Again.
I mean, yeah, I guess so.
So then what happened?
What do you mean? That is the end of the story!
Yeah, but then what happened to Casey and IBB?
Oh!
That is a whole other story.
Spill it.
Okay. So, Casey and IBB are very boring people, so they decide the best thing to do is...

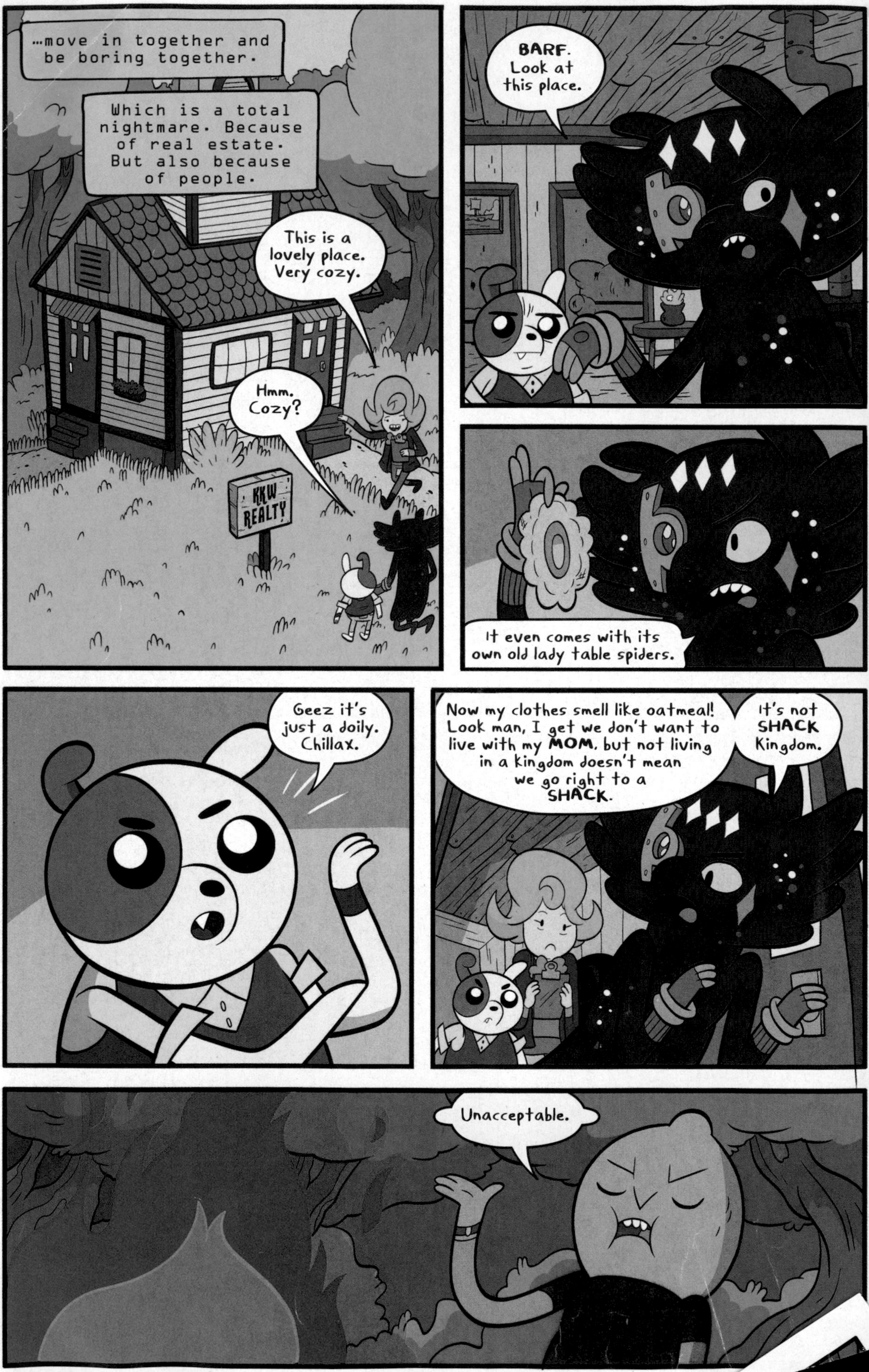

...move in together and be boring together.
Which is a total nightmare. Because of real estate. But also because of people.
This is a lovely place. Very cozy.
Hmm. Cozy?
KKW REALTY
BARF. Look at this place.
It even comes with its own old lady table spiders.
Geez it's just a doily. Chillax.
Now my clothes smell like oatmeal! Look man, I get we don't want to live with my MOM, but not living in a kingdom doesn't mean we go right to a SHACK.
It's not SHACK Kingdom.
Unacceptable.

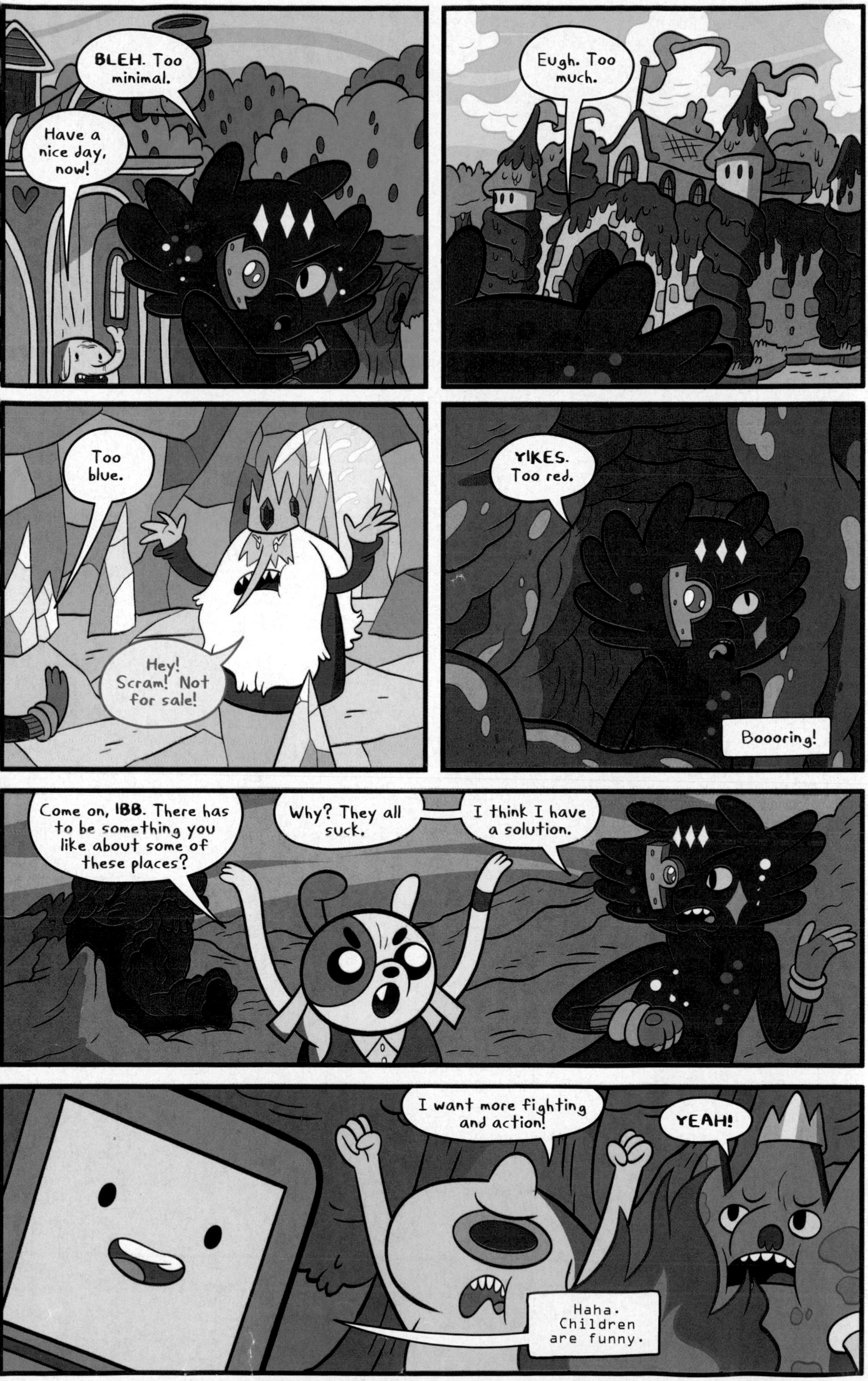
BLEH. Too minimal.
Have a nice day, now!
Eugh. Too much.
Too blue.
Hey! Scram! Not for sale!
YIKES. Too red.
Boooring!
Come on, IBB. There has to be something you like about some of these places?
Why? They all suck.
I think I have a solution.
I want more fighting and action!
YEAH!
Haha. Children are funny.

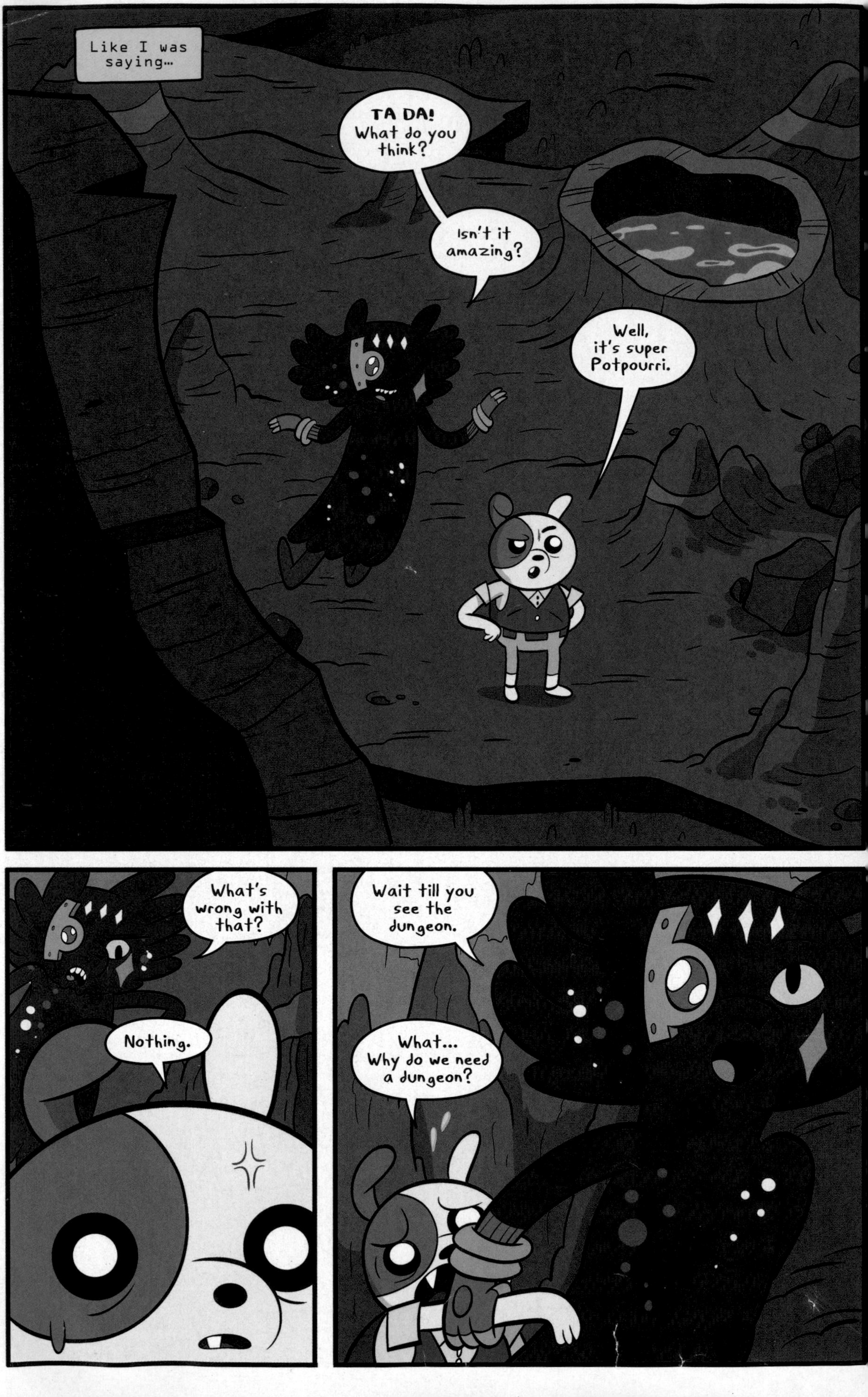
Like I was saying...
TA DA! What do you think?
Isn't it amazing?
Well, it's super Potpourri.
What's wrong with that?
Nothing.
Wait till you see the dungeon.
What... Why do we need a dungeon?

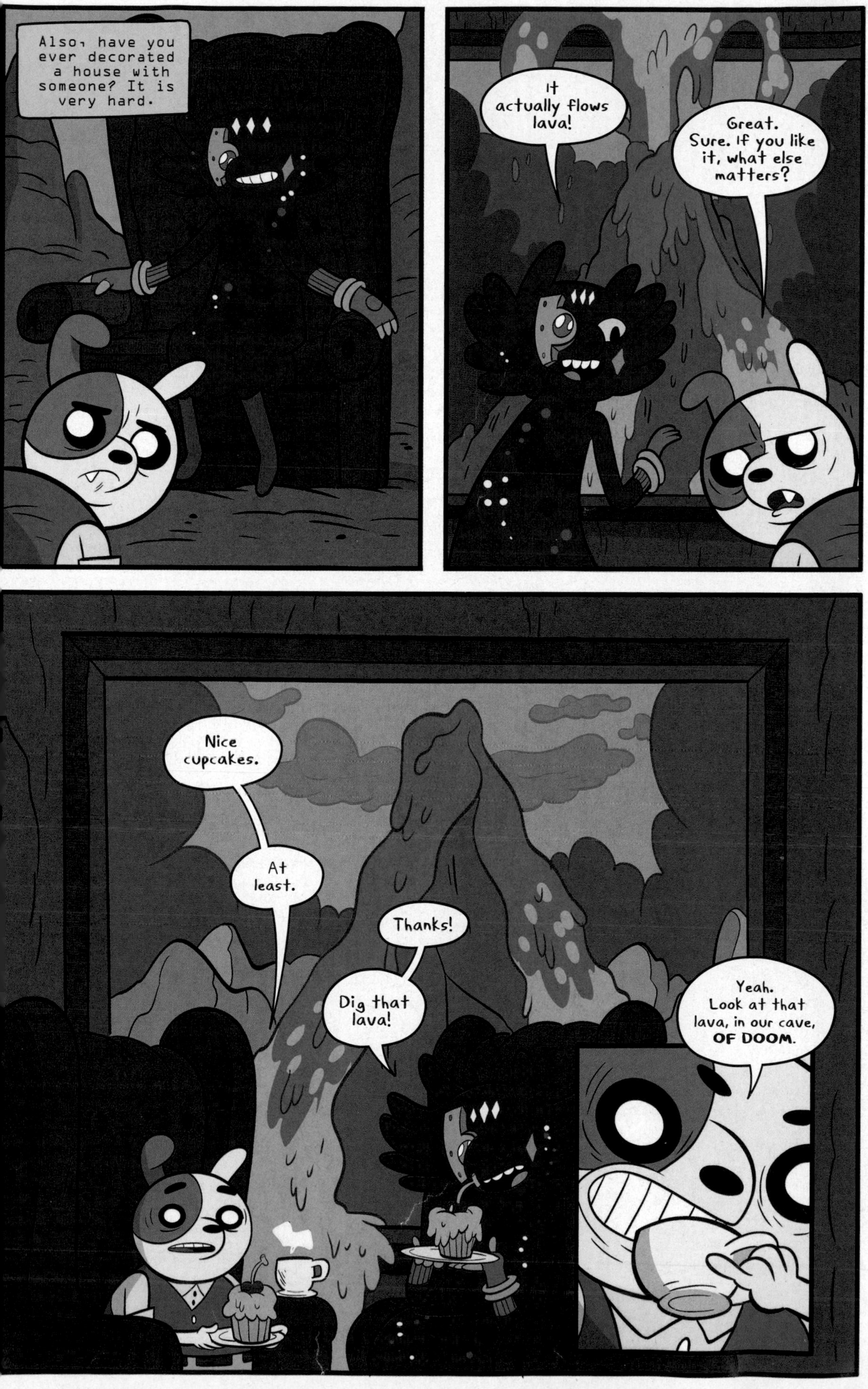
Also, have you ever decorated a house with someone? It is very hard.
It actually flows lava!
Great. Sure. If you like it, what else matters?
Nice cupcakes.
At least.
Thanks!
Dig that lava!
Yeah. Look at that lava, in our cave, **OF DOOM**.

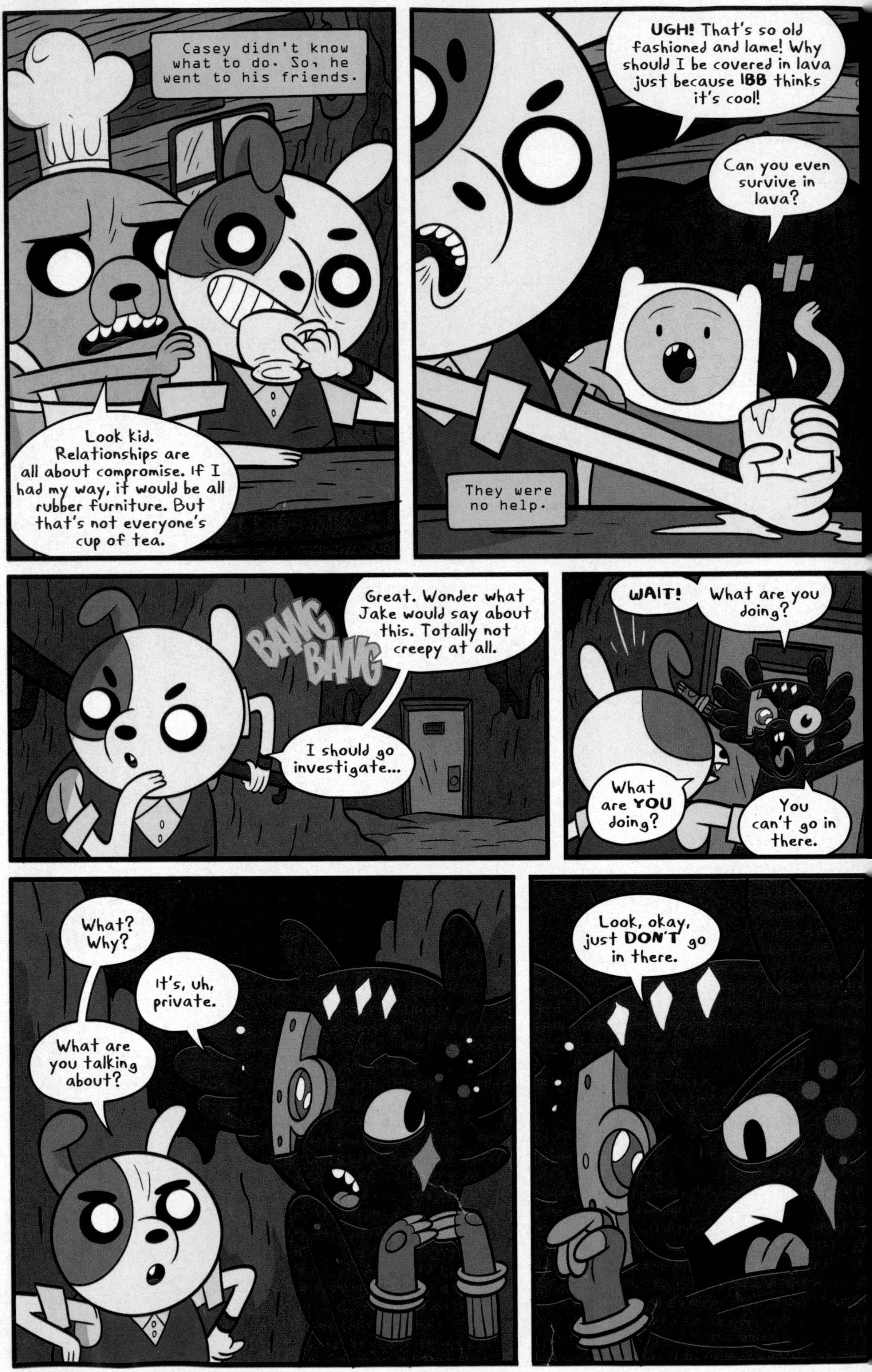

Casey didn't know what to do. So, he went to his friends.
Look kid. Relationships are all about compromise. If I had my way, it would be all rubber furniture. But that's not everyone's cup of tea.
UGH! That's so old fashioned and lame! Why should I be covered in lava just because IBB thinks it's cool!
Can you even survive in lava?
They were no help.
BANG BANG
Great. Wonder what Jake would say about this. Totally not creepy at all.
I should go investigate...
WAIT!
What are you doing?
What are YOU doing?
You can't go in there.
What? Why?
It's, uh, private.
What are you talking about?
Look, okay, just DON'T go in there.

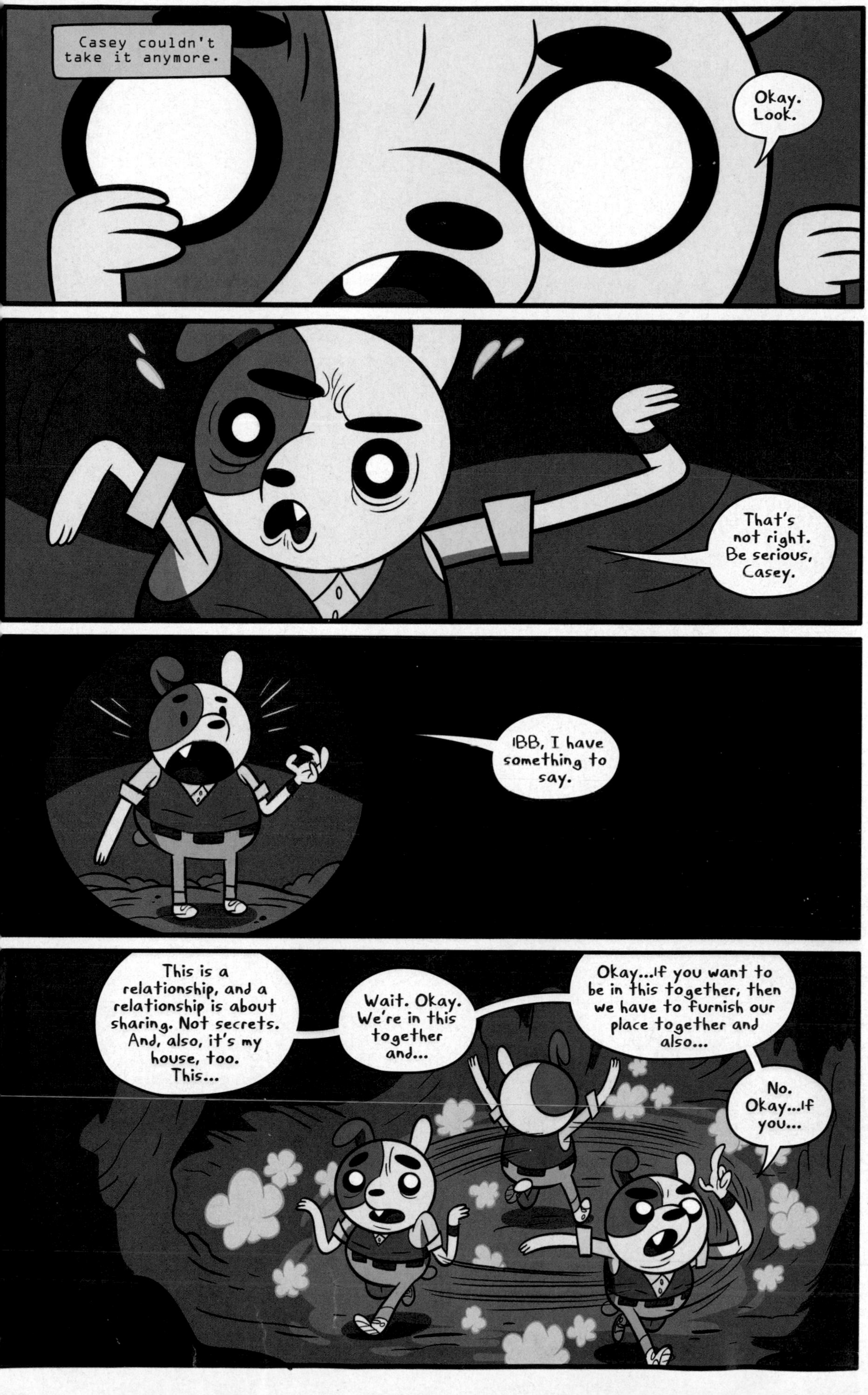
Casey couldn't take it anymore.
Okay. Look.
That's not right. Be serious, Casey.
IBB, I have something to say.
This is a relationship, and a relationship is about sharing. Not secrets. And, also, it's my house, too. This...
Wait. Okay. We're in this together and...
Okay...If you want to be in this together, then we have to furnish our place together and also...
No. Okay...If you...

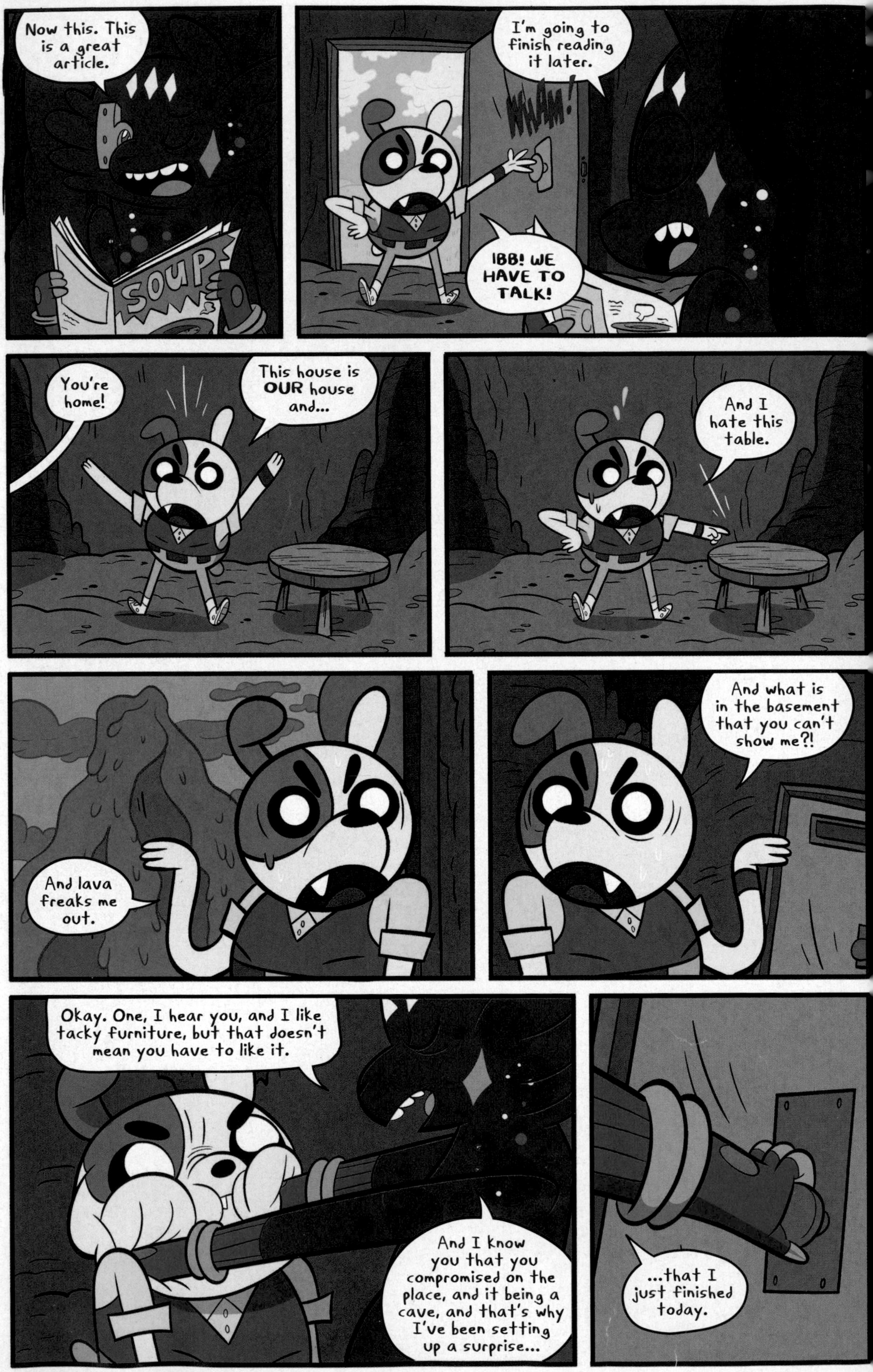
Now this. This is a great article.
SOUP
I'm going to finish reading it later.
WHAM!
IBB! WE HAVE TO TALK!
You're home!
This house is OUR house and...
And I hate this table.
And lava freaks me out.
And what is in the basement that you can't show me?!
Okay. One, I hear you, and I like tacky furniture, but that doesn't mean you have to like it.
And I know you that you compromised on the place, and it being a cave, and that's why I've been setting up a surprise...
...that I just finished today.

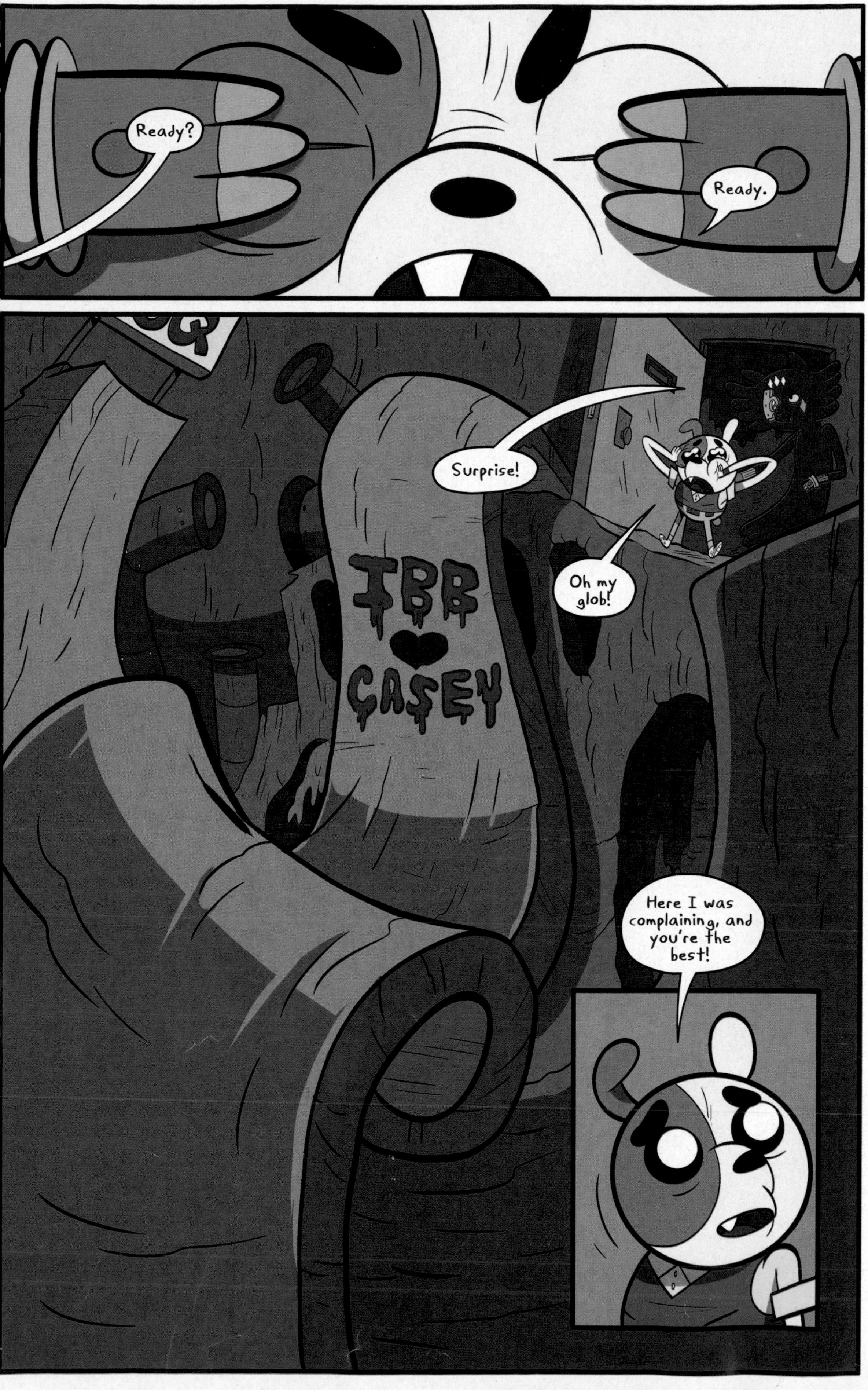
Ready?
Ready.
Surprise!
Oh my glob!
IBB
CASEY
Here I was complaining, and you're the best!

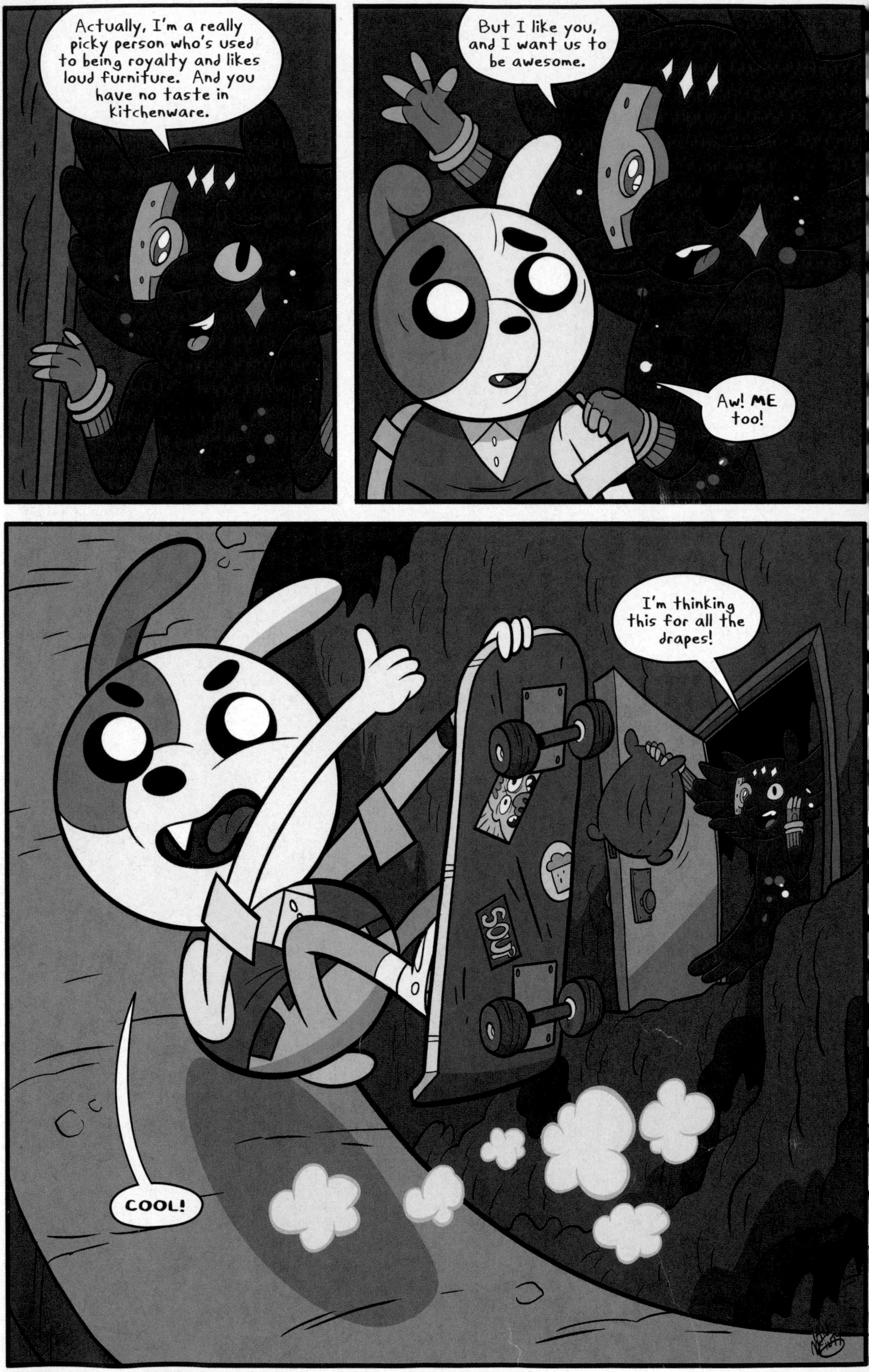
Actually, I'm a really picky person who's used to being royalty and likes loud furniture. And you have no taste in kitchenware.
But I like you, and I want us to be awesome.
Aw! ME too!
I'm thinking this for all the drapes!
COOL!
SOUP

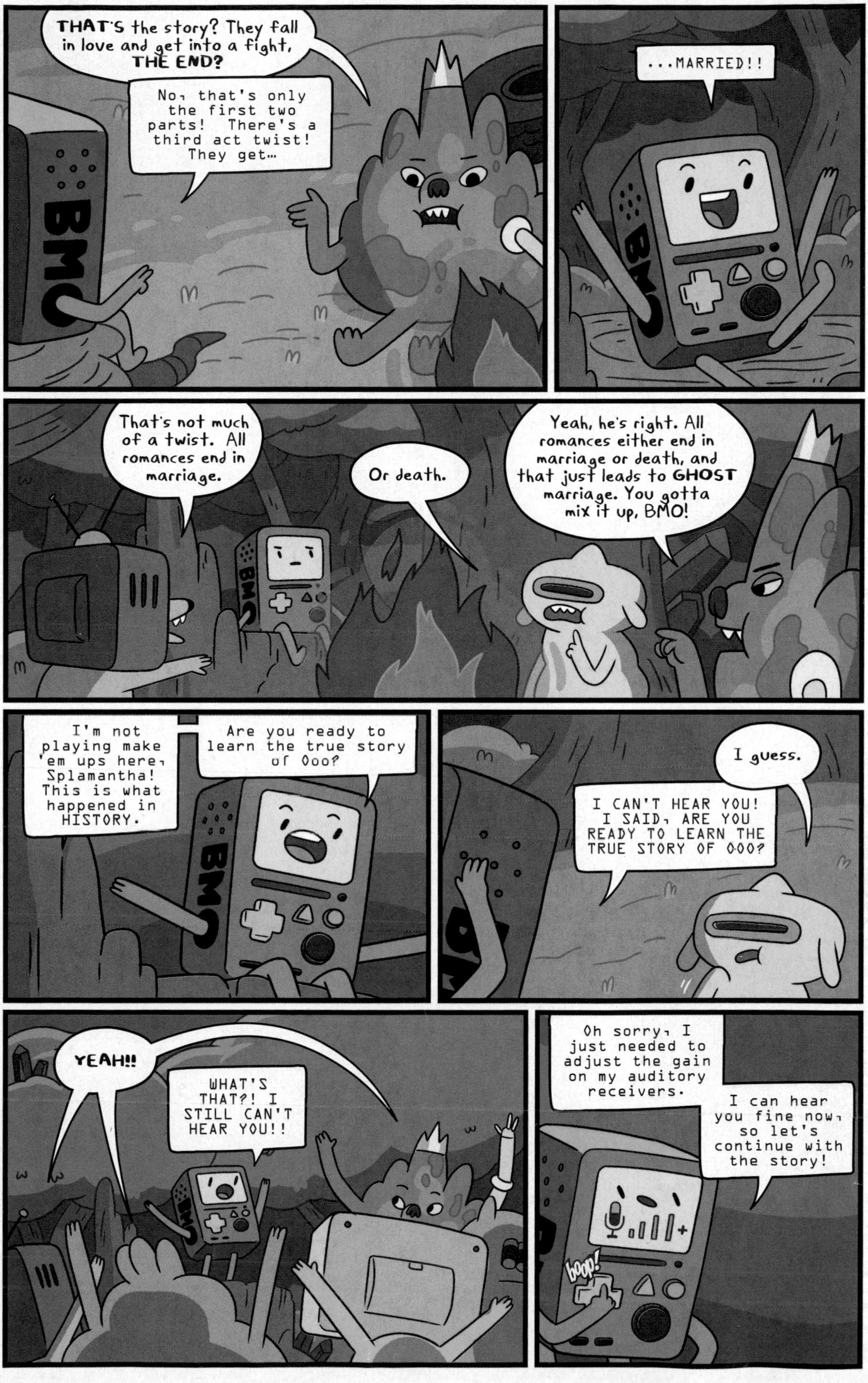
THAT'S the story? They fall in love and get into a fight, THE END?
No, that's only the first two parts! There's a third act twist! They get…
...MARRIED!!
That's not much of a twist. All romances end in marriage.
Or death.
Yeah, he's right. All romances either end in marriage or death, and that just leads to GHOST marriage. You gotta mix it up, BMO!
I'm not playing make 'em ups here, Splamantha! This is what happened in HISTORY.
Are you ready to learn the true story of Ooo?
I guess.
I CAN'T HEAR YOU! I SAID, ARE YOU READY TO LEARN THE TRUE STORY OF OOO?
YEAH!!
WHAT'S THAT?! I STILL CAN'T HEAR YOU!!
Oh sorry, I just needed to adjust the gain on my auditory receivers.
I can hear you fine now, so let's continue with the story!
boop!

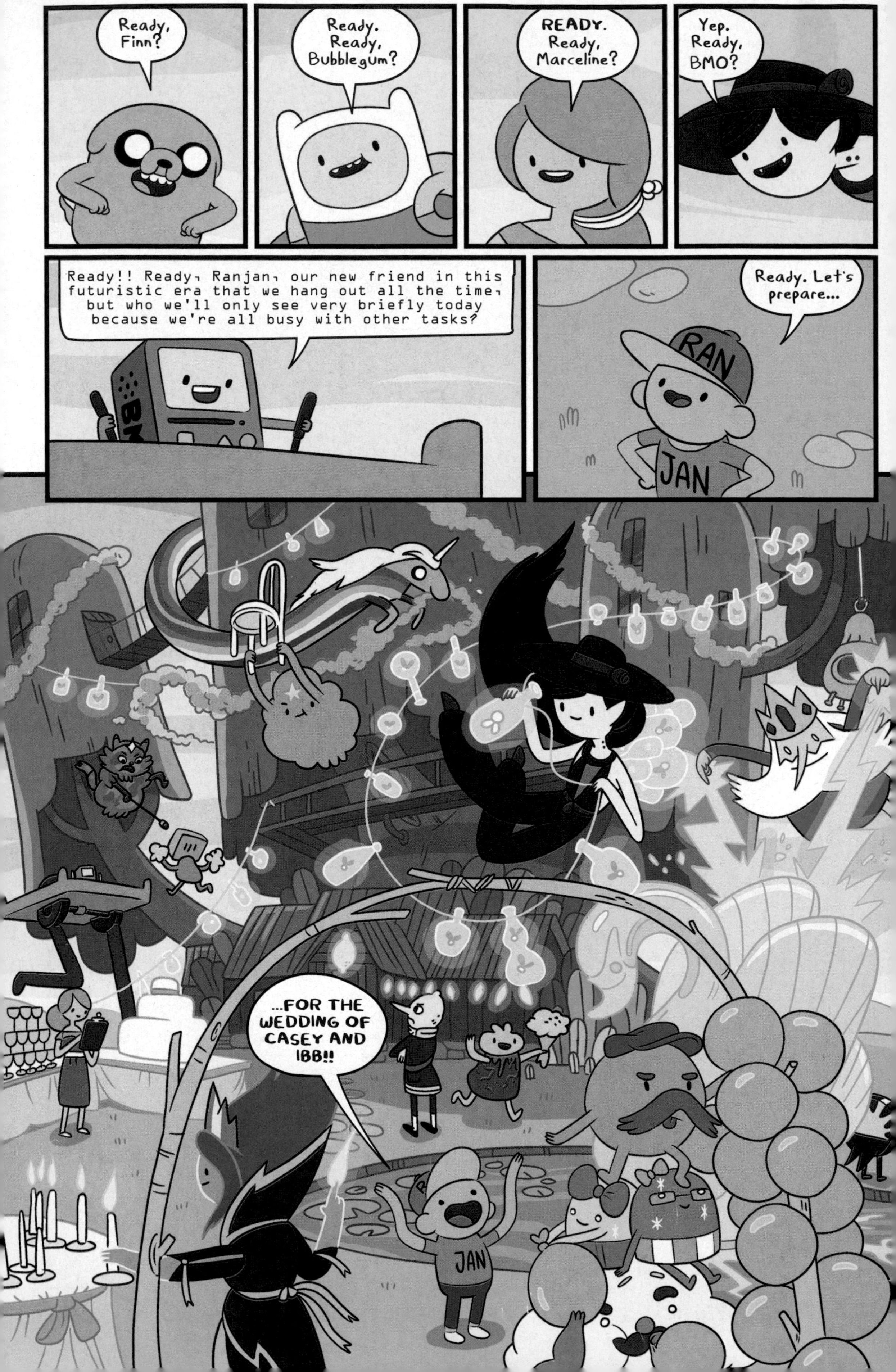

Ready, Finn?
Ready. Ready, Bubblegum?
READY. Ready, Marceline?
Yep. Ready, BMO?
Ready!! Ready, Ranjan, our new friend in this futuristic era that we hang out all the time, but who we'll only see very briefly today because we're all busy with other tasks?
RAN
JAN
Ready. Let's prepare...
...FOR THE WEDDING OF CASEY AND IBB!!
JAN

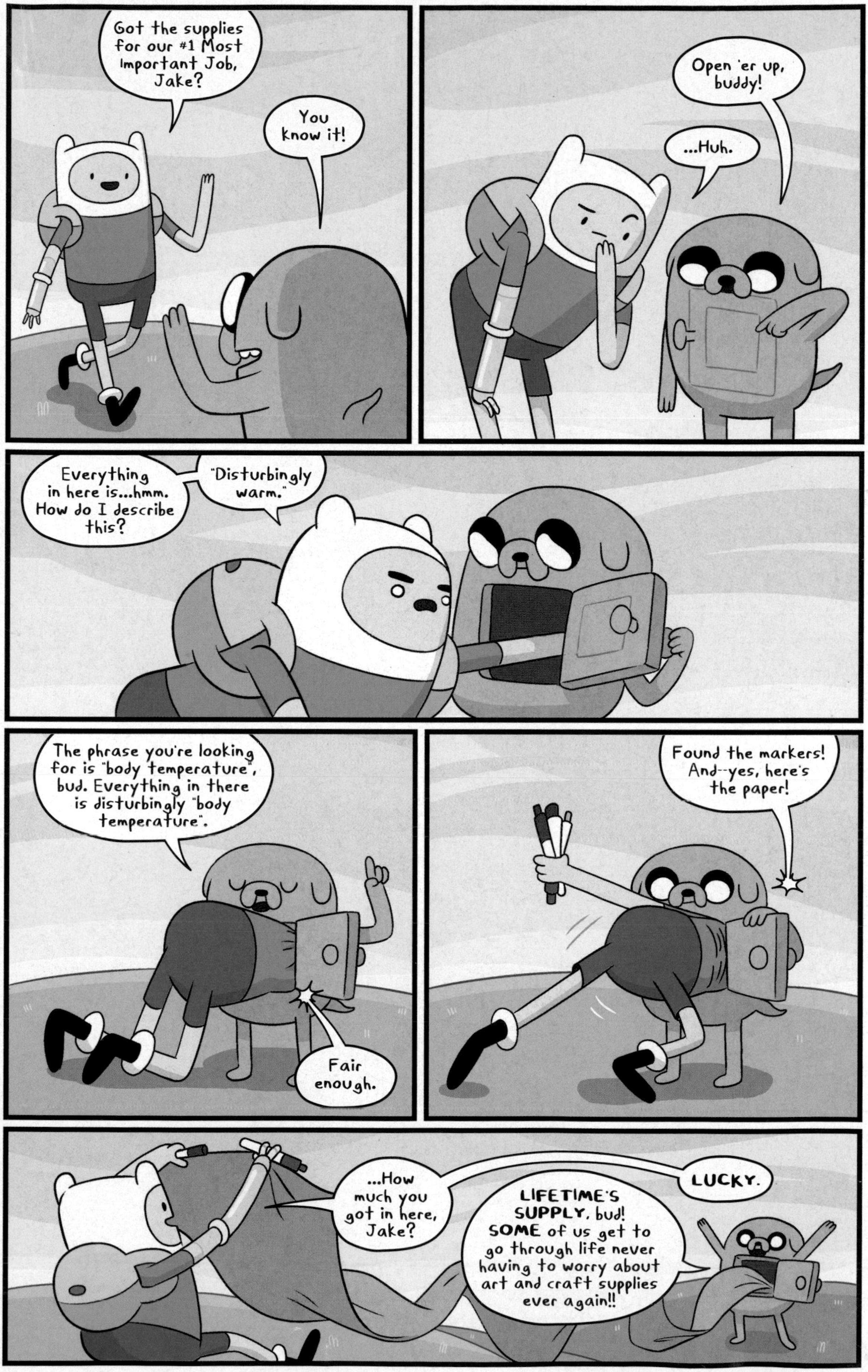

Got the supplies for our #1 Most Important Job, Jake?
You know it!
Open 'er up, buddy!
...Huh.
Everything in here is...hmm. How do I describe this?
"Disturbingly warm."
The phrase you're looking for is "body temperature", bud. Everything in there is disturbingly "body temperature".
Fair enough.
Found the markers! And--yes, here's the paper!
...How much you got in here, Jake?
LIFETIME'S SUPPLY, bud! SOME of us get to go through life never having to worry about art and craft supplies ever again!!
LUCKY.

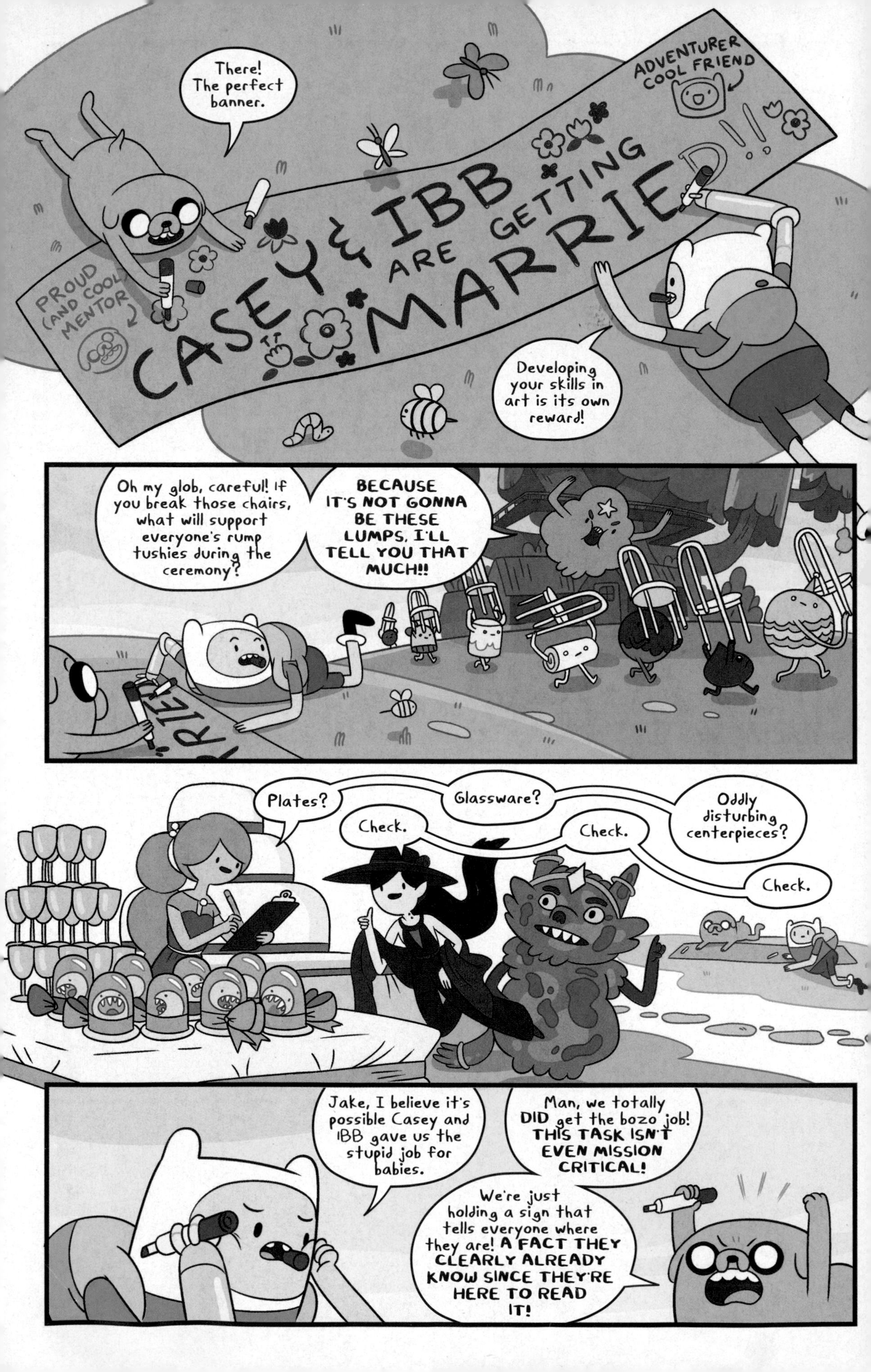
There! The perfect banner.
ADVENTURER COOL FRIEND
PROUD (AND COOL) MENTOR
CASEY & IBB ARE GETTING MARRIED!!!
Developing your skills in art is its own reward!
Oh my glob, careful! If you break those chairs, what will support everyone's rump tushies during the ceremony?
BECAUSE IT'S NOT GONNA BE THESE LUMPS, I'LL TELL YOU THAT MUCH!!
Plates?
Check.
Glassware?
Check.
Oddly disturbing centerpieces?
Check.
Jake, I believe it's possible Casey and IBB gave us the stupid job for babies.
Man, we totally DID get the bozo job! THIS TASK ISN'T EVEN MISSION CRITICAL!
We're just holding a sign that tells everyone where they are! A FACT THEY CLEARLY ALREADY KNOW SINCE THEY'RE HERE TO READ IT!

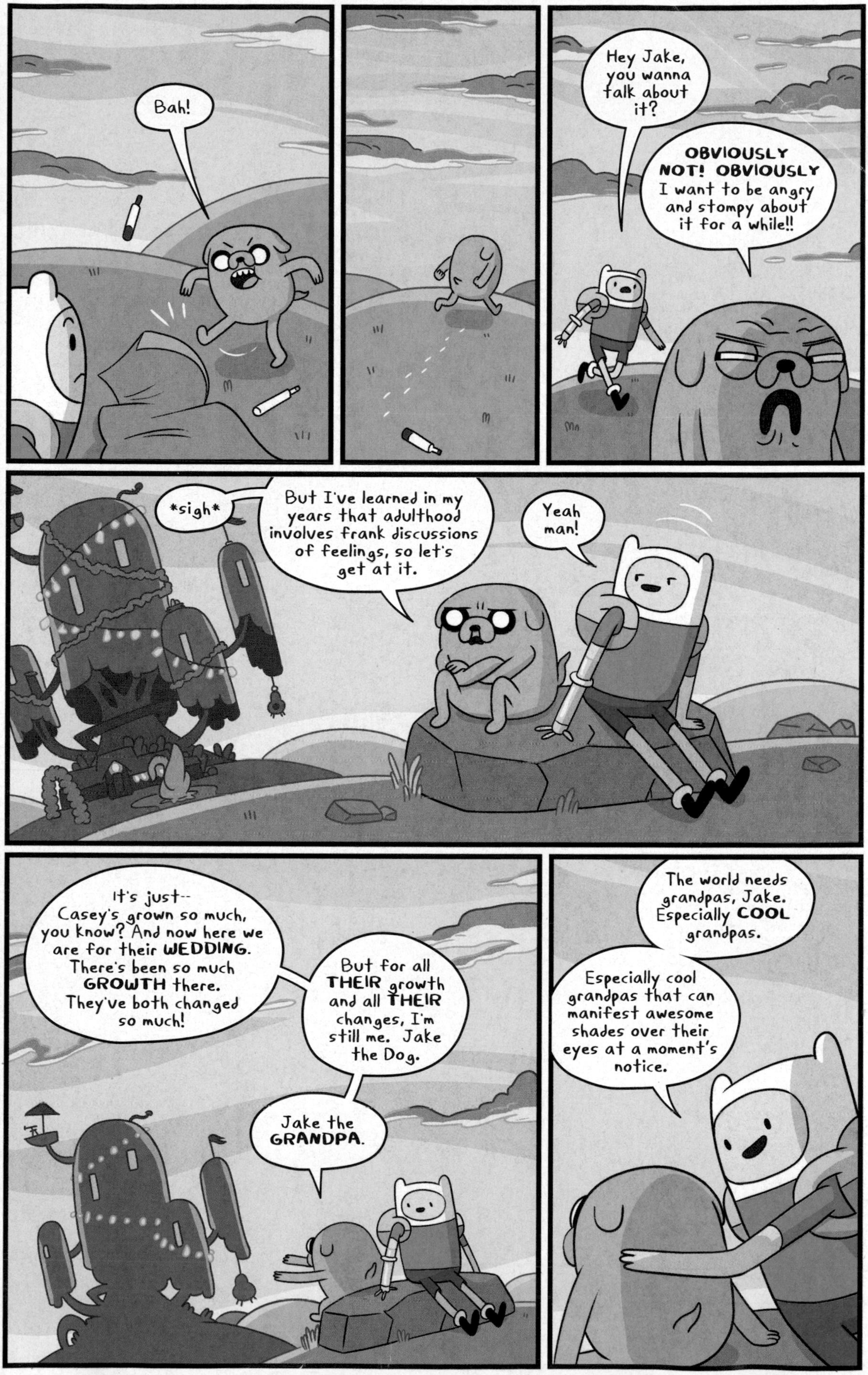
Bah!
Hey Jake, you wanna talk about it?
OBVIOUSLY NOT! OBVIOUSLY I want to be angry and stompy about it for a while!!
sigh
But I've learned in my years that adulthood involves frank discussions of feelings, so let's get at it.
Yeah man!
It's just-- Casey's grown so much, you know? And now here we are for their WEDDING. There's been so much GROWTH there. They've both changed so much!
But for all THEIR growth and all THEIR changes, I'm still me. Jake the Dog.
Jake the GRANDPA.
The world needs grandpas, Jake. Especially COOL grandpas.
Especially cool grandpas that can manifest awesome shades over their eyes at a moment's notice.

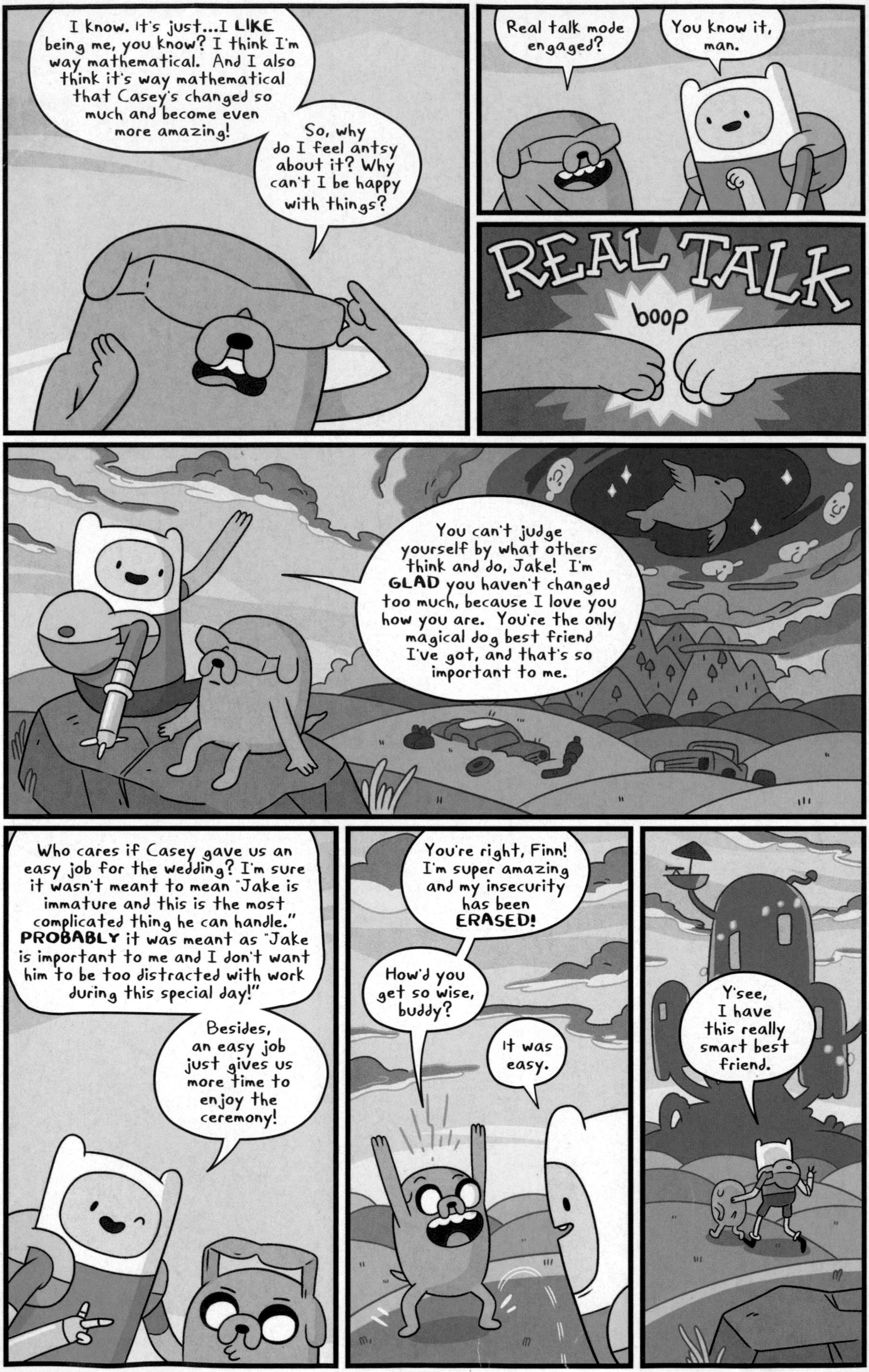
I know. It's just...I LIKE being me, you know? I think I'm way mathematical. And I also think it's way mathematical that Casey's changed so much and become even more amazing!
So, why do I feel antsy about it? Why can't I be happy with things?
Real talk mode engaged?
You know it, man.
REAL TALK
boop
You can't judge yourself by what others think and do, Jake! I'm GLAD you haven't changed too much, because I love you how you are. You're the only magical dog best friend I've got, and that's so important to me.
Who cares if Casey gave us an easy job for the wedding? I'm sure it wasn't meant to mean "Jake is immature and this is the most complicated thing he can handle." PROBABLY it was meant as "Jake is important to me and I don't want him to be too distracted with work during this special day!"
Besides, an easy job just gives us more time to enjoy the ceremony!
You're right, Finn! I'm super amazing and my insecurity has been ERASED!
How'd you get so wise, buddy?
It was easy.
Y'see, I have this really smart best friend.

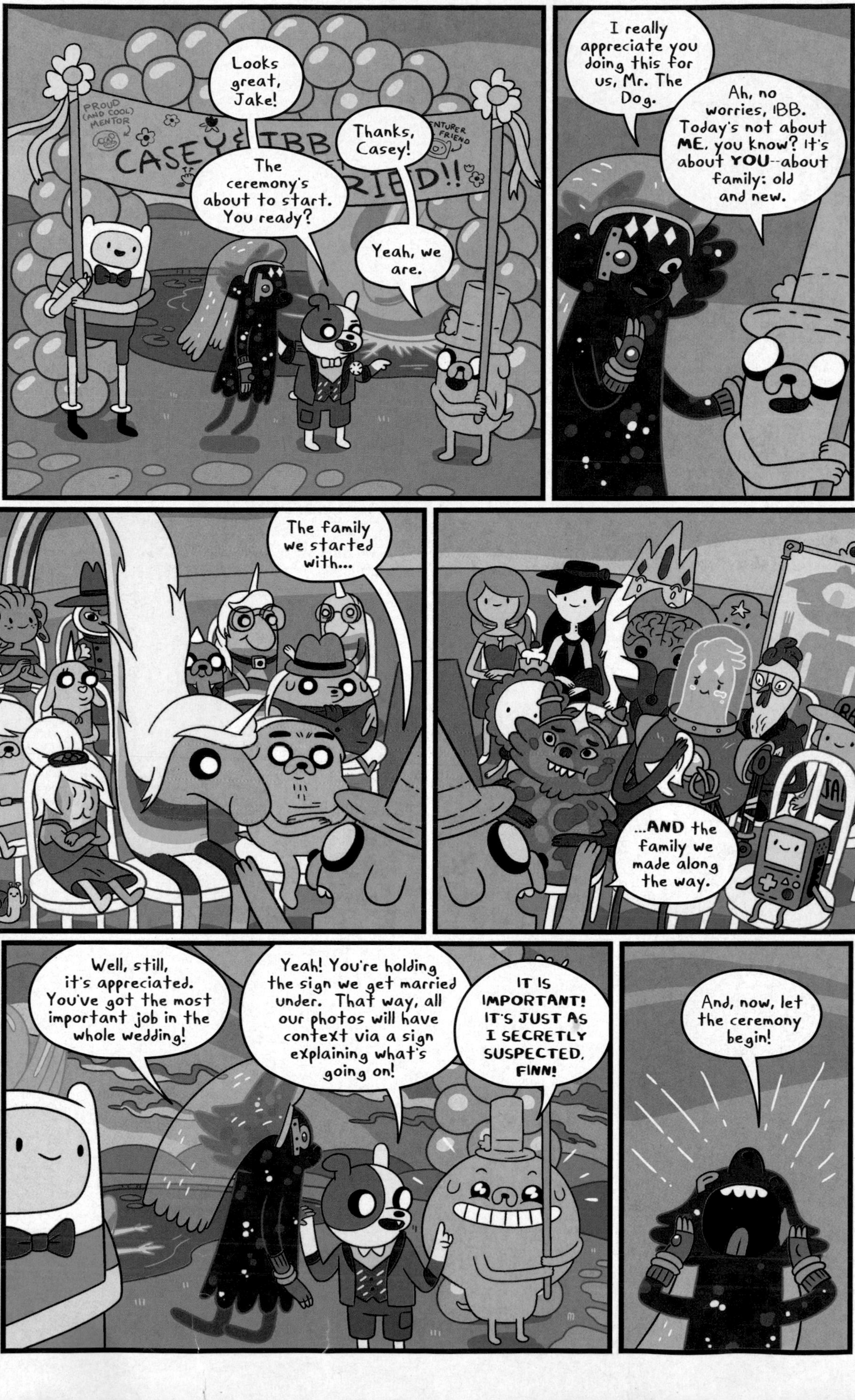
PROUD (AND COOL) MENTOR
Looks great, Jake!
Thanks, Casey!
The ceremony's about to start. You ready?
Yeah, we are.
I really appreciate you doing this for us, Mr. The Dog.
Ah, no worries, IBB. Today's not about ME, you know? It's about YOU--about family: old and new.
The family we started with...
...AND the family we made along the way.
Well, still, it's appreciated. You've got the most important job in the whole wedding!
Yeah! You're holding the sign we get married under. That way, all our photos will have context via a sign explaining what's going on!
IT IS IMPORTANT! IT'S JUST AS I SECRETLY SUSPECTED, FINN!
And, now, let the ceremony begin!

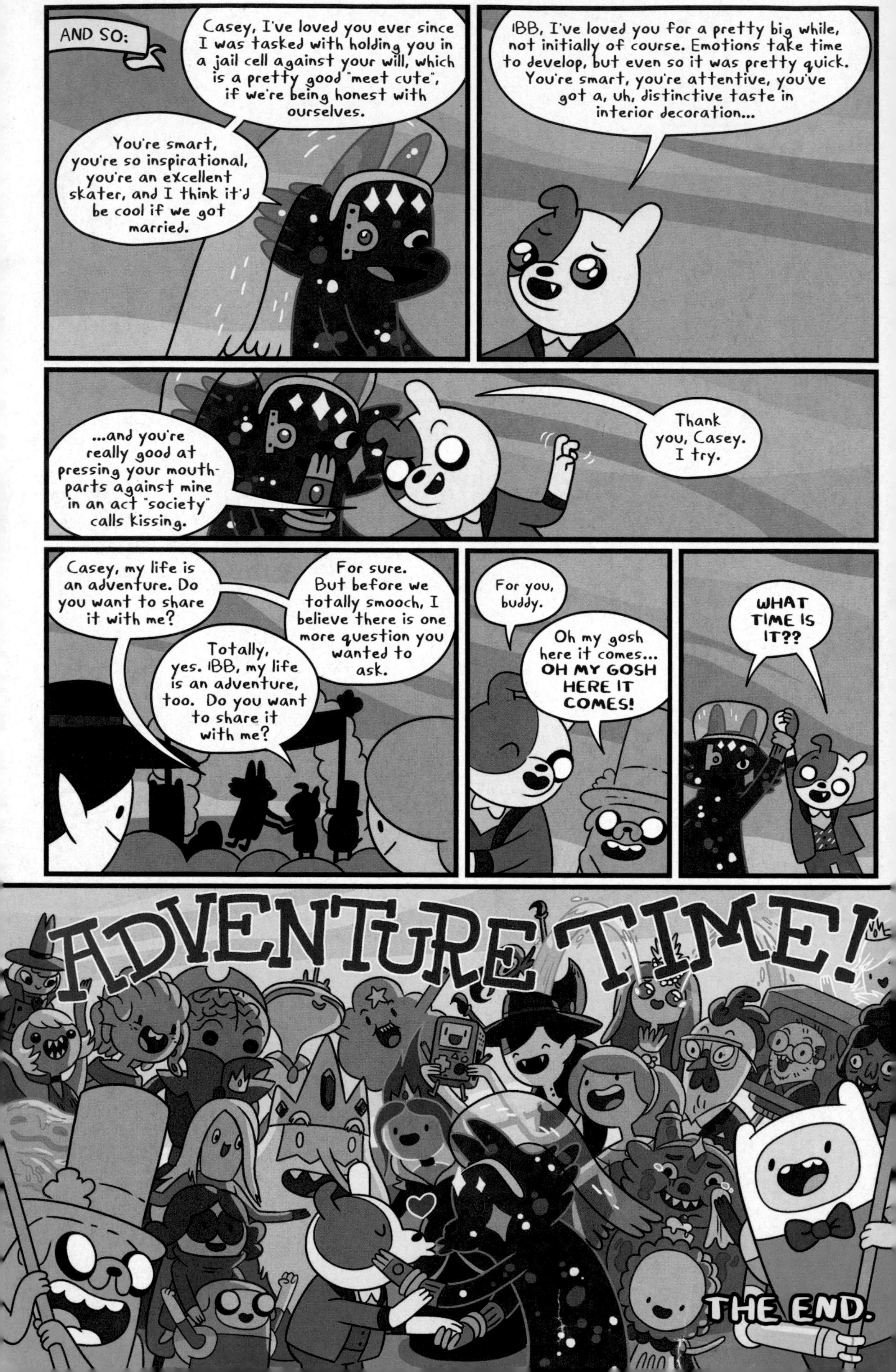
AND SO:
Casey, I've loved you ever since I was tasked with holding you in a jail cell against your will, which is a pretty good "meet cute", if we're being honest with ourselves.
You're smart, you're so inspirational, you're an excellent skater, and I think it'd be cool if we got married.
IBB, I've loved you for a pretty big while, not initially of course. Emotions take time to develop, but even so it was pretty quick. You're smart, you're attentive, you've got a, uh, distinctive taste in interior decoration...
...and you're really good at pressing your mouth-parts against mine in an act "society" calls kissing.
Thank you, Casey. I try.
Casey, my life is an adventure. Do you want to share it with me?
Totally, yes. IBB, my life is an adventure, too. Do you want to share it with me?
For sure. But before we totally smooch, I believe there is one more question you wanted to ask.
For you, buddy.
Oh my gosh here it comes... OH MY GOSH HERE IT COMES!
WHAT TIME IS IT??
ADVENTURE TIME!
THE END.

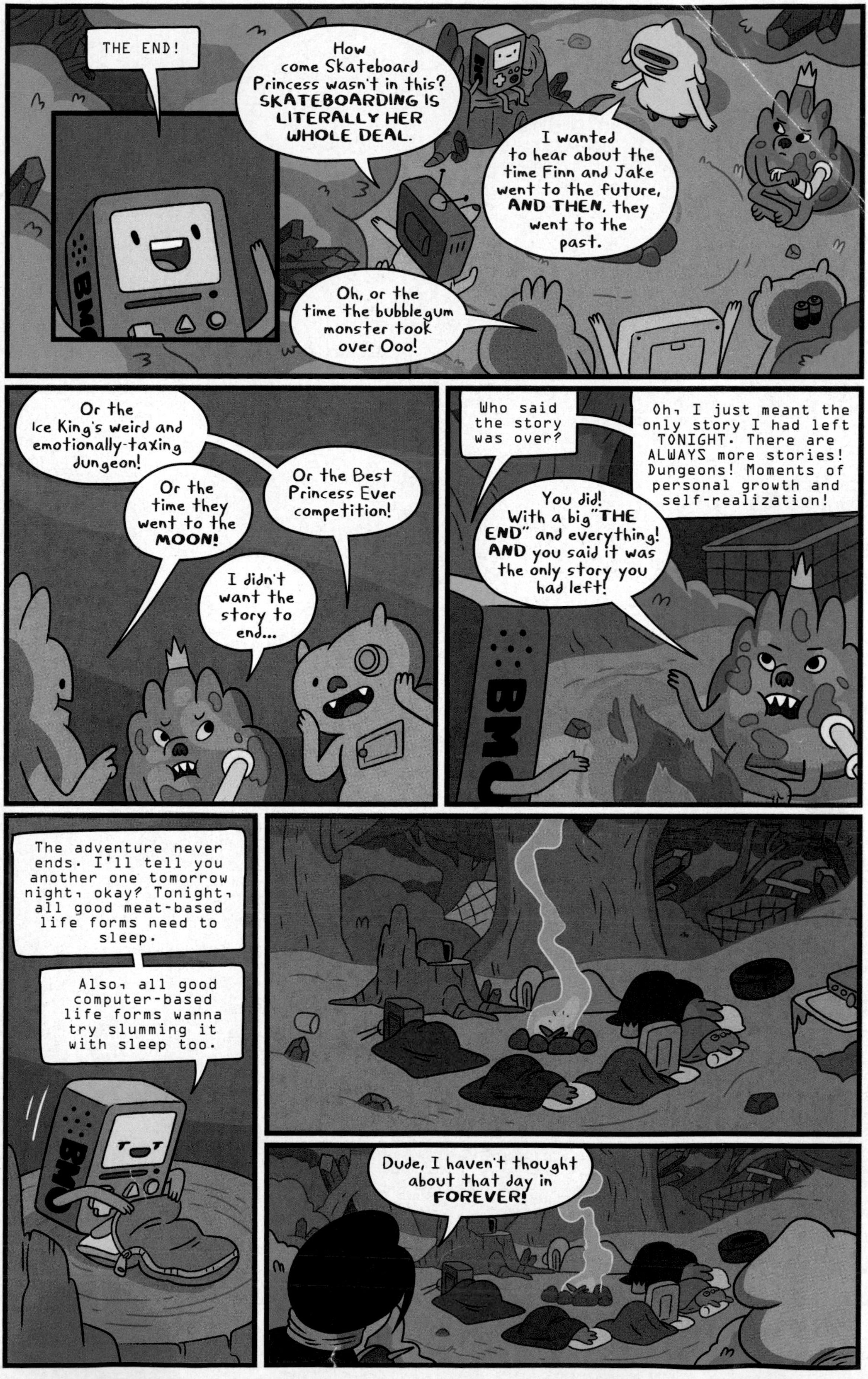
THE END!
How come Skateboard Princess wasn't in this? SKATEBOARDING IS LITERALLY HER WHOLE DEAL.
I wanted to hear about the time Finn and Jake went to the future, AND THEN, they went to the past.
Oh, or the time the bubblegum monster took over Ooo!
Or the Ice King's weird and emotionally-taxing dungeon!
Or the time they went to the MOON!
Or the Best Princess Ever competition!
I didn't want the story to end...
Who said the story was over?
You did! With a big "THE END" and everything! AND you said it was the only story you had left!
Oh, I just meant the only story I had left TONIGHT. There are ALWAYS more stories! Dungeons! Moments of personal growth and self-realization!
The adventure never ends. I'll tell you another one tomorrow night, okay? Tonight, all good meat-based life forms need to sleep.
Also, all good computer-based life forms wanna try slumming it with sleep too.
BMO
Dude, I haven't thought about that day in FOREVER!

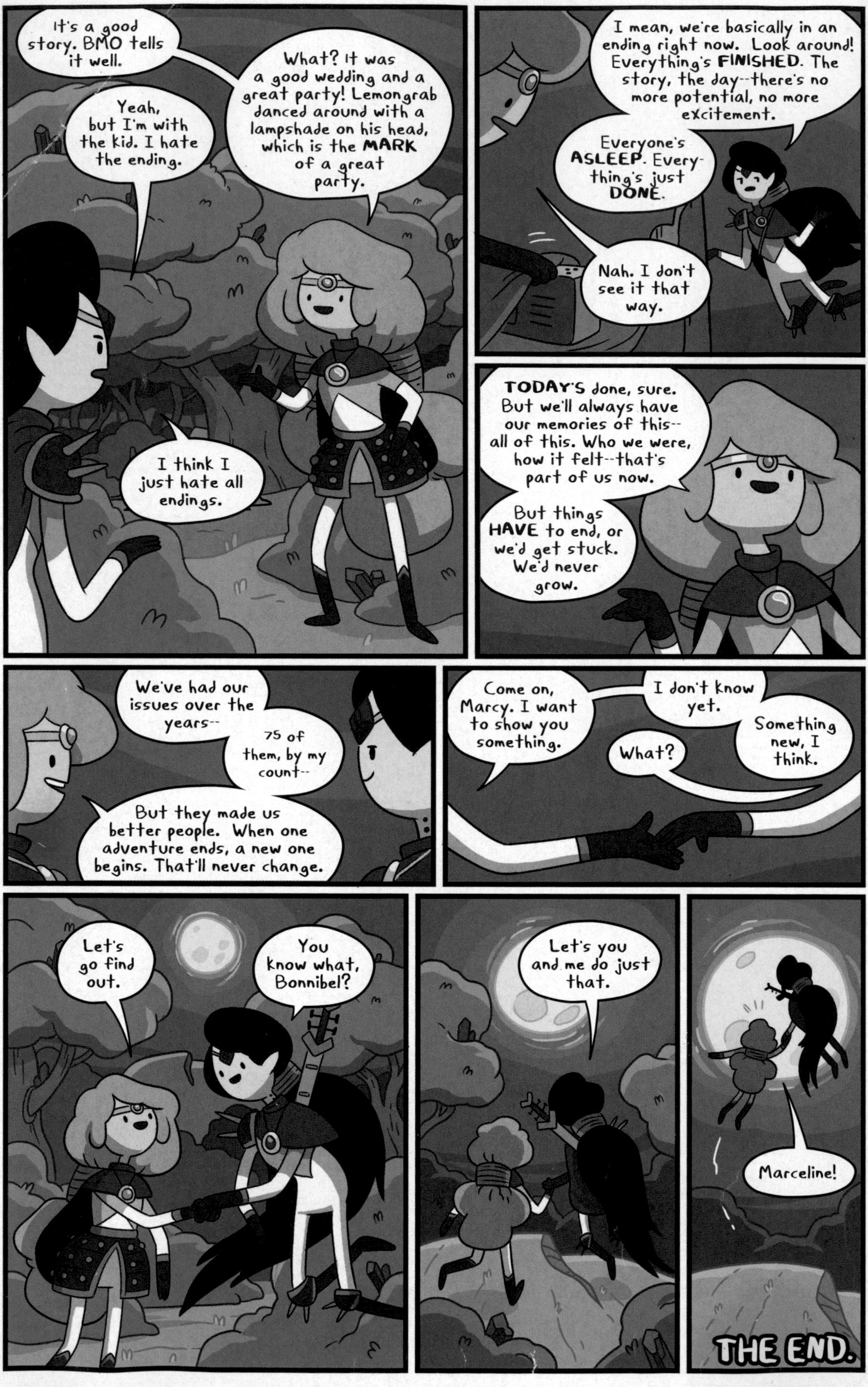
It's a good story. BMO tells it well.
Yeah, but I'm with the kid. I hate the ending.
What? It was a good wedding and a great party! Lemongrab danced around with a lampshade on his head, which is the MARK of a great party.
I think I just hate all endings.
I mean, we're basically in an ending right now. Look around! Everything's FINISHED. The story, the day--there's no more potential, no more excitement.
Everyone's ASLEEP. Everything's just DONE.
Nah. I don't see it that way.
TODAY'S done, sure. But we'll always have our memories of this--all of this. Who we were, how it felt--that's part of us now.
But things HAVE to end, or we'd get stuck. We'd never grow.
We've had our issues over the years--
75 of them, by my count--
But they made us better people. When one adventure ends, a new one begins. That'll never change.
Come on, Marcy. I want to show you something.
What?
I don't know yet.
Something new, I think.
Let's go find out.
You know what, Bonnibel?
Let's you and me do just that.
Marceline!
THE END.

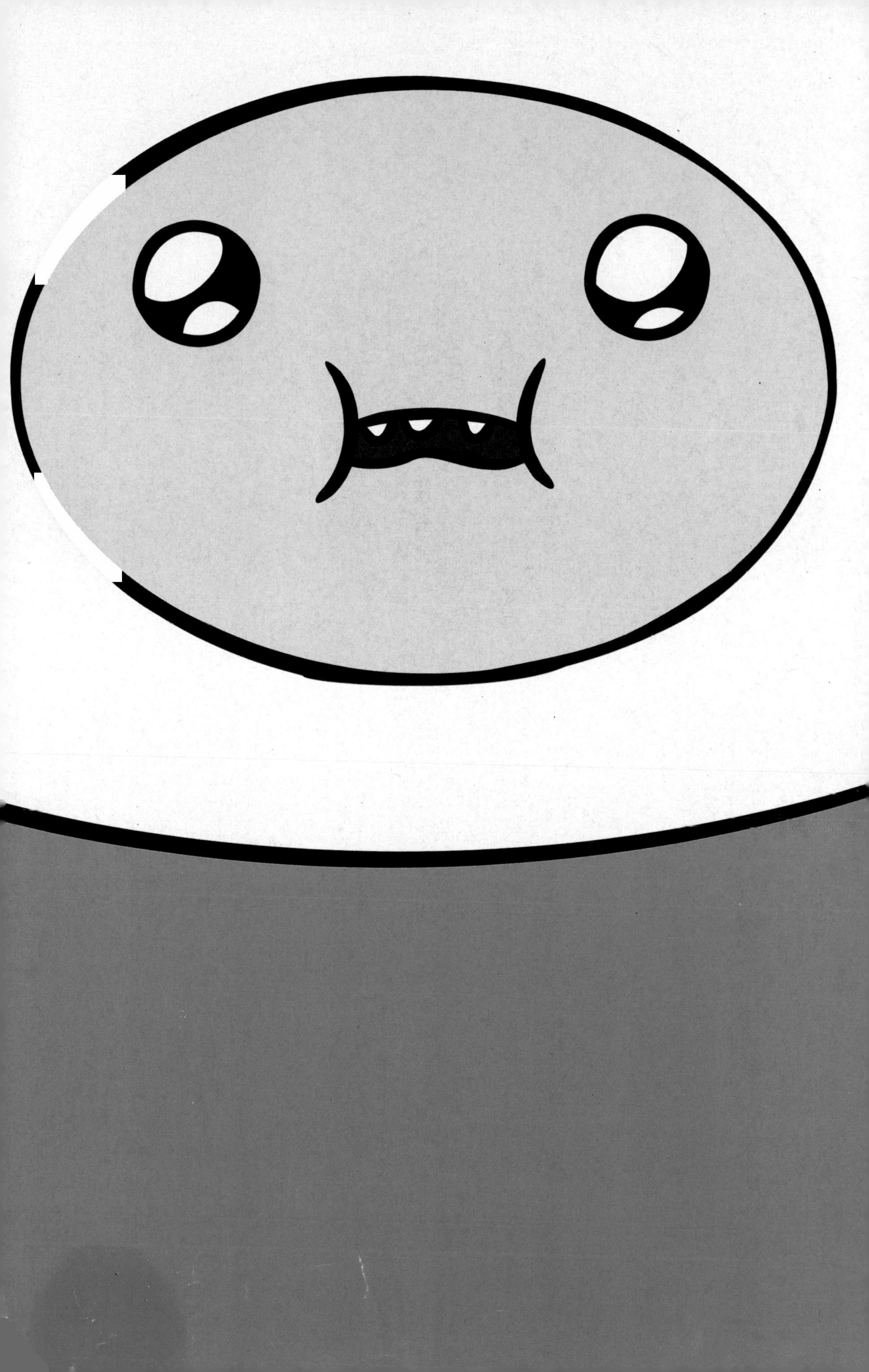

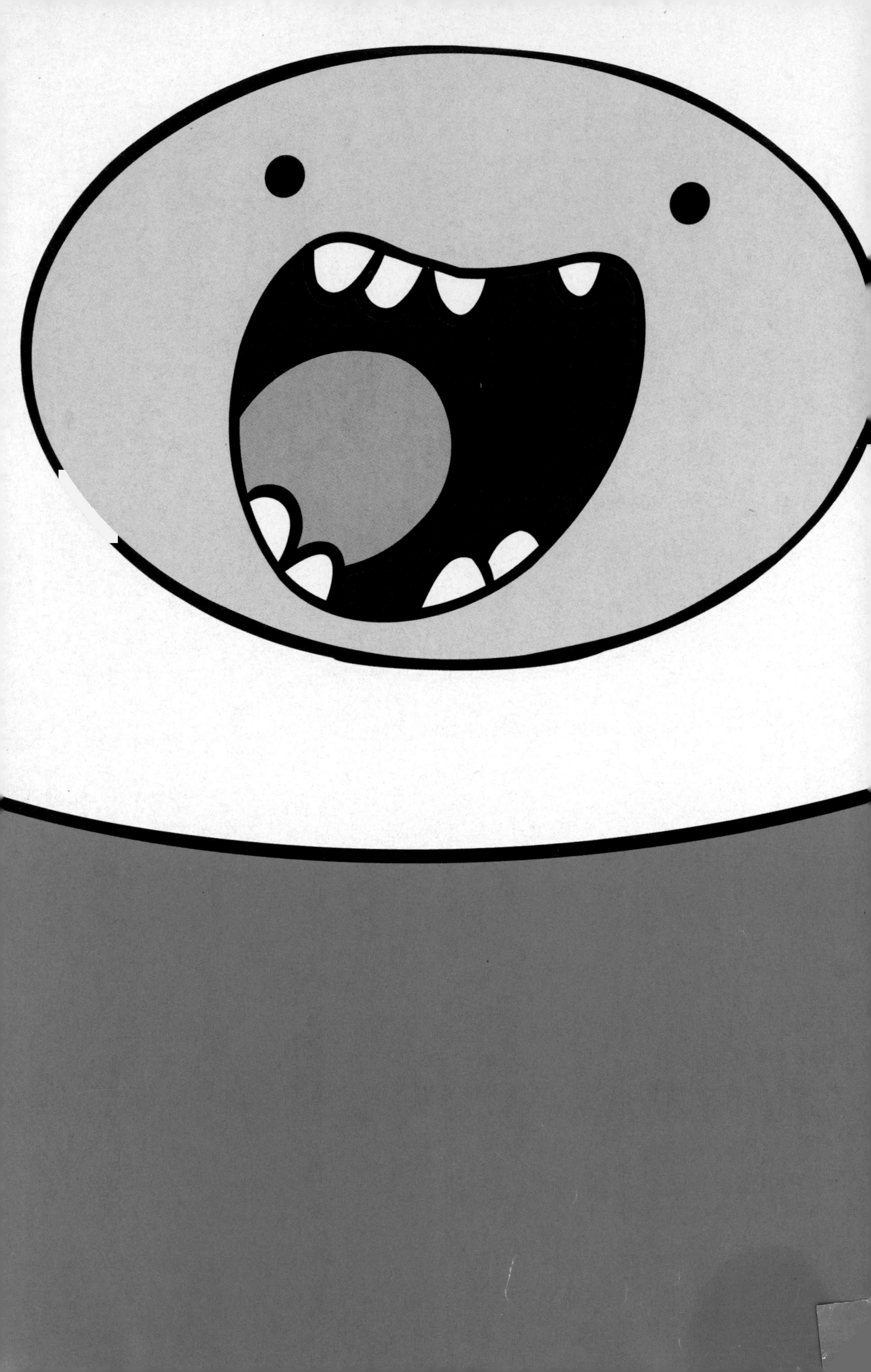

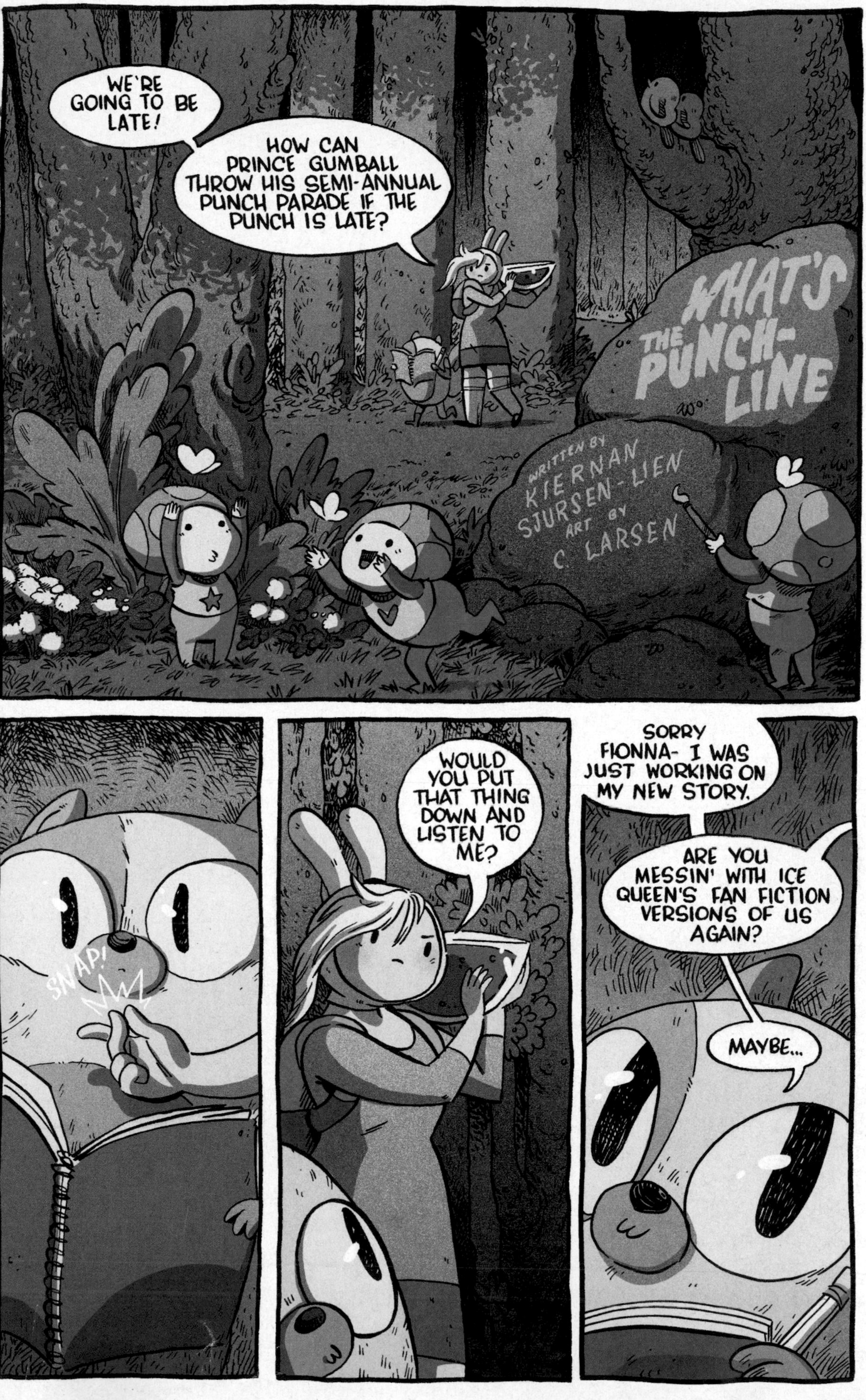
WE'RE GOING TO BE LATE!
HOW CAN PRINCE GUMBALL THROW HIS SEMI-ANNUAL PUNCH PARADE IF THE PUNCH IS LATE?
WHAT'S THE PUNCH-LINE
WRITTEN BY KIERNAN SJURSEN-LIEN
ART BY C. LARSEN
SNAP!
WOULD YOU PUT THAT THING DOWN AND LISTEN TO ME?
SORRY FIONNA- I WAS JUST WORKING ON MY NEW STORY.
ARE YOU MESSIN' WITH ICE QUEEN'S FAN FICTION VERSIONS OF US AGAIN?
MAYBE...

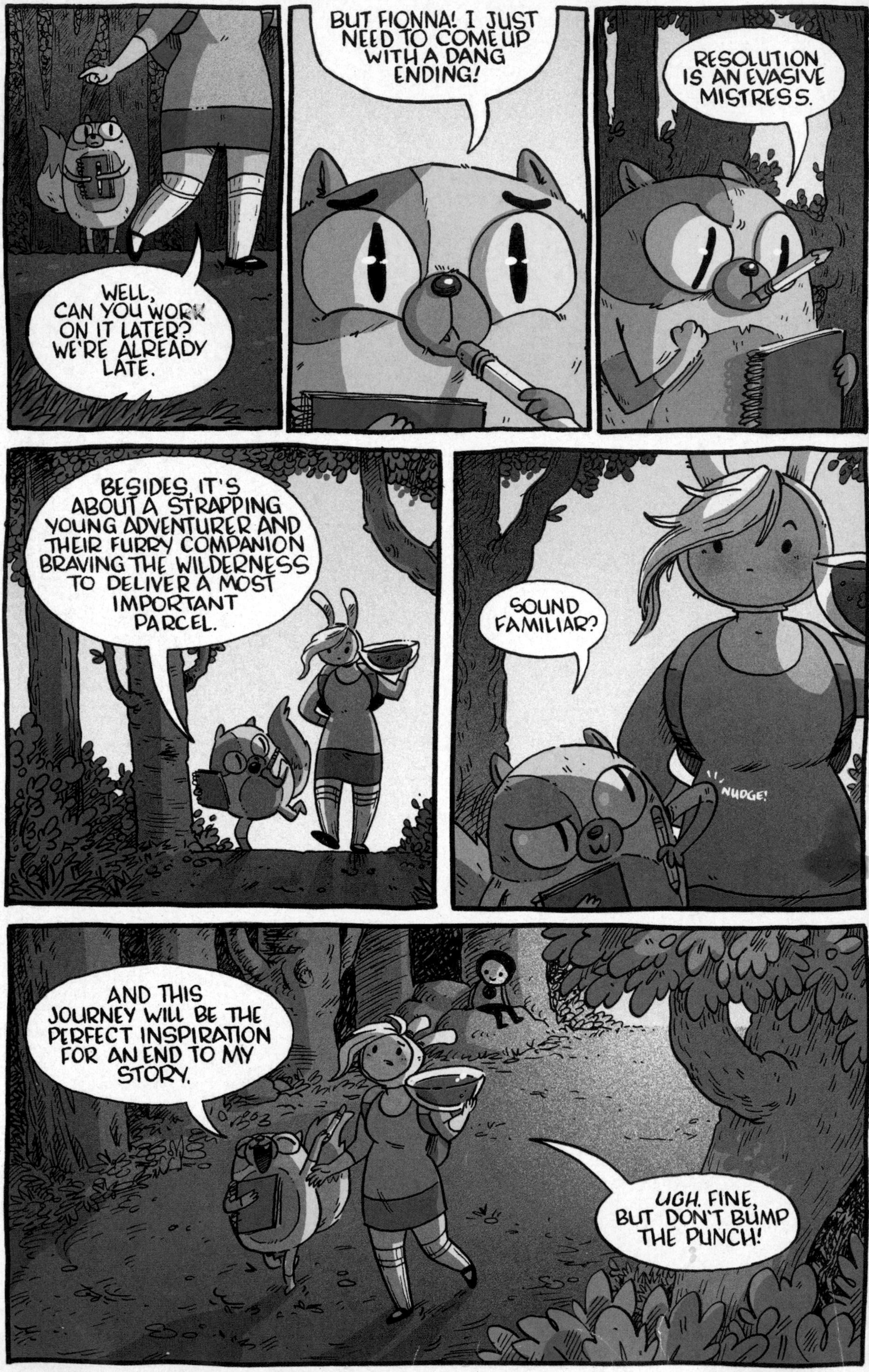
WELL, CAN YOU WORK ON IT LATER? WE'RE ALREADY LATE.
BUT FIONNA! I JUST NEED TO COME UP WITH A DANG ENDING!
RESOLUTION IS AN EVASIVE MISTRESS.
BESIDES, IT'S ABOUT A STRAPPING YOUNG ADVENTURER AND THEIR FURRY COMPANION BRAVING THE WILDERNESS TO DELIVER A MOST IMPORTANT PARCEL.
SOUND FAMILIAR?
NUDGE!
AND THIS JOURNEY WILL BE THE PERFECT INSPIRATION FOR AN END TO MY STORY.
UGH. FINE, BUT DON'T BUMP THE PUNCH!

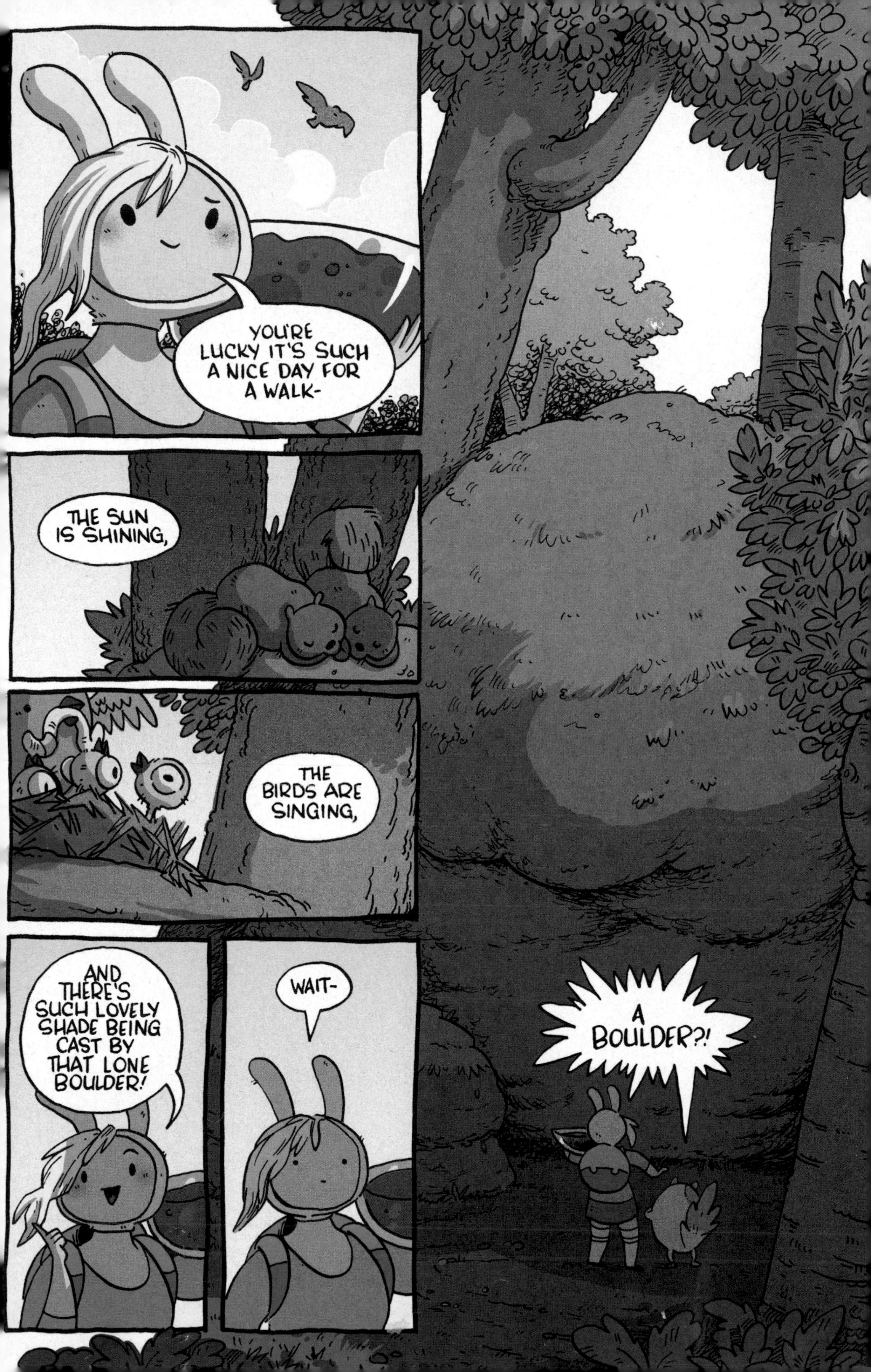
YOU'RE LUCKY IT'S SUCH A NICE DAY FOR A WALK-
THE SUN IS SHINING,
THE BIRDS ARE SINGING,
AND THERE'S SUCH LOVELY SHADE BEING CAST BY THAT LONE BOULDER!
WAIT-
A BOULDER?!

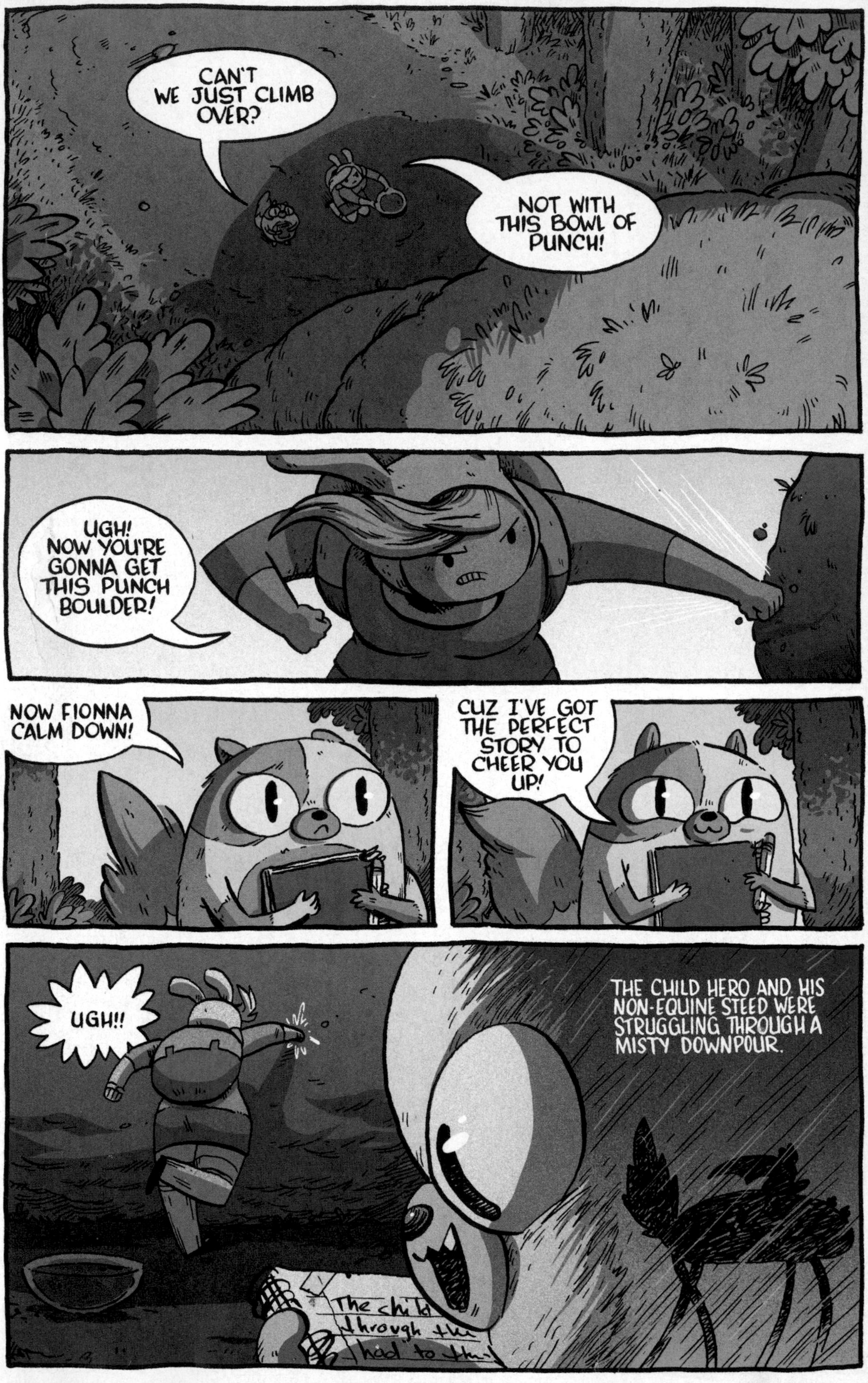
CAN'T WE JUST CLIMB OVER?
NOT WITH THIS BOWL OF PUNCH!
UGH! NOW YOU'RE GONNA GET THIS PUNCH BOULDER!
NOW FIONNA CALM DOWN!
CUZ I'VE GOT THE PERFECT STORY TO CHEER YOU UP!
UGH!!
THE CHILD HERO AND HIS NON-EQUINE STEED WERE STRUGGLING THROUGH A MISTY DOWNPOUR.

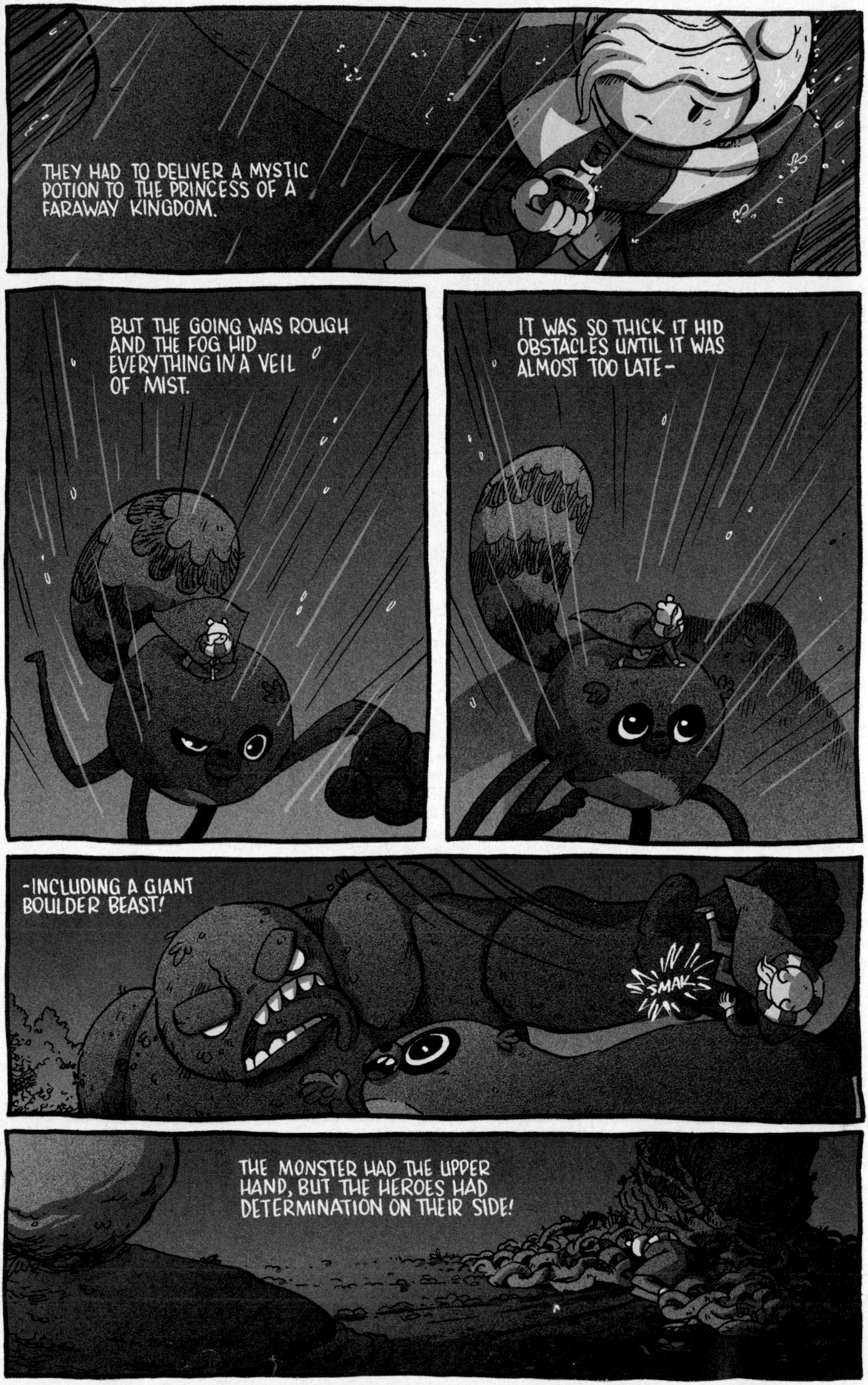
THEY HAD TO DELIVER A MYSTIC POTION TO THE PRINCESS OF A FARAWAY KINGDOM.
BUT THE GOING WAS ROUGH AND THE FOG HID EVERYTHING IN A VEIL OF MIST.
IT WAS SO THICK IT HID OBSTACLES UNTIL IT WAS ALMOST TOO LATE-
-INCLUDING A GIANT BOULDER BEAST!
SMAK
THE MONSTER HAD THE UPPER HAND, BUT THE HEROES HAD DETERMINATION ON THEIR SIDE!

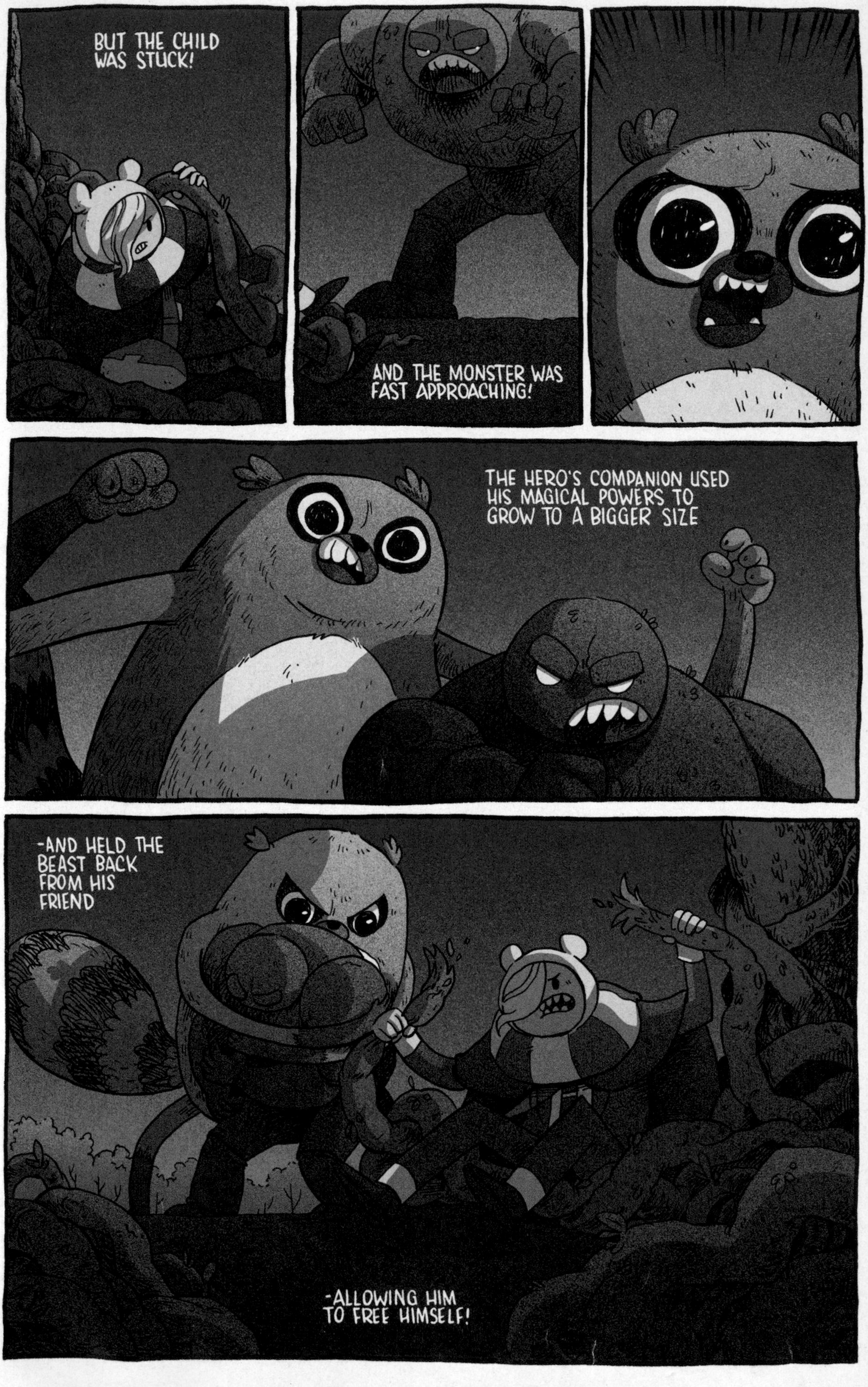
BUT THE CHILD WAS STUCK!
AND THE MONSTER WAS FAST APPROACHING!
THE HERO'S COMPANION USED HIS MAGICAL POWERS TO GROW TO A BIGGER SIZE
-AND HELD THE BEAST BACK FROM HIS FRIEND
-ALLOWING HIM TO FREE HIMSELF!

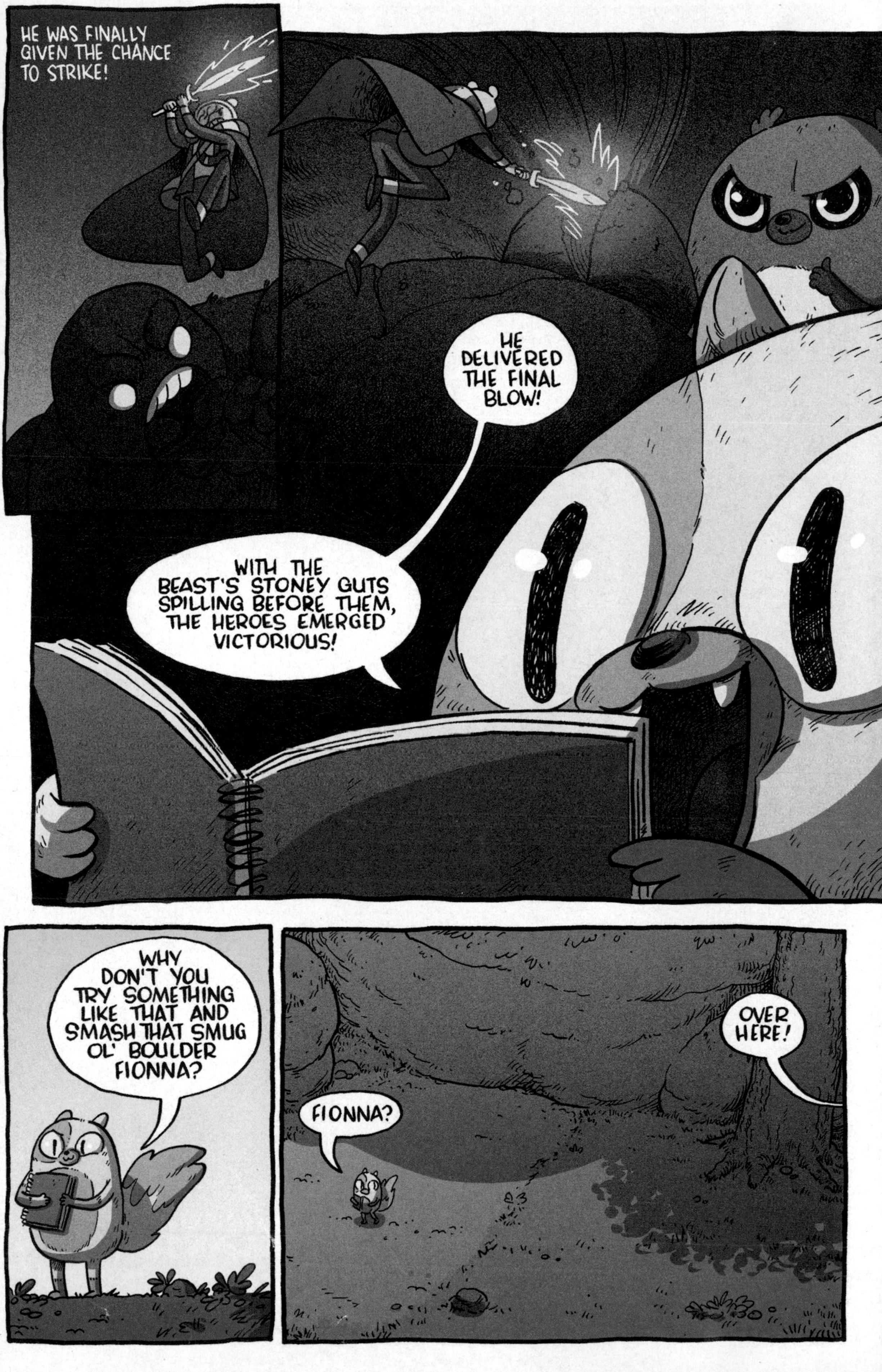
HE WAS FINALLY GIVEN THE CHANCE TO STRIKE!
HE DELIVERED THE FINAL BLOW!
WITH THE BEAST'S STONEY GUTS SPILLING BEFORE THEM, THE HEROES EMERGED VICTORIOUS!
WHY DON'T YOU TRY SOMETHING LIKE THAT AND SMASH THAT SMUG OL' BOULDER FIONNA?
OVER HERE!
FIONNA?

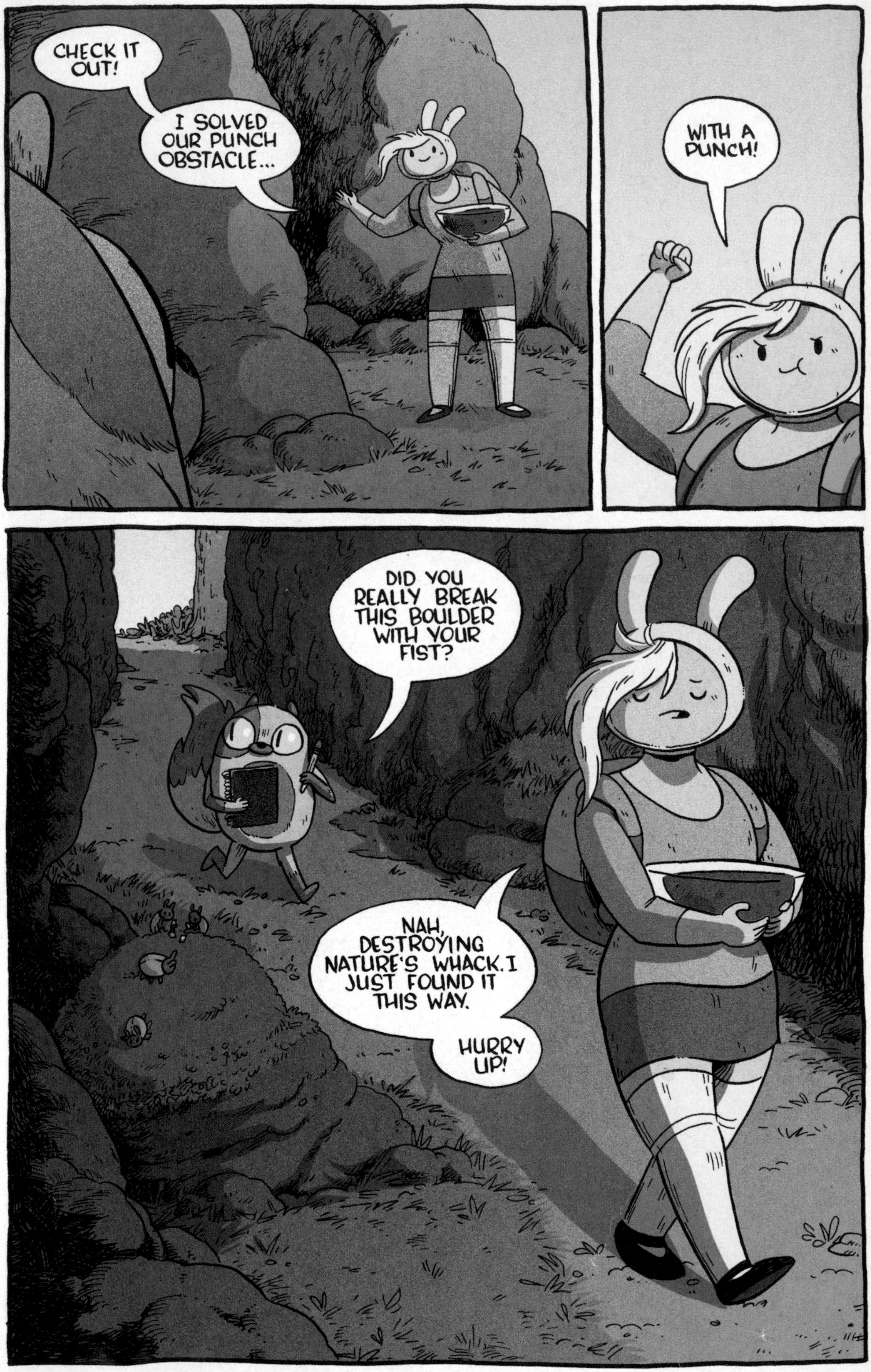
CHECK IT OUT!
I SOLVED OUR PUNCH OBSTACLE...
WITH A PUNCH!
DID YOU REALLY BREAK THIS BOULDER WITH YOUR FIST?
NAH, DESTROYING NATURE'S WHACK. I JUST FOUND IT THIS WAY.
HURRY UP!

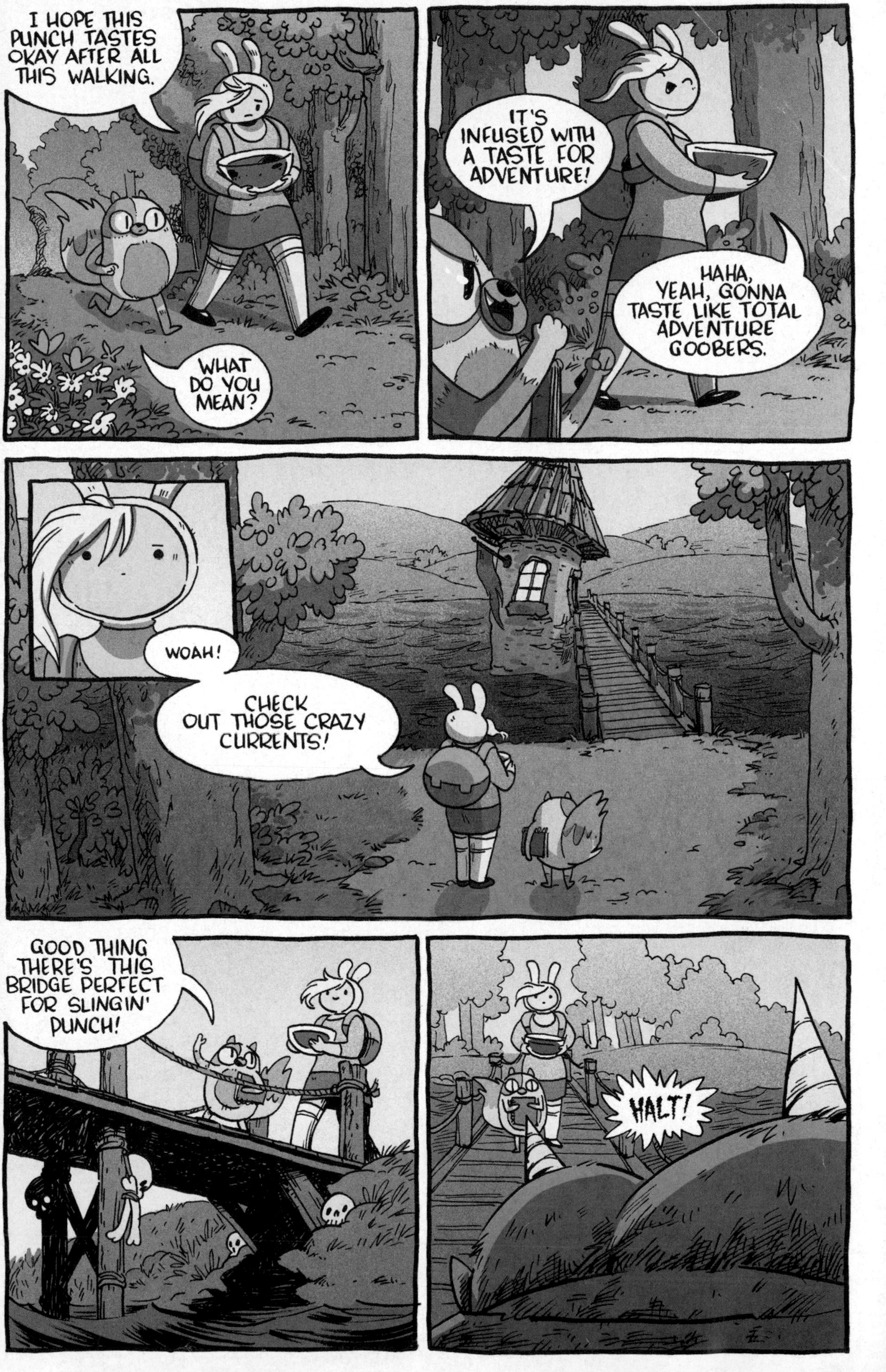
I HOPE THIS PUNCH TASTES OKAY AFTER ALL THIS WALKING.
WHAT DO YOU MEAN?
IT'S INFUSED WITH A TASTE FOR ADVENTURE!
HAHA, YEAH, GONNA TASTE LIKE TOTAL ADVENTURE GOOBERS.
WOAH!
CHECK OUT THOSE CRAZY CURRENTS!
GOOD THING THERE'S THIS BRIDGE PERFECT FOR SLINGIN' PUNCH!
HALT!

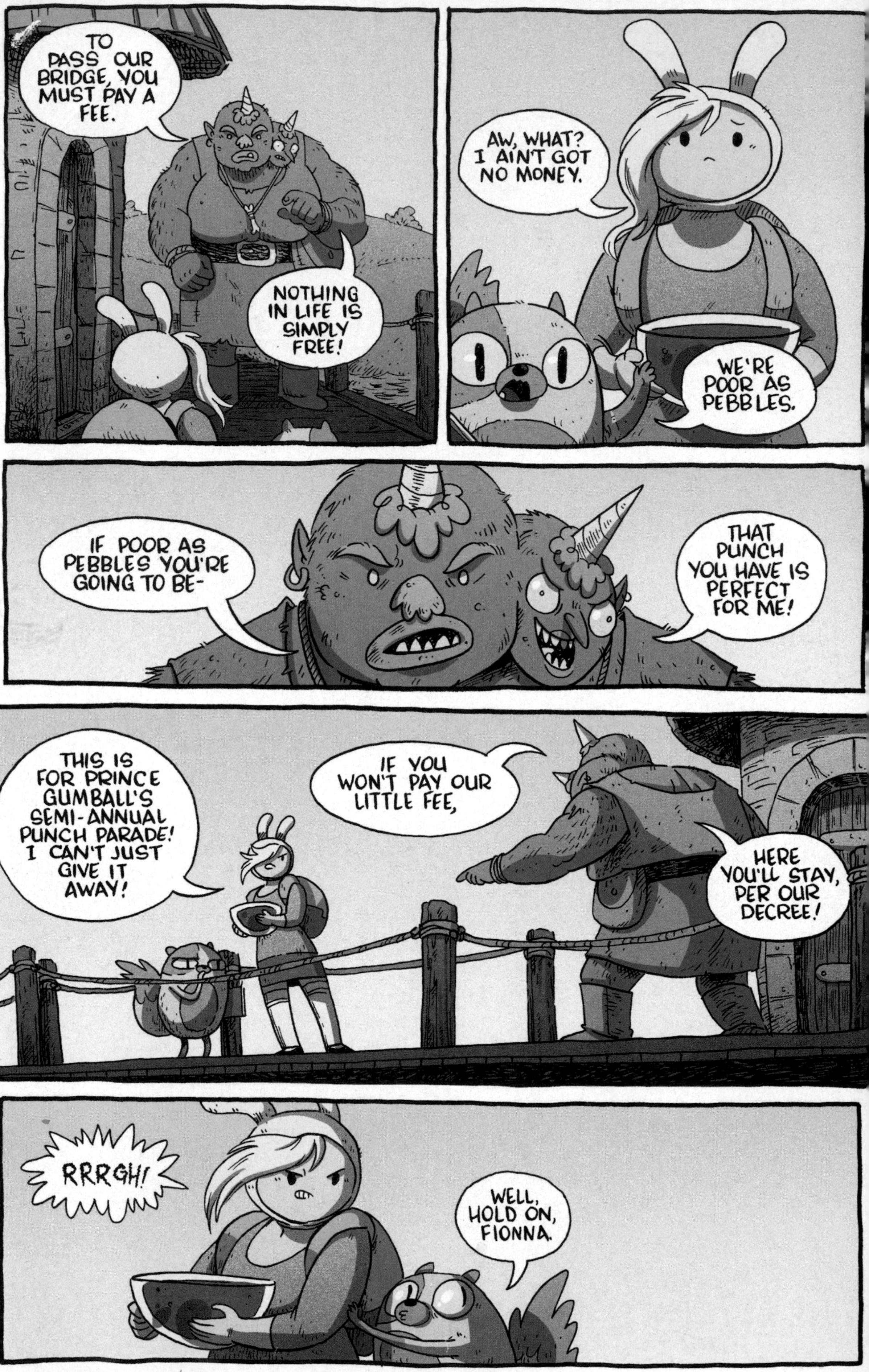
TO PASS OUR BRIDGE, YOU MUST PAY A FEE.
NOTHING IN LIFE IS SIMPLY FREE!
AW, WHAT? I AIN'T GOT NO MONEY.
WE'RE POOR AS PEBBLES.
IF POOR AS PEBBLES YOU'RE GOING TO BE-
THAT PUNCH YOU HAVE IS PERFECT FOR ME!
THIS IS FOR PRINCE GUMBALL'S SEMI-ANNUAL PUNCH PARADE! I CAN'T JUST GIVE IT AWAY!
IF YOU WON'T PAY OUR LITTLE FEE,
HERE YOU'LL STAY, PER OUR DECREE!
RRRGH!
WELL, HOLD ON, FIONNA.

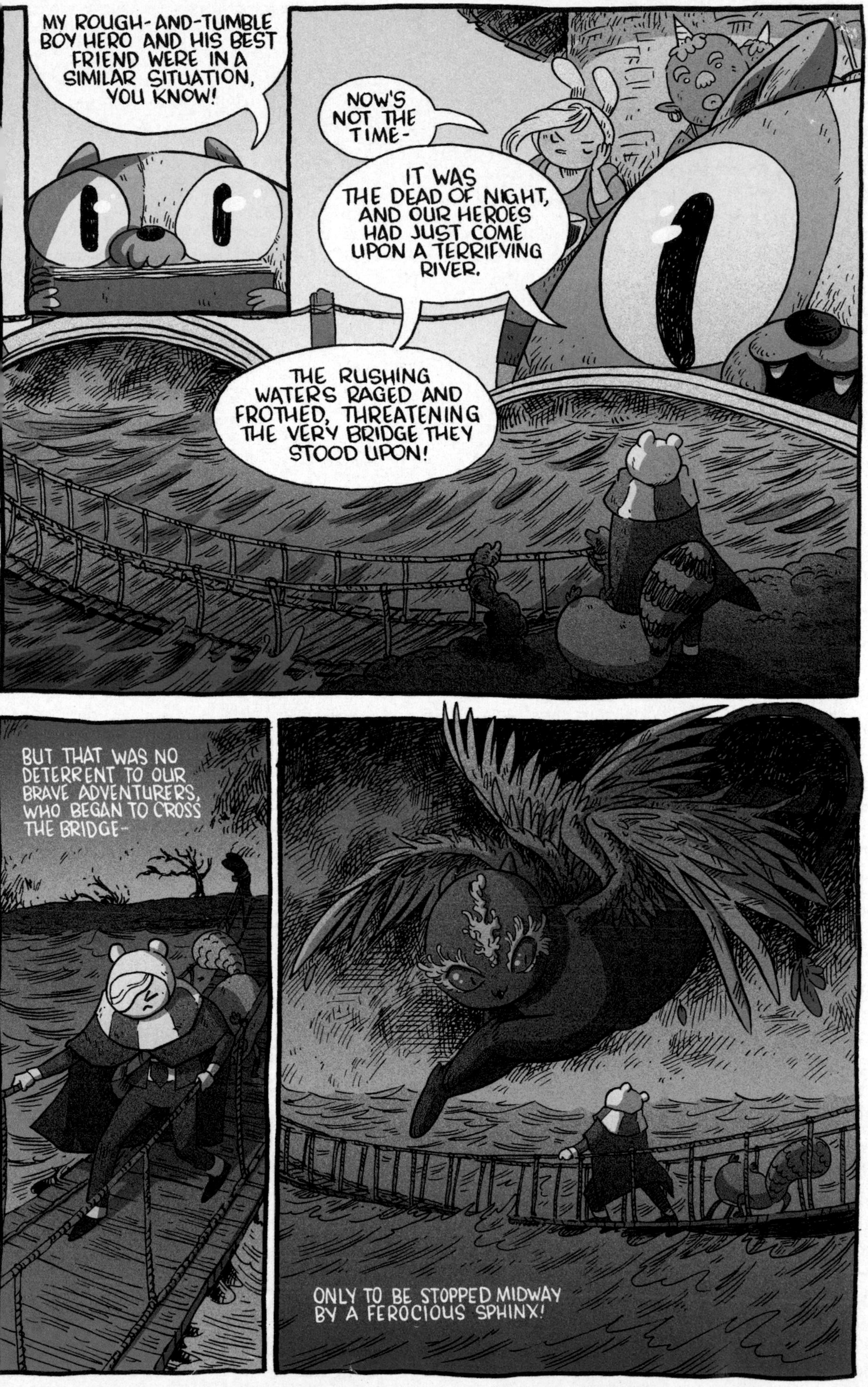
MY ROUGH-AND-TUMBLE BOY HERO AND HIS BEST FRIEND WERE IN A SIMILAR SITUATION, YOU KNOW!
NOW'S NOT THE TIME-
IT WAS THE DEAD OF NIGHT, AND OUR HEROES HAD JUST COME UPON A TERRIFYING RIVER.
THE RUSHING WATERS RAGED AND FROTHED, THREATENING THE VERY BRIDGE THEY STOOD UPON!
BUT THAT WAS NO DETERRENT TO OUR BRAVE ADVENTURERS, WHO BEGAN TO CROSS THE BRIDGE-
ONLY TO BE STOPPED MIDWAY BY A FEROCIOUS SPHINX!

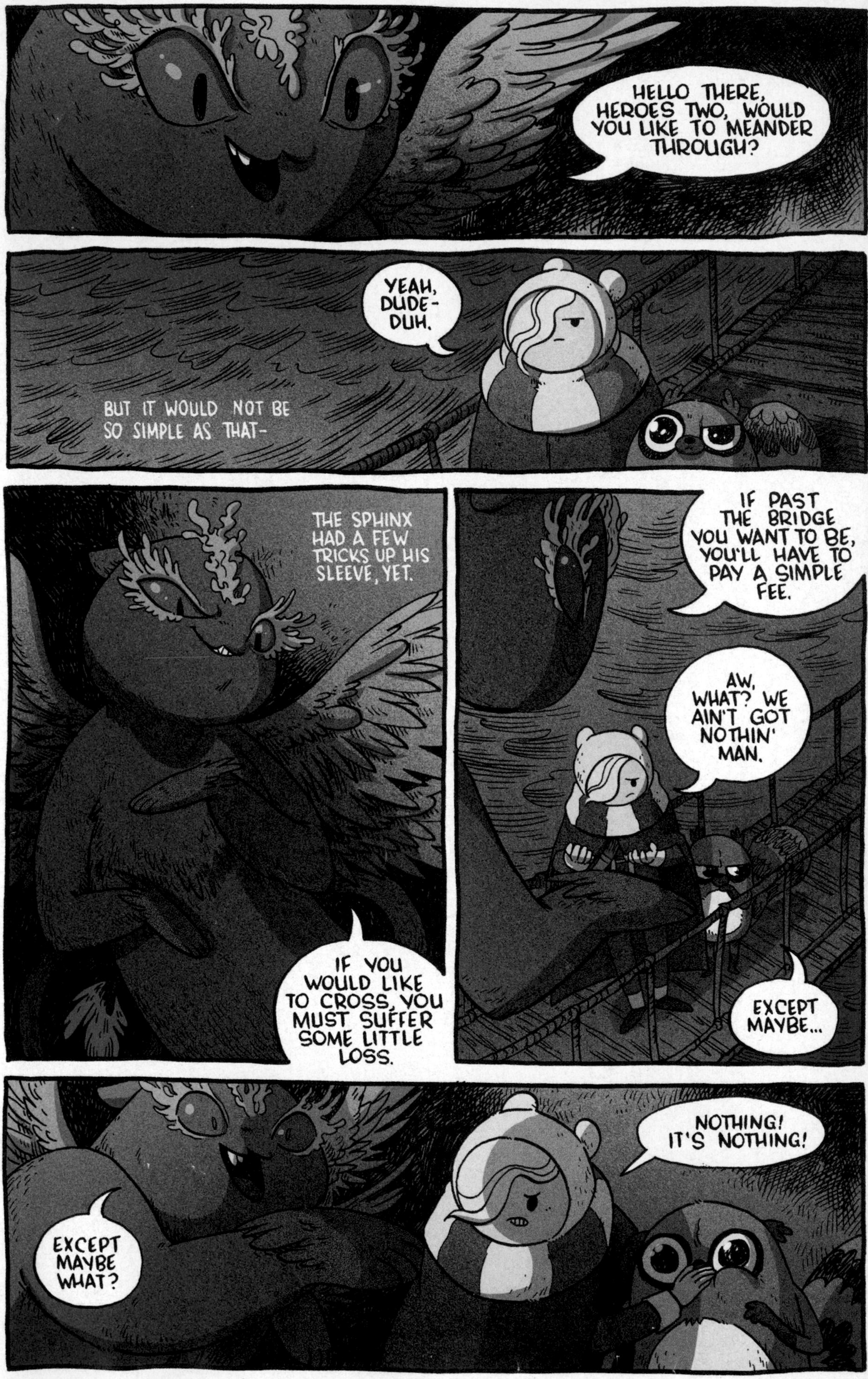
HELLO THERE, HEROES TWO, WOULD YOU LIKE TO MEANDER THROUGH?
YEAH, DUDE-DUH.
BUT IT WOULD NOT BE SO SIMPLE AS THAT-
THE SPHINX HAD A FEW TRICKS UP HIS SLEEVE, YET.
IF YOU WOULD LIKE TO CROSS, YOU MUST SUFFER SOME LITTLE LOSS.
IF PAST THE BRIDGE YOU WANT TO BE, YOU'LL HAVE TO PAY A SIMPLE FEE.
AW, WHAT? WE AIN'T GOT NOTHIN' MAN.
EXCEPT MAYBE...
EXCEPT MAYBE WHAT?
NOTHING! IT'S NOTHING!

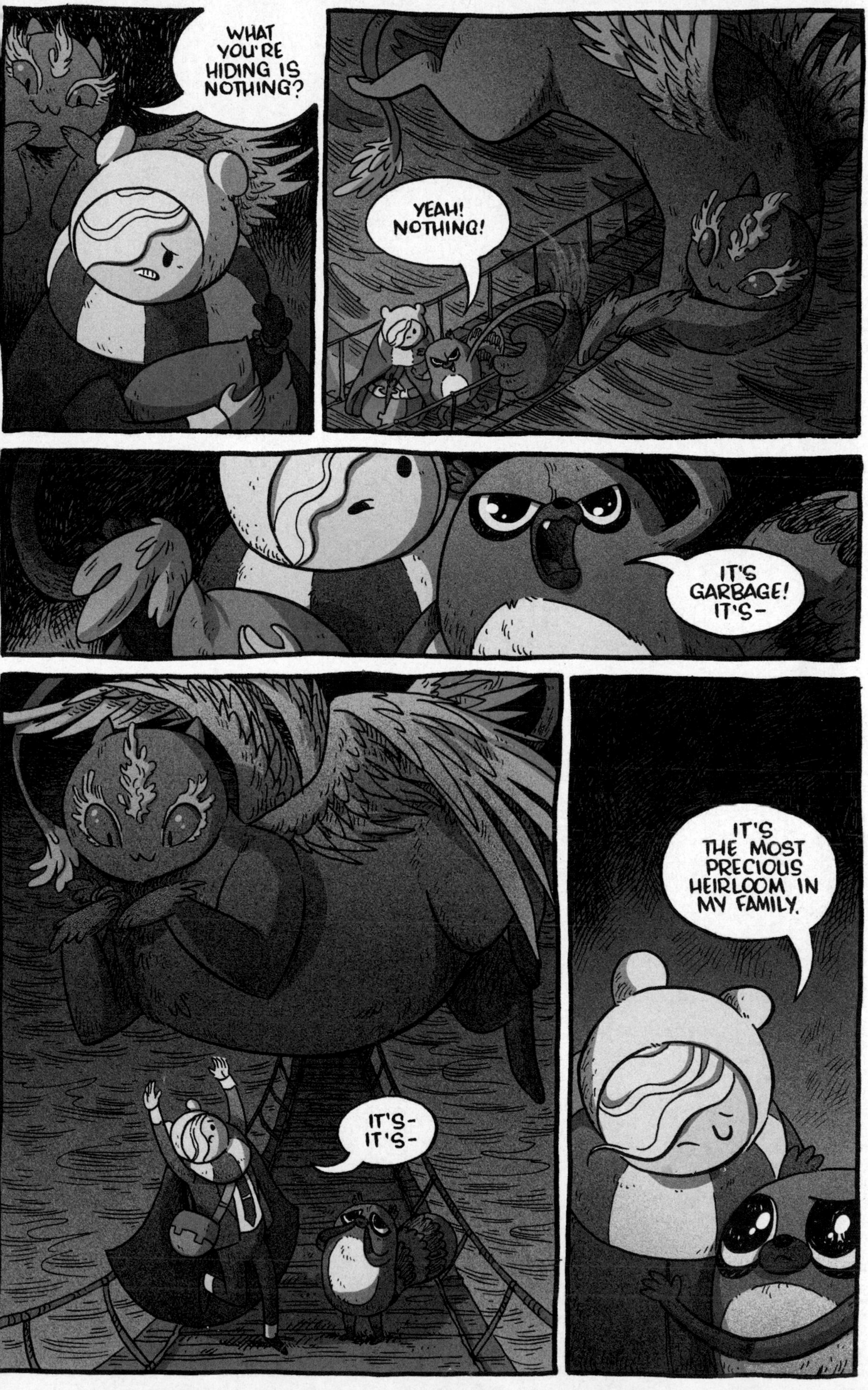
WHAT YOU'RE HIDING IS NOTHING?
YEAH! NOTHING!
IT'S GARBAGE! IT'S-
IT'S- IT'S-
IT'S THE MOST PRECIOUS HEIRLOOM IN MY FAMILY.

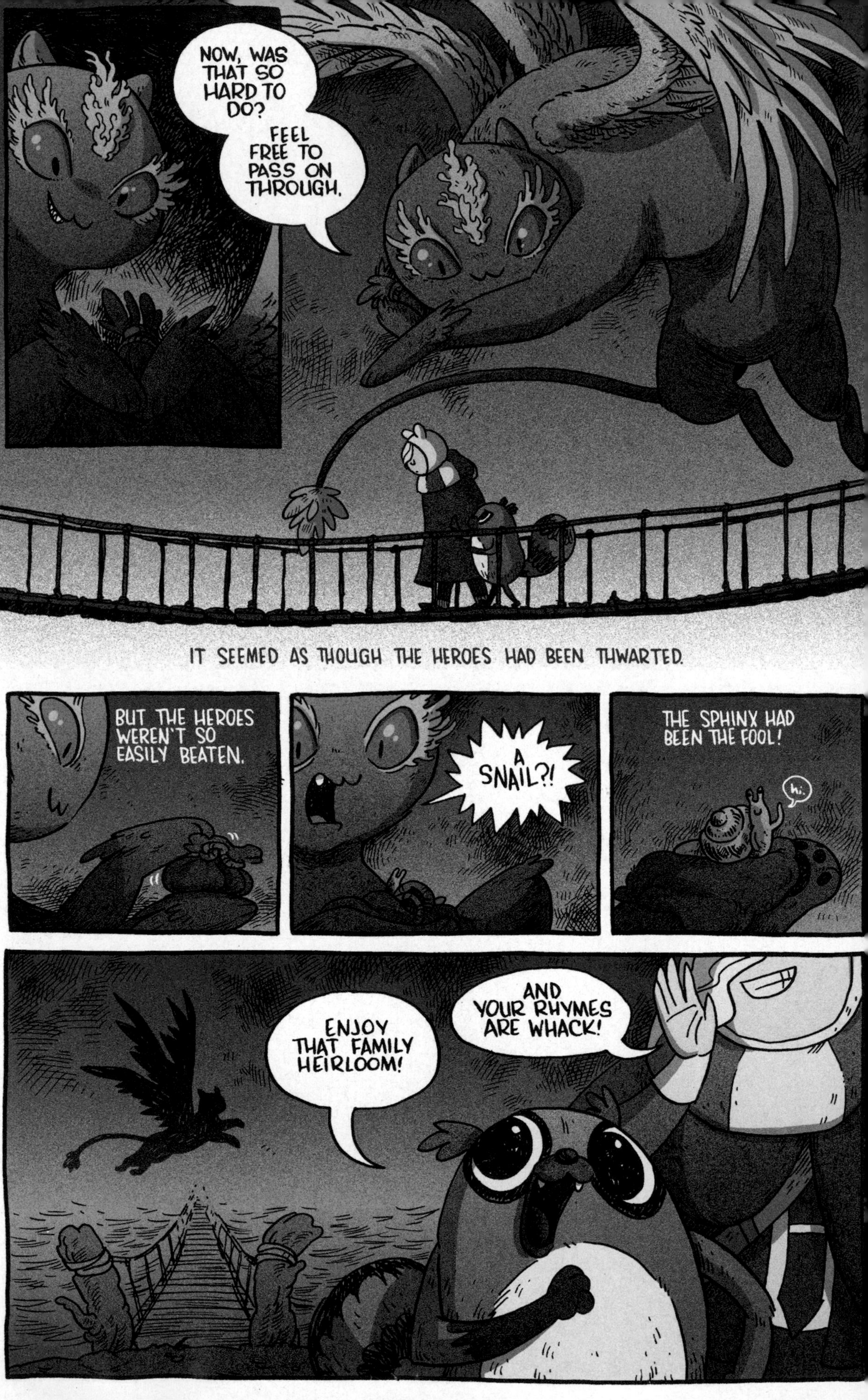
NOW, WAS THAT SO HARD TO DO?
FEEL FREE TO PASS ON THROUGH.
IT SEEMED AS THOUGH THE HEROES HAD BEEN THWARTED.
BUT THE HEROES WEREN'T SO EASILY BEATEN.
A SNAIL?!
THE SPHINX HAD BEEN THE FOOL!
hi.
ENJOY THAT FAMILY HEIRLOOM!
AND YOUR RHYMES ARE WHACK!

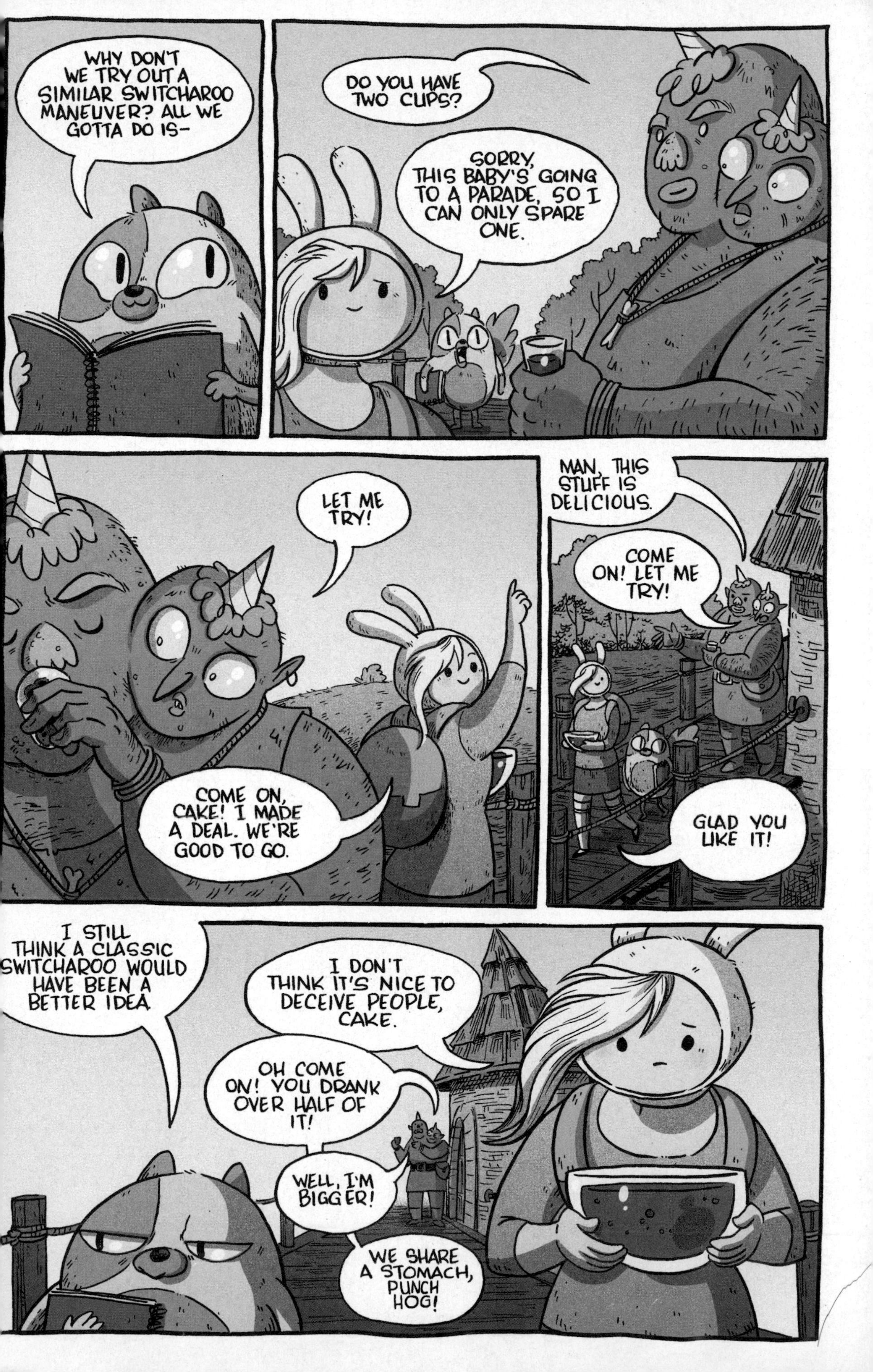
WHY DON'T WE TRY OUT A SIMILAR SWITCHAROO MANEUVER? ALL WE GOTTA DO IS-
DO YOU HAVE TWO CUPS?
SORRY, THIS BABY'S GOING TO A PARADE, SO I CAN ONLY SPARE ONE.
LET ME TRY!
COME ON, CAKE! I MADE A DEAL. WE'RE GOOD TO GO.
MAN, THIS STUFF IS DELICIOUS.
COME ON! LET ME TRY!
GLAD YOU LIKE IT!
I STILL THINK A CLASSIC SWITCHAROO WOULD HAVE BEEN A BETTER IDEA
I DON'T THINK IT'S NICE TO DECEIVE PEOPLE, CAKE.
OH COME ON! YOU DRANK OVER HALF OF IT!
WELL, I'M BIGGER!
WE SHARE A STOMACH, PUNCH HOG!

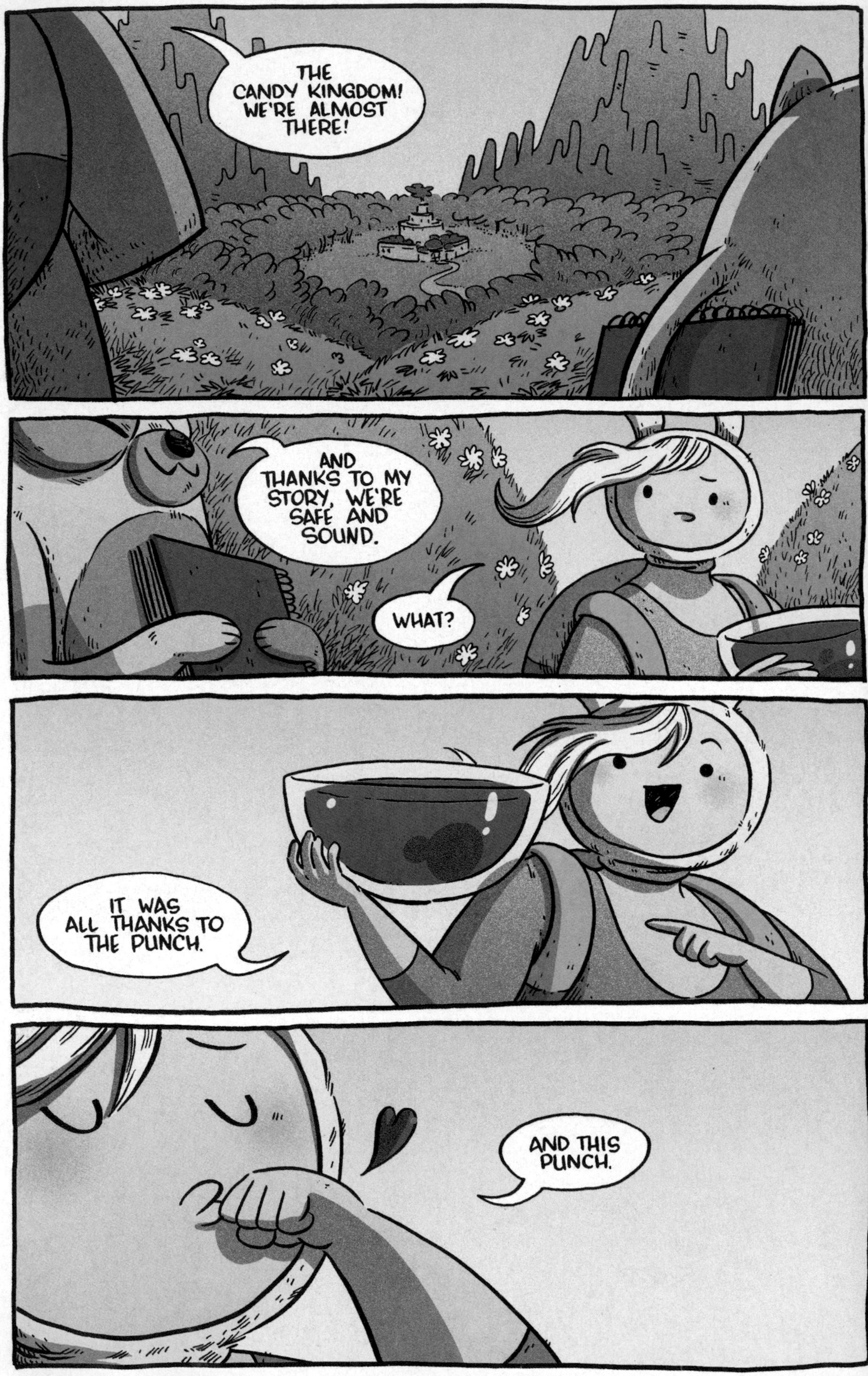
THE CANDY KINGDOM! WE'RE ALMOST THERE!
AND THANKS TO MY STORY, WE'RE SAFE AND SOUND.
WHAT?
IT WAS ALL THANKS TO THE PUNCH.
AND THIS PUNCH.

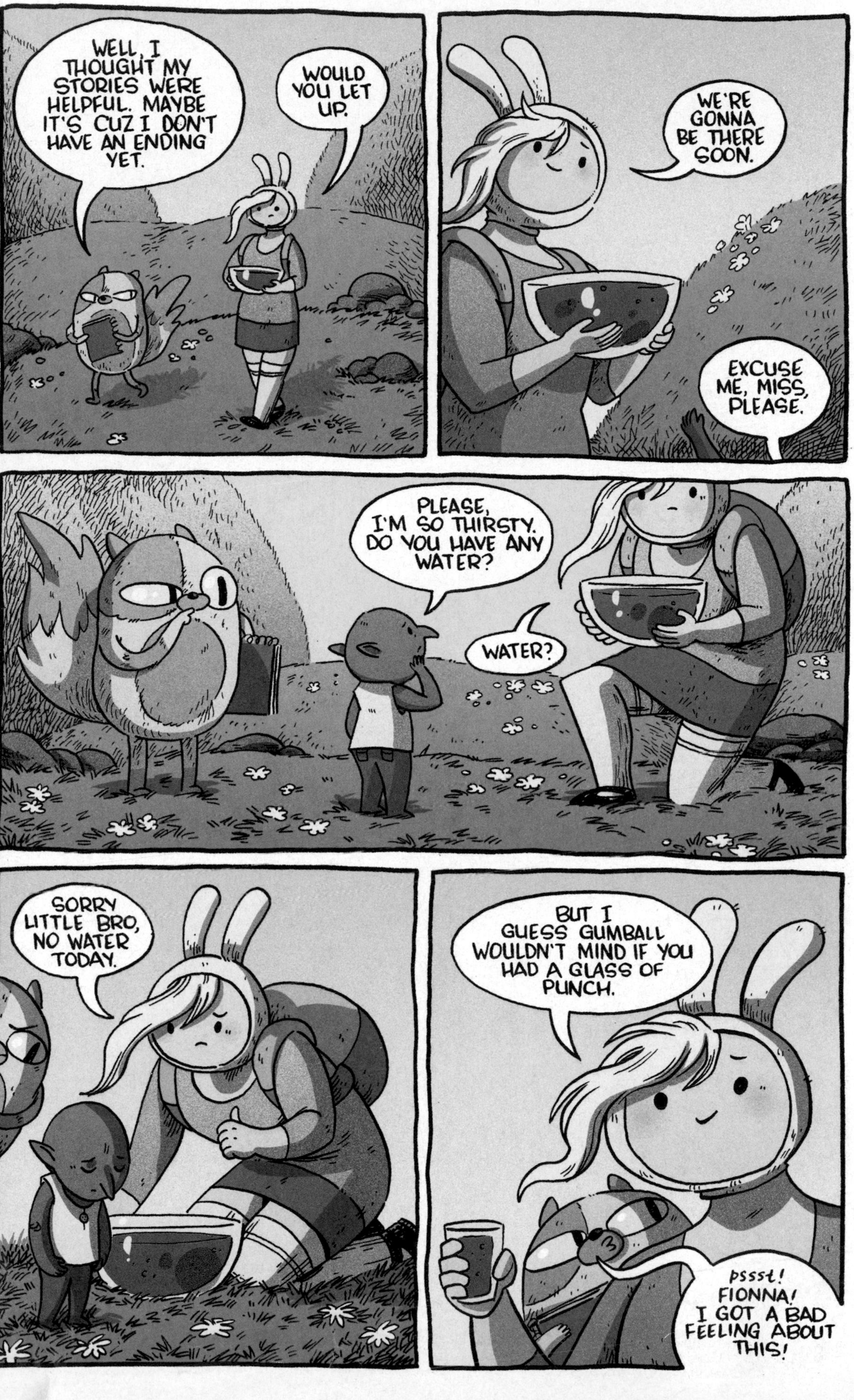
WELL, I THOUGHT MY STORIES WERE HELPFUL. MAYBE IT'S CUZ I DON'T HAVE AN ENDING YET.
WOULD YOU LET UP.
WE'RE GONNA BE THERE SOON.
EXCUSE ME, MISS, PLEASE.
PLEASE, I'M SO THIRSTY. DO YOU HAVE ANY WATER?
WATER?
SORRY LITTLE BRO, NO WATER TODAY.
BUT I GUESS GUMBALL WOULDN'T MIND IF YOU HAD A GLASS OF PUNCH.
pssst! FIONNA! I GOT A BAD FEELING ABOUT THIS!

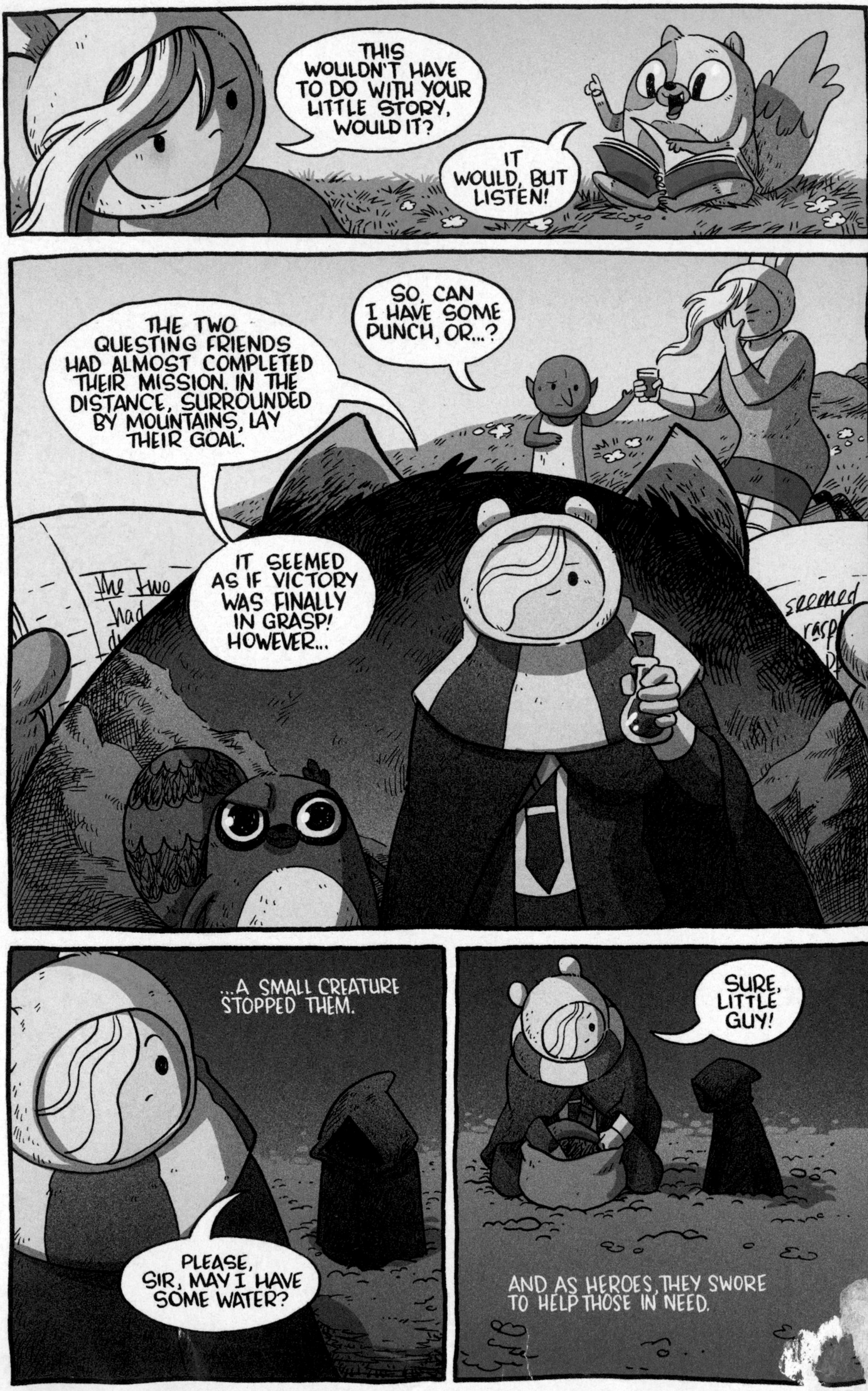
THIS WOULDN'T HAVE TO DO WITH YOUR LITTLE STORY, WOULD IT?
IT WOULD, BUT LISTEN!
THE TWO QUESTING FRIENDS HAD ALMOST COMPLETED THEIR MISSION. IN THE DISTANCE, SURROUNDED BY MOUNTAINS, LAY THEIR GOAL.
SO, CAN I HAVE SOME PUNCH, OR...?
IT SEEMED AS IF VICTORY WAS FINALLY IN GRASP! HOWEVER...
...A SMALL CREATURE STOPPED THEM.
PLEASE, SIR, MAY I HAVE SOME WATER?
SURE, LITTLE GUY!
AND AS HEROES, THEY SWORE TO HELP THOSE IN NEED.

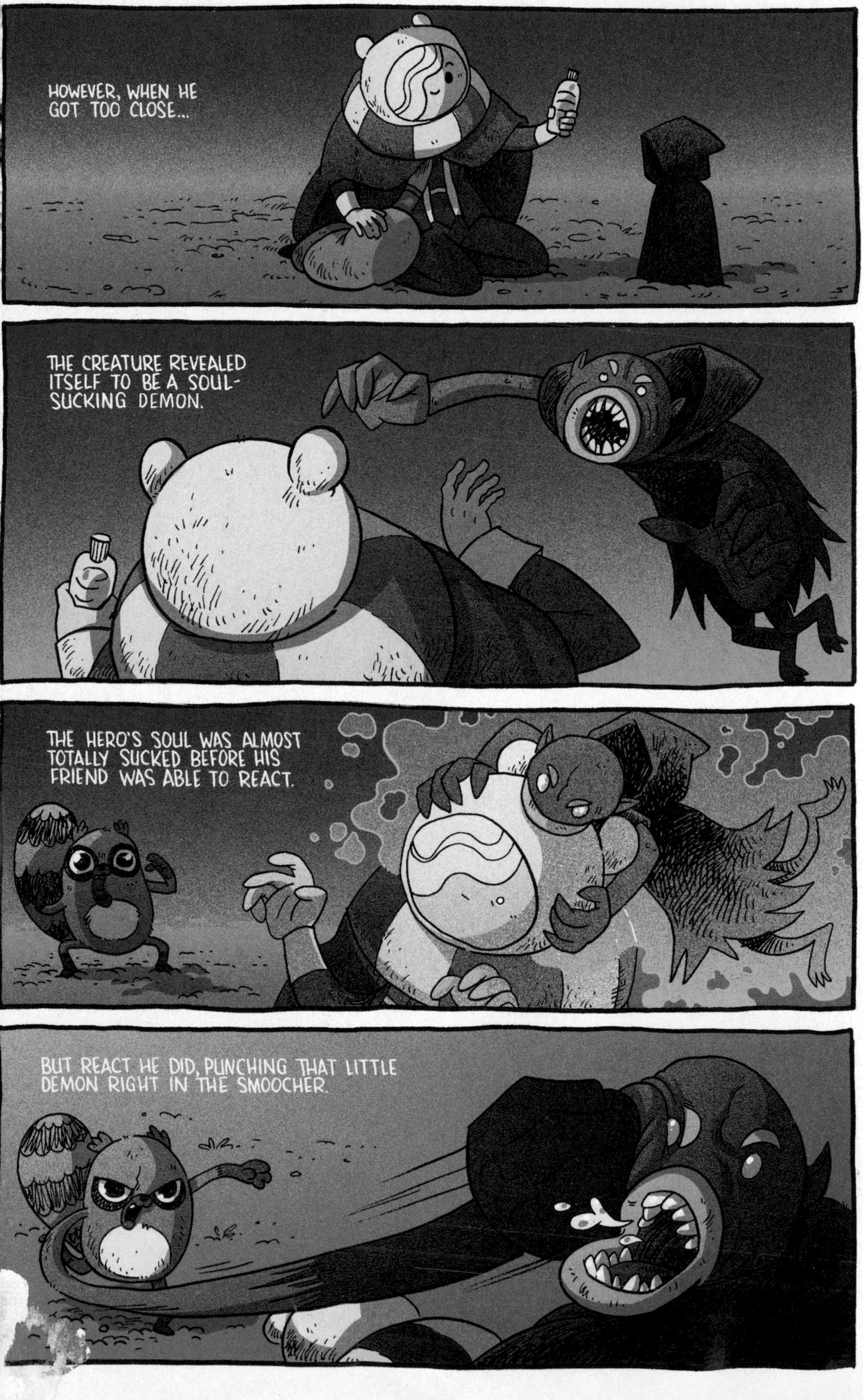
HOWEVER, WHEN HE GOT TOO CLOSE...
THE CREATURE REVEALED ITSELF TO BE A SOUL-SUCKING DEMON.
THE HERO'S SOUL WAS ALMOST TOTALLY SUCKED BEFORE HIS FRIEND WAS ABLE TO REACT.
BUT REACT HE DID, PUNCHING THAT LITTLE DEMON RIGHT IN THE SMOOCHER.

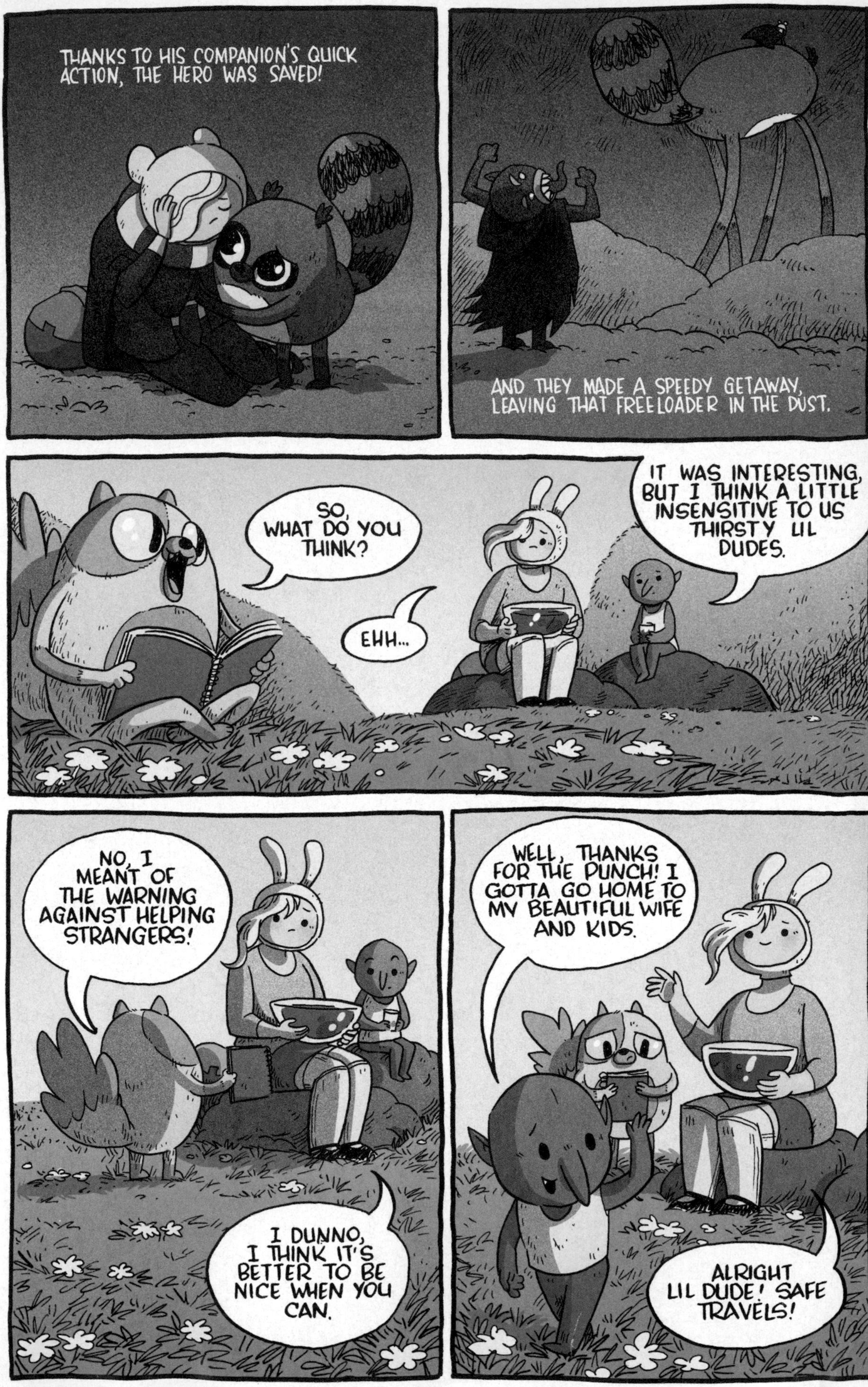
THANKS TO HIS COMPANION'S QUICK ACTION, THE HERO WAS SAVED!
AND THEY MADE A SPEEDY GETAWAY, LEAVING THAT FREELOADER IN THE DUST.
SO, WHAT DO YOU THINK?
EHH...
IT WAS INTERESTING, BUT I THINK A LITTLE INSENSITIVE TO US THIRSTY LIL DUDES.
NO, I MEANT OF THE WARNING AGAINST HELPING STRANGERS!
I DUNNO, I THINK IT'S BETTER TO BE NICE WHEN YOU CAN.
WELL, THANKS FOR THE PUNCH! I GOTTA GO HOME TO MY BEAUTIFUL WIFE AND KIDS.
ALRIGHT LIL DUDE! SAFE TRAVELS!

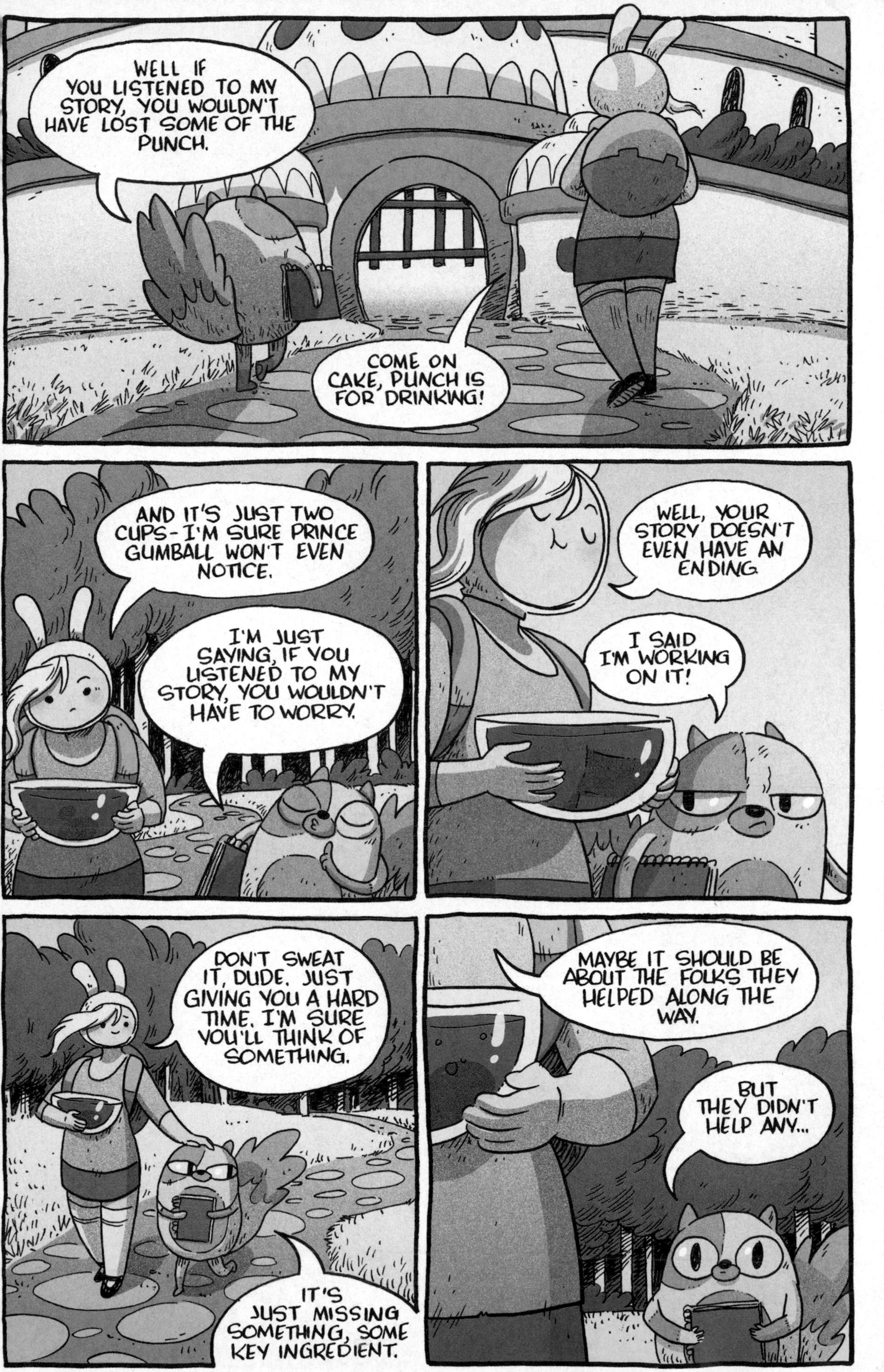
WELL IF YOU LISTENED TO MY STORY, YOU WOULDN'T HAVE LOST SOME OF THE PUNCH.
COME ON CAKE, PUNCH IS FOR DRINKING!
AND IT'S JUST TWO CUPS- I'M SURE PRINCE GUMBALL WON'T EVEN NOTICE.
I'M JUST SAYING, IF YOU LISTENED TO MY STORY, YOU WOULDN'T HAVE TO WORRY.
WELL, YOUR STORY DOESN'T EVEN HAVE AN ENDING.
I SAID I'M WORKING ON IT!
DON'T SWEAT IT, DUDE. JUST GIVING YOU A HARD TIME. I'M SURE YOU'LL THINK OF SOMETHING.
IT'S JUST MISSING SOMETHING, SOME KEY INGREDIENT.
MAYBE IT SHOULD BE ABOUT THE FOLKS THEY HELPED ALONG THE WAY.
BUT THEY DIDN'T HELP ANY...

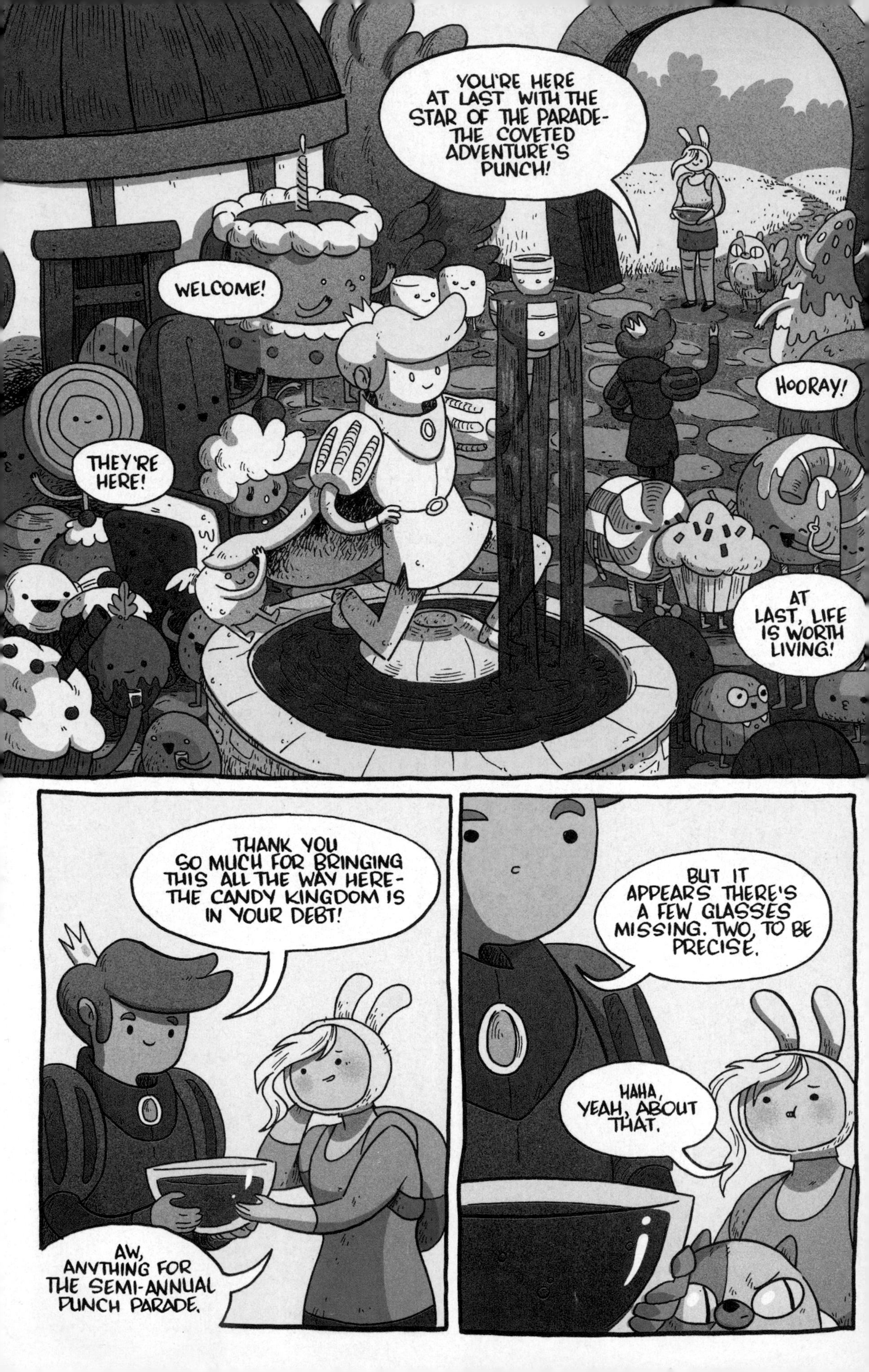
YOU'RE HERE AT LAST WITH THE STAR OF THE PARADE- THE COVETED ADVENTURE'S PUNCH!
WELCOME!
HOORAY!
THEY'RE HERE!
AT LAST, LIFE IS WORTH LIVING!
THANK YOU SO MUCH FOR BRINGING THIS ALL THE WAY HERE- THE CANDY KINGDOM IS IN YOUR DEBT!
AW, ANYTHING FOR THE SEMI-ANNUAL PUNCH PARADE.
BUT IT APPEARS THERE'S A FEW GLASSES MISSING. TWO, TO BE PRECISE.
HAHA, YEAH, ABOUT THAT.

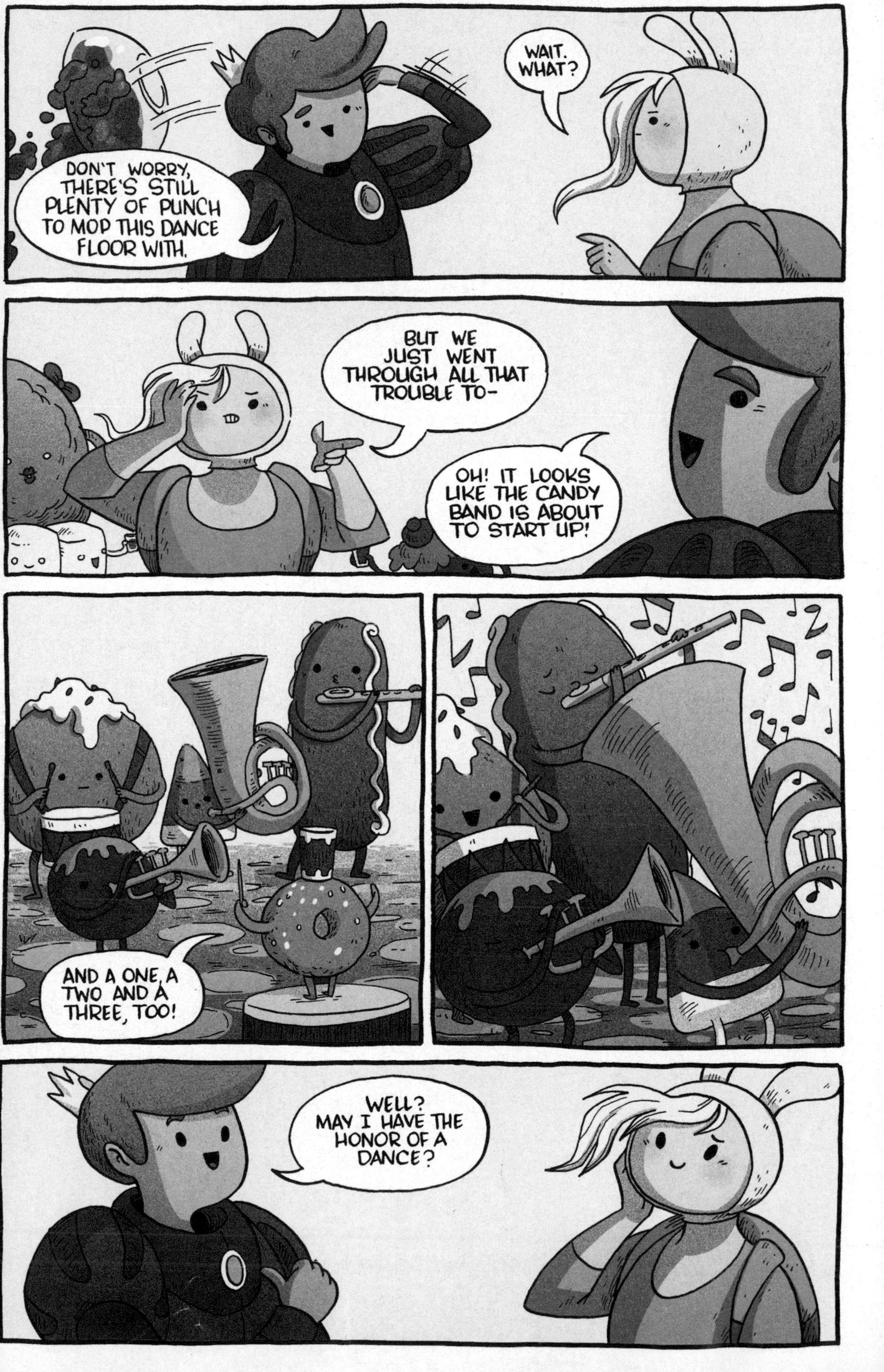
DON'T WORRY, THERE'S STILL PLENTY OF PUNCH TO MOP THIS DANCE FLOOR WITH.
WAIT. WHAT?
BUT WE JUST WENT THROUGH ALL THAT TROUBLE TO-
OH! IT LOOKS LIKE THE CANDY BAND IS ABOUT TO START UP!
AND A ONE, A TWO AND A THREE, TOO!
WELL? MAY I HAVE THE HONOR OF A DANCE?

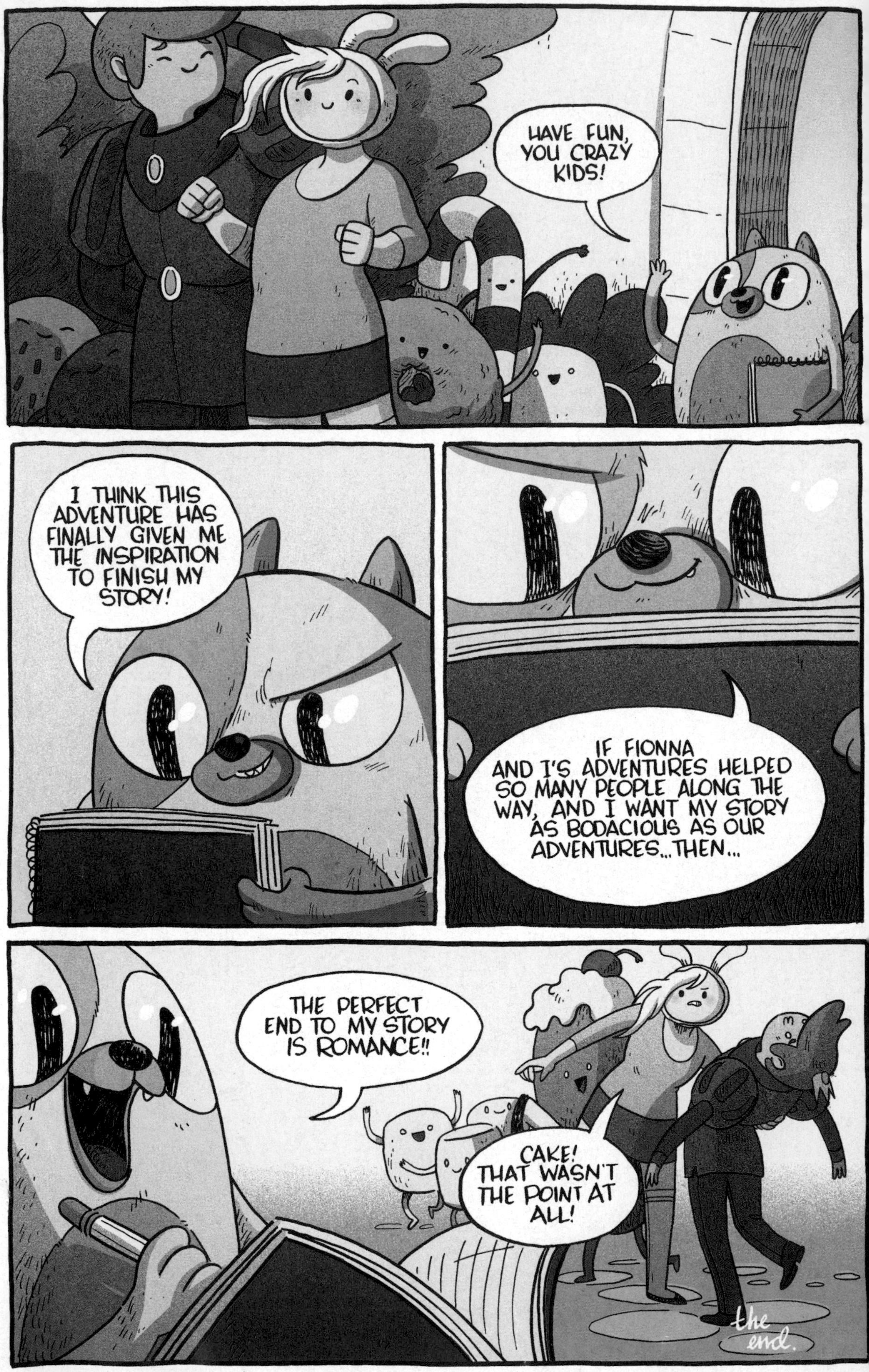
HAVE FUN, YOU CRAZY KIDS!
I THINK THIS ADVENTURE HAS FINALLY GIVEN ME THE INSPIRATION TO FINISH MY STORY!
IF FIONNA AND I'S ADVENTURES HELPED SO MANY PEOPLE ALONG THE WAY, AND I WANT MY STORY AS BODACIOUS AS OUR ADVENTURES... THEN...
THE PERFECT END TO MY STORY IS ROMANCE!!
CAKE! THAT WASN'T THE POINT AT ALL!
the end.

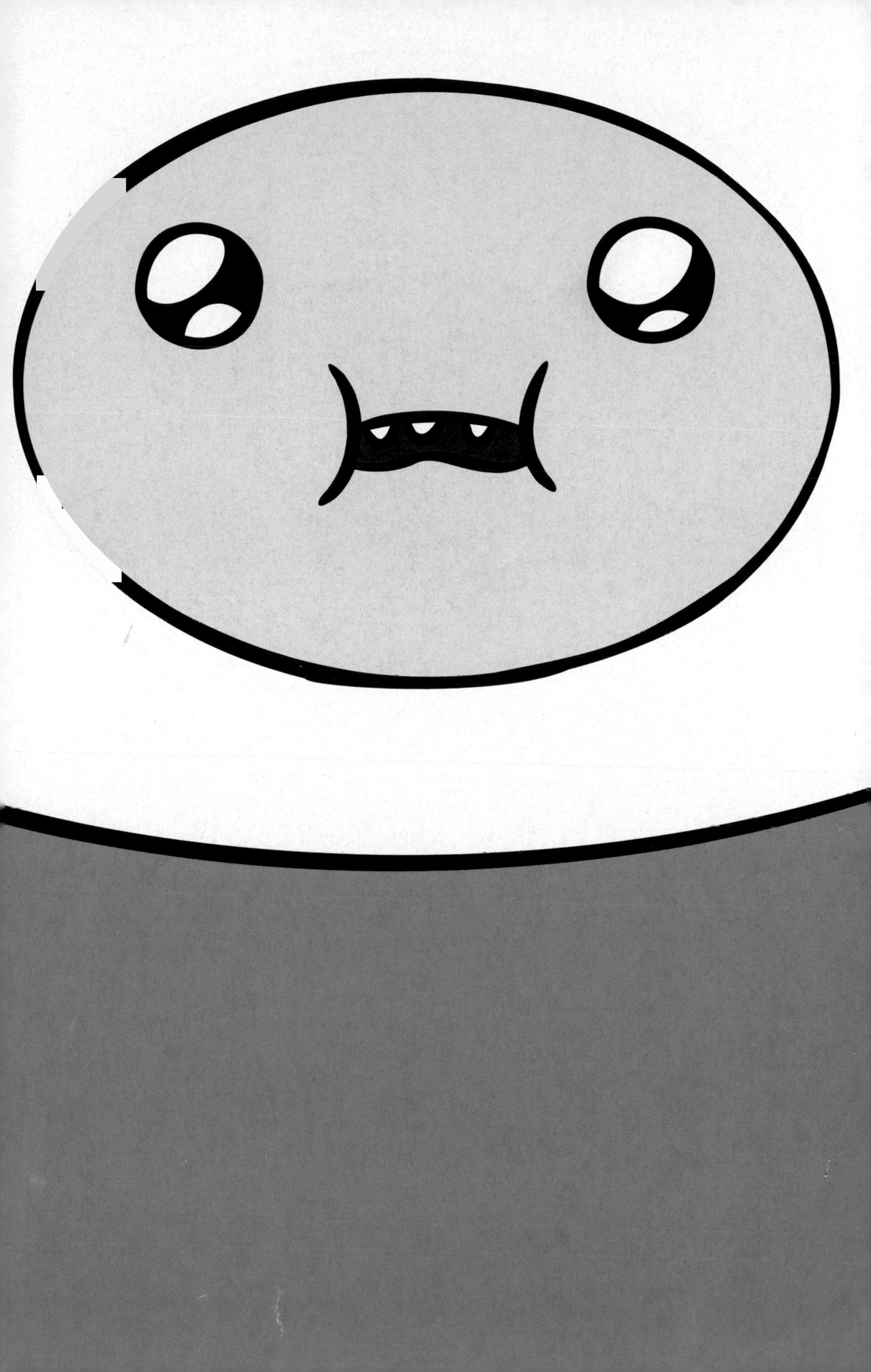

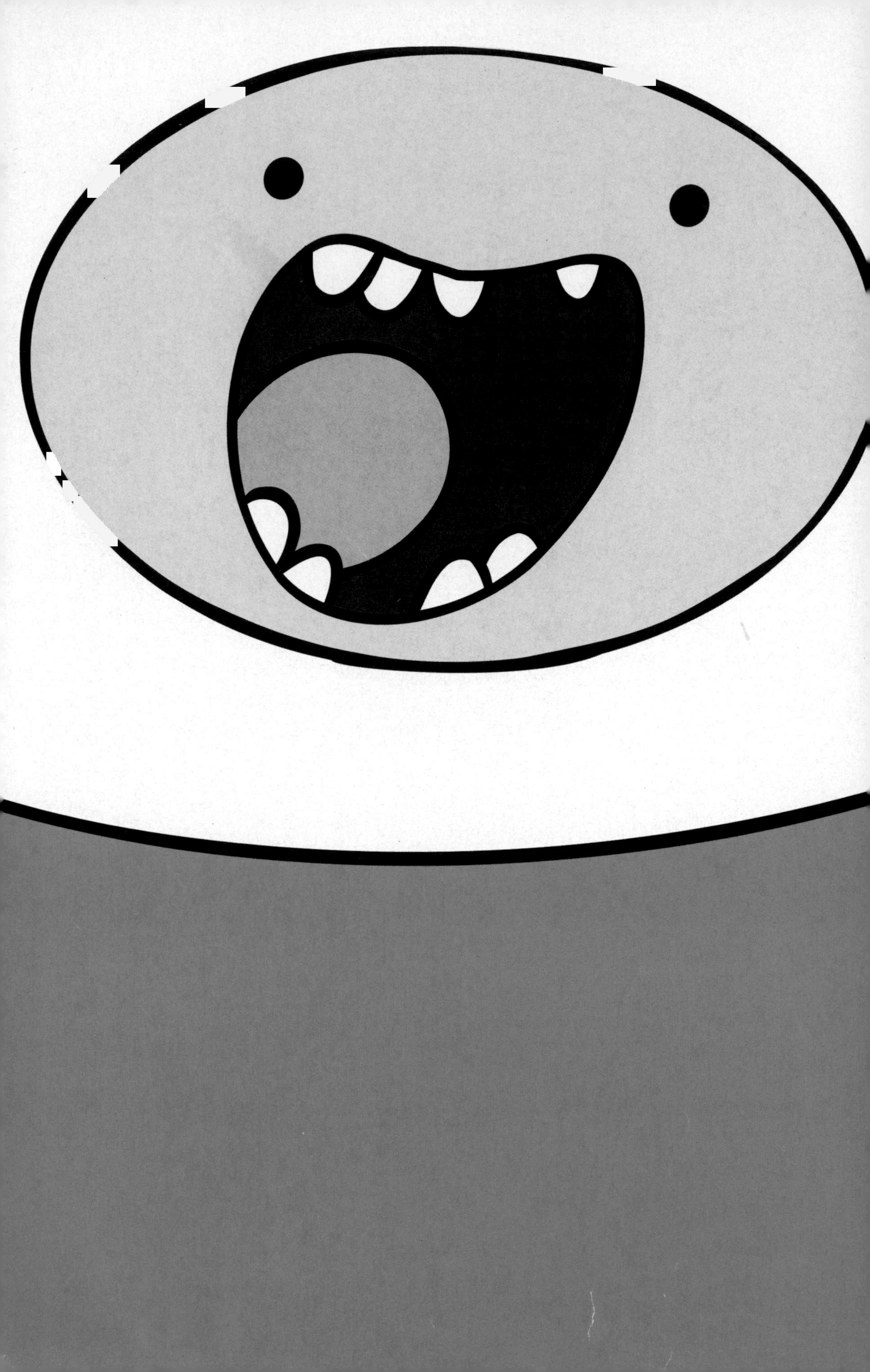

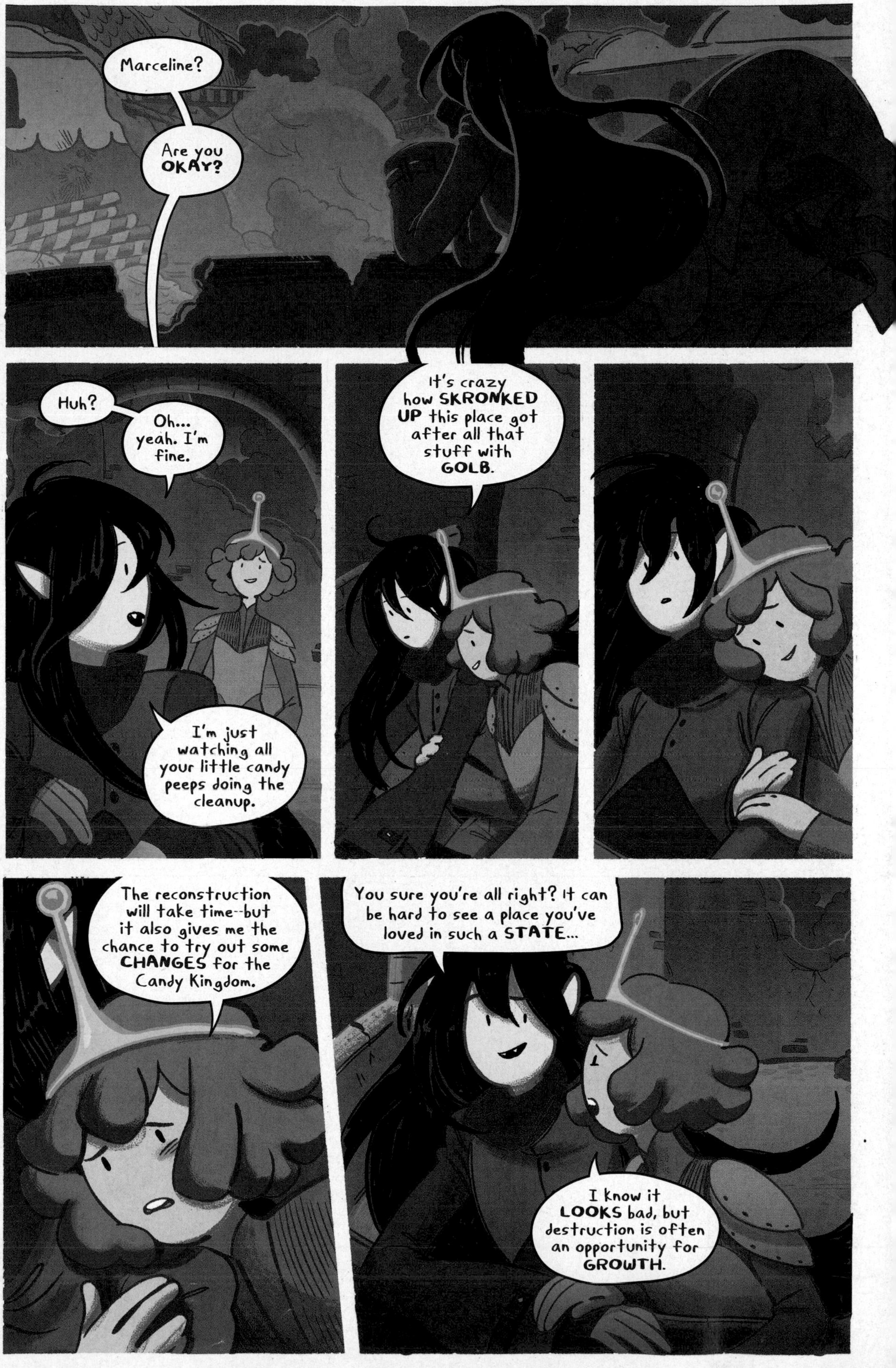
Marceline?
Are you OKAY?
Huh?
Oh... yeah. I'm fine.
I'm just watching all your little candy peeps doing the cleanup.
It's crazy how SKRONKED UP this place got after all that stuff with GOLB.
The reconstruction will take time--but it also gives me the chance to try out some CHANGES for the Candy Kingdom.
You sure you're all right? It can be hard to see a place you've loved in such a STATE...
I know it LOOKS bad, but destruction is often an opportunity for GROWTH.

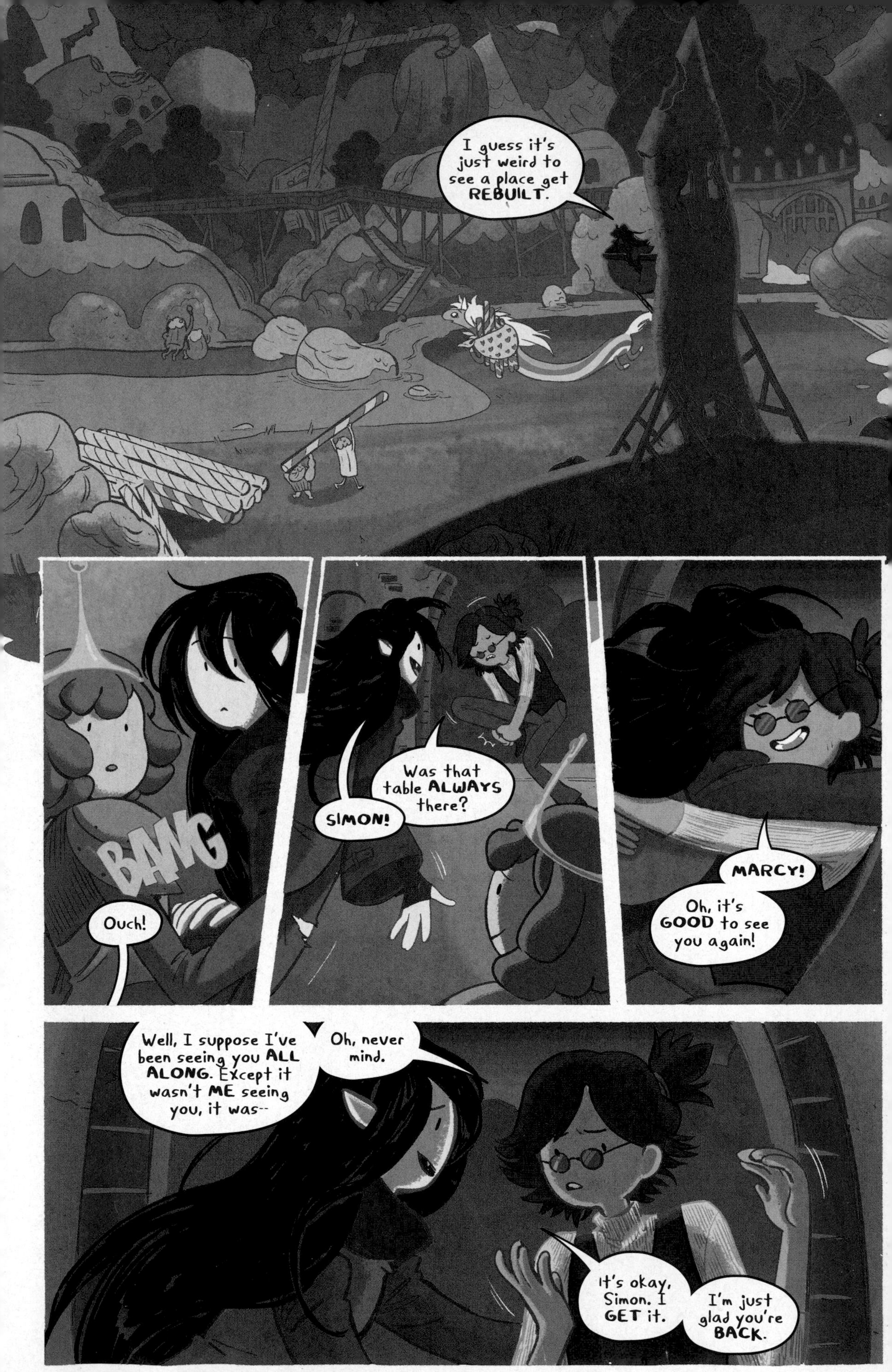

I guess it's just weird to see a place get REBUILT.
Ouch!
BANG
SIMON!
Was that table ALWAYS there?
MARCY!
Oh, it's GOOD to see you again!
Well, I suppose I've been seeing you ALL ALONG. Except it wasn't ME seeing you, it was--
Oh, never mind.
It's okay, Simon. I GET it.
I'm just glad you're BACK.

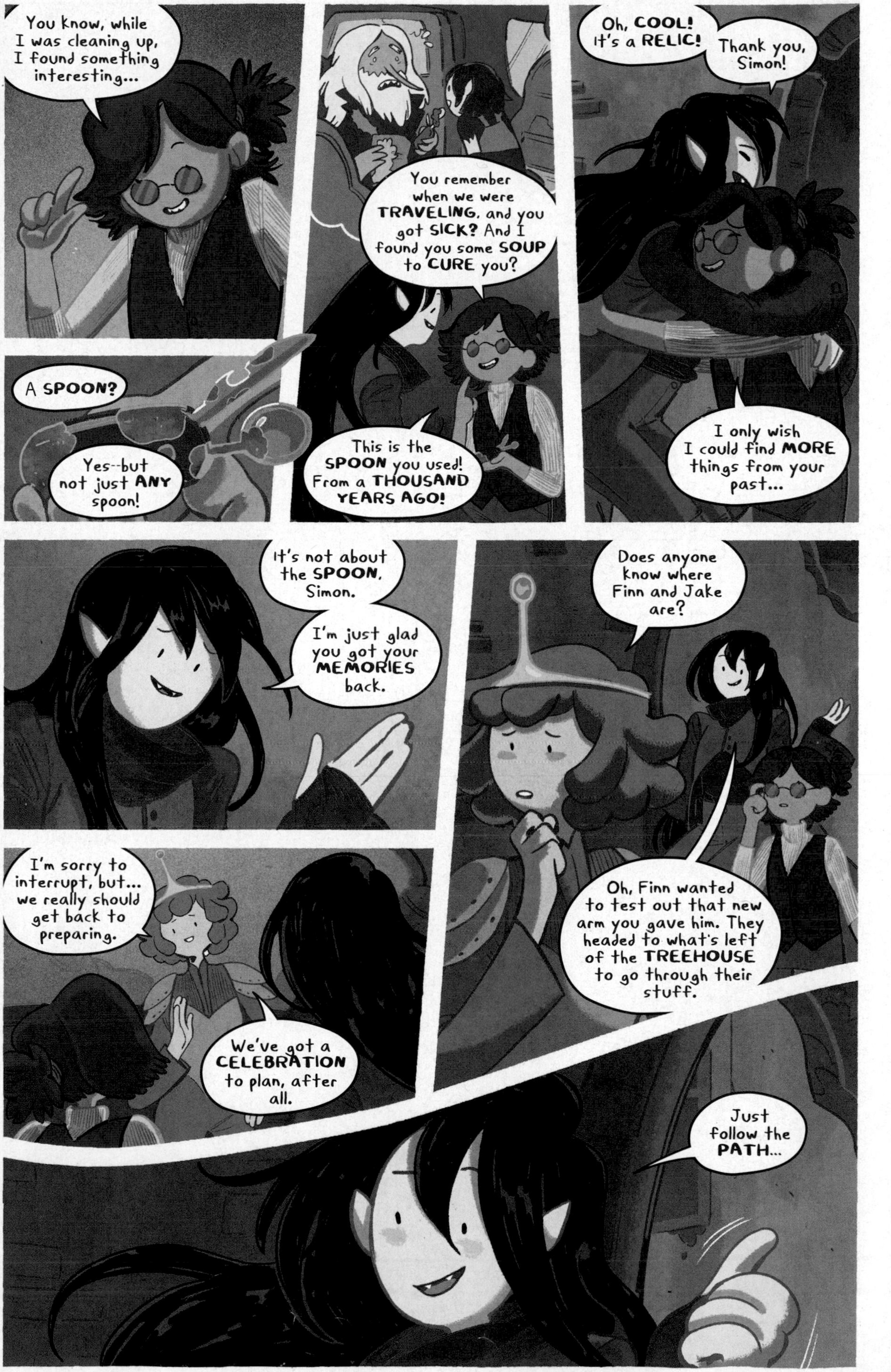
You know, while I was cleaning up, I found something interesting...
A SPOON?
Yes--but not just ANY spoon!
You remember when we were TRAVELING, and you got SICK? And I found you some SOUP to CURE you?
This is the SPOON you used! From a THOUSAND YEARS AGO!
Oh, COOL! It's a RELIC!
Thank you, Simon!
I only wish I could find MORE things from your past...
It's not about the SPOON, Simon.
I'm just glad you got your MEMORIES back.
Does anyone know where Finn and Jake are?
Oh, Finn wanted to test out that new arm you gave him. They headed to what's left of the TREEHOUSE to go through their stuff.
I'm sorry to interrupt, but... we really should get back to preparing.
We've got a CELEBRATION to plan, after all.
Just follow the PATH...

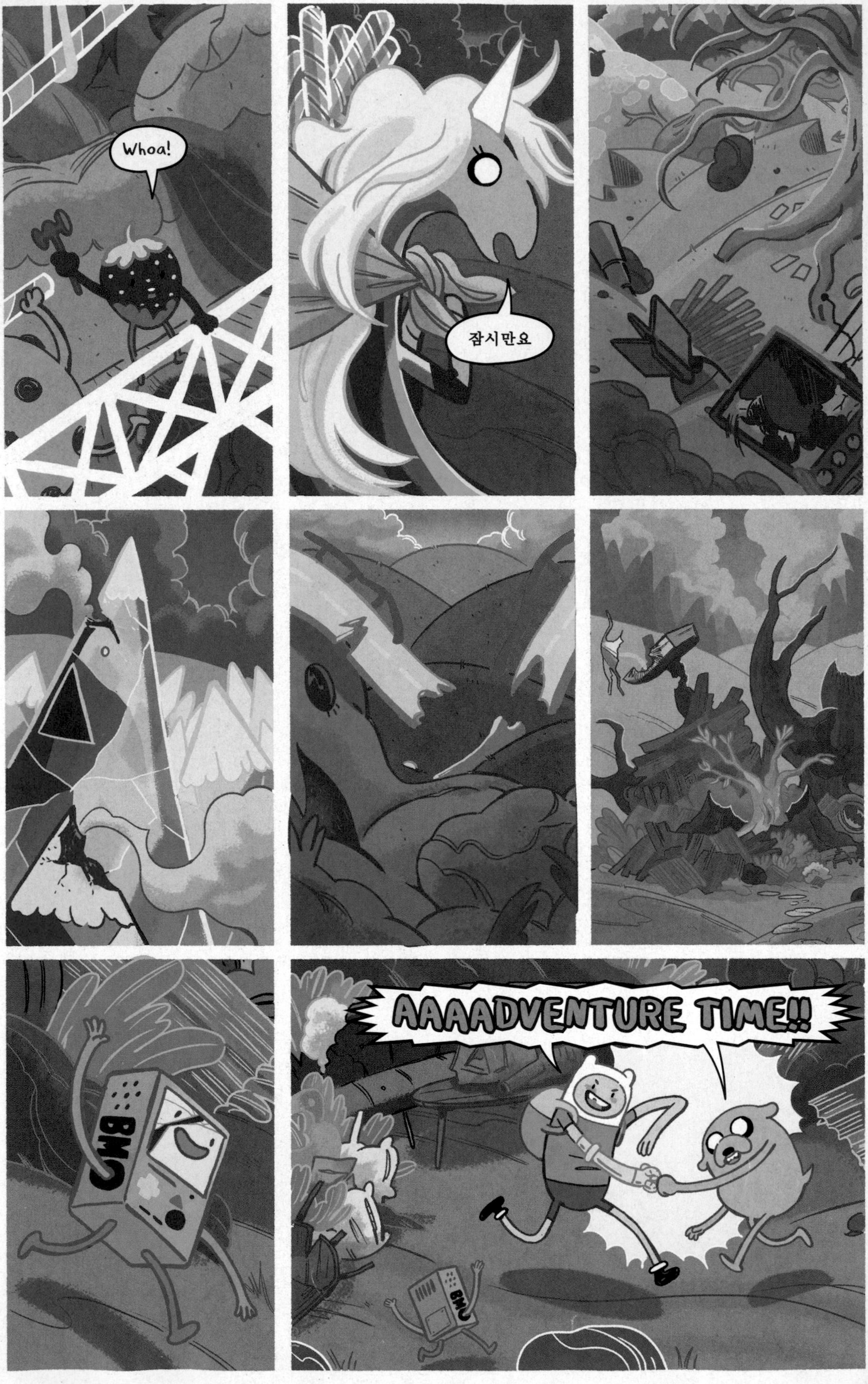
Whoa!
잠시만요
AAAADVENTURE TIME!!
BMO
BMO

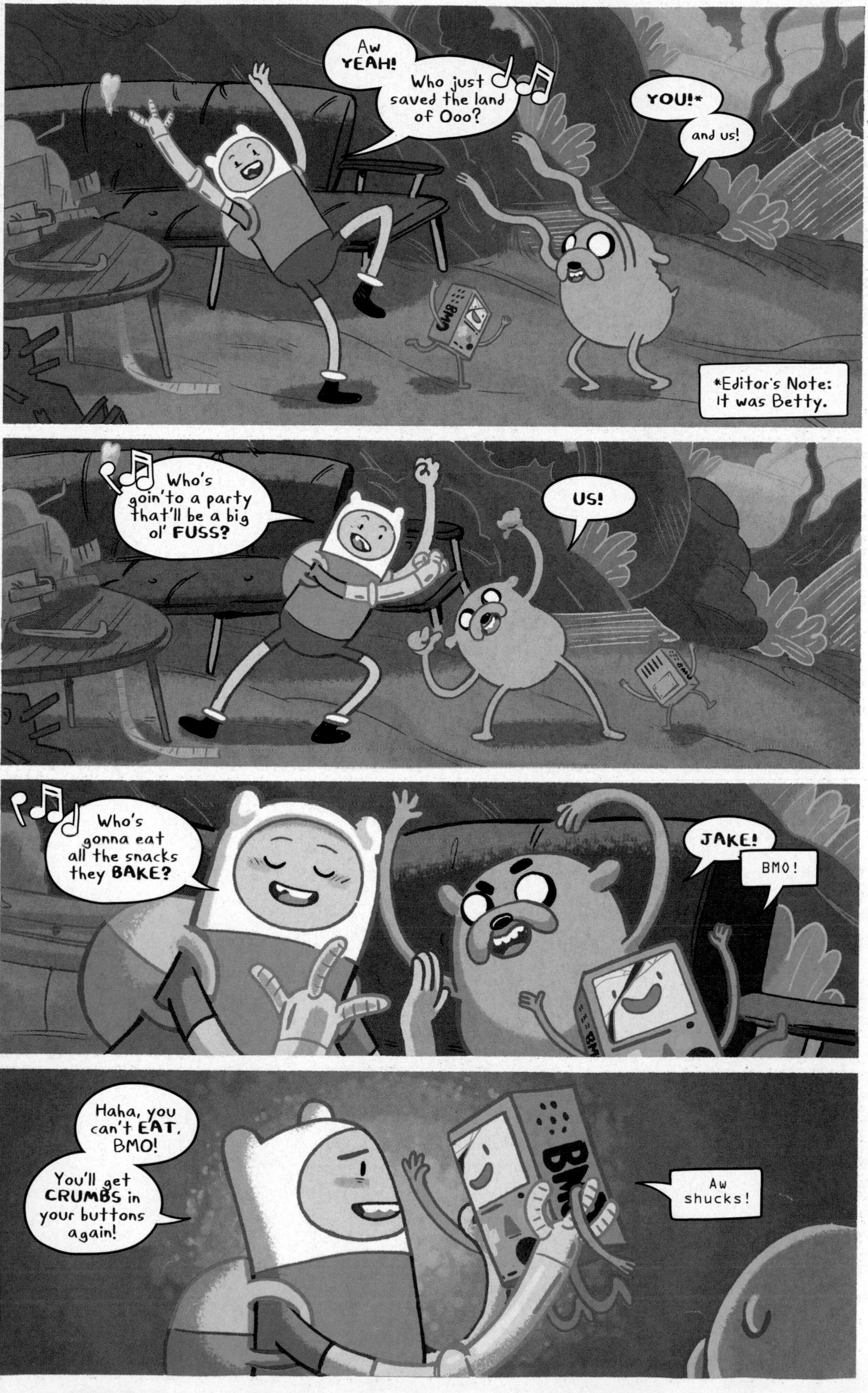
Aw YEAH!
Who just saved the land of Ooo?
YOU!*
and us!
*Editor's Note: It was Betty.
Who's goin' to a party that'll be a big ol' FUSS?
US!
Who's gonna eat all the snacks they BAKE?
JAKE!
BMO!
Haha, you can't EAT, BMO!
You'll get CRUMBS in your buttons again!
Aw shucks!

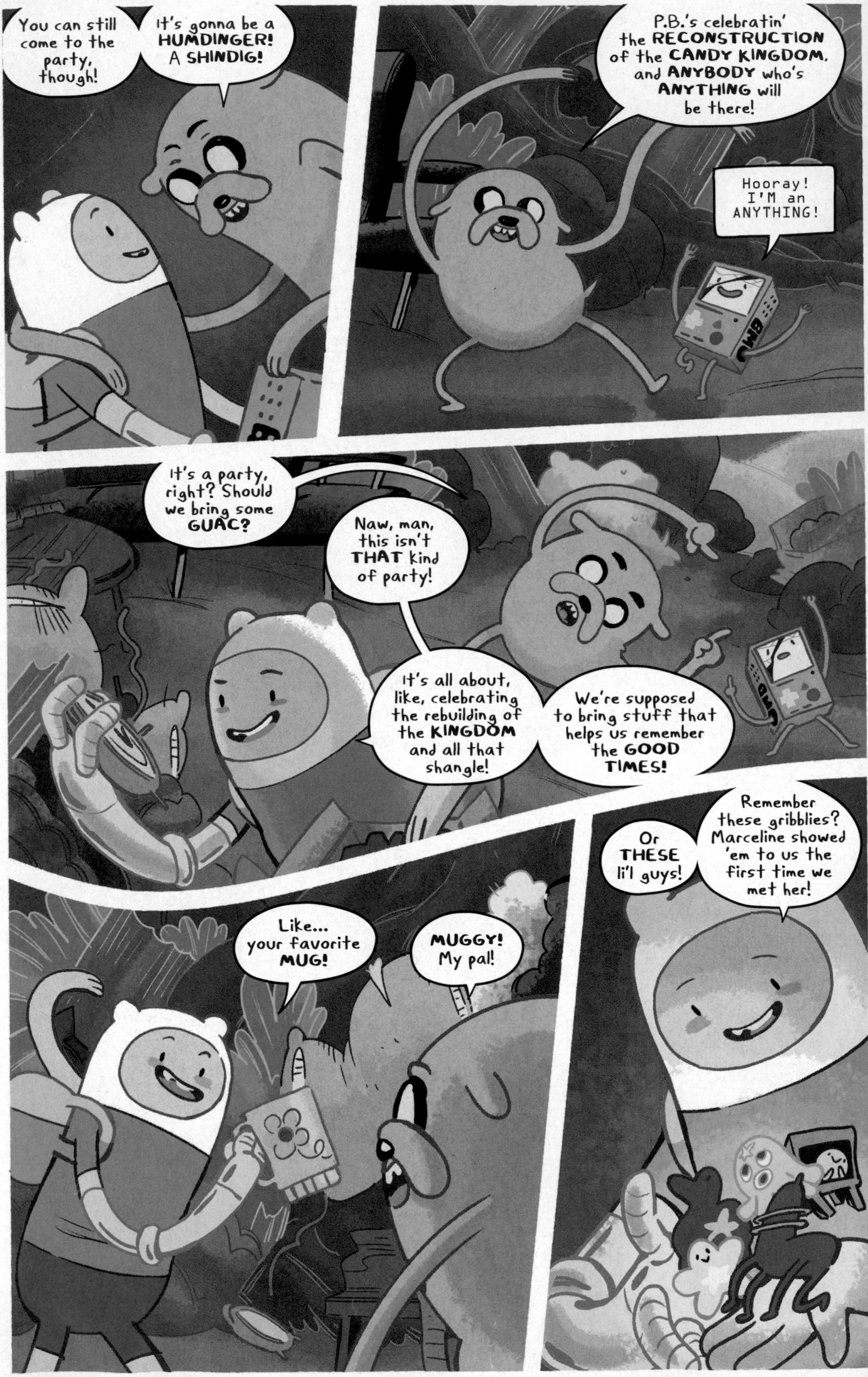
You can still come to the party, though!
It's gonna be a HUMDINGER! A SHINDIG!
P.B.'s celebratin' the RECONSTRUCTION of the CANDY KINGDOM, and ANYBODY who's ANYTHING will be there!
Hooray! I'M an ANYTHING!
BMO
It's a party, right? Should we bring some GUAC?
Naw, man, this isn't THAT kind of party!
It's all about, like, celebrating the rebuilding of the KINGDOM and all that shangle!
We're supposed to bring stuff that helps us remember the GOOD TIMES!
Like... your favorite MUG!
MUGGY! My pal!
Or THESE li'l guys!
Remember these gribblies? Marceline showed 'em to us the first time we met her!

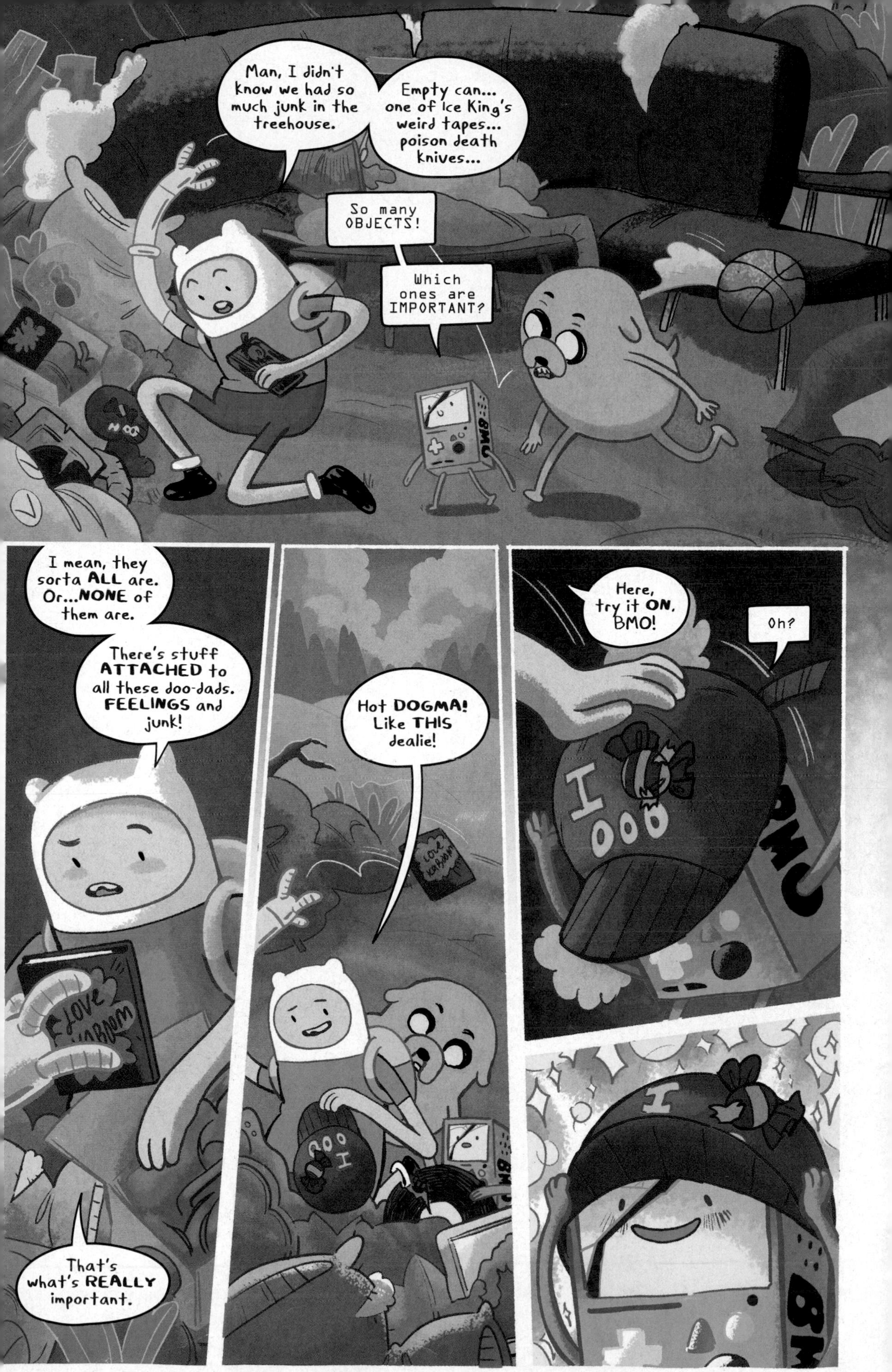
Man, I didn't know we had so much junk in the treehouse.
Empty can... one of Ice King's weird tapes... poison death knives...
So many OBJECTS!
Which ones are IMPORTANT?
BMO
I mean, they sorta ALL are. Or...NONE of them are.
There's stuff ATTACHED to all these doo-dads. FEELINGS and junk!
That's what's REALLY important.
Hot DOGMA! Like THIS dealie!
Here, try it ON, BMO!
Oh?
BMO

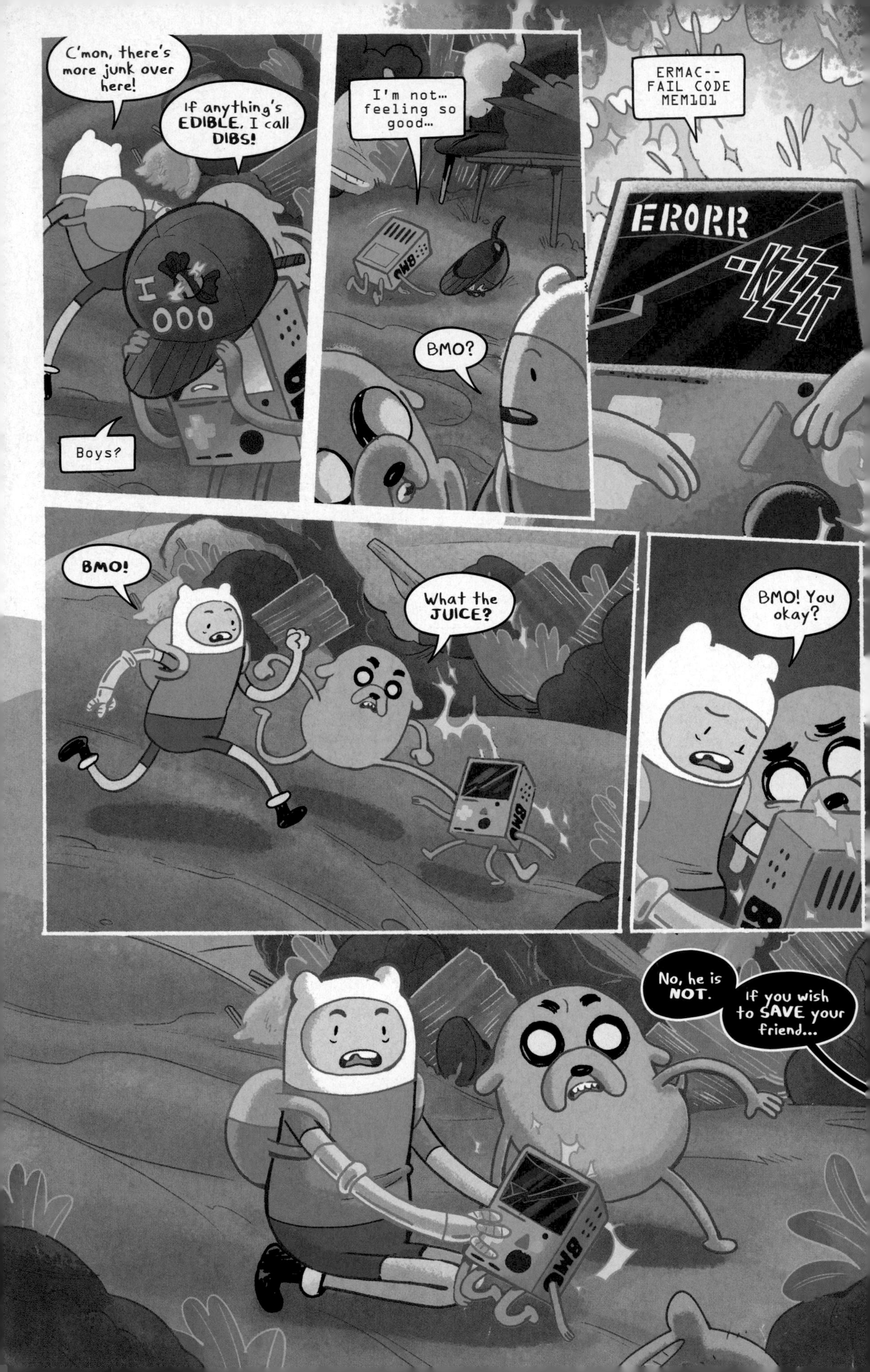

C'mon, there's more junk over here!
If anything's EDIBLE, I call DIBS!
Boys?
I'm not... feeling so good...
BMO?
ERMAC-- FAIL CODE MEM101
ERORR
-KZZT
BMO!
What the JUICE?
BMO! You okay?
No, he is NOT.
If you wish to SAVE your friend...

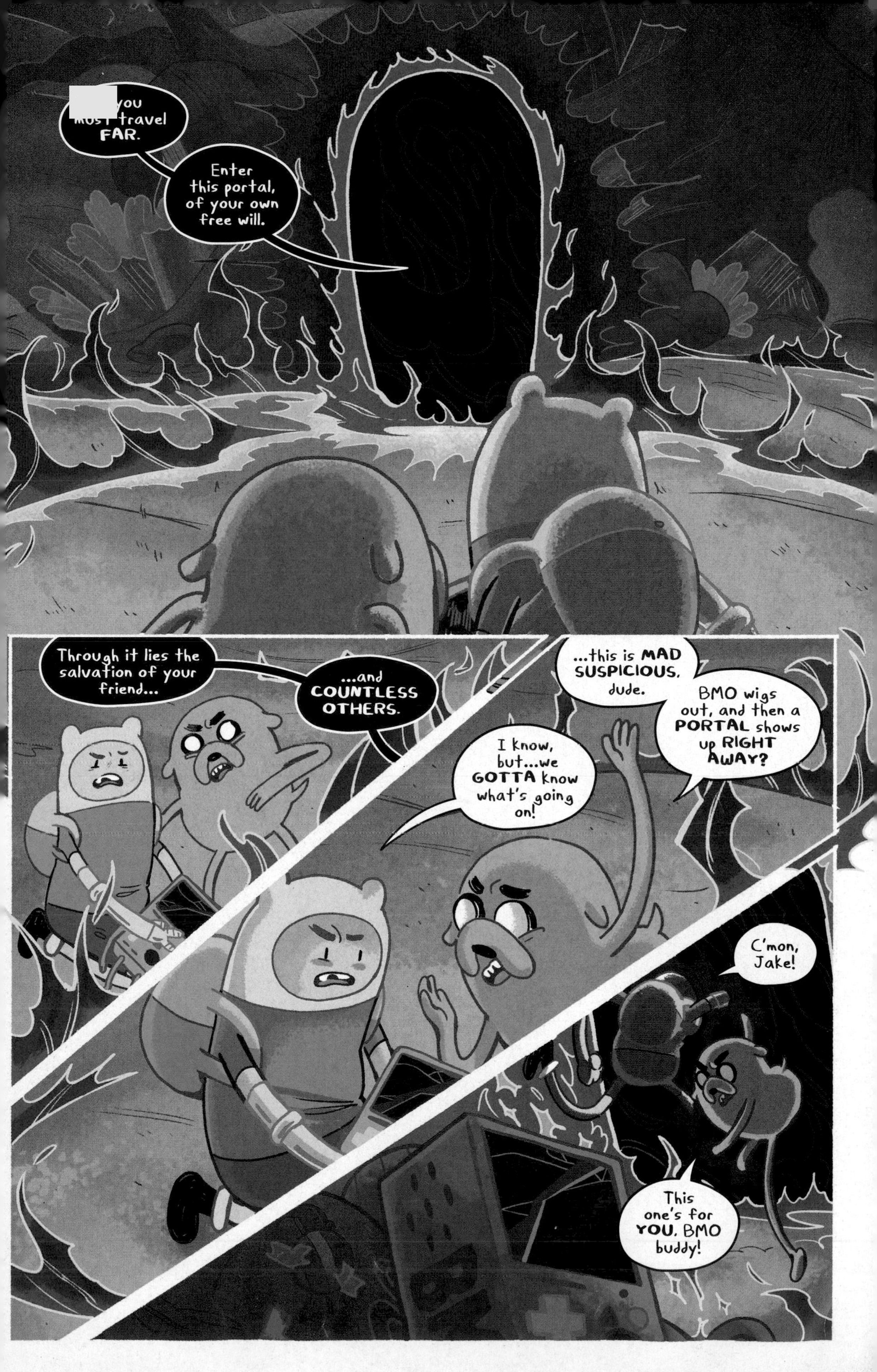

you must travel FAR.
Enter this portal, of your own free will.
Through it lies the salvation of your friend...
...and COUNTLESS OTHERS.
...this is MAD SUSPICIOUS, dude.
BMO wigs out, and then a PORTAL shows up RIGHT AWAY?
I know, but...we GOTTA know what's going on!
C'mon, Jake!
This one's for YOU, BMO buddy!

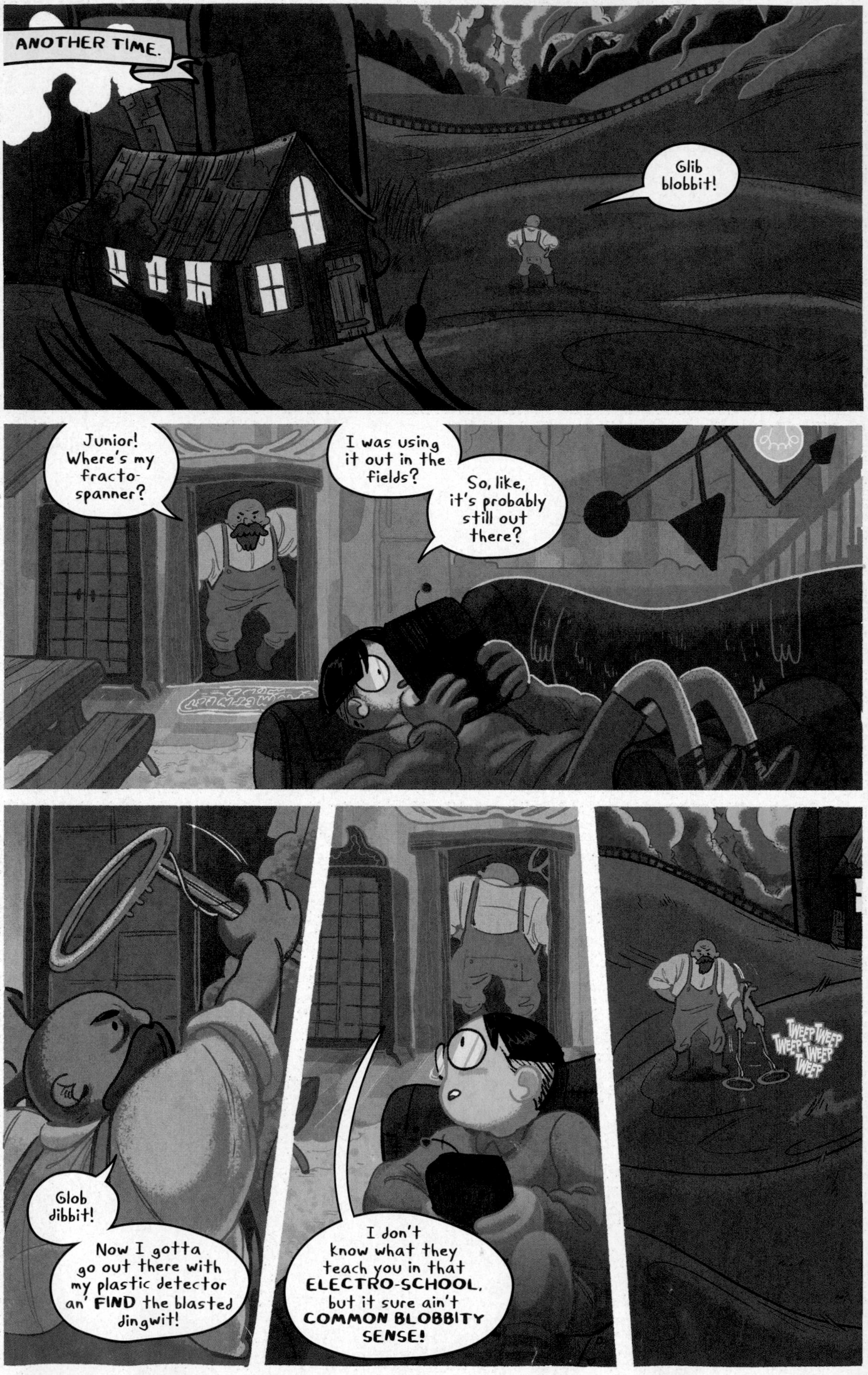
ANOTHER TIME.
Glib blobbit!
Junior! Where's my fracto-spanner?
I was using it out in the fields?
So, like, it's probably still out there?
Glob dibbit!
Now I gotta go out there with my plastic detector an' **FIND** the blasted dingwit!
I don't know what they teach you in that **ELECTRO-SCHOOL**, but it sure ain't **COMMON BLOBBITY SENSE!**
TWEEP TWEEP TWEEP TWEEP TWEEP

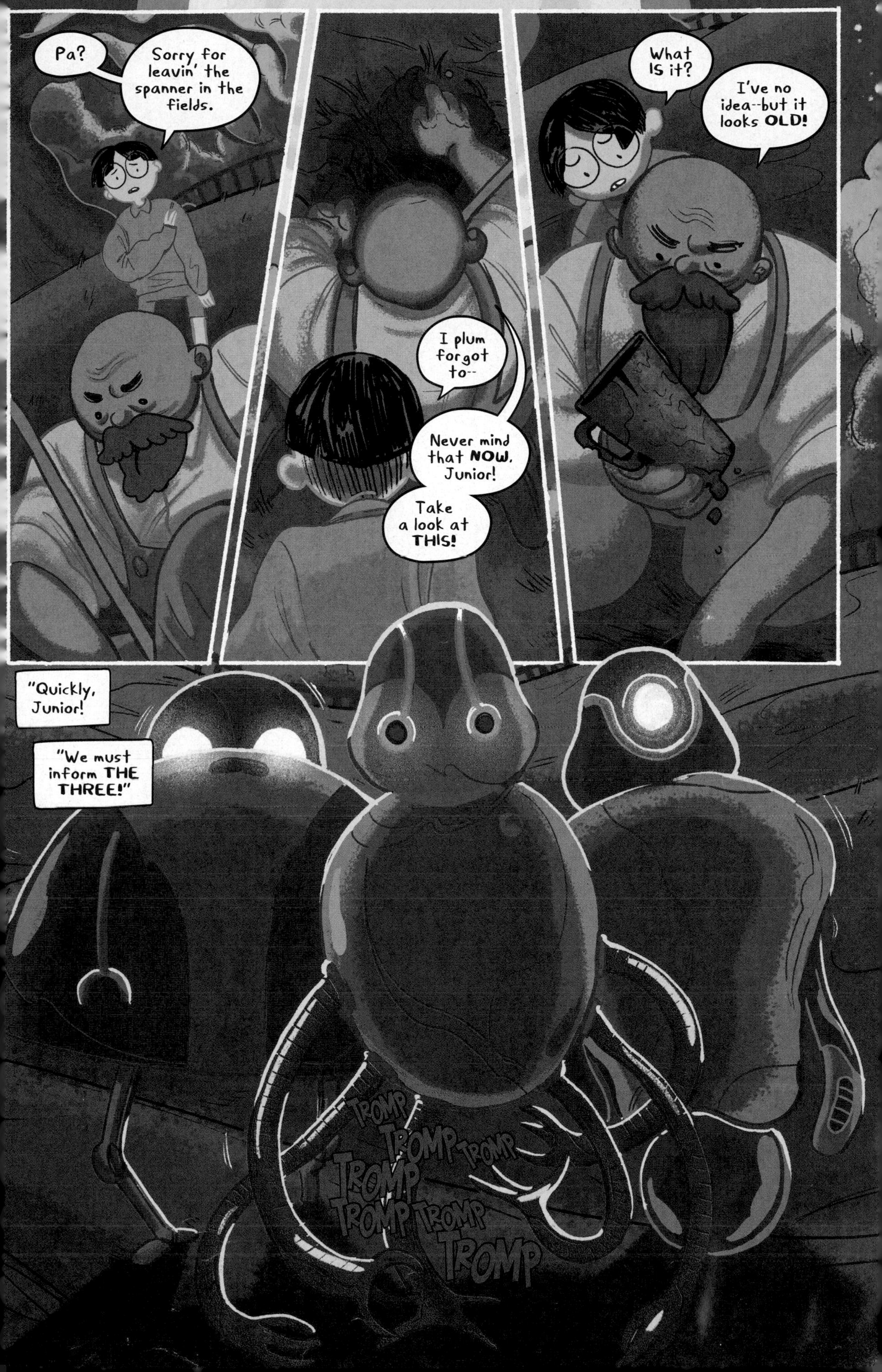
Pa?
Sorry for leavin' the spanner in the fields.
I plum forgot to--
Never mind that NOW, Junior!
Take a look at THIS!
What IS it?
I've no idea--but it looks OLD!
"Quickly, Junior!
"We must inform THE THREE!"
TROMP TROMP TROMP TROMP TROMP TROMP TROMP

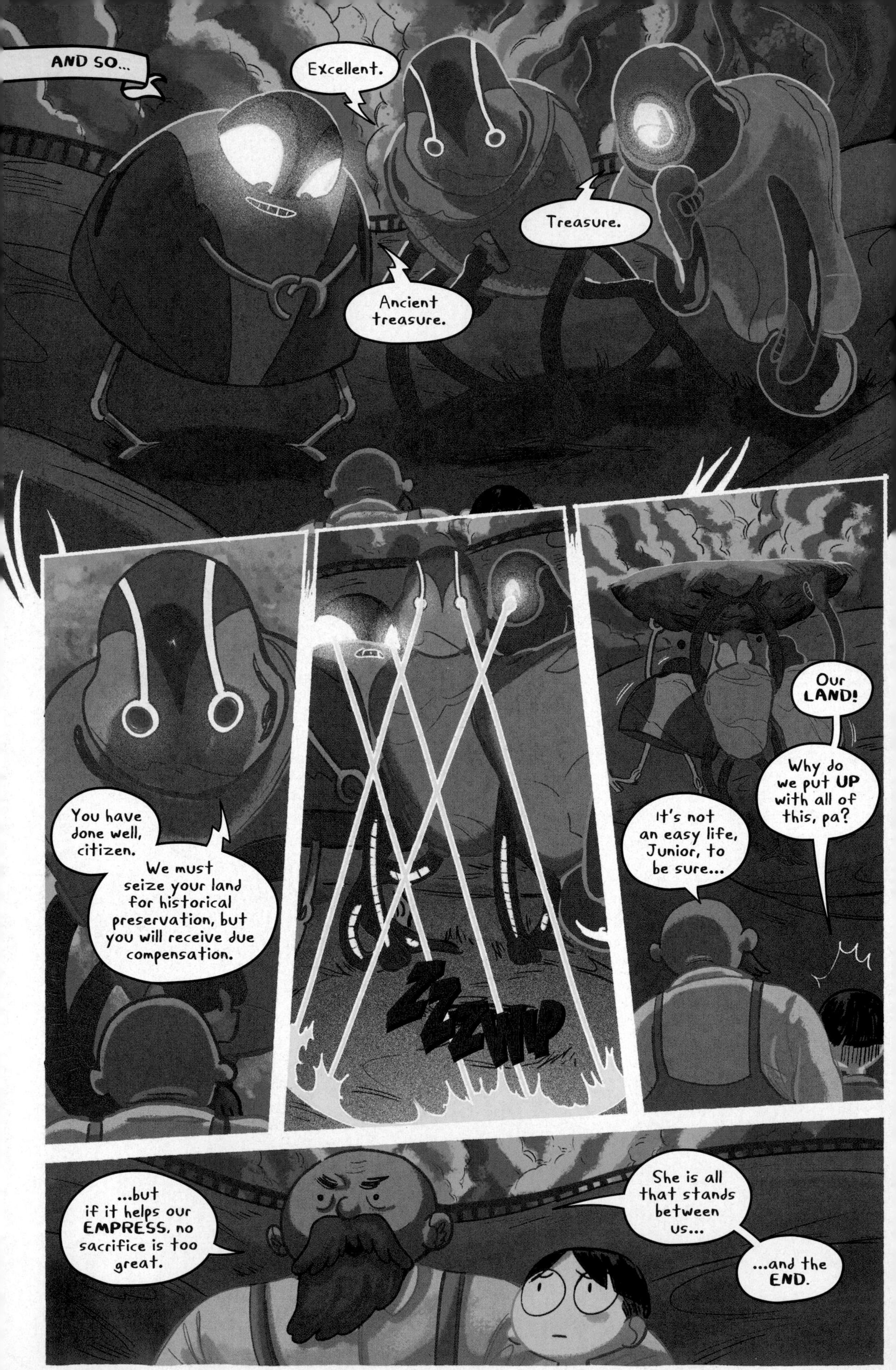
AND SO...
Excellent.
Treasure.
Ancient treasure.
You have done well, citizen.
We must seize your land for historical preservation, but you will receive due compensation.
ZZZWWP
Our LAND!
Why do we put UP with all of this, pa?
It's not an easy life, Junior, to be sure...
...but if it helps our EMPRESS, no sacrifice is too great.
She is all that stands between us...
...and the END.

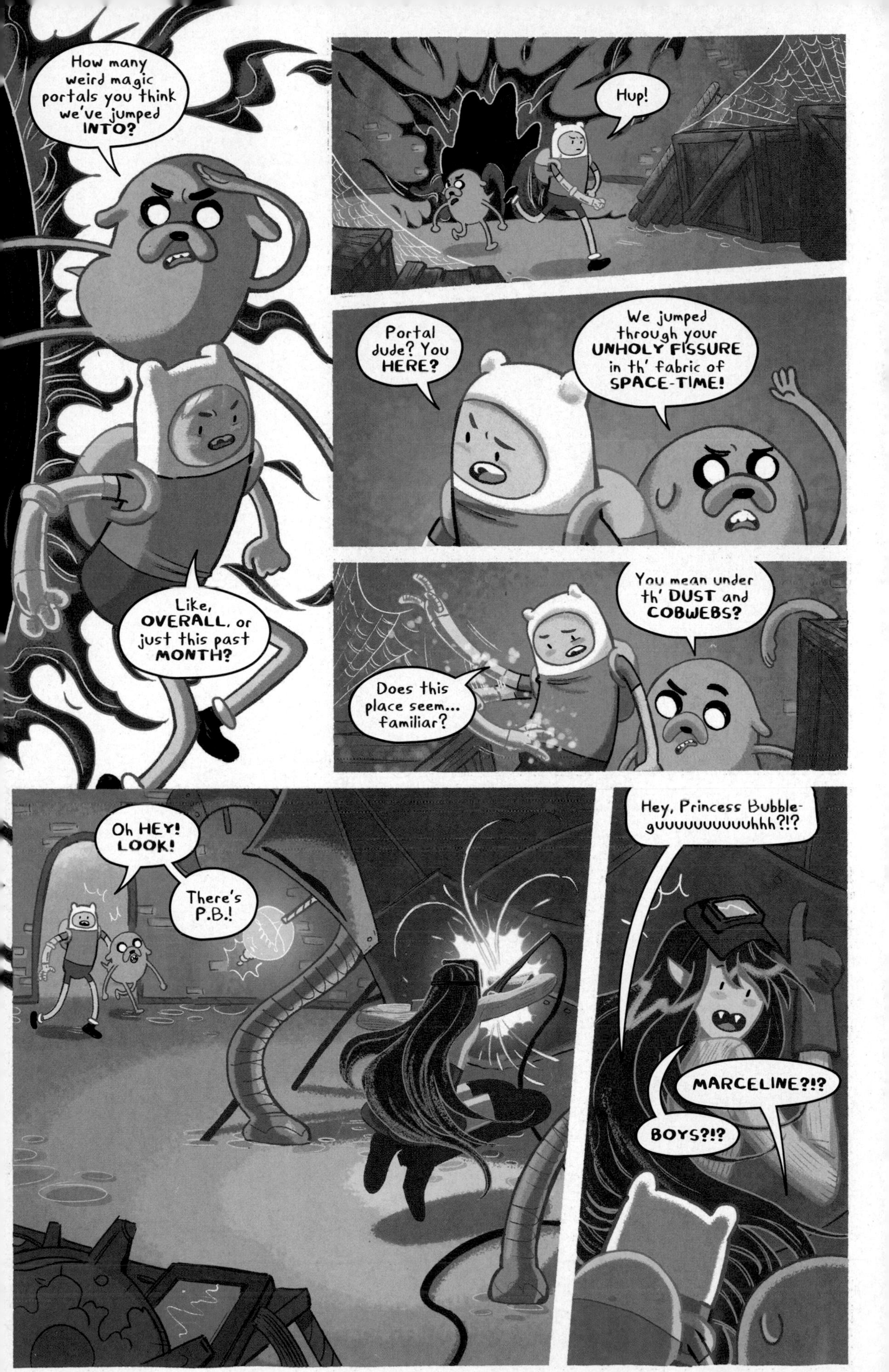
How many weird magic portals you think we've jumped INTO?
Like, OVERALL, or just this past MONTH?
Hup!
Portal dude? You HERE?
We jumped through your UNHOLY FISSURE in th' fabric of SPACE-TIME!
You mean under th' DUST and COBWEBS?
Does this place seem... familiar?
Oh HEY! LOOK!
There's P.B.!
Hey, Princess Bubble-guuuuuuuuuhhh?!?
MARCELINE?!?
BOYS?!?

COVER GALLERY

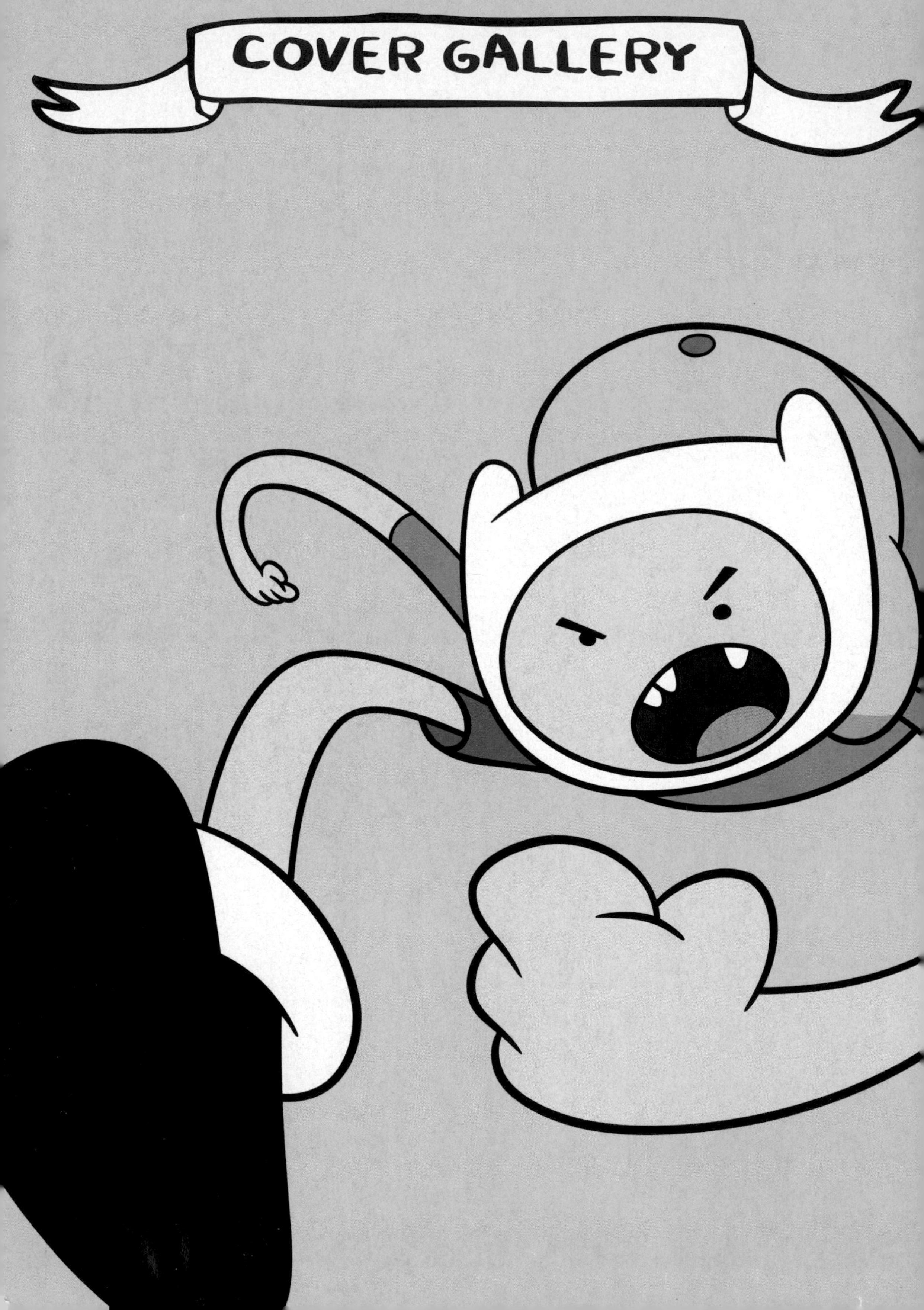

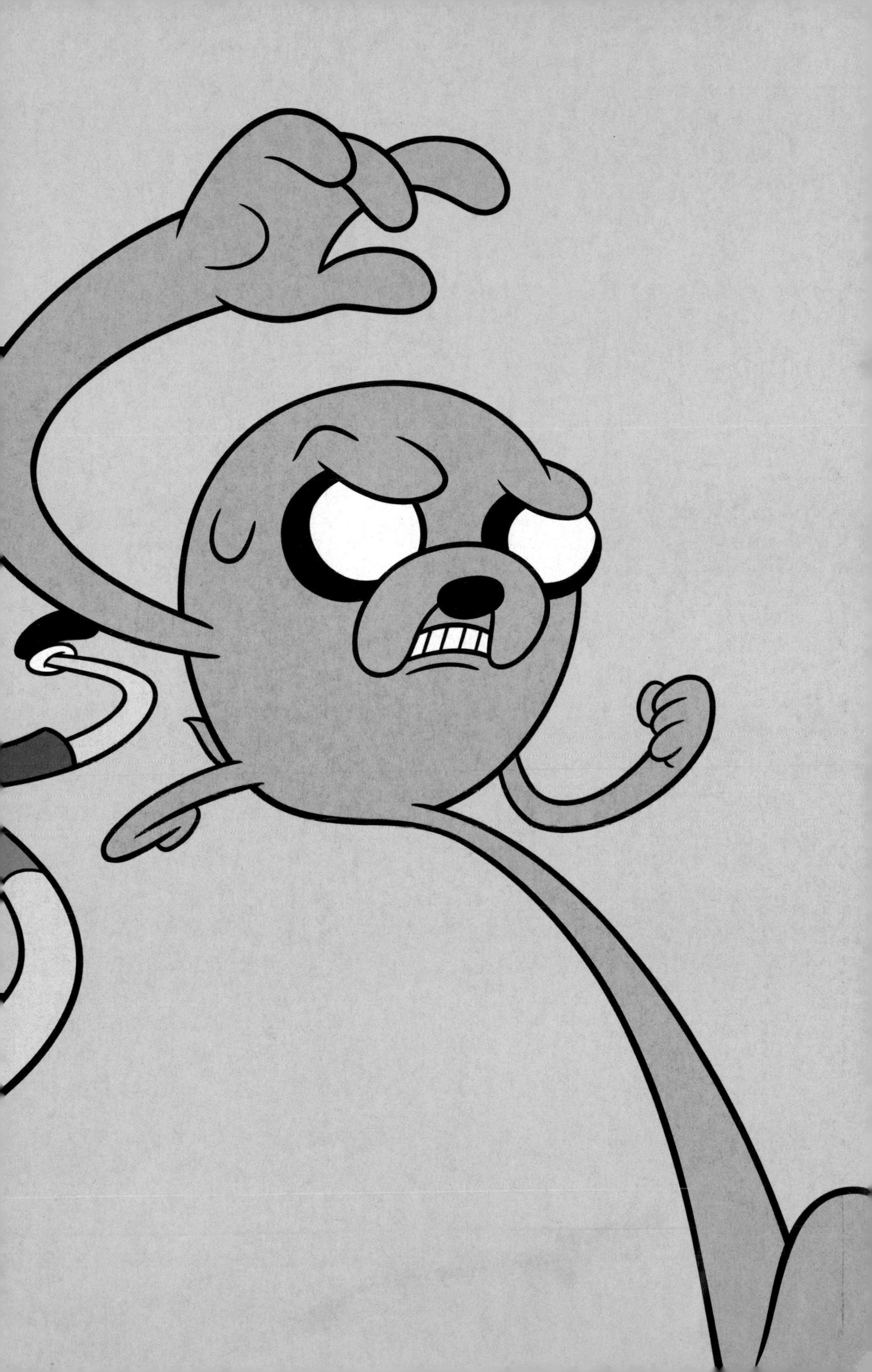

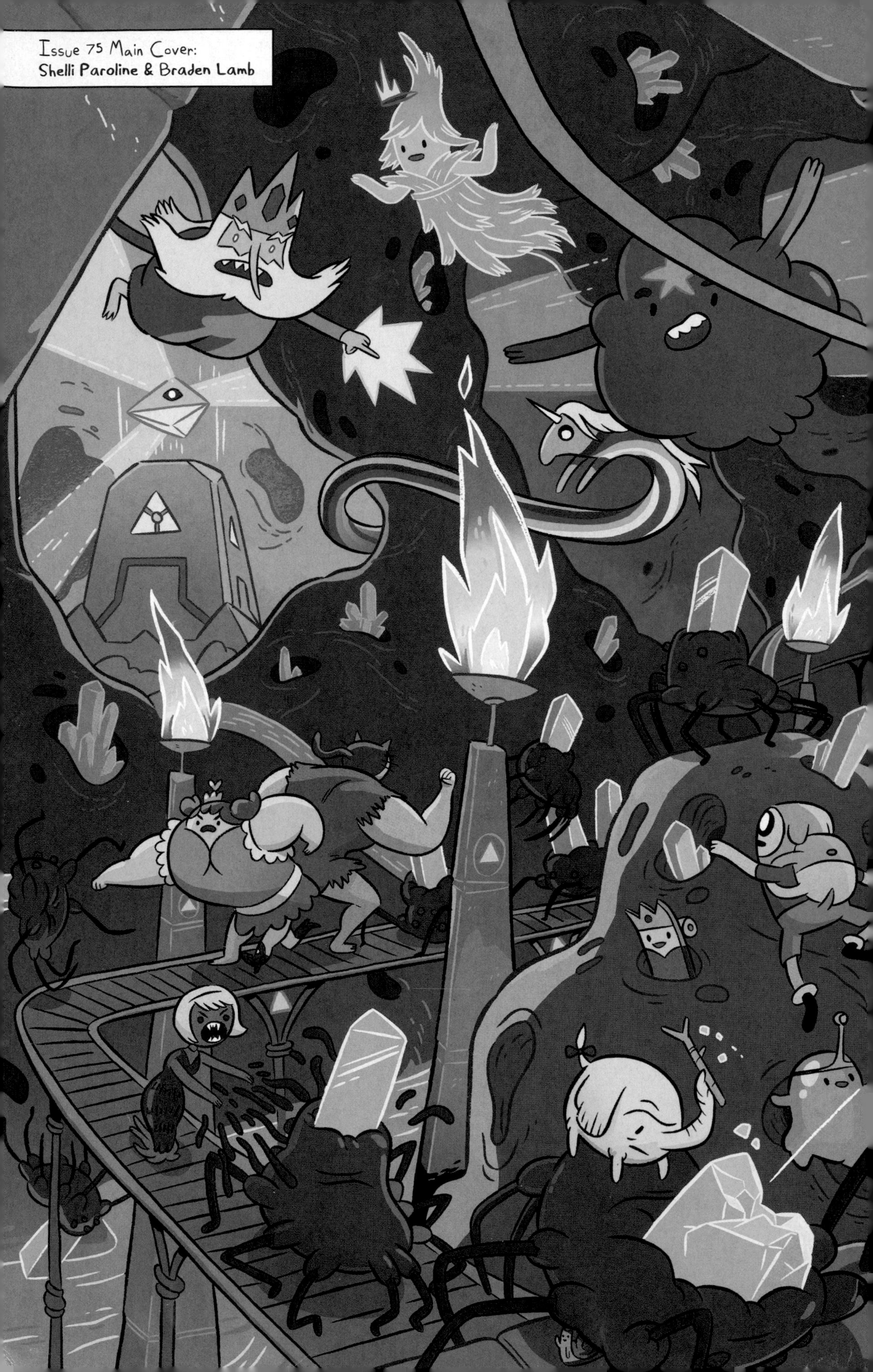

Issue 75 Main Cover:
Shelli Paroline & Braden Lamb

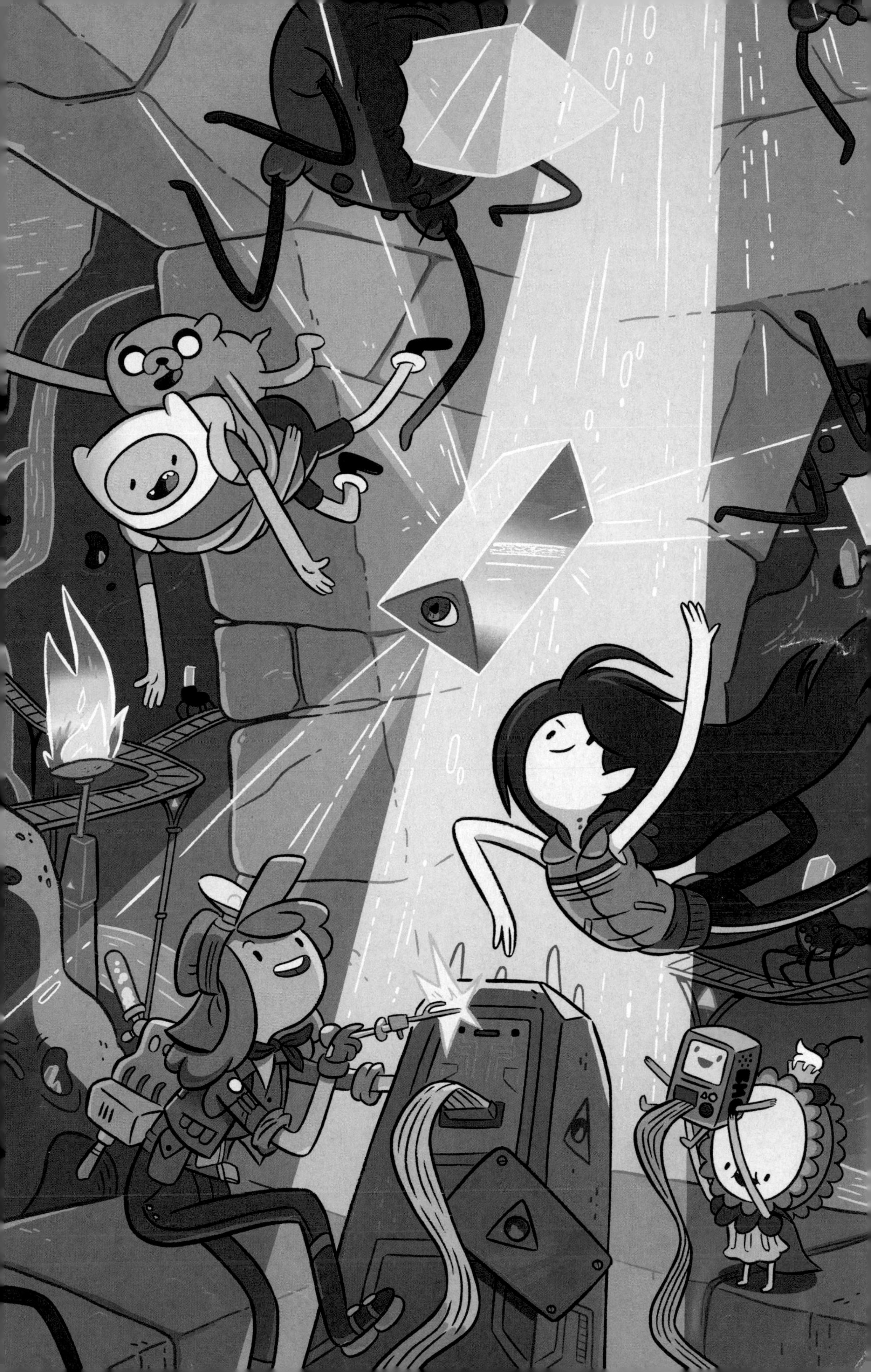

Issue 75 Celebration Wraparound Cover:
Grace Park

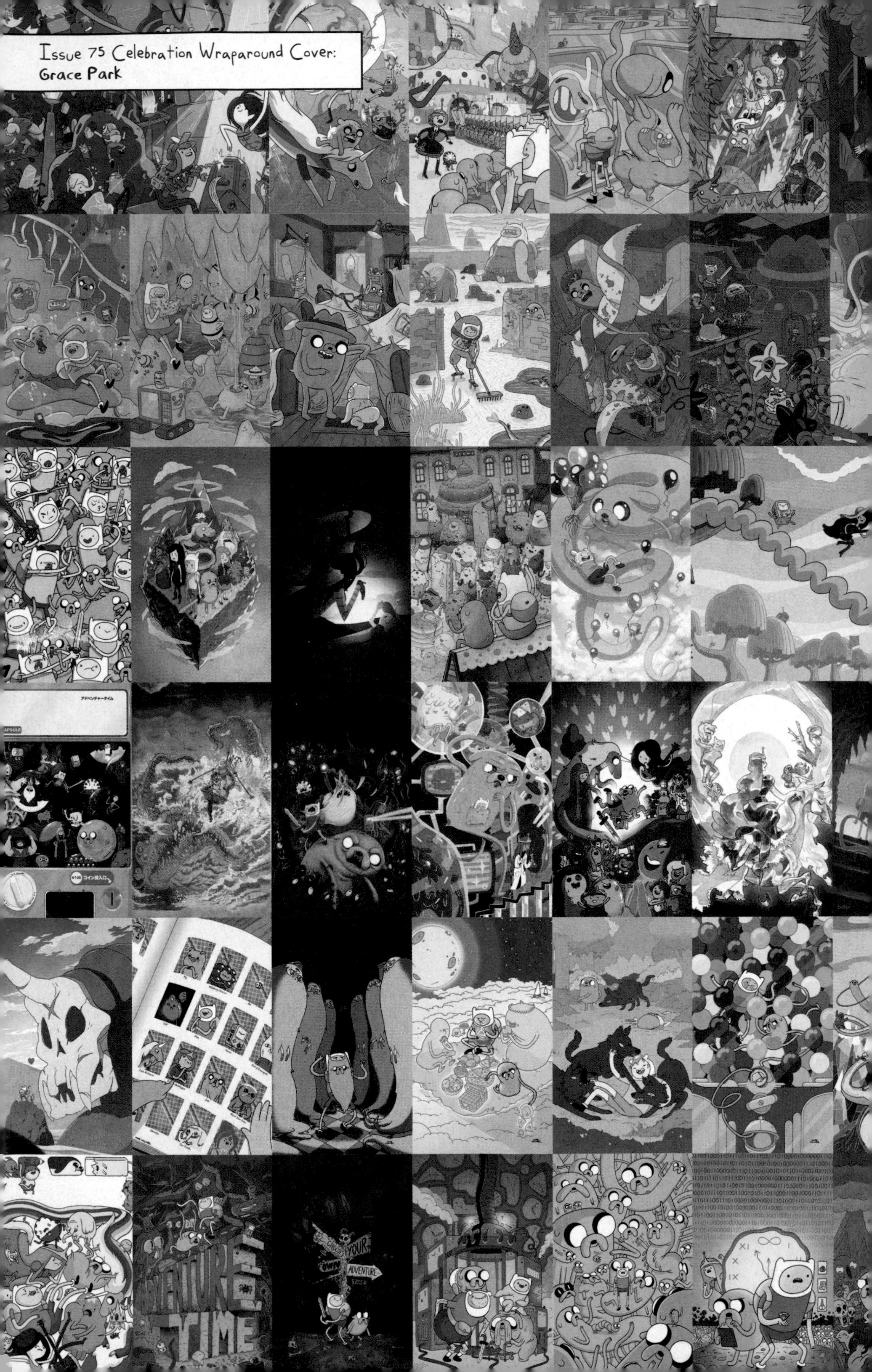
ADVENTURE
TIME

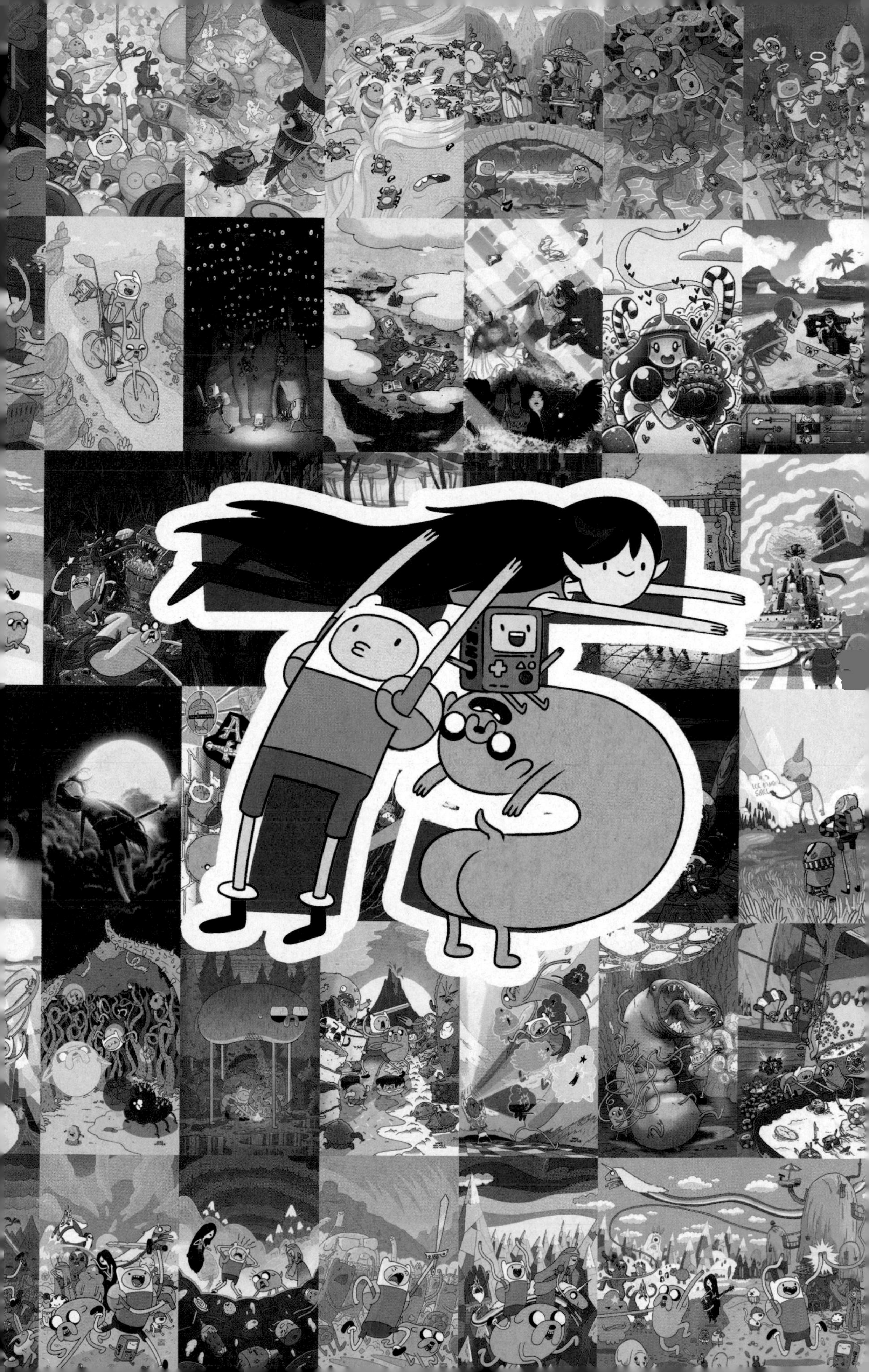

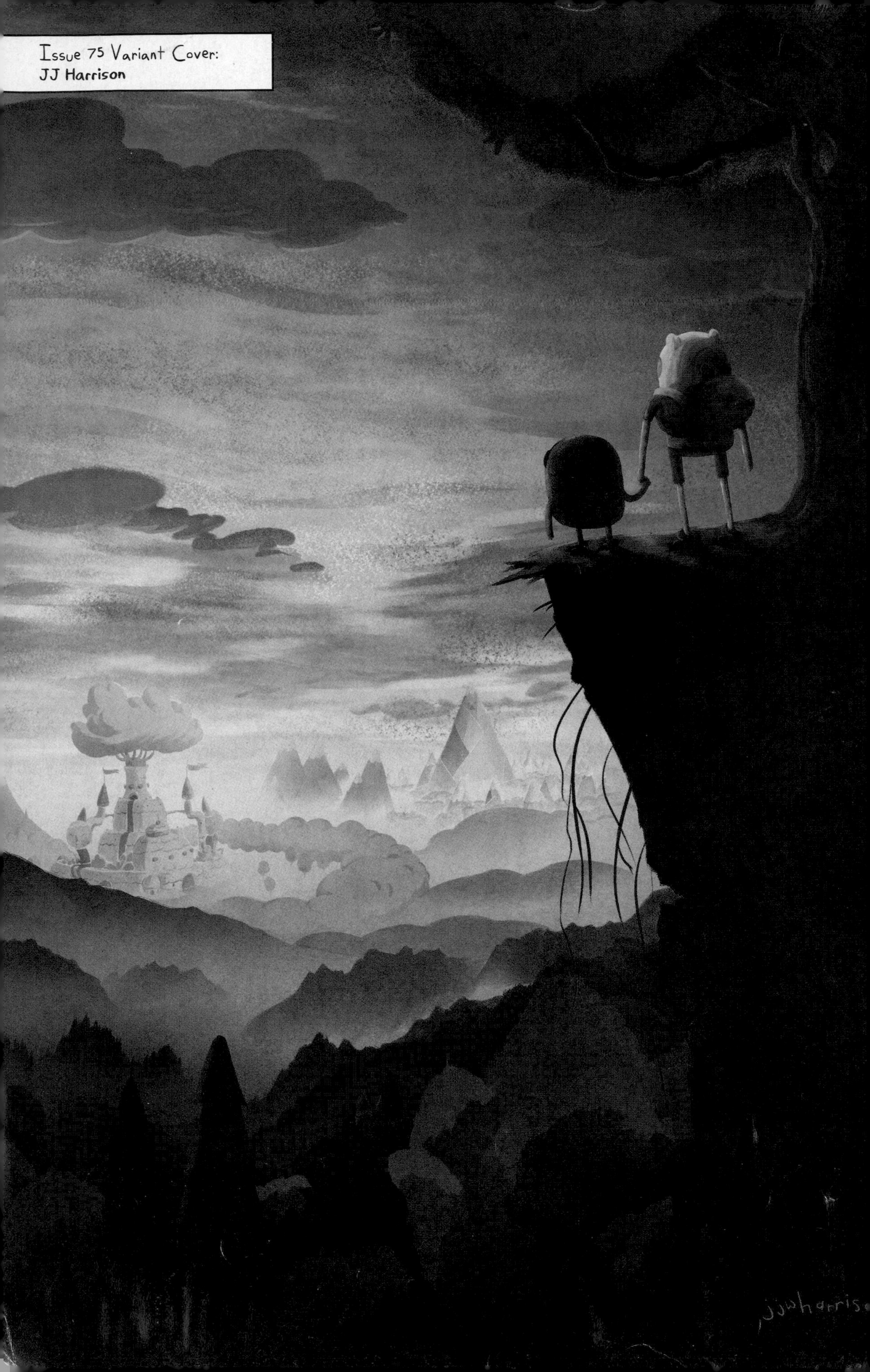

Issue 75 Variant Cover:
JJ Harrison

Issue 75 Subscription Cover:
Pius Bak

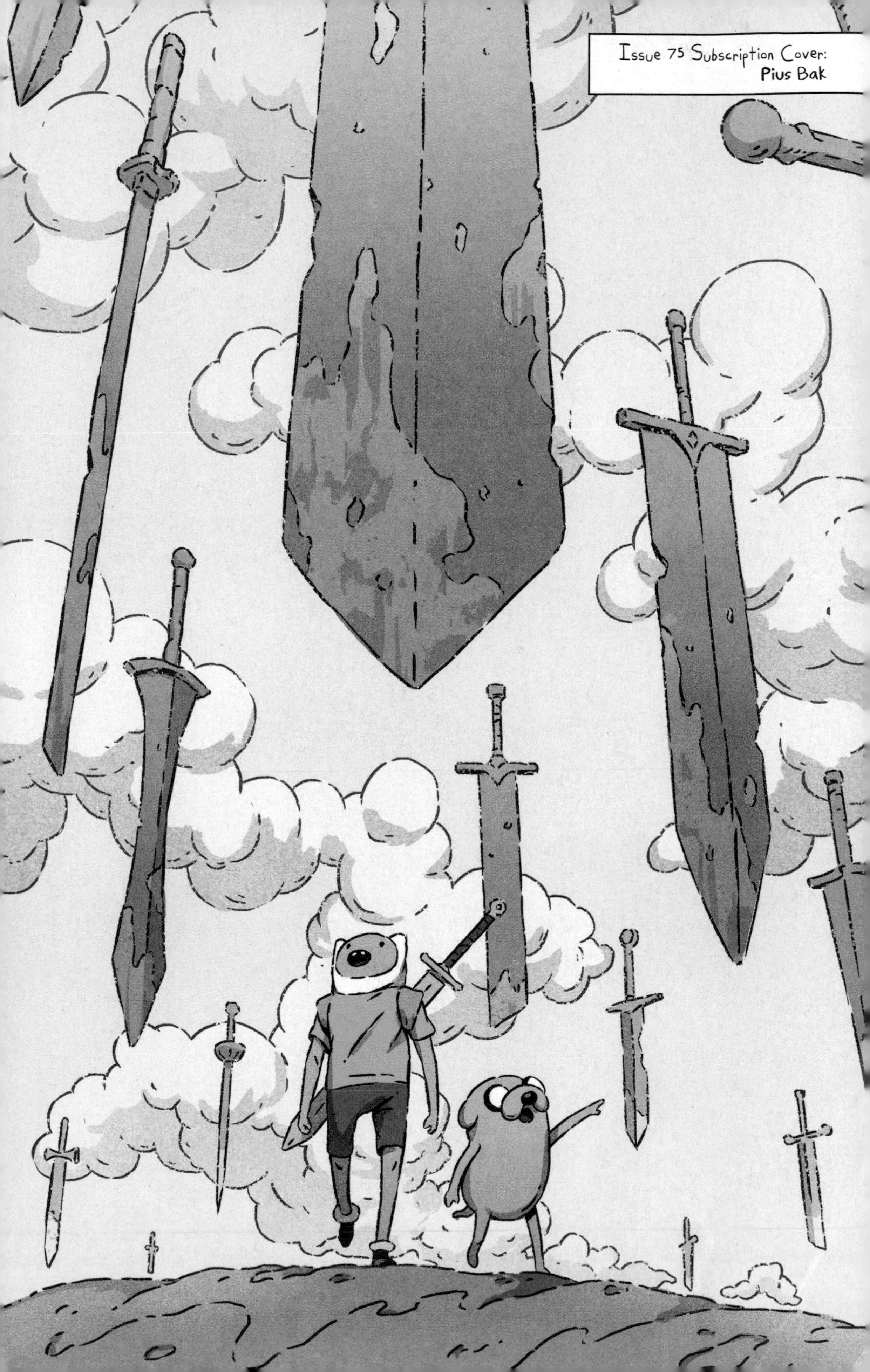

Issue 75 Unlocked Retailer Variant Cover:
Jeffrey Brown

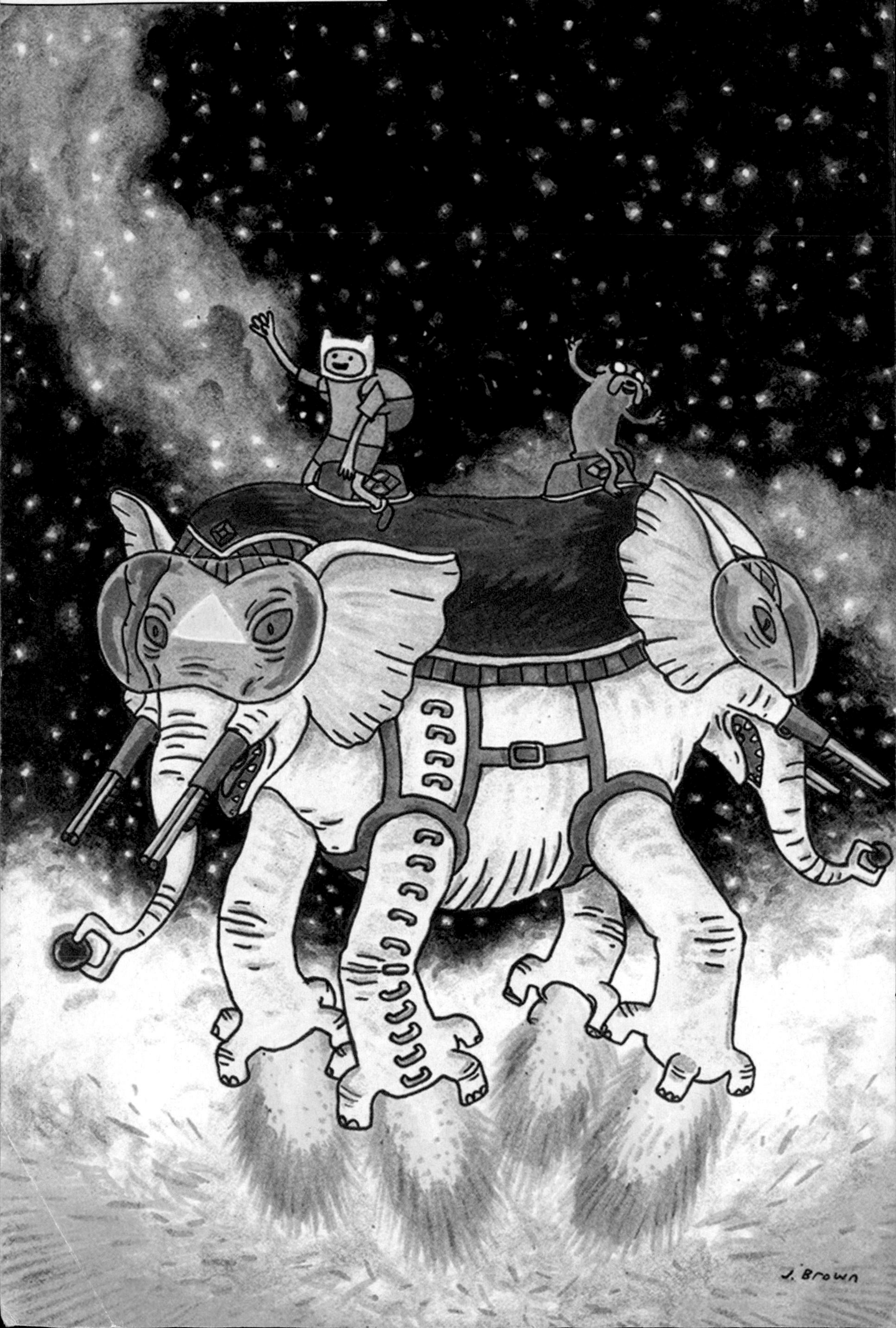
J. Brown

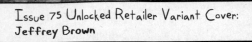

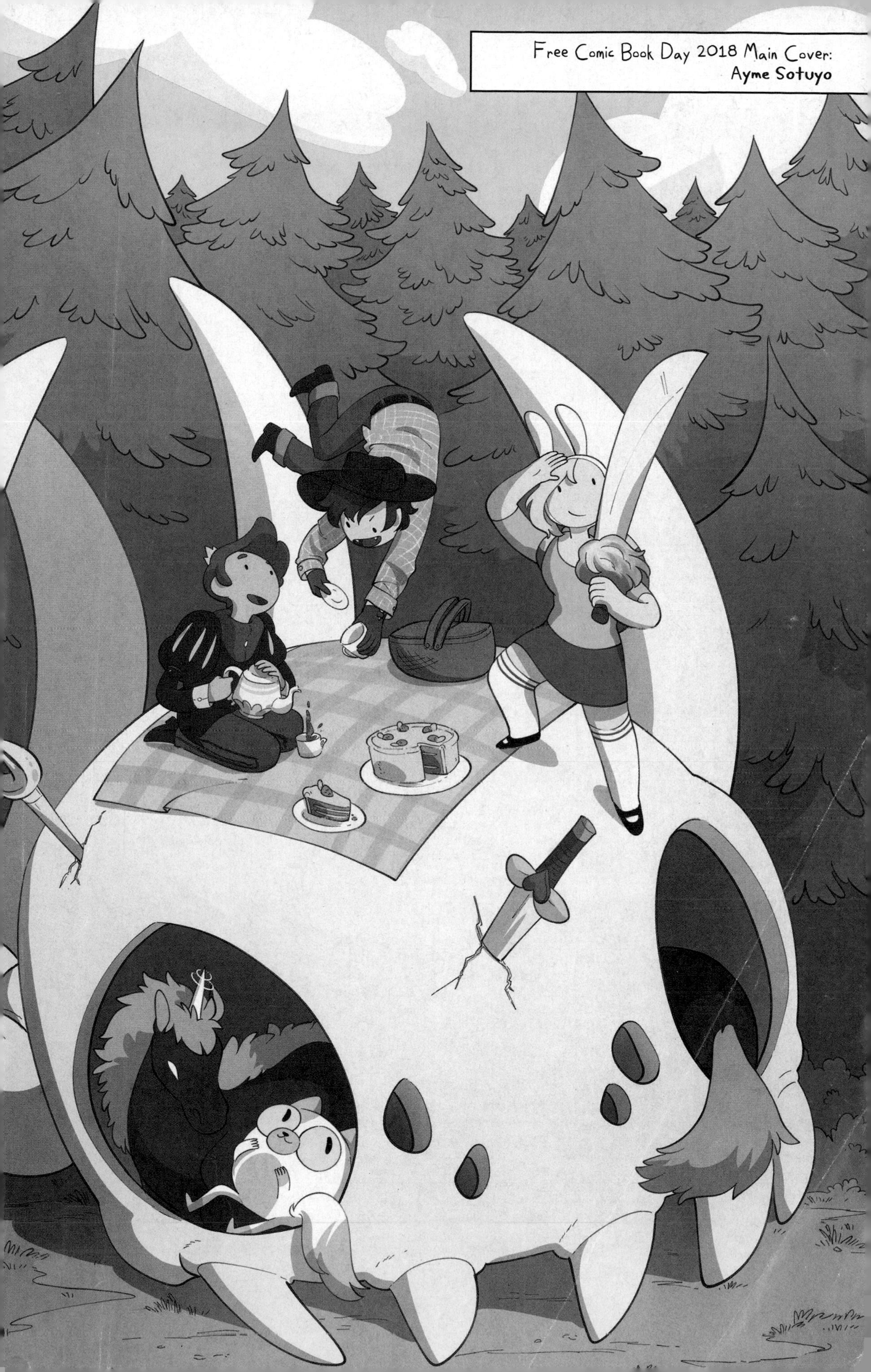
Free Comic Book Day 2018 Main Cover:
Ayme Sotuyo

DISCOVER MORE ADVENTURE TIME

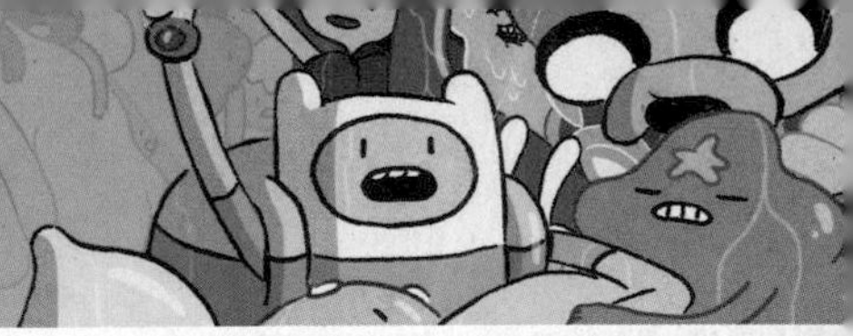

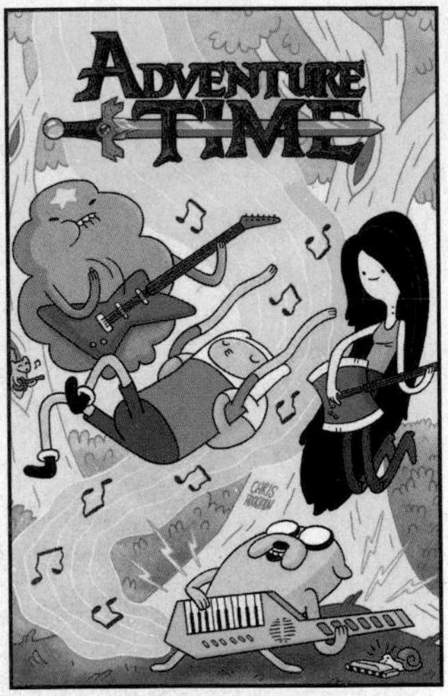
ADVENTURE TIME

Adventure Time

Volume 1
ISBN: 978-1-60886-280-1 | $14.99 US

Volume 2
ISBN: 978-1-60886-323-5 | $14.99 US

Volume 3
ISBN: 978-1-60886-317-4 | $14.99

Volume 4
ISBN: 978-1-60886-351-8 | $14.99

Volume 5
ISBN: 978-1-60886-401-0 | $14.99

Volume 6
ISBN: 978-1-60886-482-9 | $14.99

Volume 7
ISBN: 978-1-60886-746-2 | $14.99

Volume 8
ISBN: 978-1-60886-795-0 | $14.99

Volume 9
ISBN: 978-1-60886-843-8 | $14.99

Volume 10
ISBN: 978-1-60886-909-1 | $14.99

Volume 11
ISBN: 978-1-60886-946-6 | $14.99

Volume 12
ISBN: 978-1-68415-005-2 | $14.99

Volume 13
ISBN: 978-1-68415-051-9 | $14.99

Volume 14
ISBN: 978-1-68415-144-8 | $14.99

Volume 15
ISBN: 978-1-68415-203-2 | $14.99

Volume 16
ISBN: 978-1-68415-272-8 | $14.99

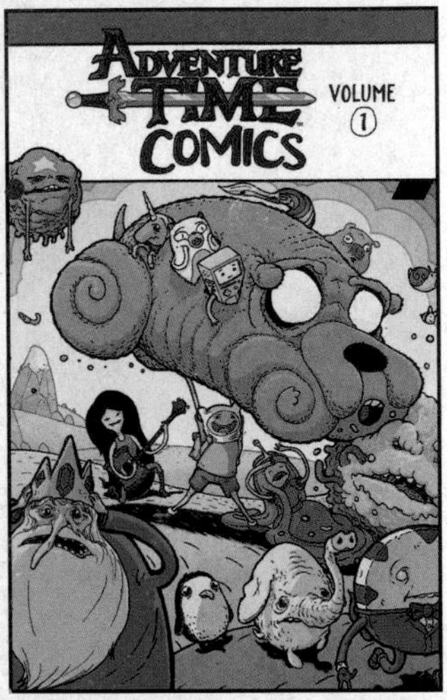
ADVENTURE TIME
COMICS
VOLUME 1

Adventure Time Comics

Volume 1
ISBN: 978-1-60886-934-3 | $14.99

Volume 2
ISBN: 978-1-60886-984-8 | $14.99

Volume 3
ISBN: 978-1-68415-041-0 | $14.99

Volume 4
ISBN: 978-1-68415-133-2 | $14.99

Volume 5
ISBN: 978-1-68415-190-5 | $14.99

Volume 6
ISBN: 978-1-68415-258-2 | $14.99

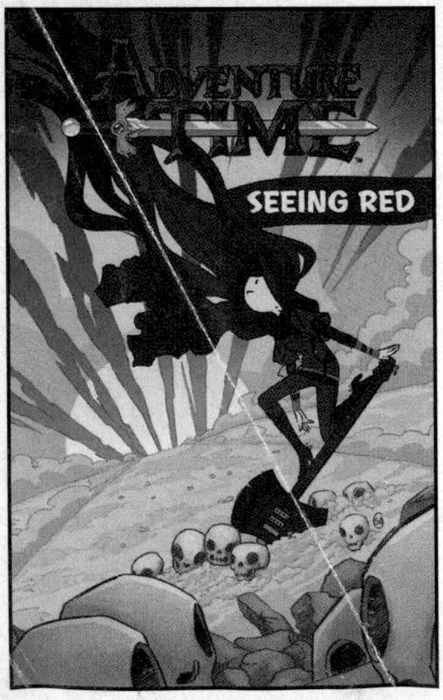
ADVENTURE TIME
SEEING RED

Adventure Time Original Graphic Novels

Volume 1 Playing With Fire
ISBN: 978-1-60886-832-2 | $14.99

Volume 2 Pixel Princesses
ISBN: 978-1-60886-329-7 | $11.99

Volume 3 Seeing Red
ISBN: 978-1-60886-356-3 | $11.99

Volume 4 Bitter Sweets
ISBN: 978-1-60886-430-0 | $12.99

Volume 5 Graybles Schmaybles
ISBN: 978-1-60886-484-3 | $12.99

Volume 6 Masked Mayhem
ISBN: 978-160886-764-6 | $14.99

Volume 7 The Four Castles
ISBN: 978-160886-797-4 | $14.99

Volume 8 President Bubblegum
ISBN: 978-1-60886-846-9 | $14.99

Volume 9 The Brain Robbers
ISBN: 978-1-60886-875-9 | $14.99

Volume 10 The Orient Express
ISBN: 978-1-60886-995-4 | $14.99

Volume 11 Princess & Princess
ISBN: 978-1-68415-025-0 | $14.99

Volume 12 Thunder Road
ISBN: 978-1-68415-179-0 | $14.99

kaboom!
A BOOM! Studios Imprint

AVAILABLE AT YOUR LOCAL COMICS SHOP AND BOOKSTORE

WWW.BOOM-STUDIOS.COM

CARTOON NETWORK